D0309256

DIRTY WAR

STEPHEN LEATHER
DIRTY WAR

HODDER &
STOUGHTON

First published in Great Britain in 2022 by Hodder & Stoughton
An Hachette UK company

1

Copyright © Stephen Leather 2022

A CIP catalogue record for this title is available from the British Library

Hardback ISBN 978 1 529 36736 2
Trade Paperback ISBN 978 1 529 36737 9
eBook ISBN 978 1 529 36738 6

Typeset in Plantin Light by
Palimpsest Book Production Limited, Falkirk, Stirlingshire

Printed and bound in Great Britain by Clays Ltd, Elcograf S.p.A.

Hodder & Stoughton policy is to use papers that are natural,
renewable and recyclable products and made from wood grown in sustainable
forests. The logging and manufacturing processes are expected to conform
to the environmental regulations of the country of origin.

Hodder & Stoughton Ltd
Carmelite House
50 Victoria Embankment
London EC4Y 0DZ

www.hodder.co.uk

AUGUST, 2021

The Bomber took a deep breath and exhaled slowly. His IED was almost half a kilometre away, buried by the side of the narrow road that twisted its way through the desert. It was a big bomb. Not the biggest he had ever built, but big enough to destroy any vehicle that the Americans had. The explosive had come from Russian MON-50 anti-personnel mines, concave rectangular devices that were copies of American Claymores. Each MON-50 contained 700 grams of RDX explosive and either 540 steel balls or 485 short steel rods, depending on which version it was. The Bomber had carefully prised open fifty of the mines, giving him close to thirty-five kilos of high-grade explosive. The RDX had been placed in the centre of six 42-gallon oil barrels and surrounded with homemade ammonium nitrate/fuel oil explosive. There were detonators in each of the barrels, all connected to the command wire which led from the road to the trigger in his right hand.

The barrels had been buried at the side of the road and a spade had been used to cut a slit six inches deep in the sand for the wire. Four men had toiled through the night and by dawn the desert wind had smoothed over all traces of the work. The Bomber was kneeling by the window of an abandoned shepherd's cottage that had been pockmarked with rifle fire.

The building had been stripped, either by the former occupant or looters, and even the doors and window frames had been ripped out.

They were in the desert, about thirty miles north of Pul-e-Khumri, capital of the northern province of Baghlan. The Bomber squinted as he peered into the distance. American Humvees were coming down the road, at speed, with plumes of dust spiralling in the air behind him. He counted six. He twisted around to look at the three men standing behind him. 'This time?' he said.

The man in the middle of the three had an eyepatch over his left eye and there was a thin scar running across his cheek. His thinning hair was swept back and his greying beard was almost a foot long. They called him the Butcher because of the way he liked to torture captured soldiers. The Americans had put a price on his head. It had initially been half a million dollars, but over the years they'd increased it to 2 million. Two bodyguards stood with the Butcher, cradling AK-47s, their eyes ever watchful. They had arrived in a white SUV which was parked out of sight behind the cottage. The Butcher shook his head. No. Not this time.

The men who had helped build and bury the bomb had left in their pick-up truck at first light. Three snipers had arrived in a black SUV which was parked behind another abandoned cottage a few hundred yards away. One of the snipers had stayed with the vehicle, the other two were on the roof above the Bomber's head. They were armed with Dragunov rifles, with comfortable wooden handguards and skeletonised wooden stocks. Rounds were fed into the weapons from detachable curved magazines, containing ten rounds, in a staggered zig-zag pattern and they had PSO-1 optical sights. The snipers were capable of taking out targets more than 800 yards away, so the road was well within range.

The Bomber looked back at the convoy, which was now speeding parallel to the house. Young men in Kevlar helmets and vests were standing in bulletproof turrets covering the area with their heavy machine guns. They turned to look at the shepherd's cottage but there was nothing to arouse their suspicions and within a minute they were speeding away towards Kabul, the clouds of dust dispersing behind them.

The Bomber knew exactly where the bomb was. He had placed two empty water bottles about fifty yards apart on the other side of the road. If he looked directly at the bottles from his window, where his gaze intersected the road is where the bomb was buried. He looked up at the clear blue sky. The one worry he had was that a drone high overhead might see the parked vehicles and the snipers on the roof, but the Butcher had assured him there would be no drones in the area that day. The Bomber didn't know how the Butcher knew that, but he believed him.

He peered down the road again. There was a vehicle coming from the direction of the Humvees. It was big, a transporter. As it got closer, he recognised it as an Afghan Army Navistar truck, which weighed more than four tons. There was no way of knowing if it contained troops or supplies. The Bomber looked over his shoulder and this time the Butcher smiled and nodded. This one.

The Bomber nodded and looked back through the window. His right thumb was pressing against the top of the trigger. His mouth had gone dry and he licked his lips. The Navistar was hurtling down the road at about fifty miles an hour. Timing was vital. Too soon and the driver might have time to turn the vehicle to the side, too late and the truck would be driving away from the explosion. The Bomber's eyes were flicking from the bottles to the truck and back again. He was holding his breath now, every fibre of his being focused on the fast-approaching truck. Two hundred yards. A hundred and fifty. A hundred. He licked his lips again. Fifty yards. Twenty. He pressed the trigger. The bomb exploded with a muffled thud that he felt as much as heard. There was an eruption of sand and rocks and the truck flipped on to its side and scraped along the road. The truck was on fire, what was left of it. The cab had been virtually destroyed and most of the roof had been ripped off to reveal metal boxes and wooden crates inside. A man crawled from the cab, dragging himself away from the burning truck. A Dragunov cracked from the roof and the man went still. The truck continued to burn and a thick column of smoke wound up into the air. No one else emerged from the wreckage.

'Congratulations, Abdul Qadir Akbari,' said the Butcher. 'That was perfect. It was everything I had hoped for. You truly are a skilled craftsman.'

The Bomber stood up, still holding the trigger. He frowned. 'But that is not my name.'

The Butcher patted him on the shoulder. 'Abdul Qadir Akbari is who you are from this day forth. And it is Abdul Qadir Akbari who will serve Allah in a way that you never could. Inshallah.'

The Bomber nodded. Inshallah. God willing. The Bomber didn't fully understand what he was being asked to do, but he knew that he had no choice other than to obey.

They thought long and hard about where to seize the target. They could have just entered the Ministry of Defence building in Whitehall, gone up to the fourth floor, and arrested him. But that would have attracted attention. They could have carried out an early morning raid at the target's first-floor flat in Belsize Park, but that too would have caused a stir. If a passing stranger captured the moment on a phone, it would all be over.

A surveillance team had been following the target for four days. He left his flat at eight o'clock in the morning, assembled his folding bike, and rode the four and a half miles to Whitehall in about twenty-five minutes. There he would disassemble his bike and enter the building. He generally took half an hour for lunch, during which he would walk to a local sandwich shop. He would leave his office between six-thirty and seven and cycle back to Belsize Park. He took the same route each time: through Soho and Marylebone and along the east side of Regent's Park, before heading north through Primrose Hill and Chalk Farm.

The decision was taken to carry out the abduction in the park. They performed a dry run and did it for real the following day. They used a six-man team. Three were on bicycles, dressed in Lycra and wearing helmets. They waited down the road from the Whitehall building and mounted up when the target appeared. He assembled his bike, put clips on his suit trousers, and put on his helmet. It was black with yellow stripes and the followers had designated the target as Wasp One.

As he started pedalling away from the building, the three cyclists followed, keeping a safe distance. There was no need to stay close, the target always took the same route.

The van was parked up close to the Royal College of Physicians, at the south-east corner of the park. There was a woman in the driving seat and a man in overalls sitting next to her, and in the back was another man wearing overalls. The driver was in radio contact with the three cyclists. Alpha, Bravo and Charlie. The rider with the designation Charlie was actually called Charlie too, a coincidence that had raised smiles at the lunchtime briefing.

Alpha, Bravo and Charlie took it in turns to take the lead, never getting closer than six car lengths behind the target. Once the target had crossed Marylebone Road, the van pulled out and began driving north along the Outer Circle. The van was in the livery of a bicycle repair company and the occupants of the van had the company's logo on their overalls.

As the target cycled along the Outer Circle, Alpha, Bravo and Charlie edged closer. The van stopped and Alpha pedalled faster. Bravo and Charlie followed, riding two abreast.

When they were fifty yards from the van, Alpha accelerated and drew level with the target. The target turned to glare at Alpha once he realised he was keeping pace with him.

'I need you to pull over, Craig,' said Alpha. He had a gruff Glaswegian accent and it was a voice that was used to being obeyed.

'What?' said the target.

'Pull the fuck over. We need to talk to you.'

The van was now about twenty yards away.

The target frowned in confusion.

'Pull the fuck over!' shouted Alpha. He moved his bike closer. 'Do as you are fucking told!'

'Okay, okay,' said the target. He braked and turned towards the pavement. Alpha moved with him. Bravo and Charlie pulled up behind them and got off their bikes. The target looked at them nervously.

'What's going on, guys?' asked the target, his voice trembling.

Alpha waved at the van and the reversing lights came on. The van started to reverse towards them. Bravo and Charlie moved close to block the view of any traffic coming up behind them.

The van stopped a couple of yards from them and the rear doors opened. The man in overalls inside beckoned for the target to join him. His eyes were hidden behind black Ray-Bans.

'Get in the van, Craig,' said Alpha.

'Who are you?'

'Get in the van. If you don't get in the van we'll Taser you and drag you in, and if we do that you'll piss and shit yourself – and we don't have a change of clothes for you.'

The man in the van pulled a Taser from his overalls. He pressed the trigger and sparks crackled between the metal prongs.

'I'm not getting into . . .'

Alpha's gloved left hand clamped around the target's throat and his right fist thudded out like a piston, slamming into his solar plexus. As the target started to double over, Alpha, still astride his bike, pushed him towards the van.

The man in the van reached out, grabbed the target by the shoulders and hauled him inside.

Alpha picked up the target's bike and swung it into the van. The man inside slammed the doors shut and the van drove off. Alpha looked around. Several cars had driven by but Bravo and Charlie had managed to hide the fracas from view.

The three cyclists began pedalling again as the van disappeared into the distance.

Dan 'Spider' Shepherd was sitting at a table with his back to the window, facing the door. The blinds had been drawn and two lights with LED bulbs had been placed behind Shepherd, so that when the team brought Craig McKillop into the room the lights would be shining in his face. It was all about keeping him off balance and insecure. Shepherd had gone for a *Men in Black* look with a dark suit, a white shirt and a black tie, but had decided against sunglasses.

Sitting to Shepherd's right was Ciara Kelly. Ciara was a recent recruit and had joined MI5 after realising she didn't really want a career in accounting. She had been briefed to listen and say nothing, but to flash McKillop sympathetic smiles from time to time. Good cop, bad cop. Or more accurately, cute cop, bad cop. McKillop was a sucker for a pretty face, and Ciara definitely had that, along with a pixie haircut and bright red fingernails. She smiled nervously at Shepherd.

He winked at her. 'You'll be fine.'

She took a deep breath and nodded. 'I hope so.'

There was a loud knock on the door and it opened. It was one of the snatch team. Bernie Quinn. He'd been designated Alpha on the operation. He was still wearing his cycling gear and Shepherd couldn't help but grin at the bulge in Quinn's Lycra pants. Quinn was a former British Transport cop who'd got bored with dealing with drunks on trains and was often called in when muscle was needed. Quinn nodded but didn't say anything. The team had been instructed to say nothing once they had the target in custody.

A second member of the team was standing behind Quinn. Charlie Raines. He was holding McKillop, who had a black hood over his head. Quinn stepped to the side and Raines brought McKillop into the room and sat him down on the wooden chair facing Shepherd. Shepherd gestured at the hood and Raines ripped it off. McKillop blinked. 'Who are you?' he asked.

Shepherd nodded at Quinn and Raines and they left the room, pulling the door closed behind them.

'Who are you?' repeated McKillop. He was trying to sound assertive but the tremble in his voice belied his fear. He was scared witless.

'I'm the man who's here to sort your life out, Craig. You've made a few bad choices and we've pretty much reached the end of the line.'

McKillop stole a quick look at Ciara before continuing. 'You've kidnapped me,' said McKillop. 'What's this about? Money? Because you're wasting your time, I've got no money.'

There was an A4 Manila envelope on the table. Shepherd took out a photograph and slid it across the table. It was a head-and-shoulders shot of a blonde woman in her early thirties. Her hair was cut short and she had an upturned nose and full lips. McKillop squinted at the photograph. 'Friend of yours?' asked Shepherd.

'Obviously you know she is, why else would you be showing me her photograph?'

'What's her name?'

McKillop sneered at him. 'Seriously, you have her photograph but you don't know her name? Sounds like you haven't thought this through.' He was starting to regain his confidence, presumably because no one had slapped him across the face or threatened to break his fingers.

'You think this is funny?'

'I was grabbed off the street and thrown into the back of a van, so I know it isn't a joke. I'm just waiting for you to get to the point.'

Shepherd tapped the photograph. 'She's the point. Anna Schneider.'

'Then you do know her name?'

'Actually that's not her name. It's the name she uses with you.'

McKillop's jaw tightened as he stared at the photograph. 'What's her real name?'

Shepherd shook his head. 'I'm the one who'll be asking the questions,' he said. 'Who is she? What does she do? For a living?'

'She's an analyst. She works for a think tank.'

'In London?'

McKillop nodded. 'They're based in Berlin but they have offices in most European capitals.' He frowned as he stared at the photograph. 'What's her real name if it's not Anna?'

'When did you start passing information to her?'

McKillop folded his arms and didn't answer.

'How did that work? She told you what intel she wanted and you downloaded it from the MoD computer? Did she give you a shopping list?'

McKillop looked up from the photograph. 'That's what this is about? Me sharing data with another analyst? Look, I'm an analyst with the MoD, she's an analyst with a German think tank, every now and again we meet for a drink and we share data. It's not as if sharing information is illegal, is it?'

'Well, the Official Secrets Act – which you signed when you joined the MoD from university – would disagree with you.'

McKillop snorted. 'I wasn't giving her secret information. The data we shared wasn't even classified.'

'You say "shared". What information did she share with you?'

'She told me about the reports she was compiling, things she was working on. We're friends, we chat. Like people do.'

'But you did more than just chat about your work, didn't you?'

'That was mainly it.'

'But you gave her MoD data when she asked for it?'

'I helped her with her reports, one analyst to another. I'm sure if I'd needed help she would have helped me.' He unfolded his arms and leaned forward. 'Look, I don't see what the issue is here. She's German, working for a company here in London. I know that we've left the EU but we're still all Europeans, aren't we? Germany isn't the enemy, despite what you might read in the *Daily Mail*.'

Shepherd held the man's look for several seconds before speaking. 'The woman you know as Anna Schneider works for the Russian Federal Security Service. What used to be the KGB in the bad old days.'

'What? No.' McKillop grimaced as if he had a bad taste in his mouth. 'No fucking way.'

'Yes. She works for the Russians. Which means you, my friend, have been a Russian spy for the past few months. So it's not just a matter of you breaching the Official Secrets Act, you are a full-blown traitor. And you're facing life imprisonment.'

McKillop shook his head. 'No, you're just trying to confuse me. She's German. No question. She was born in Berlin, she talked about it all the time. I know the city really well and she was never wrong, not once.'

Shepherd smiled. 'I didn't say she *was* Russian. I said she worked *for* the Russians.'

'No. The think tank that employs her is a real thing. I checked it out on the internet. They have an office in Victoria, they have a website, all sorts of publications.'

'Mostly funded by Moscow,' said Shepherd. He took a

second picture from the envelope, this time of her standing outside the Russian Embassy in Kensington Palace Gardens, at the north-west edge of Hyde Park. She was lighting a cigarette.

McKillop frowned as he stared at the picture. 'She doesn't smoke.' He looked at Shepherd. 'She said she'd never smoked.'

'Look, if it makes you feel any better, you're not the only agent that they're running. We've found another three being run through the think tank and there are almost certainly more.'

McKillop sat back in his chair and folded his arms defensively. 'I'm not an agent.'

'Yes you are,' said Shepherd. 'And Anna is your handler.'

'I was just helping her with her research.' His voice was trembling again.

'By passing on official secrets. Secrets which went straight to Moscow.'

'You keep saying that, but Anna is German. Why would she be working for the Russians?'

'Lots of people work for the Russians who aren't Russian. The history of MI5 and MI6 is littered with examples.'

'I'm not a traitor,' said McKillop firmly.

Shepherd ignored the statement. 'How and when did you meet her?'

'At a function at the German Embassy, about four months ago. There was an exhibition of young German painters and I was invited.'

'Was that normal? To be invited to the embassy?'

'I get several invitations a year. And the office knows about my interest in Germany and all things German, and they pass unwanted invitations on to me.'

'That's right. You got a first in Modern Languages at Oxford with a specialism in German, and a PhD in some obscure German author.'

McKillop sighed. 'Theodor Fontane is generally regarded as the most important German language author of the nineteenth century,' he said. 'Hardly obscure.'

'Obscure to me,' said Shepherd. 'What about Anna?'

'What about her?'

'Was she aware of Theodor Fontane?'

McKillop screwed up his face. 'Maybe. I'm not sure.'

'Come off it. You devoted several years of your life to the guy, you would have mentioned it. Or did she mention it first?'

'I think we talked about my doctorate. That's what people do when they meet. They talk about each other.'

'And Anna seemed interested in you?'

McKillop narrowed his eyes. 'What are you getting at?'

'It's a simple question. You met by chance at an art exhibition at the German Embassy. Presumably there were a lot of people there. What do you think attracted her to you?'

'I don't know. We were looking at a painting and we began chatting.' He avoided Shepherd's icy look and stared at the tabletop.

Shepherd pushed the photograph of Anna towards McKillop. 'She's a nine, going on a ten.'

'What do you mean?' muttered McKillop.

'You know what I mean, Craig. She's a beautiful girl. A head-turner. But you, even on a good day you're barely a four. You must know that. Receding hairline, massive forehead, weak chin, nerd glasses, sloping shoulders – I mean you were obviously at the back of the queue when the DNA was being handed out. Didn't alarm bells start to ring the moment she expressed any interest in you?'

'We had a lot in common,' said McKillop. He looked across at Ciara and his cheeks flushed red.

'Well of course you did. She was primed. She was a bloody sex torpedo launched right at you.'

McKillop looked up and glared at Shepherd. 'We never had sex,' he hissed.

'Well more fool you, mate, because she'd probably have been up for it to get what she wanted. She was a honey trap. Plain and simple. So what happened after the exhibition?'

'We went for a drink.'

Shepherd smiled thinly. 'And whose idea was that?'

'Hers. Mine. I don't know. We had a couple of glasses of wine.'

'And talked about what?'

'Brexit, mainly. She couldn't understand why Britain was so keen to leave the EU.'

'And you put her right?'

McKillop laughed harshly. 'I told her that there's no point in asking the Great British public what they want, because they don't know. They should never have been asked. The referendum was a stupid idea and now we're paying the cost.'

'You were in agreement? About Brexit?'

'Of course. Biggest mistake we've ever made.'

'Okay. And how do we get from there to you offering to supply her with MoD databases?'

'That's not what happened.'

'Well, actually it is,' said Shepherd. 'Though we might disagree about the terminology. When did she say she needed your help?'

'It wasn't like that.'

'Tell me what it was like.'

McKillop swallowed. His Adam's apple wobbled as if it had a life of its own. 'We talked about our jobs, like people do. She was having problems getting information, problems that were a direct result of Brexit. Before we left the EU, she had no problems getting information from government departments. But post-Brexit, often the only way she could get government data was by issuing a freedom of information request. Basically she compiles reports for the German government and for German companies. Say the German government wants to know how the UK's electricity consumption is rising and what scope there is for German companies to supply power stations. She would talk to the UK's electricity companies, universities, government officials, and compile a report.'

'Right. But you work for the MoD. So power stations aren't your brief.'

McKillop sneered at Shepherd. 'You asked how the conversations went. I'm telling you.'

'But eventually she wanted MoD data, right?'

McKillop sighed. 'She was compiling a report on how Covid had affected the armed forces. Not just in the UK, she wanted to compare the figures of armies throughout the world. She had applied for the MoD figures but they weren't forthcoming so I offered to help.' Shepherd opened his mouth to speak but McKillop held up a hand to silence him. 'They weren't confidential, never mind secret,' he said. 'They were there on the MoD mainframe and I had no problems accessing the files. She would have got the information eventually, I just speeded up the process.'

'And how did you give her the data?'

McKillop frowned. 'What do you mean?'

'Email? Thumb drive? How did you get the intel to her?'

'It wasn't intel. Why do you say that? It was data.'

'Semantics,' said Shepherd. 'But the question is simple enough. How did you pass the data to her?'

'I took photographs. Screenshots. And then I sent them to her through WhatsApp.'

'And was that your idea or hers?'

McKillop shrugged. 'I don't know. I can't remember.'

'You were already using WhatsApp?'

'Yes. And she gave me her number and we used to chat that way.'

'She never mentioned to you that WhatsApp is encrypted so it's a safe way of sending information clandestinely?'

'No. And I wasn't sending it clandestinely, as you describe it. I'd just call up the information, take a screenshot, and send it to her. Look, there was nothing remotely sensitive about what I was sending her. If she'd been asking me about contracts or procurements then of course I would have said something. If she was looking for information on troop movements or battle readiness, then I would have ended the relationship immediately. I was just helping her with her projects. Why would the Russians care about how Covid spread through the UK's armed forces?'

Shepherd ignored the question. 'What was the most recent report she asked for help with?'

He sighed again. 'She was researching asylum seekers, in particular from Afghanistan. The Germans have a much more sympathetic approach to asylum than the UK, and she was looking for facts and figures to illustrate how the Brits were coping with refugees from there. She wasn't having much luck getting statistics on the Afghan Relocations and Assistance Policy and on the more recent Afghan Citizens Resettlement Scheme.'

'And so she asked for your help.'

McKillop nodded. 'The ARAP scheme was designed to resettle interpreters and others who had helped the army, so the MoD had to comment on all applications. A lot of applicants who are claiming on the ACRS scheme also have links to the military so again the MoD would have to comment.'

'And she couldn't get the information from anywhere else?'

'She could, but the Home Office and the MoD were insisting on freedom of information requests so it was taking forever.'

'So you offered to help?'

'Why not? It wasn't as if it was secret. It was just data on refugees.'

'And what sort of data did she want?'

'Basic statistics. Age, sex, work background, marital status, educational qualifications.'

'And the MoD database had those breakdowns?'

'No, we just had the applications. But she said if I sent as many as I had, she would break down the statistics.'

'And that didn't seem a strange thing to ask?'

'Not really. If I'd have had to do the breakdowns, it would have taken forever. She said I could just send over the applications and she'd get an intern to do the work.'

'And how many applications did you send to her?'

McKillop wrinkled his nose. 'I don't know. A lot.'

'There were about eight thousand Afghans who applied for the ARAP scheme.'

'Yeah, I gave her pretty much all of them. And I'm still working my way through the ACRS applications.'

Shepherd frowned. 'You sent her eight thousand screenshots? That would have taken forever.'

McKillop shifted uncomfortably in his chair. 'I had to use a flash drive for that,' he said quietly.

'Because there were too many pages to send by WhatsApp?'

McKillop nodded. 'But she wasn't interested in the specifics. She just wanted a statistical breakdown. As I said, she's getting an intern to run a spreadsheet that'll show up all the characteristics.'

'How many flash drives have you given her?'

'Four so far. Each with two thousand applications on them.'

'And how did you give them to her?'

McKillop frowned. 'What do you mean?'

'I mean did you post the flash drives? Hand-deliver them? Or use a dead drop?'

'What's a dead drop?'

'Just tell me how you gave her the flash drives.'

'I handed them to her. There was nothing secretive. I wasn't doing anything wrong, I was just sharing data with her.'

'And where were you when you handed them over?'

'We'd have coffee or a drink. A couple of times we had a meal.'

'Did she pay or did you?'

'I did. Why?'

'I'm just trying to get a feel for what she was doing.'

'She's a researcher. I was helping her. That's all there was to it. And I don't understand why you think Anna works for the Russians.'

'I don't *think* she works for the Russians. I *know* she does. She's a Federal Security Service officer who has previously worked in Berlin, Vienna and Paris.' Shepherd took three more photographs from the envelope and spread them out in front of McKillop. The photographs were of the woman standing outside the Russian embassies of the three cities. In one of the pictures – the one taken in Paris – she was lighting a cigarette. 'She arrived in the UK just two weeks before she met you at the embassy, which suggests she was specifically sent to target you.'

'But why?'

'Because you had access to the information they wanted,' said Shepherd. 'And because you are clearly gullible. How could you possibly think it was okay to be taking files from the MoD and passing them to anybody? You signed the Official Secrets Act.'

'But I wasn't passing on secrets, was I? It was just data. Lists of names, that's all. And I thought she was German, I told you that. Obviously if I'd known she was working for the Russians I would have handled it differently.'

Shepherd shook his head in disbelief. 'You really have no idea what you've done, do you?'

McKillop wiped his sleeve across his glistening forehead. 'What do you mean?'

Shepherd leaned towards him. 'Moscow has been passing the data you gave them on to the Taliban. And the Taliban are using the information as a death list. So far as we know, the Taliban have executed a dozen of the names you gave Anna. Men who were still waiting to be extracted from Afghanistan. Along with their families, wives and children.'

McKillop shook his head. 'No way.'

'The men were killed, their wives and children were raped, some were murdered, others were sent to be the wives of

Taliban fighters. I'd say that so far you are directly responsible for the deaths of more than thirty people.'

McKillop sneered at Shepherd. 'That makes no sense at all,' he said. 'Why would the Russians give the information to the Taliban?'

Shepherd smiled coldly. 'Lithium,' he said.

McKillop frowned. 'What?'

'Lithium. It goes into rechargeable batteries, the sort that power electric cars. Afghanistan might be one of the poorest countries in the world, but under the desert are mineral deposits worth more than a trillion dollars. Iron, copper, gold and lithium. While the Americans and the Brits were running the show, the mineral rights were off limits. But once Trump unilaterally announced that the US forces were pulling out, everything changed. The Chinese are itching to get their hands on the mineral rights and the Russians have been trying to get a jump on them. And they've done it by supplying them with a list of what the Taliban sees as collaborators and traitors. In a way you have to admire the Russians – they get an agent to persuade you to hand over the information which they promptly pass on to the Taliban in exchange for hundreds of millions of dollars in mining rights. And how much did they pay you?'

'I wasn't doing it for the money. I was doing it . . .' His voice trembled and he couldn't finish the sentence.

'To help a pretty German girl?' Shepherd finished for him. 'Yeah, see I'm not sure how good a defence that'll be. To be honest with you, I have trouble believing it myself.'

'And who are you?'

'Me? I'm the guy who might just be able to offer you a way out. But it's up to you.' Shepherd shrugged. 'The ball is in your court.'

McKillop sniffed. 'What do you want me to do?'

'You can carry on meeting Anna. But we'll give you a phone to carry with you that will record everything you say.'

'Like a wire?'

'Like a wire, but it will look just like your usual phone and you won't have to switch it on. You just keep the phone with you.'

'That means you'll know where I am every minute of every day, and what I'm doing?'

'A bit like prison, but in your case you'll be able to pop into a pub whenever you want.'

'And then what? What do I do?'

'Exactly what you've been doing these past three months. You find out what she wants and you give it to her. Except you tell us first and we put our own information on to the flash drive. My colleague here will be your point of contact. She might even take you for a drink or treat you to a meal.'

McKillop looked across at Ciara and smiled nervously. Ciara nodded and returned his smile. McKillop looked back at Shepherd. 'And if I do that, if I cooperate, what happens to me?'

'That depends on how productive your cooperation is. If we shut them down as a result of your help, I don't see there'd be any value in prosecuting you. But that would be down to the Crown Prosecution Service.'

'I could still go to prison? Even if I help you?'

'Look, mate, if you don't cooperate, you'll be behind bars for the rest of your life. Or at least the greater part of it. That's a given.'

'I didn't say I wouldn't cooperate.' McKillop leaned forward and looked pleadingly at Shepherd. 'You know I didn't realise I was dealing with the Russians, right? You believe me?'

'I want to believe you, Craig. You seem like a decent enough guy to me. But what I believe isn't really the issue. It's down to you to try to put things right, and you do that by cooperating with us.'

'And what if they find out that I'm double-crossing them?'

Shepherd opened his mouth to reply but stopped when his phone began to ring. He took out his phone and looked at the screen. It was his boss, Giles Pritchard. Shepherd nodded at Ciara. 'I've got to take this.' He left the room and took the call. 'How's it going?' asked Pritchard.

'Yeah, he'll turn,' said Shepherd. 'Ciara will keep an eye on him. I'm not sure that you'd want him running for more than a few weeks, I get the feeling he'll fold like a cheap deckchair if he's under pressure.'

'Can you come to Thames House, right away?'

'Sure. What's up?'

'I'll fill you in when you get here.' He ended the call. Shepherd smiled ruefully. Yes, probably best not to ask for an MI5 briefing over an open line.

The safe house where McKillop was being questioned was in Hampstead, not far from the heath. Shepherd walked for half a mile before calling an Uber. The traffic was light and within half an hour he was walking into Thames House. He went through security and took the lift up to Pritchard's floor. His secretary, Amy, looked up when he walked through the door. 'He says to go straight in.'

'Thanks, Amy,' said Shepherd. Amy Miller was in her sixties, and rumoured to have been one of MI6's top agent-runners in East Germany before the Berlin Wall was torn down. Shepherd knew nothing about her family situation but she was one of the first to start work each day and one of the last to leave. It was after eight o'clock at night and she was clearly in no rush to go home.

MI5 director Giles Pritchard was sitting at his desk, his attention flicking between two computer monitors. His shirt collar was done up but his White's tie was at half mast, always an indicator that his stress levels were rising. He smiled when he saw Shepherd, ran a hand through his greying slicked-back hair and nodded at the two chairs facing the desk. He took his metal-framed glasses off his hawk-like nose and began to twirl them. 'How did it go with McKillop?' he asked as Shepherd sat down.

'He'll cooperate. And Ciara will have no problems handling him. He's a sucker for a pretty face. She and Amar will fix him up with the phone and set him loose.'

'He's still passing Afghan names to the Russians?'

Shepherd nodded. 'He swears blind that he thought she was just a German researcher and I believe him. He's given her all the names on the ARAP database, which is why the Taliban managed to get hold of so many of the translators the UK left behind. The database has everything – names, addresses, fingerprints and photographs.'

'Luckily we managed to get most of them out,' said Pritchard. 'There's still about a hundred trying to get on to the airport. The problem is, the Taliban checkpoints almost certainly have the ARAP files.' He shook his head sadly. 'I don't understand why the MoD didn't have a higher classification on the files. We had a duty to protect those people and their families. And what about the ACRS database?'

'We've removed it from the MoD mainframe and are adjusting it as we speak. We've got a team removing the details of anyone at risk and once that's been done we'll add to it details of Taliban fighters and organisers that we'd like to see disrupted.'

Pritchard smiled thinly. 'That's a tactful way of putting it.'

'It should work, for a while at least. So far all the intel the Russians have been feeding to the Taliban has been kosher. It'll be some time before they realise that the well has been poisoned and by that time hopefully they'll have killed dozens of their own people.'

'And what happens to the Russian agent then? Her bosses will realise that McKillop has been feeding her false intelligence and the Russians have a tendency to be ruthless with their people when they make mistakes.'

'It'll be a good opportunity to turn her,' said Shepherd.

Pritchard nodded. 'The timing will be crucial. They'll prob-ably ship her to Moscow the moment they realise she's been blown. We'll need to keep a close eye on her.'

'I'd suggest not having her followed,' said Shepherd. 'If she's Moscow trained there's a good chance she'll spot a tail. Best to monitor her conversations with McKillop. Once she realises there's a problem her manner will change. She'll be less trusting and we should be able to spot that.'

Pritchard nodded. 'At which point we pick her up and make her an offer she can't refuse. Work for us or take a one-way trip on Aeroflot.' He nodded again. 'You're right. She isn't Russian-born, I think she'll be easy enough to turn when the time's right.'

'And what about McKillop?' asked Shepherd.

'What do you mean?'

'A lot of people died because of what he did. Including women and children who were raped and murdered.'

'But he didn't know that would happen, did he?'

Shepherd shrugged. 'I don't think ignorance is reason enough to give him a pass.'

'You want to put him on trial? The *Guardian* will have a field day.'

'So it gets swept under the carpet?'

'If McKillop does what he can to put this right, and if he's open and honest about everything, then I don't have a problem in giving him a clean slate.' Pritchard leaned forward. 'I can see you're not happy about this.'

Shepherd grimaced. 'There isn't much to be happy about, is there?'

'I disagree. If a senior army officer out in Kabul hadn't realised that our former interpreters were being picked up by the Taliban we'd never have discovered the data leak. And you were able to link McKillop with the Russian agent in double-quick time, which means we can now plug the leak. And we have the opportunity to do some damage ourselves.'

'It's an ill wind . . .'

'Try to look on the bright side, that's all I'm saying,' said Pritchard. He leaned back in his seat. 'Anyway, there's a reason I needed you back here ASAP. You worked with MI6's man in Marbella, a few years ago. Tony Docherty.'

'Yeah. Good guy.'

'Well Docherty has come a cropper in Afghanistan.'

'Afghanistan?'

'He's been based at the embassy in Kabul for the last two years.'

'He's married with three kids.'

'Four.'

'Then what was he doing out in a war zone?'

Pritchard shrugged. 'That was my first question, too. One that has yet to be answered. Anyway, he left the embassy to pick up his translator and his family who have been approved for resettlement in the UK. Docherty arrived in their village at the same time as the Taliban and they had to take cover in a basement. They're not armed so someone has to go in and get them out.' He smiled. 'And by someone . . .'

'Surely there are people on the ground in Kabul?'

'You've seen what's happening at the airport? The regular troops can barely hold the perimeter and those that do go out aren't venturing out of Kabul. The SAS is stretched thinly and are flying in all the men they can as we speak. There's a flight leaving Brize Norton in two hours with four SAS guys on board. The plan is for you to take them to Docherty and to bring him to the airport with his translator and the translator's family.'

'Where is he exactly?'

'He's in a village outside a town called Charikar, a ninety-minute drive north of Kabul. Charikar is on the main Afghan ring road that links Kabul to the northern province, and the Taliban swept through there two days ago. He was on the way there when the Taliban appeared but managed to get into a shophouse and lock himself in a basement with the translator and his family. We have his location but his sat-phone ran out of power yesterday and there's no mobile phone signal where he is, so we've no way of contacting him.'

'That's awkward.'

'Well, yes, but we have his location and he won't be going anywhere. He'll stay put until extracted.' He looked at his watch. 'We have a C17 Globemaster on standby to fly to Kabul as part of our evacuation plan. The SAS men on board will offer you every assistance and Major Gannon is arranging for you to be met in Kabul by an SAS trooper on the ground. Hopefully he'll have a helicopter ready by the time you land.'

Shepherd nodded. 'So the plan is that I fly in, extract Docherty and his translator and family, and get them to Kabul Airport?'

'Exactly. You can get on the next flight back to the UK with them. If all goes to plan you'll be back here within forty-eight hours.'

'Flying into an airport surrounded by Taliban fighters, what could possibly go wrong?'

'So far they haven't been shooting at anything – people, choppers or planes. They're just making it difficult for people to get on to the airfield. It looks worse than it is.'

'I hope so,' said Shepherd. He looked at his watch. 'I'd better be going.'

'The traffic's not great heading to Brize Norton, so I've arranged police bikes to get you there. Wheels up the moment you're on board.'

Shepherd nodded and stood up. 'I'll need Docherty's exact location.'

'The SAS guy in Kabul will have everything you need by the time you land.' He flashed Shepherd a smile. 'Break a leg.'

There were three police motorcyclists waiting outside Thames House. Two were on their bikes, the third was standing by his and holding a white full-face helmet with a tinted visor. Shepherd walked over. 'I guess you're my ride,' he said.

The officer handed him the helmet. 'Our instructions are to get you to Brize Norton ASAP, sir, so it'll be blues and twos all the way.'

Shepherd put on the helmet.

'There's a radio in there so you'll hear what we're saying,' said the officer, sitting astride the bike. 'The airport is seventy-two miles from here and we've got a pool going. I'm reckoning on fifty-eight minutes.' Shepherd sat behind him and put his arms around the officer's waist. 'You've been on a bike at speed before, sir?' asked the officer.

'A few times,' said Shepherd.

'Great. Just lean into the turns and we'll be fine.' He gunned the engine. 'Take the lead Alpha One. Alpha Three to follow.'

'Alpha One taking the lead,' said a voice in Shepherd's helmet.

The three bikes moved off, along Millbank. Almost immediately their sirens and blue lights kicked in.

They reached the gates of Brize Norton in fifty-two minutes and the pool was won by Alpha One. They had cut through the London traffic, using their sirens to zoom through any red lights, to get to the A40. They had spread out along the outside lane and their sirens and lights had everyone pulling over to the left, which meant they could reach speeds of close to ninety miles an hour. Once the A40 became the M40, they upped their speed and for most of the way were above a hundred miles an hour. They'd had to slow as they approached Oxford, but they were still able to keep their speed above seventy over the last few miles to the airport.

The airport security people were clearly expecting them. As they approached the main entrance the barrier lifted up and two armed guards waved them through. They drove past the main terminal towards a parking area where a massive C17 Globemaster was waiting with its rear ramp down. It was much bigger than the Hercules that the SAS generally used to transfer men and equipment around the world, with a fifty-two-metre wingspan and four huge Pratt & Whitney turbofan engines.

Shepherd climbed off the back of the bike, took off his helmet and handed it to the officer. 'Thanks, that was . . . exhilarating.'

'Just glad we got you here in one piece, sir,' said the officer. He nodded at the plane. 'Good luck.'

The three bikes drove away as Shepherd walked towards the plane. The loadmaster was standing at the top of the ramp. He was barely out of his teens with close-cropped red hair and a sprinkle of freckles across his nose, and was wearing a headset with a microphone. He waved for Shepherd to come up.

As Shepherd walked up the ramp, the plane's engines burst into life.

'Better late than never!' somebody shouted from inside the plane.

'Yeah, there's always one, isn't there?' shouted another voice. 'Probably overslept.'

Shepherd reached the top of the ramp and grinned when he recognised the two men. One was Matt Standing, whose anger-management issues had seen him twice lose his sergeant's stripes. The other was Terry 'Paddy' Ireland, a broad-shouldered bruiser of a man wearing a quilted jacket and jeans. Both were sitting with their backs to the fuselage. Ireland stood up and fist-bumped Shepherd. 'How are they hanging, Spider?' he said in his strong Norfolk accent.

'Straight and level, Paddy,' said Shepherd.

'You never did turn up for that drink.'

'Yeah, sorry about that.' The two men had worked together in London as part of an operation to thwart a jihadist drone attack on the capital. The SAS team had been victorious, but it had been a close call. Shepherd had given the celebratory drinks a miss.

Standing got to his feet and fist-bumped Shepherd. 'Good to see you again, Spider. I should have guessed you'd be our VIP on this mission.'

'Is that what they said? VIP?'

Standing grinned. 'Words to that effect. And you obviously dressed for the part. Is that Savile Row?'

'Guys, I need you to fasten yourselves up!' shouted the loadmaster. He pressed a button and the ramp began to withdraw into the fuselage.

'I was keeping your seat warm for you, Spider,' said Standing. He moved to the next seat along and dropped down. Ireland also sat down and fastened his harness.

'The good news is that Penny is no longer the oldest member of the team,' said Standing. He gestured at a grey-haired man in his forties who was wearing a North Face fleece over a black polo neck sweater. He was stretched out on the opposite side of the fuselage, his arms folded and his head down. Shepherd grinned when he realised who it was.

'Bloody hell, Penny, are you still going?' said Shepherd. 'You're like the Energiser Bunny.' Andy 'Penny' Lane had been with the Regiment for more than twenty-five years. He had joined six months after Shepherd and they had been on several missions together. He was a talented linguist, fluent in several European languages along with Russian, Arabic and Kurdish. Whereas Shepherd had left the Regiment to join the police and eventually MI5, Lane had stayed where he was and had served with distinction in Afghanistan, Iraq, Libya and half a dozen other war zones.

'Penny's the unit's signals specialist,' said Standing. 'He tells me that big bulge in the front of his pants is the sat-phone.'

'Sir, please buckle up!' shouted the loadmaster. 'We're on a tight schedule here.'

'Sorry,' said Shepherd. He dropped down on to the seat and fastened the harness.

The ramp clicked into position. Shepherd looked over at the fourth member of the team, who was sitting two seats along from Lane on the other side of the fuselage.

'That's Karl, Karl Williams, the group's medic,' said Ireland.

Williams gave Shepherd a laconic wave. He was in his late twenties, tall with a close-cropped beard. 'I've heard a lot about you,' said Williams. 'Living legend.' He had a strong Bristol accent and large slab-like teeth.

Shepherd laughed. 'If it's Matt who's been talking, he's not a reliable source,' he said.

'Nothing wrong with a little embellishment if it adds to the story,' said Standing. 'Karl used to be a dairy farmer, which accounts for his milkmaid complexion. He's new to the Regiment so this is his first time in Afghanistan.'

'You picked a good time to pop your cherry,' said Shepherd.

'I'm a long way from being a sandpit virgin, I've been to Iraq twice and did a month in Syria,' said Williams.

'Kabul is a whole different ball game at the moment,' said Standing. 'We're flying right into the lion's den.'

'I've always thought of the Taliban as hyenas rather than lions,' said Lane. 'They only fight in packs and they run the moment they face any real opposition.'

'How much have you been told about our mission?' asked Shepherd.

'Just that it's an extraction, outside the airport,' said Standing. 'And that you're calling the shots.'

'We're meeting one of your guys in Kabul, he should have the heli sorted,' said Shepherd.

Standing nodded. 'Yeah, that'll be Clint. Brian Heron. He joined the year before me. Good guy. He's the spitting image of Clint Eastwood. The *Dirty Harry* years.'

'"Are you feeling lucky, punk?"' said Lane. 'That was a great movie.'

The engines started to roar and the plane edged forward. It was too noisy to talk so Shepherd settled back. They had a long flight ahead of them. As the crow flew, Kabul was just over 3,500 miles from Brize Norton. Massive jets didn't tend to fly in exactly the same way as crows and had to stick to approved flight paths, so the true distance would probably be closer to 4,000 miles. The plane had a cruising range of about 2,800 miles, so it would have to refuel at least once on the way. Incirlik Airbase in Turkey was just about midway, but that would mean arriving in Kabul with tanks less than half full, which wouldn't be ideal. Presumably the pilots had done the necessary calculations.

With a cruising speed of just over 500 miles an hour, they'd be in the air for about eight hours, plus whatever time was needed for refuelling. Possibly an hour in all to get the 30,000 gallons of fuel into the tanks. So nine hours in total to reach Kabul. Shepherd looked at his watch. It was just after half past nine. Kabul was three and a half hours ahead of London, which meant an arrival time of about ten o'clock in the morning. Shepherd wasn't happy about mounting a rescue operation during daylight but the clock was ticking and they might not have the luxury of being able to wait until dark.

He looked around. The Globemaster came with fifty-four sidewall seats, twenty-seven on each side. The interior could be left empty and used to carry vehicles and cargo, but for this mission it had been filled with another eighty seats. That meant a total of 134 passengers, a big improvement on the ninety-two that could be carried on a Hercules. Shepherd had been on several missions where the much larger Globemaster had been used and he had become a fan. It could carry larger loads than the Hercules, and was able to operate with a much smaller aircrew – two pilots and a loadmaster, compared with the two pilots, navigator, flight engineer and loadmaster needed to crew a Hercules.

The biggest improvement so far as soldiers were concerned was the fact that the Globemaster had an actual toilet with a sink and lockable door. The Hercules only had a urinal and toilet hidden by a curtain, tucked away in the cargo area, and most soldiers preferred to hold it in rather than suffer the torrent of abuse aimed at anyone who went behind the curtain. There were also bunks behind the Globemaster cockpit so that the crew could catch some sleep, along with an oven and a fridge. All the comforts of home.

The C17 came to a halt. After a few seconds the engines went to full power and the plane rolled forward. They were taking off. The plane powered down the runway then the nose lifted and they were in the air. Standing and Ireland had their heads close together and were deep in conversation, but Lane and Williams were already fast asleep. The loadmaster had his head bent down over a tablet and was tapping on it. Shepherd leaned back and stretched out his legs.

He began planning the forthcoming operation, running through a list of kit they would need. They would pick up weapons and communications gear at the airport, courtesy of Brian 'Clint' Heron. The SAS had plenty of equipment in Kabul so they'd be spoiled for choice. But for a simple extraction, carbines and sidearms would hopefully be all they'd need, with a few grenades as back-up. The big question – still to be decided – was whether to go in during the day or to wait until nightfall.

As Shepherd was considering his options, the plane levelled off. Ireland and Standing opened their eyes as the engine sound changed. The loadmaster put his tablet into one of his jumpsuit pockets and unfastened his harness. He made his way over to Shepherd and flashed him a reassuring smile. 'Right, guys, we're at cruising altitude. We're now en route to Germany where we'll refuel inflight, and from there will be flying into Doha to refuel on the ground.'

'Doha?' said Ireland.

'A deer,' said Standing.

'A female deer,' added Ireland.

'Far, a long long way to run,' they chorused.

The two men laughed. It was clearly an old routine for them. Even the loadmaster couldn't help but smile.

'Why the inflight refuelling?' asked Shepherd.

'They've been wanting to practise Globemaster refuelling for a while so this will kill two birds with one stone. You probably won't even be aware of it happening, though the airspeed will maybe drop a bit.'

'And Doha rather than Incirlik?' said Shepherd.

'Apparently the Qataris have been really helpful and Incirlik is getting backed up with American planes. Distance-wise there isn't much to choose between them. The problem is that even full tanks won't be enough to get us from Doha to Kabul and back, especially if we're fully loaded on the return trip. That means refuelling in Kabul.' He grimaced. 'No one's happy about that prospect, obviously.'

'I was told the Taliban haven't been firing at planes,' said Shepherd.

'Not yet, no,' said the loadmaster. He looked at his wrist-watch, a chunky Breitling. 'Our ETA at Kabul is approximately 0720 Zulu time, but that could well change. I'll keep you updated as we go. While we're cruising feel free to stretch your legs. There's no inflight entertainment but there are soft drinks, water and sandwiches in the fridge. Please don't take anything that's been labelled, the crew are really touchy about that. Other than that, just help yourself. The toilet's over there.' He pointed at the closed door. 'Don't put anything other than paper down, it has a tendency to block and it's a long flight. Any questions?'

Lane raised a hand. 'It's okay to shit in there, right? When you said only paper, you didn't mean only paper, did you? Turds are okay?'

The loadmaster shook his head contemptuously. 'That probably depends on how big your turds are,' he said. 'I'm guessing yours would be the size of a small dog.'

The SAS men laughed as the loadmaster walked back towards the rear of the hold.

Shepherd was woken from a dreamless sleep by the loadmaster shaking his shoulder. He blinked a couple of time to focus his eyes, and grinned. 'Was I snoring?'

'Quiet as a mouse,' said the loadmaster. 'Which is more than can be said for your colleagues.' He gestured over at Lane and Williams who were both stretched out with their heads back, snoring loudly. A trickle of saliva had run from Lane's mouth and dribbled down his jacket. 'Just to let you know we're going to be starting our approach to Doha in about five minutes. They're geared up for a quick refuel so the pilots would prefer everybody to stay on board.'

Shepherd nodded. 'Not a problem.'

'Flight time from Doha to Kabul is about three hours, so we're still on track for a 0720 Zulu arrival. The pilots are worried about a possible missile attack at Kabul, even though everything appears to be quiet around the airport. The plan is to keep high on the approach, then to come down fast and hard with a couple of corkscrew turns, then to lose the power and put on full flaps. It can be a bit disconcerting.'

'I've done it a few times,' said Shepherd. 'In Afghanistan and in Sarajevo.'

'If you like I can wake you guys up about ten minutes before landing so that you can prepare yourselves.'

Shepherd grinned over at his sleeping colleagues. 'That's okay, I'll handle that,' he said.

The loadmaster flashed him a thumbs-up and went back to his seat at the far side of the plane. He strapped himself in and began talking through his headset.

Shepherd settled back in his seat. After a few minutes he felt the plane bank to the left and start to descend. He felt his ears pop and the engine roar quietened a little, and after a few minutes he heard the flaps grind into position for landing, then the thumps of the landing gear coming down.

The massive airplane weighed close to 130 tons, but the landing was so soft that Shepherd was barely aware of the wheels touching the tarmac. They taxied for a few minutes and then came to a halt. Almost immediately he heard a truck outside and commands being shouted. He unbuckled his harness and went over to the fridge. He opened it and peered inside. The loadmaster hadn't been joking about the crew labelling their refreshments. There was even a handwritten note – DON'T EVEN THINK ABOUT IT – taped to a Tupperware container filled with sandwiches.

Everything on the lower three shelves was label free so Shepherd helped himself to a bottle of water, a pack of cheese sandwiches and a banana. Standing joined him and grabbed ham sandwiches and a Coke. 'This is a step up from the old Herc, isn't it?' said Standing.

'Travelling in style,' said Shepherd.

'I can't get over the fact that they actually installed a real toilet. I might even give it a go.'

'First time on a C17?'

'Yeah. Though I hear they're phasing out the Hercs so the C17 will be the norm.'

The loadmaster joined them and helped himself to a bottle of water. 'We'll be wheels up in about fifteen minutes,' he said. 'Just to confirm, we'll only be on the ground in Kabul for about six hours.'

'You won't be waiting for me?' asked Shepherd.

'I'm afraid not,' said the loadmaster. 'The airport is under American military control. They're assigning departure slots as planes arrive and the planes have to stick to those times. Zero flexibility. We had one flight out with just one passenger on board and I'm told other countries have been forced to fly out planes empty.'

'Fucking Yanks,' said Standing. He popped the tab on his can of Coke and drank. A loud groaning sound filled the fuselage, like an animal in pain. 'What the hell's that?'

The loadmaster laughed. 'It's the pressure relief vents,' he said. 'As the fuel goes in it forces the air out. The Yanks reckon it sounds like a moose on heat so they call the C17 "the Moose".'

'What's the story with the evacuees?' asked Shepherd. 'They're at the airport waiting to be flown out, right?'

'The ones who have been processed are good to go,' said the loadmaster. 'Then there are others who are being processed, and more outside trying to get in. It's a major cock-up. We can only take people who have been fully processed. Doesn't matter who they are or what their circumstances are; no paper-work, no flight. That's why we've had near-empty planes flying out.'

'This isn't your first Kabul evac flight?' asked Shepherd.

'It's my third. On the first we only had twelve passengers, all embassy staff. There were Afghans waiting to be processed but we weren't allowed to take them. The second time we managed to get more than four hundred on.'

'You're joking.'

The loadmaster shook his head. 'Four hundred and thirty-six souls. Three times our regular capacity and a new RAF record – the biggest-capacity flight in the RAF's history.'

'That's impressive,' said Shepherd. 'And dangerous.'

The loadmaster sipped his water. 'We had to rip all the seat palettes out. But the Yanks did even better. They managed to cram eight hundred and twenty-three on to a C17. Eight hundred and twenty-three.' He shook his head. 'They must have been crammed in like sardines. I can't imagine how they managed to get that bird in the air.'

'The pilots probably told them to lift their feet off the floor,' said Standing. 'Lighten the load.'

The loadmaster opened his mouth to reply but then realised that Standing was joking. 'You are funny guys,' he said, as he walked back to his seat.

Standing took a bite of his sandwich.

'How have you been, Matt?' asked Shepherd.

'All good. Back up to sergeant, which is nice. We'll see how long it lasts.'

'Anger management still working?' Standing had a reputation for flying off the handle, especially with incompetent officers, but was one of the Regiment's best combat soldiers.

Standing grinned. 'Yeah, I'm good.' He took a swig of his Coke. 'This Afghanistan thing is a bloody mess.'

'Yeah.'

'That's where you took a bullet, right?'

Shepherd nodded and felt a sudden twinge in his shoulder as if the wound was reminding him that it was still there.

'So many good soldiers died out there, and for what?' said Standing. 'The Taliban were controlling things when we went in, and twenty years later they're still in charge. Nothing has changed.'

'We took out a lot of bad guys,' said Shepherd.

Standing grinned. 'Yeah, we did that.'

'That has to count for something. But I take your point. This is a defeat no matter how you look at it. And no soldier likes a defeat.' He peeled his banana and took a bite. 'What are your orders on this?'

'To help you get this MI6 spook on to a plane back to the UK and then protect the ambassador and his people until they're ready to fly out. With any luck we'll be on the plane with him because I really wouldn't want to be left behind.'

'Just walk to the border and write a book about it,' said Shepherd. 'It could be a whole new career for you.'

'I think they've put a stop to memoirs like that,' said Standing. 'But there's no way they'll be leaving me or my guys behind.'

'You'll be fine,' said Shepherd.

They went back to their seats and strapped themselves in. They had just finished their food when the engines restarted and the plane moved forward. Ten minutes later they were back at cruising altitude, heading for Kabul.

Shepherd yawned, stretched, and checked his watch. They must be getting close to their destination. He looked over at the loadmaster who was talking on his headset. The loadmaster nodded at Shepherd and held up his hand, fingers splayed. 'Five minutes,' he mouthed.

Shepherd flashed him an 'okay' sign. He turned to see Standing looking at him.

'Shall I wake the guys?' asked Standing. Ireland was snoring and Williams and Lane were stretched out, their eyes closed. Saliva was again dribbling from Lane's mouth.

Shepherd shrugged. 'They're professionals, they'll be fine.'

Standing grinned. 'Exactly what I was thinking.'

They tightened their harnesses and checked that their rubbish was stowed. The descent started a few minutes later. There was a slight change in engine noise and then the plane went into a steep dive. The engines began to scream and the whole plane vibrated.

Ireland's feet lashed out and his eyes sprang open. 'What the fuck!' he shouted.

The dive steepened and Shepherd felt the harness bite into his shoulders.

Lane and Williams both woke up and began flailing about. At that moment the Globemaster went into a steep right turn that slammed Shepherd back against the bulkhead. Lane and Williams were thrown forward. As Lane had his harness loose his backside slipped off the seat and he yelped in pain.

The two men looked across at Shepherd and Standing who were both laughing. 'You bastards!' shouted Lane. 'Some warning might have been nice!'

'Caught me by surprise, too!' Shepherd shouted back.

Lane pushed himself back into his seat as the plane came out of its tight turn. It was still in a steep dive.

The loadmaster was laughing and Lane threw him an angry look. 'Next time I'm flying easyJet!' he shouted.

The plane levelled off for ten seconds, then it began to dive. The engines roared as once again it went into a tight turn and again Standing and Shepherd were flattened against the bulkhead. 'Are we being shot at?' asked Ireland.

'I think it's just better safe than sorry,' said Standing. 'Either that or the pilots just like fucking with us.'

The tight turn continued for almost a minute, then the nose came up and the engines throttled back. As soon as the speed had slowed there were loud thumps from both wings. The flaps. They were coming in to land. A few seconds later the landing gear rumbled into position, then there was a bump as the wheels hit the tarmac followed by the squeal of rubber as the brakes were applied.

They turned off the runway and taxied, then turned right and slowed. The moment they stopped, the loadmaster was on his feet. 'That wasn't so bad,' said Standing, unfastening his harness.

'I've had worse,' said Shepherd. He released his harness,

stood up, and stretched. The ramp was lowering, giving them their first glimpse of the Afghan sky, bright blue with just a few wisps of cloud. The hot air billowed in along with the smell of aviation fuel.

The loadmaster came over. 'Pleasure having you guys on board,' he said. 'Good luck with whatever you've got planned.'

'You too,' said Shepherd.

Lane and Williams were already at the bottom of the ramp where a tall, thin man in desert fatigues was waiting for them. Shepherd knew immediately it was Brian Heron – he really did look just like a young Clint Eastwood.

Lane and Williams bumped fists with Heron, who then turned to look at Standing. 'You can't stay away from the sandpit can you, Matt?' he said.

'Just when I thought I was out, they pull me back in,' said Standing, in a half-decent Al Pacino impression. He nodded at Shepherd. 'This is Spider, he's running the show.'

'I've been expecting you,' said Heron. He bumped fists with Shepherd and nodded over at Ireland. 'Good to see you back, Paddy. You can pay me that fifty quid I lent you.'

'You'll take a cheque, yeah?' said Ireland.

'Short arms, long pockets,' Heron said to Shepherd with a grin. 'I've managed to requisition a room for your briefing and I have a Puma on standby. The crew are from 230 Squadron so they're used to special ops missions and are up for anything. What's your time-frame?'

'Still to be decided,' said Shepherd. 'But I'm thinking the sooner the better.'

'I'll take you straight there,' said Heron.

Lane and Williams stepped off the ramp on to the tarmac and Shepherd, Standing and Ireland followed them. A plane took off to their right. It was another Globemaster, with American markings. There were more transport planes lined up by the terminal, some of them in the process of being refuelled, and half a dozen civilian jets.

They ducked instinctively as they heard a rattle of an AK-47 in the distance. Heron smiled tightly. 'The Taliban fire into the air every now and again to keep the crowds under control,' he said. 'There are thousands of men, women and children outside trying to get in.'

There were groups of Afghans sitting on the tarmac close to the planes in ordered lines. There was no shade and most of them had their heads covered. US Army personnel were distributing bottles of water. More soldiers stood around in full battle gear, their carbines at the ready. Shepherd did a quick count – there were a dozen groups, each of several hundred evacuees.

'Would you look at that,' said Williams.

'I'm looking,' said Standing. 'And what I'm seeing is mainly men of fighting age who should be out there defending their country. And where are the women and children? It's ninety per cent men.'

Lane laughed. 'You're surprised? You've always known what the Afghans are like. They're not great fighters, never have been.'

'There were ninety thousand men in the Afghan Army,' said Standing. 'Last I heard the Taliban had fewer than thirty thousand. And the Taliban had twenty-year-old AK-47s and the Afghans had billions of dollars of state-of-the-art equipment. Yet these bastards are running away without firing a shot.' He waved his hand at the crowds around the terminal. 'Look at that. There's thousands of them. They should be out there fighting for their country. Pricks.'

'Relax, Matt,' said Shepherd.

'It just annoys me, Spider. We've had mates die out here, and for what?'

'Ours is not to reason why.'

'Yeah, I know. We just do what our masters tell us. But this is fucked up. Imagine if this lot were in England during the Second World War. They see Germany preparing to invade England, what do you think they'd do? Pick up a gun and defend our country? Or grab a dinghy and paddle over to Ireland and demand asylum?'

Shepherd patted him on the back. 'Let's stay focused on the job in hand, yeah?'

The group followed Heron across the tarmac to a line of buildings separate from the main terminal. There were several SUVs lined up outside. 'Clint, what happens to all the kit?' asked Shepherd.

'Most of it is being left behind,' said Heron. 'We're only evacuating people.' He grinned. 'Though the Afghan president has flown to Dubai with 170 million dollars packed up in crates.'

'So the captain isn't going down with the ship?' asked Standing.

'He was one of the first rats to leave,' said Heron. 'That's really when the rot set in. When the Afghan troops heard he'd done a runner they figured there was no point in fighting.'

'Probably more worried that they weren't going to get paid,' said Standing.

Heron took them to a door and opened it. They were immediately hit by a blast of cold air. Heron had left the aircon running. 'I don't think anyone's going to be worried about the electricity bill,' he said.

Shepherd went in first. It was a large room that had obviously been an office. Four desks had been pushed against a wall along with filing cabinets, a large photocopier and an industrial-sized shredder. There were several black garbage bags stacked on the desks. One of them had ripped open and a stream of shredded paper had spilled out. 'The RAF used this for admin but all the clerks have shipped out,' said Heron.

Ireland was the last in and he closed the door. There was a single table in the middle of the room with a large-scale map and half a dozen aerial photographs taken either from a satellite or a drone. More aerial photographs had been taped to a wall. One of them was an overhead shot of the airport. Shepherd went over to look at it. Two shipping containers had been placed at the entrance to the airport, blocking the way in but for a small gap just a few feet wide. Beyond the containers were thousands of people, obviously desperate to get to the planes. 'The army put the containers there,' said Heron. 'The crowds were crushing against the gates and there was a danger of them collapsing.'

Shepherd looked closer at the photograph. There were dozens of Afghan men with guns standing by the containers. 'The Taliban are controlling the entrance? They say who gets in and who doesn't?'

Heron nodded. 'They're in control outside the containers. They decide who goes through. Then there's a sort of no-man's land between the containers and the gate and fence. That's controlled by the US Army. It's a bit surreal because they're sometimes just a few feet away from the Taliban and everyone is armed to the teeth. Just a few days ago they'd have been shooting each other, today they're cooperating. And the Taliban have checkpoints on all the roads leading to the airport. Basically they're in charge of everything outside the perimeter.' Heron tapped on a photograph where three pick-up trucks flying Islamic State flags had blocked the road and bearded men with guns were checking cars and pedestrians. Most of the civilians were waving sheets of paper. 'They probably have to get through four of five roadblocks just to get to the front of the airport.'

'How do they choose who to let through?'

'They need paperwork from the relevant embassy, plus cash or jewellery or maybe a blowjob. It's a jungle out there. And even if they do make it through the checkpoints there's no guarantee that they'll get into the airport and on to a plane. It's a mess.'

Shepherd surveyed the photographs, then turned to look at the map on the table. 'Thanks for this,' he said. 'I know it's all been kick-bollock-scramble.'

'It's getting worse by the hour,' said Heron. 'So far Terry Taliban has only been shooting into the air, but if he decides to have a pop at us, we'll be sitting ducks. They already had RPGs but the Yanks have left behind a shed load of missiles. If they start taking pot-shots at the helis or God forbid the planes, then everything changes.'

'Is anyone talking to them?' asked Shepherd.

'The rumour is that MI6 and the CIA are in contact, trying to put some sort of deal in place.'

'What sort of deal?'

Heron shrugged. 'It's way above my pay grade. But there's a rumour that the CIA is saying they'll leave behind all the guns and equipment, undamaged, if the Taliban allow everyone out.'

'They're bribing them with Humvees and M4s?' said Standing. 'I can't see how that'll end badly, can you?' He shook his head. 'That bastard Biden has a lot to answer for. What the hell was he thinking?'

Ireland laughed scornfully. 'You've seen him, right? The guy's got late-stage dementia, he's not thinking about anything.'

'The prime minister is no better,' said Lane. 'It wasn't that long ago that he was telling Parliament there was no military path to victory for the Taliban.' He snorted scornfully.

'How could they not have seen this coming?' said Williams.

'Guys, there's no point in asking how we got here,' said Shepherd. 'All that matters is getting the job done.' He turned to Heron. 'How long to reach the target?' he asked.

'Fifteen minutes in a heli.' He pointed at the map on the table and they all gathered around it. They heard the roar of engines as another plane took to the sky. 'This is Charikar, a town on the Afghan ring road. It's on the main route to Kabul from the north, so it's chock-a-block with Terry.' He ran his finger across the map and tapped again. 'The spook is here in a small village. Just a few dozen houses, a school, a few shops and a medical centre. It's about three miles to the east of Charikar. The surrounding area is mainly agricultural.'

He reached over and picked up one of the satellite photographs. He placed it on the map. 'This is a satellite image taken yesterday,' he said. There was a two-lane dirt road running through the middle of the picture, with a building and a large yard at the bottom and a long building with a paved area in front of it. Smaller single track roads led off the main road. He tapped the long building. 'The spook was in the area to pick up his translator and his family. They live outside the village but when they got to this street they saw Taliban in the area and left the vehicle. He managed to get into a shophouse and lock himself in a basement with the translator and his family. We have his location but his sat-phone ran out of power yesterday and there's no mobile phone signal where he is, so we've no way of contacting him. We are pretty sure he's in the third shophouse from the right but there's a possibility it could be one either side.'

Shepherd narrowed his eyes as he looked at the photograph. 'I don't see Taliban in the area.'

'The Taliban that are there are mobile,' said Heron. He pulled over another photograph. It showed a pick-up truck with two men and a heavy machine gun in the back driving down the road. 'There aren't any checkpoints in the area and most people seem to have fled from the village itself. But Taliban fighters are driving around and will be an ongoing problem.' He tapped his finger on the building at the bottom of the picture. 'There's a school opposite but that's shut now. There's a sizeable playground in the school where the heli can land, but I wouldn't recommend hanging about.'

'Do you think a day or night extraction would be best?' asked Shepherd.

Heron shrugged. 'Six of one,' he said. 'The heli pilots are happy to fly at night, more than half their missions are after dark. And they're familiar with the area.'

'Enemy fire?'

'So far no helis have been shot at and they're arriving and leaving all the time. The Yanks are mainly using Chinooks to fly in their people so they're all buzzing around. But I can't guarantee what will happen if the Taliban catch you on the ground.'

Shepherd nodded. 'What's the moon situation?'

'There's some moon and the skies are fairly clear,' said Heron. 'But you'll still need night vision gear – there's no street lighting out there.'

'Never been a fan of night vision,' said Standing. 'Too easy to trip over something in unfamiliar territory.'

'Looks like there's a lot to trip over, too,' said Lane. 'All sorts of crap littered about and potholes everywhere.'

Shepherd nodded. Night vision goggles did what they were supposed to, but they limited vision to what was directly ahead of you, which meant no peripheral vision and no way of seeing where you were placing your feet. The trick was to check the ground a few yards ahead of you and remember where any obstacles were. It was perfectly doable but it slowed you down in combat. 'Is everybody happy with a daytime extraction?' asked Shepherd. 'Because with the way things are going I reckon that's the better option.'

All the men around the table nodded.

'A daytime extraction means that we can do a fly-around and check for opposition,' said Ireland. 'At night we won't know who's there waiting for us.'

'Daytime it is,' said Shepherd. 'What about you, Clint? Are you coming with us?'

'I'd love to but I'm under orders to stay on the airfield,' said Heron. 'I'm in charge of the ambassador's close protection team.'

'Shitting himself, is he?' asked Standing.

Heron laughed. 'And some. At the first sign of the collapse, he abandoned the embassy and was about to get on a plane to the UK. The PM phoned him and ordered him to stay put so long as there were British citizens at risk and visas to be processed. The ambassador tried to refuse but they compromised by agreeing that he could stay at the airport with round-the-clock SAS protection. The moment it looks as if the airport is being breached, our orders are to get him and his staff on the next plane out.'

'So it's the five of us. How are we fixed for equipment?'

'Anything you want, within reason.'

Shepherd studied the map. 'Looks to me like the best place for the heli to land is in the school grounds. There's plenty of room and no obvious obstacles. We cross the road and head into the building. I'm presuming Docherty will open the door when we knock. He's in the basement, right?'

Heron nodded. 'Last message we had, yes.'

'I'm thinking in and out within ten minutes,' said Shepherd.

'Assuming no opposition,' said Standing.

'We'll know from the recce if there's Taliban around,' said Ireland.

'What if there is?' said Lane.

'Depends on the level of opposition,' said Shepherd. 'If it's just a couple of guys with AK-47s, we can handle it. If there's more in the vicinity we can look for a drop zone further away and come in on foot. But from the pictures, the area looks pretty clear. Assuming we don't see any problems, the heli can land in the school grounds and wait for us.'

'And if Terry turns up while we're in the basement?' said Lane.

'The pilots can retreat and come back for us when it's clear,' said Shepherd.

'I'm not comfortable with the idea of us being out there with no transport at hand,' said Lane. 'What do we do if the shit hits the fan? Run for it?'

'If there's an RPG in the vicinity and they shoot down the

heli, we'd be in the same position,' said Shepherd. 'But we'd have a dead heli crew too. Better they go back up and stay out of range of any possible enemy fire.'

'If they hover above the school, even a thousand feet or so above it, they'll attract more Taliban,' said Heron. 'They either stay put on the ground or get well away and return to pick you up.'

'How about this?' said Ireland. 'Get the guys we're picking up to come to us. They can meet us at the school, we swoop down and pick them up laying down whatever fire is necessary. Job done.'

'Except we have no way of contacting them,' said Shepherd. 'Their sat-phone is dead. We literally have to knock on their door.'

Shepherd wasn't the least bit fazed by the questions. It was standard practice before an SAS mission, a procedure known as a Chinese Parliament. Every member of the team was encouraged to speak and to offer up suggestions and reservations. It didn't matter how much experience they had or what rank they were, everyone was listened to. The final call would be Shepherd's – it was his op – but everyone had their say.

He looked down at the map again. 'Okay, maybe I'm being too pessimistic about the timing. Let's suppose we hit the ground running. We get to the school gate in ten seconds. Cross the road in less than five. Straight into the shop and find the basement door. Another ten seconds? I bang on the door, Docherty opens it and sees it's me. Another five seconds. We get them out and run back to the heli. If it goes like clockwork, we could be in and out in a minute. Sixty seconds.'

'Yeah, but when does it ever go like clockwork?' asked Standing.

Ireland nodded. 'Best laid plans.'

'Yeah, but if we've done the recce properly there won't be any Taliban within range during that time. So the heli can wait for us with instructions to take off if we're delayed and Terry's approaching.' He tapped the school gate on one of the photographs. 'Paddy, you can stay here and keep an eye out for Terry.' He nodded at Heron. 'We're okay for comms?'

'Standard SAS kit. Plus I've got a sat-phone for you.'

Shepherd looked back at Ireland. 'Paddy, you keep watch. We cross the road and go into the house. He nodded at Karl. 'Karl, you stay outside the shop. You and Paddy will have a full view of the road and you can tell us if there's a problem.' He looked at Standing and Lane. 'Matt, you and Penny come to the basement with me.'

Both men nodded.

'Unless there's a problem, the heli stays. Anything more than a stray jihadist or two and the heli can fly off and RV with us later. All good?'

The men nodded. 'Excellent. Now in terms of kit, carbines and handguns should be enough.' He looked at Heron. 'Grenades?'

Heron nodded. 'All you want.'

'I'm thinking just a few in case we meet an armed truck.'

'They've got Humvees already,' said Heron. 'The Yanks are leaving everything behind.'

'If they come in a Humvee, we'll see them for miles,' said Shepherd.

'I'd feel happier with a grenade launcher,' said Ireland. 'Just to be on the safe side.'

Shepherd looked at Heron. Heron smiled. 'I've got M203s and all the HEDP rounds you can use.'

Shepherd nodded. The M203 grenade launcher could be fitted underneath the barrel of an M16 assault rifle to fire a wide range of grenades, including CS gas, smoke and the high-explosive dual-purpose round that Heron had mentioned. The HEDP could penetrate five centimetres of armour plate when aimed at a vehicle and had a kill radius of five metres when fired at personnel. 'Paddy?'

'Perfect,' said Ireland. 'I'm a big fan of the M203. It'll ruin anybody's day.'

'You should be able to take out any contact on wheels,' said Shepherd. 'Just make sure you don't point it at the heli.' He looked at the faces of the men around the table. 'I think we're good to go, guys,' he said. 'Any questions?'

All the men shook their heads.

'When can we go, Clint?' asked Shepherd.

'The Puma is fuelled and ready when you are. The Yanks are being more flexible about helis so you can go when you want.'

'Let's get kitted up,' said Shepherd.

The Puma's twin turbines roared and the helicopter lifted into the air. They had left the doors open on both sides to improve visibility. Shepherd and Standing were sitting towards the front. They were both carrying Heckler & Koch 417 assault rifles. Next to them was a crew chief in an olive jumpsuit and a helmet with a microphone.

Ireland, Williams and Lane were further back, peering out of the open doors. Ireland was cradling an M16 with the M203 grenade launcher attached and had three nylon pouches containing the HEDP grenades on his belt. Lane was cradling his favourite weapon for close-quarter combat, a Mossberg

590M pump-action shotgun with a magazine holding twenty shells. Like Shepherd, Williams had chosen an HK417. They all had Glock 17s and their holsters of choice. Standing had his on his left hip. Shepherd had his on his right thigh, as did Lane and Ireland. Williams had his under his arm. Standing and Lane both had two fragmentation grenades and Lane had the sat-phone clipped to his belt. They were all wearing Afghan clothing – long jackets and baggy trousers, and black-and-white scarves around their necks. There were no foreign troops outside the airport so there was no chance of friendly fire, and the local clothing would confuse any contacts, at least until they got close enough to see that they were Westerners.

They all had headsets connected to transceivers on their belts and they had tested them before getting on board. Heron would be listening in, but once they were out of range they would use the sat-phone to stay in touch.

Shepherd's jaw dropped as they approached the airfield perimeter. There were tens of thousands of men, women and children trying to get in, with more pouring in along the roads. It was like a scene from a zombie apocalypse movie. The higher they climbed, the more people they saw, most carrying bags or pushing trolleys containing what few possessions they hoped to take with them. Most of them were trying to get to the main entrance but there were desperate people all around the perimeter.

The crowd trying to get into the main entrance was more than a hundred deep, with more arriving all the time. Shepherd could only imagine what it must feel like to arrive with a family and see a crowd that big between you and safety.

The helicopter banked to the right, heading west. Down

below, two men were fighting, clawing at each other's faces, surrounded by screaming onlookers.

'Survival of the fittest,' said Standing.

'How did it get to this?' said Shepherd. 'They've known the troops were pulling out since the Doha Agreement in February 2020. They've had more than enough time to get everybody out.'

'The Afghans just gave up,' said Standing. 'Even the Taliban were caught by surprise. They were assuming they'd be in Kabul by the new year but it's August and here they are.'

The helicopter straightened up and headed west, still climbing. Two Chinooks passed them, a thousand feet above them and heading towards the airport.

All the roads leading to the airport had been blocked with checkpoints and there were lines of cars and trucks waiting to be processed. Many had been abandoned at the roadside, the occupants obviously deciding they'd be better off on foot.

The Puma banked to the right again, heading north and still climbing. Shepherd peered down through the open door, the wind tugging at his hair. The streets below were surprisingly regular with a grid plan that resembled an American city. There was a single flat-roofed house on each plot, many of them dotted with satellite dishes and washing lines, and mosques everywhere. More than 4 million people lived in Kabul but the streets away from the airport were practically empty, and the only vehicles Shepherd could see appeared to be carrying Taliban fighters.

The helicopter levelled off at 3,000 feet. To their left was the Asian Highway 76, the main route connecting Kabul to the north. There was virtually no northbound traffic through

– all the vehicles on it were Taliban trucks, heading to the capital.

Soon they had left the urban sprawl behind and were flying over farms and crops grown in fields as neatly ordered as the streets of Kabul. After ten minutes the helicopter began to descend. Eventually the crew chief tapped Shepherd on the shoulder. 'Coming up to the village now!' he shouted. 'We're going to do a full circuit at two thousand feet and then another at five hundred.'

Shepherd flashed him an 'okay' sign. The Puma began a slow descent. They were still flying over agricultural land and down below goat herders were tending their flocks. Charikar was off to the west. It was quite a large town with close to 200,000 inhabitants. Running through it was Highway One, part of the largest ring road in the world, connecting Kabul with most of the country's major cities. Two-thirds of the country lived within twenty miles of the 1,300-mile road.

The Puma began a slow clockwise turn and all the men peered out of the doorway on the right. The school was easy to spot, as was a mosque a couple of hundred yards from it. The road in front of the school was clear, and so were the side roads leading off it. Shepherd scanned the surrounding area. There was a single truck with a dozen goats in the back heading towards Charikar. Peering off into the distance, he could see plenty of traffic along Highway 1, mainly trucks and Taliban military vehicles. There were several Humvees, presumably left behind by the Americans. The occupants would have been able to see the Puma, but hopefully they would continue driving to Kabul.

The Puma finished its first circuit and went into a steep descent before levelling off at 500 feet. This time they went into an anti-clockwise turn and the men all looked out of the left doorway. They had a clear view of the school. It was deserted. Shepherd frowned as he realised that there were no vehicles parked anywhere near the building where Docherty was holed up. Presumably he had driven there to pick up his translator, so where was the vehicle?

'Looks clear,' said Standing.

Shepherd nodded. 'We're good to go.' He flashed the crew chief a thumbs-up and the man spoke to the pilot through his headset.

The Puma finished its second circuit, then the engines quietened and it began to descend again. Shepherd quickly checked that everyone was ready. Lane and Williams were grinning, eager to get going. Ireland nodded and kissed his grenade launcher.

The Puma slowed as it approached the school, then hovered over the yard, its main rotor blades kicking up swirls of dust and sand. Standing was first out, even before the Puma's wheels had touched the ground. Shepherd followed him, bending double at the waist. Lane and Williams jumped out of the other door and ran around the front of the helicopter, as Ireland brought up the rear.

The rotors slowed but continued to turn. Standing and Shepherd ran out of the school gate and looked left and right. No traffic. Shepherd pointed at the shophouse, Standing nodded, and they ran across the road. Lane and Williams followed. Ireland stopped at the gate and stood with his M16 across his chest.

The shophouse sold charcoal, metal pots, oil lamps and candles. The door was locked. Shepherd peered inside. The shop didn't appear to have been looted, there were full shelves and a cash register sitting on a wooden table. He took a step back and kicked the door just below the lock. The wood splintered but the door stayed put. His second kick did the trick and the door crashed to the floor. He walked over it, his boots crunching on the wood. Standing followed him. They did a quick recce of the ground floor. There was a back room that was being used for storage, and a basic bathroom. 'I don't see a basement,' said Standing.

Shepherd nodded grimly. 'Must be next door.'

They went back into the main part of the shop where Lane was waiting for them. Williams was outside, standing with his back to the window, his head swivelling from side to side. 'Wrong place,' Shepherd said to Lane. 'You and Matt check the shop on the left, Karl and I will go right.'

They walked over the broken door, back into the sunlight. Standing and Lane immediately went into the shop on their left, which seemed to sell and repair bicycles.

Shepherd and Williams checked the window of the shop on the right. It looked as if it had once sold food but the shelves were bare. Shepherd opened the door and a small brass bell tinkled. He walked quickly across the shop, his carbine at the ready.

'There's a basement here,' said Standing in his earpiece. 'The door's open.'

Williams followed Shepherd. A large rat scuttled along the wall to their left and disappeared through a hole in the floor. The layout of the shop was similar to the one they had just been in, though the back room was being used as a bedroom. There was an old chest of drawers that had been ransacked, either by the occupants before they fled or by the Taliban if they'd come through pillaging.

'Door to the right,' said Williams, gesturing with his carbine.

Shepherd swung his weapon around. The door was behind a threadbare curtain hanging from a wooden rod.

'Basement empty,' said Standing in Shepherd's ear. 'Unless you fancy interrogating a few rats.'

'Roger that,' said Shepherd. 'We've a basement here.' He reached for the door handle, turned and pushed, but the door was either locked or bolted. He banged on it with the flat of his hand. 'Tony, are you in there?' he shouted. 'It's Spider Shepherd.'

There was silence for a few seconds, then Shepherd heard footsteps and two bolts rattle back. The door opened a few inches and Shepherd caught a glimpse of an ashen face. 'Fuck me!' said a voice. The door opened wide. It was Tony Docherty, looking considerably greyer and more stressed than the last time they'd met in Marbella. 'What the hell are you doing here?'

Shepherd grinned. 'Someone had to get your MI6 nuts out of the fire. Come on, your chariot awaits.' He stepped back as Docherty opened the door wider to reveal wooden steps leading down to the basement. There were more people standing together, looking up anxiously. Two Afghan men, two women and a group of children. 'How many of you are there?' Shepherd asked.

'Yeah, sorry about this,' said Docherty. 'There's my translator, Sayyid, and his wife and two kids. We've linked up with a British Afghan family. There's a guy – his name is Waiz – and his wife and three kids. So ten, including me. Is that a problem?'

'It's okay. We're in a Puma, there's room for everybody.'

'There's something else, Spider. Sorry. Can we have a quick word, in private?'

'Tony, mate, we need to get out of here.'

'It's important.'

Shepherd gritted his teeth, then nodded. 'Paddy, keep watch,' he said over the radio. 'We're going to be a bit longer here. Matt and Penny, can you get in here?' He turned to look at Williams. 'Get them all up and into the shop. But don't let anyone leave just yet.'

Williams nodded. Shepherd and Docherty went through to the back room. Docherty was wearing a grey linen suit that was streaked with dirt over a sweat-stained white cotton shirt. 'Have you got any water?' he asked.

Shepherd shook his head. 'Sorry.'

There was a small bathroom to the left and Docherty went in and ran a tap, drinking a little water and splashing some over his face.

'Is that safe to drink?' asked Shepherd.

'Beggars, choosers,' said Docherty. 'I'll take the tablets when I'm out of here. Okay, so here's the thing. I left to pick up Sayyid and his family. The paperwork hadn't been done so I was going to drive him into the embassy. There were already checkpoints being set up and he was worried they wouldn't let him go to the airport. So I drove out, but on the way things took a turn for the worse. The ambassador and his staff fled to the airport.'

'Yeah, I heard. Apparently he tried to get on a plane but the PM stopped him.'

'I didn't know that, but I heard that he was abandoning the embassy. He and his staff should have destroyed anything sensitive including the computers and stuff, but there's a briefcase in my office that they won't have known about. It's in a floor safe so there's a chance any looters won't find it, but if they do . . .' He shrugged. 'There's some sensitive stuff there. Really sensitive.'

'Shit,' said Shepherd.

'Yeah. Exactly. There are some papers and documents, but the really sensitive stuff is on a couple of thumb drives. Details of assets within the Afghan government, village elders who have been helping us, council officials and so on. If the Taliban get hold of it . . .'

'Why didn't you destroy it, Tony?'

'When I left the embassy, everything was still relatively secure. But the Taliban moved faster than anyone expected. There was no resistance and they cut through the country like a knife through butter. I only found out that the ambassador had bailed after the event. Look, I need you to get me into the embassy to get that briefcase.'

'The Taliban are everywhere now. They've surrounded the airport so I'm sure they're all over the embassy.'

'We can't let them get their hands on that intel, Spider.'

Shepherd nodded. 'I understand. Where is your office?'

'Second floor, at the rear of the main building.'

'And if we take the helicopter, where can it land? On the roof?'

'The roof is cluttered with containers and satellite dishes. The tennis court is better.'

'Okay, let me run it by the guys. Now this Waiz, what's his story?'

'He'd been visiting his family out in the sticks. They were on their way back to Kabul when the Taliban came through here. He panicked and hid in this shop. We busted in a few hours later.'

'We didn't see your vehicle outside?'

'We left it around the corner. Ran here on foot. There were Taliban everywhere but we were lucky and got into the shop without anyone seeing us. It was a decent SUV so the Taliban probably took it.'

Shepherd went back through to the shop. Standing and Lane were by the door. Williams had gathered the people from the basement and they were grouped together against a wall lined with wooden shelves. To the left was an Afghan man in his thirties, dark-skinned and bearded, wearing a grey shalwar kameez, a long tunic over loose pyjama-style trousers. Next to him was a woman in her twenties wearing a blue pullover and Levi jeans, her hair covered with a pale blue hijab. She had her hands on the shoulders of two young boys, one maybe six years old, the other about four. The kids were both wearing Paw Patrol sweatshirts and jeans and were staring wide-eyed at Shepherd's gun. Shepherd assumed it was the interpreter and his family. 'You're Sayyid?' he said to the man.

The man smiled showing gleaming white teeth. 'Yes, sir.' He put his arm around the woman. 'This is Laila, my wife.'

She smiled at Shepherd. 'Pleased to meet you,' she said hesitantly as if she was unsure of her English.

'Pleased to meet you, too,' he said. He smiled at the two boys. 'Don't worry boys, we'll soon have you out of here.'

Sayyid translated and the two boys nodded, but they were clearly scared.

Shepherd looked at the other Afghan man. 'You're Waiz, right?'

The man nodded. 'Yes. I am Mohammed Waiz Gulzar.' He was short and fat, probably less than five feet six and tipping the scales at a hundred kilos or so, and the black thobe dress that covered his bulk gave him the look of a walking barrel.

He had deep-set eyes, bushy eyebrows that almost met above his nose, and a straggly beard.

'Mr Docherty tells me you're British. What exactly are you doing in Afghanistan?'

Gulzar reached into his thobe and brought out a British passport, one of the dark blue ones that had been issued post-Brexit. He waved it in the air. 'Yes, I am British. British citizen.'

He shouted over at his wife in Pashto. She opened her bag and took out four passports and held them up. She was a couple of inches taller than her husband and considerably thinner, her face and body covered with a full black burkha. Their three children were standing behind the woman – a young girl also in a full black burkha and two boys in their early teens wearing thobes like their father's, and grey skullcaps. 'My wife is British. My children are British. You need to get us out of here. We are in danger.'

'Yes, I understand that,' said Shepherd. 'But what are you doing here?'

'I come to my brother's wedding. Last month. Big wedding. Very big wedding.'

Standing walked over to the man and took the passport from him. He frowned as he looked at it. 'When did you get this, mate?' he asked.

'Two years ago. I am British now.'

'You were what, an asylum seeker?' He flicked the passport open. 'You were born in Afghanistan?'

Gulzar nodded. 'Yes. I flee the Taliban. We cross Europe to France and then we go to England.'

Standing nodded. 'And you claimed asylum when you got to England?'

The man nodded. 'Yes. Of course. I am asylum seeker.'

'Let me get this straight, pal. You fled the Taliban because you were in fear of your life. You crossed Europe, passing through half a dozen perfectly safe countries, then you put your family in a little rubber dinghy and crossed the English Channel?'

'A lorry. We pay to go in the back of a lorry.'

'Dinghy, lorry, whatever. But you get to England and we offer sanctuary to you and your family, we give you a house, we let you use our health service and our schools, and we give you a nice shiny passport.'

The man nodded enthusiastically. 'Yes, we are British! British citizens!'

'Matt,' said Shepherd. 'Go easy.'

Standing ignored Shepherd and continued to glare at the man. 'And after all that, the first thought in your head was to fly back to Afghanistan to go to a fucking wedding? And to take your wife and your kids with you?'

'My brother, he was getting married.'

'Yes, mate, but you fled a war zone. This war zone. That's why we gave you asylum. That's why we gave you this passport.' He threw it at the man's face and it fell to the floor. The man scrambled to pick it up.

'Leave it out, Matt,' said Shepherd.

'Yeah? Almost five hundred of our lads died fighting for these people, including guys we served with, and they died to protect fuckwits like this who think it's a good idea to come here on holiday. And when the shit hits the fan he waves his passport and says he's British and we have to get him out.'

'That's right,' said Shepherd quietly. 'That's our job. To protect people no matter how stupid they are. Now get a grip and let's put a plan of action together.'

Standing gave the man a final glare and nodded. 'Okay,' he said.

'Right, over here guys,' said Shepherd, gesturing at the corner of the shop furthest away from the civilians. The team gathered around him and he quickly explained what Tony Docherty needed them to do. They listened without interrupting. 'The way I see it, we have two objectives here. We need to get everyone to the airport and get them on planes to the UK. And we need to get to the British Embassy to destroy any intel still there, and retrieve Tony's briefcase. Transport isn't an issue, we can call the heli when we need it. The question is, do we go to the airport first, drop the civilians and then return to the embassy? Or do we hit the embassy first and then head to the airport?'

'Will the Taliban be at the embassy?' asked Standing.

'Almost certainly,' said Shepherd. 'But other than intel there's nothing of value so hopefully just a token presence.'

'I'd rather we got the civilians out of harm's way first,' said Docherty.

'Yes!' shouted Gulzar. 'We must get to the airport. We have to leave Kabul now.'

The Afghan interpreter glared at Gulzar and spoke to him in Pashto. The man began to argue but the interpreter shut him down by shouting at him and pointing at his face. Shepherd's Pashto was rudimentary at best but he picked up enough to realise that the interpreter was telling him to shut the fuck up.

'The civilians will just hold us up if we take them to the embassy,' said Williams.

'But the longer the heli is in the air, the more vulnerable it is,' said Standing. 'The Taliban have all the gear dropped by the Afghan Army so we're talking RPGs, the works.'

'From what I've been told, they're not shooting at planes or helicopters,' said Shepherd. 'Not yet at least.'

'How long do you think we'll need at the embassy?' Lane asked Docherty.

'To get my briefcase, a few minutes. But I'd like to check that nothing else sensitive was left behind. Ten minutes. Fifteen maybe.'

Shepherd nodded. 'And the airport is how far from the embassy?'

'Five kilometres.'

'We could do it on foot in an hour if necessary?'

'Except that the airport is surrounded by armed Taliban,' said Lane.

'Yes, but we're wearing Taliban gear,' said Shepherd.

'Which is fine at a distance,' said Standing. 'But close up, we won't be fooling anybody.'

'We can grab a vehicle,' said Williams.

'There are roadblocks outside the airport,' said Lane. 'And there are just too many people to shoot our way through. Why not get the heli to wait for us?' He looked over at Docherty. 'There are places a heli could land in the compound, right?'

'There's a tennis court.'

'Perfect,' said Lane. He looked at Shepherd. 'The heli can land and wait. Simples.'

'Except that it'll be a sitting duck on the ground and we'll have attracted attention to ourselves,' said Shepherd. 'The pilots won't want to hang around. And who knows how long it'll take us to get everything done. It's open-ended.'

Standing nodded. 'So, the heli drops us at the embassy and then continues to the airport. The heli drops off the civilians at the airport and waits for us to call them back.'

'That's assuming they come and pick us up here,' said Lane.

'Oh ye of little faith,' said Shepherd. 'But it sounds like we have a plan.'

'Contact, contact, contact,' said Ireland in Shepherd's earpiece. 'We've got company, Spider.'

Shepherd opened the shop door and peered out. Ireland was on the other side of the road, looking to his right. He opened the door further and peered down the road. A Humvee was heading their way. Three Taliban fighters were sitting on the roof and it was slowing as it approached the school. Ireland raised his right hand and waved. One of the Taliban fighters waved back. At a distance they might well mistake Ireland for one of their own, but close up they'd spot the pale skin and the M16. And even if they didn't realise he wasn't a jihadist, the guys sitting on top of the Humvee would be sure to see the helicopter.

'Take it out, Paddy,' said Shepherd over the radio.

'Roger that,' said Ireland. He pointed his weapon towards the approaching vehicle and pulled the trigger. An HEDP round erupted from the barrel of the grenade launcher, arced through the air and hit the windscreen of the Humvee. It exploded and the three fighters on the roof flew through the air like broken dolls. Ireland let loose a second round and it hit the nearside wing, blowing apart the wheel so that the front tipped to the ground, ripping though the road surface.

Shepherd stepped out of the shop, followed by Standing. Shepherd moved to the right, Standing to the left, and Lane followed, moving between the two of them so that they all had separate lines of fire.

The Humvee came to a halt in a cloud of dust. The rear

doors opened and fighters appeared brandishing Kalashnikovs. They were covered in blood from the first grenade explosion, but were very much alive. Ireland fired a short burst with his M16 and took out the man on the right. Shepherd raised his carbine but Standing beat him to it, firing two shots into the chest of the man who had exited the door on the left. Standing started moving, running in a crouch, and when a third man appeared he shot him twice in the chest. Both men collapsed into the road. The Humvee's radiator was hissing and white steam was pouring from the ripped bonnet. Standing moved closer to the vehicle to get a better view of the men in the front seats but he lowered his weapon when he saw the damage the grenade had done. 'All good,' he shouted.

'Right, let's get everyone on the heli,' said Shepherd. He and Lane stepped aside and encouraged Docherty and the Afghans to cross the road. 'Fast as you can!' shouted Shepherd.

The Afghans hurried over to Ireland who waved them through the gate. Docherty and Williams ran after them. Standing was looking down the road, his carbine at the ready. 'So far, so good,' he said over the radio. 'But they'll have heard the explosions on the road so they'll be heading this way.'

Shepherd took a look to the right. The road there was clear. He and Lane ran to the gate. Standing waited until they were in the schoolyard before turning and following them.

As Shepherd jogged across the schoolyard, Docherty and Williams were helping the children into the helicopter. The translator was helping his wife to climb up but the other Afghan, Gulzar, was already strapping himself into his seat despite the fact that his wife and three kids still hadn't got on board.

'There's no women and children first with this lot, is there?' said Lane.

Shepherd nodded at the translator, who was now helping the two teenage boys up into the helicopter. 'They're not all like that,' he said.

Shepherd waved the crew chief over and quickly briefed him on what he was to tell the pilots. The crew chief flashed him a thumbs-up and relayed the message through his headset.

Eventually all the civilians were on board and strapped into their seats. The SAS guys climbed in. Standing was waiting at the gate, checking that the road was clear.

'Let's go, Matt,' said Shepherd over the radio.

Standing nodded and then ran over to the Puma. The engines roared and the rotors span, kicking up flurries of dust. As Standing jumped on board the helicopter lifted up and made a slow turn to the left. Shepherd squinted out of the door. As they climbed higher he saw two more Humvees heading their way but there was no way they could follow the helicopter.

'Everyone okay?' said Shepherd into his headset.

Standing, Lane, Ireland and Williams all flashed him 'okay' signs.

Shepherd leaned towards Docherty. 'You okay?' he shouted over the roar of the engines.

Docherty nodded. The crew chief slid the door shut and fastened his harness. They were almost a thousand feet above the village and still climbing.

Shepherd put his head closer to Docherty's. 'Look, mate, we don't know how much opposition we'll be up against, do you want a weapon?' He patted the Glock on his thigh. 'I can give you this.'

'I'm not firearms trained,' said Docherty. 'I'd probably do more harm than good.'

Shepherd grinned. 'That was my thought exactly, but I wanted to give you the option. Just stay close to me, no matter what happens.'

Docherty nodded. He was clearly worried but he forced a smile.

'You'll be fine,' said Shepherd. He switched seats to sit next to the interpreter. 'Everything okay, Sayyid?' he said.

The man nodded enthusiastically. 'Very good,' he said. 'Thank you for helping us. The Taliban would surely kill me and my family if . . .' He grimaced and left the sentence unfinished.

'I know,' said Shepherd. 'Don't worry about it. We'll have you and your family at the airport in a few minutes and then a plane will fly you to England.'

The translator nodded again. 'Thank you,' he said. 'Alhamdulillah.'

Shepherd knew the phrase. Allah be praised. Thanks be to God. Shepherd wasn't sure what part if any Allah had played in the man's rescue, but he wasn't prepared to argue the point. 'Right, this is what's going to happen. The helicopter is going to drop Tony and us at the British Embassy. It will then fly you and your family to the airport. When the helicopter lands you are to look for a soldier called Brian Heron. He's tall with black hair, wearing fatigues. He should be there waiting for you, but if not, just ask for him. Brian Heron.'

'Brian Heron,' the translator repeated. 'Yes. Thank you.'

'He's working with the British ambassador. He'll make sure you and your family are put on a plane.'

Gulzar leaned towards Shepherd. 'What about us?' he

shouted above the noise of the turbines. 'We need to get out too.'

'You'll be taken care of,' said Shepherd. 'Just go with him.' He pointed at the interpreter.

Gulzar glared at Shepherd. 'Why is he in charge? He's just an Afghan. I'm a British citizen.'

Shepherd opened his mouth to snap at the man, but then just smiled thinly. 'Because he fought for his country and you are just a tourist,' he said. He moved seats so that he was back next to Standing.

'How upset would you be if I put a bullet in that twat's head?' Standing asked him.

'Very,' said Shepherd. 'I'd hate to see you lose your sergeant's stripes again.'

Standing grinned. 'It'd be worth it,' he said.

The crew chief leaned over and pointed at the window. 'We're coming up to the airport on our left,' he shouted. 'The embassy will be on our right in about two minutes. Look for the swimming pool. They'll do a quick circuit at two thousand feet and then drop you off. They say they'd rather not land so if you could disembark on the move, that would be great.'

'Not a problem,' said Shepherd. He and Standing peered out of the window. Ahead of them an Air France Boeing 777 was climbing into the clear blue sky, heading west. Further west at about 6,000 feet he saw a drab grey Hercules heading towards the airport. Beyond it was another plane. And another. All heading towards Kabul in a last ditch effort to rescue as many people as possible.

Standing tapped him on the shoulder and pointed at a three-storey flat-roofed building topped with what looked like shipping containers and a huge satellite dish pointing upwards.

There were other smaller dishes scattered around the roof. The building was behind a high wall on which were perched several viewing towers. In the grounds, close to the main building, was a swimming pool, and further away there was a red-brown tennis court.

The Puma began a slow turn to the right. There were vehicles moving on the roads, mainly pick-up trucks flying Taliban flags and Humvees. Most of the parked cars were saloons and SUVs that appeared to have been abandoned, either by people trying to get into the embassy before it closed or trying to reach the airport on foot.

The helicopter continued its clockwise turn. The grounds appeared to be clear but they weren't able to see if there was anyone inside. Docherty joined them at the doorway. He pointed at the building next to the British Embassy. 'That's the Bulgarian Embassy,' he said. 'But their diplomats are long gone.'

'Assuming we're dropped off on the tennis court, what's the best way into the building?' Shepherd asked.

'The rear entrance is to the left, through to the kitchen,' said Docherty. 'To the right are French windows leading into an office area. It depends on how conscientiously they locked up.' He forced a smile. 'I guess a locked door isn't going to stop you guys.'

'And where are the stairs?'

'In the main hallway. You can get there from the kitchen or the offices.'

As the helicopter continued to turn, they could see the main entrance to the compound. There were four vehicles parked in a line inside the wall. 'Tony, do they look like embassy vehicles to you?' asked Shepherd.

Docherty frowned. 'I can't tell, sorry. But there were plenty of white SUVs in the pool.'

'One of them's a Humvee,' said Standing.

'We didn't use Humvees,' said Docherty.

'I see Terry, next to the gate,' said Standing.

Shepherd narrowed his eyes. Standing was right. An Afghan man in tribal clothing was smoking a cigarette, an AK-47 over his shoulder. 'There could be more inside,' said Shepherd.

'You want to call it off?' asked Standing.

'We can't,' said Shepherd. 'Too much at stake.'

'Okay. How about I skirt the outside and take care of any Terry near the gates? Then go in through the front door.'

'You could take Paddy with you.'

'No need. You'll need all hands to protect Secret Squirrel. I'll be okay, they won't be expecting me. And I move faster solo.'

Shepherd considered it for several seconds, then nodded. 'Okay. But make sure you announce yourself when you come into the building. We can do without any surprises.'

'Roger that.'

The door to the Puma was already wide open as it swooped down over the tennis court. It slowed to almost walking pace when it got to six feet above the ground. Standing leapt out and ran towards the main embassy building, bent over his carbine. Lane followed Standing, then Shepherd jumped out. The rotor was sending dust, twigs and leaves whirling through the air, so Shepherd kept his mouth closed and his eyes narrowed. Docherty stood in the doorway, the wind tugging at his hair, then he jumped. His feet hit the ground and he stumbled but Shepherd reached out and grabbed him and started him running. The helicopter was lower now, just a couple of feet from the ground, and moving so slowly that Ireland and Williams didn't even break stride as they jumped out and ran after Shepherd and Docherty.

Standing went left and headed around the side of the building. Behind them the turbines roared and the Puma picked up speed and lifted back into the air. Ireland and Williams caught up with Shepherd. They were all checking out the windows as they ran, alert for any sign of movement.

The tennis court gave away to rough grass. There was no cover so they kept on going. Lane reached the kitchen door. He pulled at the handle but it was obviously locked. 'French windows are a better bet,' said Shepherd over his radio.

Lane turned and ran along the rear of the house. There was a small paved terrace outside the French windows and Shepherd and Docherty reached it at the same time as Lane. There were four oil barrels lined up on the terrace, stained with soot and full of ashes. Lane tried the handles but it was locked.

'I'll do the honours,' said Ireland. He took a step back, lifted his right leg and kicked out. The two doors flew open with the sound of splintering wood.

Lane and Williams went through first, weapons at the ready. Lane went left, Williams went right. 'Clear,' said Lane over the radio. Shepherd and Docherty stepped over the threshold. Ireland brought up the rear, his eyes scanning the embassy grounds. Inside, there were two dozen workstations, grey partitions separating desks with computer terminals. On the right was a wall of filing cabinets. Several of the drawers were open and empty. Six large shredders had been placed on a table and there were black garbage bags bursting with shredded paper and cardboard. Shepherd took a quick look at one of the terminals. The hard drive had been removed.

'Where are the stairs, Tony?' Shepherd asked.

Docherty pointed at a pair of double doors at the far end of the room, then flinched at the sound of two gunshots outside. Shepherd recognised the sound immediately – it was Standing's HK417. Presumably he had double-tapped the jihadist by the gate. He cocked his head on one side as he listened. If there were more jihadists, there'd be more shooting.

'Front gate clear,' said Standing in his earpiece. 'Moving towards the front door.'

Shepherd pointed at the double doors. 'Penny, Karl.'

The two men nodded and moved forward. Lane stood to the side and opened the door on the right. Williams went through first, low and fast, his carbine sweeping in all directions. 'Hallway clear,' he said.

Shepherd heard two more gunshots. 'I was optimistic about the all clear,' said Standing in his ear. 'Terry with a gun in one of the trucks. Moving towards the front door now.'

Lane followed Williams through the door. Shepherd and Docherty jogged across the office and again Ireland was tail-end Charlie. There were offices off to the left and a stairway ahead of them. To the right was another set of double doors with a sign that said 'STRICTLY NO ADMITTANCE' above them. The doors were open and the floor was littered with shredded paper and discarded cardboard files. 'That's the ambassador's residence and office,' said Docherty.

Lane and Williams went up the stairs. 'Coming your way,' said Standing over the radio, then a door opened at the far end of the corridor and he appeared. He closed the door and jogged towards Shepherd.

'The road's clear,' said Standing. 'I think we're—'

He was interrupted by the sound of Lane's shotgun upstairs, quickly followed by the thwack-thwack of an HK417. 'Contact, contact, contact,' said Williams over the radio. He voice was low but Shepherd could hear the tension. The shotgun fired again then there was the crack of an AK-47.

Shepherd opened his mouth to tell Standing to move but Standing was already sprinting towards the stairs. 'Go with him, Paddy,' said Shepherd. 'I'll stay with Tony.'

Ireland ran after Standing. Upstairs they heard the shotgun blast again. Then a Kalashnikov being fired on fully automatic. Shepherd's stomach turned cold. A Kalashnikov being fired indoors was as lethal a weapon as you'd meet. He desperately wanted to ask for a sit-rep but he knew they were professionals and that they had more pressing issues than dealing with his inquiry.

There were four shots from an HK417, two sets of two, then silence.

Shepherd looked at Docherty. 'Stay close, and stay behind me,' he said. Docherty nodded nervously. Shepherd jogged over to the stairs, put his carbine to his shoulder and took the stairs two at a time. He reached the top and his eyes began to water from the cordite in the air.

Standing was ahead of him, his gun up. Ireland was down on one knee, to Standing's left. As Shepherd moved closer he saw two dead jihadists, their tunics soaked in blood. Further along the corridor he saw two men in combat trousers and sweatshirts, holding their hands high. Behind them were Lane and Williams. Lane had the barrel of his shotgun pressed against the neck of the older of the two men. There were two more dead jihadists behind the SAS men.

The ceiling overhead had been raked by shots, presumably from one of the AK-47s.

The younger of the two men shouted at the top of his voice in Russian. Shepherd knew enough of the language to realise the man was begging not to be shot. Williams was aiming his carbine at the man's head.

'Hold your fire!' shouted Shepherd.

Lane and Williams relaxed a little but kept their fingers on the triggers of their weapons. There was a scuffling sound from behind Shepherd. He whirled around to see a jihadist run out of an office, his eyes wide and staring, a Kalashnikov in his hands. Shepherd's finger slipped over the trigger of his carbine but Standing reacted immediately and shot the man twice in the chest. The jihadist staggered back, slammed into a wall and slid down to the floor leaving a red streak on the plaster.

The young Russian began screaming, his hands on his head. He had close-cropped hair and a square jaw with a large dimple in the middle. Shepherd turned to Lane. 'Penny, ask him who they are and why they're here.'

Lane shouted at the man in Russian. The man immediately stopped screaming and frowned at Lane. He said something in Russian and Lane replied.

The older man began speaking in Russian and the younger man deferred to him. He was obviously the more senior of the two. He was a big man with a weightlifter's forearms and slightly bowed legs. His head was shaved and there was an ugly rope-like scar across the back of his right hand, and what looked like shrapnel scars on his left cheek.

Shepherd waited as the Russian and Lane talked back and forth. Standing prowled up and down, his carbine at the ready.

Ireland moved back down the corridor, listening intently for the sound of more intruders.

Eventually Lane turned to Shepherd. 'They say they're diplomats from the Russian Embassy. They're getting ready to pull out but their bosses told them to check to see if the British had left anything of interest behind when they left.' He shrugged. 'It's bollocks of course.' He pointed at two black nylon holdalls. 'They were carrying these.'

Shepherd bent down and unzipped one. There were a dozen or so files inside, along with a number of notebooks, diaries and a portable hard drive.

Lane gestured at the dead Taliban fighters. 'They're presumably not from the Russian Embassy.'

'We've got Russians with a Taliban escort?' said Ireland. 'That's weird. I thought the Taliban hated the Russians as much as they hate the West.'

'The Russians will be looking to get a foot into Afghanistan now that we're pulling out,' said Docherty. 'But these two are quick off the block.'

'They're almost certainly security services,' said Shepherd. 'They're not armed so I don't think they're Spetsnaz. GRU maybe. Or SVR.' The GRU was the Main Directorate of the General Staff of the Armed Forces of the Russian Federation, basically military intelligence. Their assassins were the men – and women – who killed the country's enemies overseas. The SVR was the Foreign Intelligence Service of the Russian Federation, and was the external intelligence agency that concentrated mainly on civilian affairs. 'Either way they almost certainly speak English.' He was watching the younger Russian from the corner of his eye as he spoke to Lane and caught the merest flicker of a smile.

The older Russian patted his trouser pocket and said something to Lane in Russian.

'He says he can show you his embassy ID if you want.'

Shepherd shook his head. 'No point,' he said. 'Okay, no matter who they're working for we're not in the business of slotting unarmed men.' He looked at Williams. 'Karl, get something to tie them up with.'

'Will do,' said Williams. He disappeared into an office.

Docherty took out his phone. Before the Russians could react, he took photographs of them. They both turned away, hiding their faces, but Docherty grinned. 'Got you,' he said. He saw Shepherd frowning and his grin widened. 'Intelligence gathering,' he said.

Shepherd nodded. 'Matt, you and Karl stay here just in case there are more of them. Penny, Paddy and I will take Tony to his office. RV back here.'

'Roger that,' said Standing.

As Shepherd and Docherty headed down the corridor with Lane and Ireland in tow, Williams reappeared with several lengths of cable. The corridor branched left and right. Shepherd motioned for Docherty to wait, then he checked that both sides were clear before gesturing for Docherty to go ahead. He took them to the left.

Docherty's office had no name on the door, just a number. He tried the handle and it was locked. 'That's a good sign,' he said. He pulled a set of keys from his pocket and unlocked it. Lane stood guard at the door while Shepherd and Ireland followed Docherty inside.

There were three identical metal desks with high-backed office chairs, a line of filing cabinets and a map of Afghanistan dotted with pins of different colours. There was a computer terminal on each desk. A single-barred window overlooked the wall that surrounded the embassy grounds. Docherty went over to the far corner and pulled back a rug. Set on to the floor was a metal door with a combination lock. He dialled in the combination and pulled open the door, then reached in and took out a brown leather briefcase. He sat back on his heels, checked the contents, and nodded at Shepherd. 'All good,' he said. He stood up. 'Give me a minute,' he said. He went over to the map, pulled out all the pins, and dropped them into a wastepaper bin. 'Spider, could you do me a favour and disable the computers?' he said.

'No problem,' said Shepherd. He nodded at Ireland and together they began smashing the computers with the butts of their carbines. Docherty went over to one of the desks, opened a drawer and took out a diary, a notebook and a couple of wallets and put them into his briefcase, then stepped back to allow Shepherd to smash his computer.

'On the way out can we just check the ambassador's office?' asked Docherty.

'Sure, but let's not hang about,' said Shepherd.

Docherty headed out and turned left. Lane hurried to overtake him, his shotgun at the ready. Shepherd and Ireland followed.

They went back along the corridor. Williams had finished tying up the two Russians with cables as Standing stood guard.

'Tell them we won't gag them, but if they start shouting before we've left, I'll personally come back and put a bullet in their heads,' said Shepherd.

As Lane began to translate, they heard the crack-crack-crack of an AK-47 in the distance. Shepherd looked at Standing.

They had the same thought – were the shots from inside the building or outside?

'From the street, I think,' said Standing. 'You want me to check?'

Shepherd nodded. 'Take Paddy with you. His grenades might come in handy if we've got visitors.'

Standing and Ireland ran towards the stairs. Lane finished talking to the Russians. 'Right, let's get Tony down to the ambassador's office,' said Shepherd. 'Penny, bring those bags with you.' He led the way, with Docherty close behind him and Lane and Williams bringing up the rear. Lane had his shotgun hanging from its sling and had a holdall in each hand.

They reached the hall on the ground floor and jogged along to the open double doors. Shepherd motioned for Docherty to stand to the side and then he went through, keeping to the left while Williams went right. It was a large room with a dozen desks and filing cabinets against one wall. There were more industrial-sized shredders and overflowing garbage bags bursting with shredded paper.

Docherty pointed at a door to the left. 'That's the ambassador's office,' he said. 'I just want to check that it's been stripped.'

'Let me clear it first,' said Shepherd. The door was ajar and he kicked it open, then stepped inside, his carbine at the ready. There was a computer on the desk but it had been smashed and the hard drive removed. Docherty had a quick look around. 'It looks okay,' he said.

'We'll make sure,' said Shepherd. 'Penny, dump the holdalls on the desk.'

Lane did as he was told. Shepherd took out a fragmentation grenade. 'Back to the hall,' he said.

Williams, Lane and Docherty headed out as Shepherd pulled
the pin from the grenade and placed it on top of one of the
bags. He ran for the door, counting in his head. He pulled the
doors shut and followed the others into the hall. The grenade
exploded on five, a muffled thud that he felt as much as heard.

Shepherd and Docherty ran along the corridor, followed by
Lane and Williams. 'We've a problem on the street,' said
Standing in Shepherd's ear. 'Terry in four trucks. Mob-handed.'

Shepherd stopped and held up his hand, fist clenched.
Everyone halted. Lane and Williams looked around, their
fingers on the triggers of their weapons. 'Heading this way?'
asked Shepherd.

'Roger that,' said Standing.

'Can you hold them off?'

'Not for long,' said Standing.

Shepherd looked across at Lane. 'Penny, talk to the heli. We
need it here now and we'll have to do an evac from the roof.'

Lane nodded. He moved away and began to talk on the
radio.

'How do we get to the roof?' Shepherd asked Docherty.

'Top floor, at the back, there's a staircase that doubles as a
fire escape.'

'Okay, take us there.'

Docherty took them back to the hall and they all headed
up the stairs. There was the crack of gunfire outside, the
rat-tat-tat of an HK417 followed by the dull thud of a grenade
exploding. 'Matt, we're heading to the roof. We'll lay down
covering fire from there.'

'Soon as you can,' said Standing calmly.

'Heli's on the way.'

There were more shots, followed by several Kalashnikovs firing in concert.

They sped up the stairs to the top floor, then Docherty pointed down a corridor at a single door with 'AUTHORISED PERSONNEL ONLY' stencilled on it.

'I guess we're authorised,' said Williams. He kicked it open. Metal stairs led up to another door, this one with 'FIRE EXIT' on it. Williams opened it and stepped on to the roof, his weapon up at his shoulder.

'Heli's on its way,' said Lane. 'ETA five minutes.'

'Finally some good news,' said Shepherd. 'Tony, get to cover. Penny, Karl, with me.' He ran across the rooftop which was dotted with shipping containers that had been modified as sleeping quarters, presumably for the added embassy security that had become necessary once the Taliban started moving towards Kabul. He reached the edge of the building and looked over the chest-high concrete parapet. A Humvee was on fire, destroyed by one of Ireland's grenades. There were three pick-up trucks parked outside the main gate. One had a heavy machine gun in the back, though the operator was slumped over the weapon, his head a bloody mess. As Shepherd watched, the truck with the machine gun reversed out of view.

The Taliban fighters had positioned themselves behind the remaining trucks and were shooting at Standing and Ireland. Shepherd couldn't see the SAS men but figured they would have taken cover. The Taliban fighters were firing haphazardly on fully automatic, while Standing and Ireland were returning fire calmly and methodically, choosing their targets carefully and using single shots. As Shepherd peered down he heard the crack of an HK417 and one of the fighters fell back, blood pouring from his throat.

'Nice shot, Matt,' said Shepherd over the radio.

'We try to please,' Standing replied.

Ireland switched to his grenade launcher and sent a HEDP round over the gate and into one of the trucks. The vehicle exploded and tipped on to its side. One of the jihadists was killed instantly, and another caught fire and ran down the road with flames covering his upper body. Williams fired twice, hitting the man in the back, and he went down.

Lane held his fire. His Mossberg shotgun was lethal at short range, but even with its three-inch rifled slugs it wasn't accurate much beyond a hundred yards.

Shepherd and Williams started firing quickly before the jihadists had time to react. From their vantage point they were able to pick off several Taliban fighters. Shepherd caught two with head shots and Williams picked off three. Then the remaining jihadists worked out where the shots were coming from and changed positions.

Shepherd sighted on one of them. He was a teenager with pale skin and a neatly-trimmed beard. He was peering out from behind the rear of a blue pick-up and had fallen into a pattern. He remained hidden for three seconds, then took a quick look, then hid again for three seconds, then he would stick the barrel of his AK-47 around the truck and fire a short burst.

The teenager fired and pulled back. Shepherd started counting, keeping his Heckler aimed at the spot where he knew the man would appear. He pulled the trigger on three, just as the man's face came into view. The bullet smacked into his nose and he fell back into the road.

'We've got company, Spider,' said Williams. 'Your two o'clock.'

Shepherd looked to his right. Half a dozen vehicles were heading down the road to the embassy, clouds of dust billowing behind them. The first two were Humvees, the rest were pick-up trucks. The Humvees were flying Taliban flags.

'Paddy, more trucks and Humvees on the way,' Shepherd said over the radio. 'They'll be here in a couple of minutes.'

'Visibility's not great from here, Spider. Unless they're directly outside the gate I'm firing blind.'

'Heli incoming,' said Lane.

Shepherd looked over his shoulder. The Puma was at about 3,000 feet and probably half a mile away.

'Paddy, can you get up here with us? You'll get a better view. Matt, can you hold the fort solo for a while?'

'Roger that,' said Ireland. 'Cover me, Matt.'

Standing began to fire single shots half a second apart, ensuring that the Taliban fighters kept their heads down while Ireland made his run to the embassy front door.

'I'm inside, coming up,' said Ireland after a few seconds.

'When you get to the top floor, go right, then left,' said Shepherd. 'There's a door marked "AUTHORISED PERSONNEL ONLY" then stairs leading up to the roof.'

'On my way,' said Ireland.

'The pilots are asking if the area is hot,' said Lane. 'What do I tell them?'

'Tell them we'll try to cool it down,' said Shepherd. He squinted at the fast-approaching Taliban convoy. The machine guns on the Humvees and the trucks were effective up to about 6,000 feet, though the rounds could travel as far as 25,000 feet on a good day. Either way, they were more than capable of hitting the helicopter if it attempted an extraction while they were in range. They were about a mile away now, so maybe two minutes. 'Tell them to come in now, quick as they can.'

'Roger that,' said Lane.

'Karl, we need to concentrate on the convoy as soon as it's within range,' said Shepherd. 'The AK-47s aren't going to do much damage but those heavy machine guns could ruin our day.'

'Roger that,' said Williams.

'Matt, the heli's inbound,' Shepherd said over the radio. 'I'll lay down covering fire in six, okay?'

'Roger that.'

'Six, five, four, three, two, one . . .' Shepherd began firing at the trucks outside the compound, aiming for human targets if he saw them, hitting the trucks if he didn't. He emptied his magazine and slapped in a new one.

'I'm inside, coming up now,' said Standing in his earpiece.

'Penny, you're never going to hit the convoy, but start blasting away so that the guys out there keep their heads down.'

Lane nodded and started firing his shotgun.

Shepherd sighted on the lead Humvee in the convoy. The HK417 was effective up to about a thousand feet against human targets, but the 7.62mm Nato rounds would have little or no effect on an armoured Humvee. Even the Kevlar tyres were designed to run flat. The windows were practically bullet-proof, but a few shots to the glass tended to make a driver slow down, so that was where he aimed.

He and Williams let loose a few rounds but the vehicles were still too far away to see if the shots were striking home.

Ireland appeared at the doorway and ran over to take up position next to Williams. 'Keep their heads down,' said Shepherd. 'I don't want them to realise that we've abandoned the ground floor.' Ireland nodded and began firing single shots from his carbine. 'I might lob the odd grenade,' he said.

Shepherd grinned. 'Knock yourself out.' He could hear the Puma now. He looked over his shoulder again. It had descended to about 800 feet. The crew chief had opened the door and was looking out.

'Spider, they're saying there's too much clutter on the roof, they're going to have to use the winch,' said Lane.

Shepherd nodded. He'd already realised that. There were five containers on the roof, along with several satellite dishes, so the helicopter wouldn't be able to touch down.

Standing appeared in the doorway. He looked up at the helicopter which was now about 500 feet above them and descending quickly. The crew chief began to play out a length of rope, on the end of which was a nylon harness. 'What's the order?' Standing asked.

'Paddy should go first,' said Shepherd. 'Then Tony. Then Karl. Then Penny. Then you. Then me.'

'Roger that,' said Ireland. He sent a grenade arcing over the wall and it exploded with a dull thump.

'I'll go last,' said Standing. He took up position on the parapet.

'Okay,' said Shepherd. 'Me, then you.' He turned to look at Docherty, who was sitting with his back to one of the containers. He had his briefcase in his lap and was holding it with both hands. Shepherd bent double and hurried over to him. 'Tony, are you okay?' Before he could answer a round smacked into the container about six feet above Docherty's head and he flinched. Shepherd patted him on the shoulder. 'We'll be out of here soon,' he said. He pointed up at the Puma, which was now only 300 feet above them. 'They'll drop down a rope and a harness and winch us up one at a time. Paddy will go first and then they'll send the rope down for you. I'll help strap you in and then the winch will haul you up. Just keep a tight hold on the briefcase and you'll be fine.'

Docherty nodded. 'Okay.'

There was another thud as Ireland sent a grenade over the wall. He was firing blind but the HEDP rounds were lethal over a wide area and there was every chance he'd hit something.

'It'll be a few seconds, that's all,' Shepherd said to Docherty. 'And once we're on board, it's a few minutes to the airport. We're almost home free.' Another round smacked into the container above their heads. Shepherd grinned. 'Seriously, mate, they couldn't hit a barn door these guys. Most of the time they're not even looking where they're shooting.'

'I didn't really sign up for this,' said Docherty.

'Trust me, you'll look back on this one day and laugh.' Shepherd patted him on the shoulder again.

Docherty gestured at the parapet. 'You know we helped form the Taliban?'

'Who do you mean by "we"?' said Shepherd.

'MI6,' said Docherty. 'Back in the eighties we were supporting the mujahideen, who were fighting the Russians. We were giving money and training to several militant Islamic groups including more than a few jihadists. The CIA were out here, too. Operation Cyclone they called it. They gave more than three billion dollars to the mujahideen, in money and arms. Once the Russians pulled out, the funding stopped, but in 1994 the mujahideen began morphing into the Taliban. Same faces, just a different name.' He grimaced. 'What goes around, comes around.'

One of the jihadists let loose a volley from his AK-47 and

the rounds smashed into the container again. 'Maybe you could ask for your guns back,' said Shepherd. He turned and went back to the parapet. The convoy was about a mile away. 'What do you think?' Shepherd asked Standing.

'They'll be here before we're all off,' said Standing.

'The heli could fire on the convoy. That might slow them down,' said Ireland.

Shepherd nodded. The Puma was equipped with two 7.62mm general-purpose machine guns, which could fire 750 rounds a minute at targets up to a mile away. The accuracy wouldn't be great but a hail of bullets might well slow the convoy down. 'Penny, ask them if they'll lay down some fire in front of the convoy.'

'Roger that,' said Lane. As Lane conveyed the request to the pilots, Shepherd sighted on one of the pick-up trucks outside the gate. He started breathing tidally as he focused on the cab, waiting for any sign of movement. He was rewarded by the black-and-white flash of a scarf around a jihadist's head. He squeezed the trigger and the back of the man's skull exploded across the road.

A second jihadist appeared by the gate and went into a crouch, firing his AK-47 from the hip, a huge mistake when you were up against professionals. The bullets went high and wide and Standing had all the time in the world to put two rounds in the man's chest.

'The pilots will fire warning shots but they've been ordered not to engage with the enemy,' said Lane.

'That's not fair, they started it,' said Williams, sarcastically.

'Warning shots will do it,' said Shepherd. 'We just need to slow them down.' He grinned at Docherty. 'You might want to cover your ears, mate.'

Docherty put his hands over his ears. Shepherd and his team followed suit. The Puma was less than fifty yards above them and the noise of the machine guns was deafening even with their ears covered. The Puma fired four short bursts. Shepherd peered into the distance and saw the rounds kicking up dirt on the road. The lead Humvee veered to the side, two of the trucks collided and one smashed into a parked car.

Standing grinned. 'That did the trick,' he said.

The Puma continued to descend and the harness was only six feet or so above their heads. The downdraft from the rotors tugged at their hair and clothes. Ireland let his weapon hang from its sling and ran in a crouch away from the parapet towards the descending rope.

The lead Humvee began to move again, but the Puma fired another burst. This time the rounds were just feet from the vehicle and it came to a halt, then went into reverse. One of the trucks pulled a tight U-turn and headed back the way they had come.

Two jihadists appeared at the gate, brandishing AK-47s. Standing took out the first one with two shots to the chest and Williams killed the other with a single round to the head.

They heard the growl of an engine and seconds later a pick-up truck reversed into view. It had been hidden by the wall but had been damaged by one of Ireland's grenades. The offside front wing and tyre had been destroyed and the axle was scraping across the road surface. Shepherd cursed as he saw there was a Taliban fighter standing behind the machine gun mounted at the rear. He took aim and fired but the truck lurched as he pulled the trigger and his shot went wide. The machine gun was splattered with the blood of the jihadist who had previously been manning it, but his replacement was taking more care. He had hunched himself down behind the metal shield mounted over the gun.

'Matt, have you got a shot?'

'Not really,' said Standing. He fired two rounds but they both screeched off the metal shield.

Shepherd looked over his shoulder. They really needed one of Ireland's grenades but he was looking up at the helicopter, preparing to grab the harness.

Standing and Williams were firing almost non-stop at the gunner but the jihadist crouched down even further as the truck continued to back away from the wall. Shepherd had two fragmentation grenades but the truck was too far away. He doubted he'd be able to get close to the wall, never mind clear it. He joined in the firing instead. The man's head was hidden by the gun and the shield but Shepherd could just about make out the man's left foot. He sighted on it and pulled the trigger but the truck was still lurching from side to side and his round thudded into the roof of the cab.

Williams fired a short burst but all the rounds went high. Standing was holding fire, hoping for a clear shot.

Shepherd caught a glimpse of sandal and he squeezed the trigger. He was rewarded by the sight of the foot exploding. The jihadist screamed so loudly that he could be heard over the roar of the Puma's turbines but he stayed behind the machine gun.

The pick-up truck was now about twenty feet from the embassy wall. Shepherd sighted on the driver and squeezed off two shots. The windscreen shattered and the driver slumped in his seat. The truck stopped moving.

The gunner swung up the barrel of his machine gun and

pulled the trigger. He clearly wasn't used to the weapon as it shuddered in his grip and the rounds sprayed everywhere, hitting the front of the embassy building, smashing the windows on the upper floor and then thudding into one of the containers on the roof.

'Got you,' whispered Standing. He pulled the trigger and the top of the jihadist's scarf flew off his head along with a chunk of skull. The jihadist's finger stayed on the trigger as he slumped forward. His weight pushed the rear of the gun down and bullets sprayed into the air. Several thudded into the side of the Puma.

Shepherd, Williams and Standing poured fire down on the jihadist and the hail of bullets knocked him back into the bed of the truck. The machine gun finally fell silent. Shepherd looked up at the Puma. Black smoke was pouring from the fuselage, close to the tail rotor. The crew chief was looking into the helicopter, the rope forgotten.

Lane looked anxiously over at Shepherd. 'They're losing oil pressure, the pilots say they've got to go,' he said.

Shepherd nodded. It was clear from the black smoke that something was very wrong. The turbines were still working and the rotors were turning, but if they lost all their oil that could change in an instant. They were only five kilometres from the airport but they were flying low and any loss of power would have them crashing to the ground in seconds.

'Good luck guys,' Shepherd whispered, as the Puma turned to the north.

'Spider, we've got a problem,' said Standing.

Shepherd laughed harshly. 'Tell me about it.'

Standing was pointing down the road. In the distance the convoy was moving again. They had seen the helicopter leave and were racing towards the embassy, clouds of dust kicking up behind them. 'That's not good,' said Shepherd.

Shepherd flinched as the .50 calibre rounds ripped into the container behind him. Docherty was still sitting with his brief-case in his lap, his hands over his ears. The rounds had a range of close to a mile but the two Humvees were only a couple of hundred yards away. Every time one of the SAS men put his head over the parapet they were greeted with a hail of bullets.

It would only be a matter of time before the jihadists got up the courage to enter the building. Then they'd come across the Russians who would be able to tell them they were only facing five armed men. True, there was only the one way up to the roof, but now that the helicopter had gone they had all the time in the world. Not to mention the fact that Shepherd and his team were running low on ammo. Very low.

'Anyone got any suggestions?' asked Shepherd.

'We either get another heli or we go downstairs and try to get over the wall,' said Standing.

'You saw the watchtowers, right?' said Williams. 'If we can reach one of them we can get over the wall.'

Shepherd looked over at Docherty. 'Tony!' he shouted. Docherty didn't react. Shepherd crawled over to him and shook his shoulder. 'Tony, the watchtowers on the walls. Can we get into them?'

Docherty nodded. 'Yeah. They're observation platforms for the guards. There are stairs inside.'

'Stairs on both sides or just inside the walls?'

'You can go down on the other side of the walls and there's a lockable steel door there. The idea was to let people in if there were problems at the main gate.'

'Good man,' said Shepherd. He crawled back to the parapet. 'I think another heli is out of the question at this short notice,' he said. 'Terry will come in eventually and when they do we're trapped here. We can hold them off for a while, but at some point we'll be out of ammo. I say we make a run for it now. Down the stairs, out the back, and over to the nearest watchtower.'

'And then what?' said Ireland.

'Grab a vehicle. Depending on how many there are at the gate, we might even be able to take a Humvee. Then we either drive to the airport or to a safer pick up point.'

Standing nodded. 'Sounds good. But I should stay here, lay down some covering fire. If it goes quiet they'll know we're up to something.'

'How much ammo do you have?'

'One full magazine plus five rounds.'

'Paddy, how many grenades do you have?'

'Four,' said Ireland.

'Paddy can stay with you, fire a grenade every six or seven seconds, then he can follow us. You keep firing for another thirty seconds, by which time we should be out of the back. You leave and join us and we head for the nearest watchtower.' He looked around. 'Everyone happy with that?'

He was faced with nodding heads. Lane's sat-phone started to ring and he pulled it out of his pocket and answered it.

'Tony, are you okay to make a run for it?'

Docherty nodded. 'I'm good.'

'Just stay close to me and you'll be fine. As soon as we get out of the back, you need to point us in the direction of the nearest watchtower that can't be seen from the main gates.'

'Spider, it's for you,' said Lane, holding out the sat-phone.

Shepherd frowned. 'What?'

'He says he wants to talk to you. Said his name's Yokely. A Yank.'

Shepherd took the phone and put it to his ear. 'Richard?' Shots thwacked into the container above his head.

'AKA your fairy godmother,' said the American. 'Looks like you've got a spot of bother, as you English say.'

Shepherd couldn't help but grin. Richard Yokely was the last person he would have expected to hear from in the midst of a firefight. The American had served in the US Army, the CIA, the DEA and the NSA, but these days he worked for Grey Fox, a super secret off-the-books agency that took care of business that the White House would prefer stayed hidden. He and Yokely went back a long way. 'Where are you?' Shepherd asked.

'Midway between Baltimore and Washington DC,' said Yokely.

Yokely was obviously at the NSA's headquarters in Fort Meade. The National Security Agency was the American equivalent of GCHQ, the Government Communications Headquarters, and between them they had the capacity to listen to every phone call and read every email in the world, twenty-four seven. Shepherd looked up into the sky. 'You're not by any chance watching me, are you, Richard?'

The American chuckled. 'As soon as it became obvious what was happening in Kabul, we moved two satellites into position to get a better look,' he said. 'And we have drones up around the clock.'

'It doesn't look good, does it?'

'It's a clusterfuck, no question about that. So you're surrounded? And under fire?'

'Yes on both counts. Our helicopter has had to turn away.'

'Yes, I saw that.'

'Richard, I have to ask, how did you know it was me?'

'We saw the Puma leave the airport and fly off after your group disembarked from the C17 flight from the UK. We watched you pick up the civilians from the village outside Charikar and saw them drop you at the UK Embassy. That's when I realised there was something going on. I put in a call to London and asked what was happening.'

'And they told you it was me?'

Yokely laughed. 'I'm on your side, remember. And Julian Penniston-Hill and I go back a long way. What is it with the security services and double-barrelled names?'

'It's a tradition,' said Shepherd.

'Well, Julian told me what you were up to, though he seemed a bit baffled that you'd gone to the embassy. He said your mission had been to rescue one of his agents. He asked me if I could offer you any assistance and of course I said I'd be delighted.'

'Okay,' said Shepherd.

'Have you finished whatever it was you were doing in the embassy?'

'We have,' said Shepherd. 'We called in our evac chopper but it came under fire and we had to abort. But then you saw that.'

'Your guys had a narrow escape,' said Yokely.

'We were just discussing requisitioning a vehicle and driving back to the airport. It's only five clicks away.'

'I'd advise against that,' said Yokely. 'We've got intel that ISIS-K are planning to attack the airport gates with suicide bombers. You've heard of ISIS-K, I assume?'

'Of course,' said Shepherd. ISIS-K – Islamic State Khorasan Province – was the most extreme and violent of all the jihadist militant groups in Afghanistan. They had targeted hospitals and girls' schools, and even shot pregnant women and nurses in a maternity ward. They had more than 3,000 hardcore fighters, mostly Afghan and Pakistani jihadists who didn't think the Taliban was extreme enough. 'We'll try going over the wall.'

'Easier said than done,' said Yokely. 'I have a better solution. I'll send someone to get you.'

'Last I heard the Americans weren't sending anyone outside.'

'Not from the airport, no. But we already have some special forces guys and choppers waiting to fly in. I can send a chopper your way.'

'It's too dangerous, Richard. Much as I appreciate the offer, obviously.'

'This chopper is a little bit special,' said Yokely. 'It's a Chinook MH-47G, on loan from USASOC. Guns-a-go-go.'

'Ah, that is special,' said Shepherd. USASOC was the US Army Special Operations Command and the MH-47G had been especially designed and built for use by special forces. It came with two M134 7.62mm air-cooled mini guns and two M240 7.62mm belt-fed machine guns mounted on either side of the fuselage. It also had defensive aids including a missile warning system, an integrated radio frequency countermeasures suite and dark flares that would – hopefully – protect the helicopter against surface-to-air and air-to-air heat-seeking missiles.

'Well, from the look of it, it does seem that you'll be wanting fries with that.'

Shepherd grinned at the joke. The special forces Chinook

did indeed come with FRIES – a Fast Rope Insertion Extraction System, including an electrically powered rescue hoist. It would be perfect for plucking them from the roof of the embassy. 'Let's do it,' said Shepherd.

'Your wish is my command,' said Yokely. 'They should be there within five minutes. There's six of you, right?'

'Yes,' said Shepherd.

'Stay safe.'

The line went dead and Shepherd gave the phone back to Lane. Everyone was looking at him expectantly. 'The cavalry's on its way,' he said.

Shepherd shuffled along the parapet, took a breath, then popped up and fired a quick shot. There was virtually no time to aim because the two Humvees had their machine guns trained on the embassy roof and at any sign of movement one or both would let loose a volley of bullets.

Parts of the parapet had already started to crumble and the shipping containers were holed like Swiss cheese. The gunners on the backs of the two pick-up trucks were also taking pot shots but their aim was poor to say the least.

Ireland nodded at Shepherd and stood up, took aim at one of the Humvees and let fly his last remaining HEDP grenade. He grinned when it hit the gun shield, blowing it, the gun and the gunner, into pieces. He ducked down just as the second Humvee fired but the rounds went high. 'Got one,' he said. 'But I'm out.'

'Chinook incoming!' shouted Lane, pointing off to the south. Shepherd looked into the sky and shaded his eyes with his right hand. The Chinook was a beast of a helicopter, almost a hundred feet long with two massive rotors. It was a workhorse, weighing close to 50,000 pounds and capable of carrying a load of almost half that. It carried over a thousand gallons of fuel and could fly at 150 mph with a full load. That full load could be 55 troops or equipment and ammunition. But the Chinook heading their way was more than a workhorse – it was a killing machine, specially adapted for US Special Forces missions.

It was flying at about 2,000 feet and descending quickly. It was coming in downwind from the jihadists so the first they knew was when rounds from the belt-fed machine guns began ripping through their bodies and blowing their vehicles apart.

Shepherd and his team kept their heads down until the firing stopped and the massive helicopter had flown overhead. They peered over the parapet. Williams whistled when he saw what was left of the Taliban convoy. The vehicles were practically in pieces and the jihadists were bleeding and broken, sprawled across the road. 'The Yanks don't fuck about, do they?' he said.

'They've always had air superiority,' said Standing. 'If they'd used it to support the Afghan Army, the country wouldn't be in the mess it is now.'

The Chinook began to descend and turn. 'Right guys,' said Shepherd. 'The heli will drop a rope with harnesses attached. Basically it will lift us all in one go.'

'Have you done this before?' Docherty asked Shepherd.

'I've seen it done, but never actually done it myself,' said Shepherd. 'We tend to lift people one at a time, like the Puma was going to do. This is a technique used more by the Navy SEALs.'

'I've done it,' said Standing. 'When I was embedded with

the SEALs a few years back. The trick is to keep your arms and legs out like a starfish. It'll stop you rotating. You attach yourself in pairs. Best I'm at the top with Penny. Karl and Paddy can be in the middle and you and Secret Squirrel can bring up the rear.'

Shepherd nodded. It made sense to have someone experienced at the top. If the men at the top started spinning then everyone would follow.

'Just so you know, the rope won't be hauled in,' said Standing. 'They extract the team on the rope and then drop them elsewhere. It's too much weight to raise safely so they'll lift us and take us to the airport and then lower us to the ground.'

'That means we'll be dangling over the Taliban,' said Ireland. 'What if they start taking pot shots?'

'I'm guessing they'll go high,' said Standing. 'Probably 3,000 feet or so.'

Shepherd smiled as the colour drained from Docherty's face. He patted him on the shoulder. 'It's just like parachuting, but in reverse.'

'I've never parachuted.'

'Bungee jump?'

Docherty shook his head.

'You'll be fine,' said Shepherd.

The helicopter was overhead now. A rope appeared from a side door just behind the front rotor. The rope swayed as it played out. There were harnesses hanging from it, in pairs.

The end of the rope hit the roof, followed by the first two harnesses. Shepherd picked up one of the harnesses and helped Docherty get into it. The rope continued to drop and it coiled on to the roof. Williams and Ireland grabbed the second set of harnesses and began fitting them as Standing and Lane seized the top set. The rope dropped another ten feet or so and then stopped.

Shepherd methodically checked all the straps around Docherty's thighs, waist and shoulders, then made sure that the carabiners were securely locked. The MI6 officer was as white as a sheet and breathing heavily. Shepherd grinned. 'Trust me, once we're in the air you'll love it.'

Docherty nodded and tried to smile but ended up just baring his teeth like a frightened dog.

Once he was satisfied that Docherty was safely strapped in, Shepherd fitted his own harness. The Chinook was about a hundred feet above them. The crew chief was leaning out of the doorway to get a better look.

Standing came over and checked Shepherd's harness. Lane had to come with him as their harnesses were attached to the same point on the rope. Standing grinned at the way Docherty was clutching his briefcase to his chest. 'You'll need to attach that, otherwise the slipstream will rip it from your hands,' he said. He unclipped a spare carabiner from his harness and used it to clip the handle of the briefcase to the strap around Docherty's waist. 'And don't forget what I said about keeping your arms and legs out. Starfish position.'

Docherty nodded. 'Starfish position,' he repeated.

'Watch and learn,' said Standing. He walked along the roof with Lane until the rope had tightened between them and Williams and Ireland, then he looked up and gave the crew chief a thumbs-up.

The crew chief repeated the gesture. Standing and Lane opened their legs wide and stretched out their arms. Williams and Ireland did the same.

The Chinook began to rise, taking the rope with it.

Shepherd and Docherty adopted the starfish position, craning their necks to keep their eyes on the helicopter.

The rope smoothly uncoiled itself, then tightened. Lane and Standing had to shuffle along and then their feet lifted off the roof.

The rope continued to tighten and then Williams and Ireland were also hoisted into the air.

Almost immediately the rope yanked at Shepherd's harness. He winked at Docherty. 'Here we go. Just relax and enjoy the ride.'

Docherty let loose a string of expletives and then he yelped as his feet left the roof. He kept his arms and legs out and the briefcase dangled from the harness. Shepherd had his back to Docherty as they rose into the air.

It was a strange sensation. Shepherd had made hundreds of parachute jumps over the years, but this was totally different. When he jumped out of a plane the only way was down, and he had control – he could move the chute through a full 360 degrees. But on the rope he had zero control. All he could do was try to stop himself spinning. They climbed quickly as they headed north-east, towards the airport. In the distance he could see more Taliban pick-up trucks leaving the main road and heading to the embassy.

They reached 3,000 feet in less than two minutes. Shepherd swung around slowly and he saw the airport ahead of them. An American Airlines jet was taking off and a Delta jet was waiting to taxi on to the main runway. There were four Globemasters parked by the terminal, and half a dozen Hercules C130s. There were jets from various European countries, and a Qantas Airbus A380. There appeared to be even more people outside the airport now than when he had left just a few hours earlier. Thousands upon thousands, mainly men. And there were queues of vehicles at all the checkpoints on the roads leading to the airport.

He began to turn. He tried forcing his arms and legs wider but it didn't make any difference. Slowly the airport moved from his view and he was looking at Kabul and the desert wilderness and rocky mountains beyond. It truly was a desolate place, and even before the Taliban had regained control he could understand why so many Afghans made the perilous journey to Europe in hope of a better life.

The helicopter began to descend and Shepherd's ears popped as the pressure inside equalised. They were over the airport now, about a hundred yards from the terminal. They dropped 2,000 feet quite quickly, but then the descent slowed. Shepherd looked down as the tarmac came towards him. He instinctively bent his knees in anticipation of the impact, but the pilots were skilled and his feet touched the ground so softly that it was only when the rope went slack that he realised he was standing. Docherty was less agile and he lost his balance, but Shepherd caught him and steadied him.

They walked backwards a few steps to take up the slack as Williams and Ireland touched down. Shepherd unfastened Docherty's harness and helped him out. By the time he had dealt with his own, Williams and Ireland were out of theirs and Standing and Lane were on the tarmac. They quickly shrugged off their harnesses, then they all looked up at the helicopter and gave the crew chief a thumbs-up. He waved back, threw them a mock salute, then a few seconds later the Chinook's turbines roared and the helicopter climbed. As they watched it fly away, Brian Heron jogged over to Shepherd. 'That was one hell of an entrance,' he said.

Shepherd grinned. 'Yeah, there was a change of plan. Did the Puma get back?'

'They did,' said Heron. 'It was a fairly rough landing, but the crew are fine.'

'They took enemy fire over the embassy.'

'Yeah, they said.' He gestured at the Chinook, which was now high in the air and heading west. 'Yanks?'

'Special forces heli. Literally pulled our nuts out of the fire. So, the Afghans, what's the story?'

'The British Afghan and his family are on the next flight to Qatar.' He pointed at a Hercules that was taxiing to the runway. 'Their passports were fine so they're out of here. They were in Kabul for a wedding?'

'Yeah.'

Heron shook his head. 'What is wrong with these people?'

Shepherd left the question unanswered. 'What about the translator and his family?'

Docherty walked over, brushing dust off his jacket with one hand, the briefcase in the other. 'I'm just asking about Sayyid,' said Shepherd.

'His case isn't as simple,' said Heron. 'He's with the ambassador at the moment. Paperwork. And the kids don't even have Afghan passports. There was a lot of humming and harring before I left.'

'I'll go and help smooth things over,' said Docherty. 'I'm not leaving Afghanistan without him.' He stuck out his hand. 'Thanks, Spider.'

'Pleasure,' said Shepherd.

They shook hands and Docherty headed over to the main terminal building.

'What about you, Spider?' asked Heron. 'Are you hanging around?'

'No, straight back to London.'

'Pity, you'd come in handy here. It looks as if it could go tits-up at any moment. The Taliban are staying outside the perimeter but if they change their mind there's no way we could stop them.'

'The Yanks have said they'll all be out by the end of the month?'

Heron nodded. 'That's the timetable we're working on. But if it seems as if the Taliban are going to breach the perimeter our orders are to get the ambassador and his team and whatever Brits we can on to the last planes and get the hell out of Dodge.' He shook his head disdainfully. 'It's the mother of all cock-ups.'

Shepherd handed his carbine to Heron, then unstrapped his holstered Glock and gave him that too.

'Your civvy clothes are in the briefing room,' said Heron. 'I can arrange a shower and a meal if you want?'

'Thanks, but I'll just change and go,' said Shepherd.

'The Hercules is leaving now but we have a slot for a C17 in forty-five minutes. I can make sure you have a seat on that.'

'You're a star, Clint.'

Standing and the rest of the team ambled over. 'The old man still has what it takes, hey,' said Standing with a grin.

'Less of the old,' said Shepherd. The two men hugged and then Williams, Lane and Ireland shook Shepherd's hand.

'You never did say where that Chinook came from,' said Ireland.

'Friends in low places,' said Shepherd. 'My guardian angel.'

'Well it would have got very interesting if it hadn't turned up,' said Lane. 'The Puma made it?'

'By the skin of its teeth,' said Heron.

'All's well that ends well,' said Standing. 'Make sure you put in a good word for us with the Secret Squirrel boys, Spider. You never know when we might need friends in low places.'

'For sure,' said Shepherd. 'And can you keep an eye on Tony? He's one of the good guys, I wouldn't want anything to happen to him.'

'We'll make sure he's safe,' said Standing. He hugged Shepherd again, then the SAS team headed to the terminal. Shepherd walked to the briefing room and changed out of his fatigues and put on his suit. Twelve hours later he was back in London.

Job done.

PRESENT DAY

'Sammy says you want to do business with us,' said Charlie Lin. 'He says you are big men in Scotland.' Lin was sitting alone at a circular table with eight chairs. He was in his seventies, totally bald and wearing a black Manchu jacket with an upright collar. Around his neck was a ring of jade on a gold chain. In front of him was a red, gold and green teapot and a matching small bowl. He looked at them over the top of his bowl as he sipped his tea. Shepherd had seen photographs of Lin but this was the first time he had been face to face with the man. Lin owned the building they were in and half a dozen others in Chinatown. He was worth several million pounds, but he also worked for China's Ministry of State Security, albeit at arm's length. They were in an office above a bustling Chinese restaurant, with two windows overlooking the street below. There was an ornate Chinese desk at the far end of the room but most of the space was taken up by the large circular table. There were three large heavies stationed around the room, big men in matching black suits and ties.

'We get around,' said Jimmy 'Razor' Sharpe. 'Plenty of irons in the fire.' Sharpe and Shepherd were both wearing suits. Shepherd had a dark blue tie and Sharpe's shirt was also dark blue. Dark blue was the colour of the day. If bullets started to fly, they hopefully wouldn't be heading in the direction of anyone sporting dark blue. That was the theory, anyway. Sharpe had his greying hair slicked back, was wearing a thick gold chain around his right wrist and had a diamond stud in his right earlobe. Gangster chic.

Shepherd was carrying a Prada briefcase containing 250,000 pounds in marked notes. His suit was Ted Baker, his shoes polished to a shine.

Lin frowned. 'Irons in the fire?' he repeated, carefully placing his tea bowl on the table.

One of the heavies said something in Chinese, obviously translating the phrase.

Lin nodded. 'We have an expression in Chinese. *Shù dà zhāo fēng.* Tall trees attract the wind. I would not want any of your irons to attract the attention of the police.'

'Oh, no need to worry on that score,' said Sharpe. 'I've never been in trouble with the law and Mr Walker here, he is just a regular businessman.' Shepherd was posing as Andrew Walker, an English businessman who lived in Edinburgh whose business was struggling and who needed to make some quick money.

'You own betting shops?' said Lin.

'A chain of them, yes,' said Sharpe. 'It's a cash business.'

'You have to be careful where you wash the notes,' said Lin.

'Not in a laundrette, then?' said Sharpe.

'This is not a laughing matter,' said Lin, his eyes narrowing. 'If you are not prepared to take this seriously, we shall do business elsewhere.' He picked up his bowl and took another sip of tea.

'Why do we have to be careful?' asked Shepherd. 'We were told that the notes are perfect.'

'They are,' said Lin. 'The polymer is good, the ink is good, all the security measures including the foil and the holograms are good.'

'But they all have the same number, right?'

Lin shook his head. 'No, the notes are individually numbered, just like the real thing.'

'Can I see?' asked Shepherd.

'First I must see your money,' said Lin, putting the bowl down.

Shepherd nodded. He was sure that the banknotes that Lin was selling were perfect in every respect. In fact MI5 was almost certain that the counterfeit notes had been printed by the Chinese government as part of a long-term plan to desta- bilise the UK. That was why MI5 had linked up with the National Crime Agency. This wasn't about criminals profiting from counterfeit currency, it was an attack by one government on another. The plan was to flood the UK with fake banknotes and at some point make the fact public. At that point the pound would collapse and the Chinese would be able to pick up British assets for a song. But so far all MI5 had was suppo- sition and conjecture – they needed hard facts.

Lin pointed at the briefcase and clicked his fingers. Shepherd swung the case on to the table and pushed it towards him.

Lin clicked open the two locks and looked down. Shepherd realised he wasn't looking at the notes, but was checking out the case.

'Do you want to count it?' asked Sharpe. 'You can if you want. It's all there.'

Lin squinted at the heavy standing between the windows and said something to him in Chinese. The man reached into his jacket and took out a small black plastic box with twin rubber aerials protruding from the top.

Shepherd tensed. He had a bad feeling about the box.

The man handed it to Lin, who pressed a button on the side. The box began to emit a low buzzing sound. Lin looked at Shepherd. Shepherd smiled, his mind racing. He looked over at Sharpe. Sharpe was also smiling, but Shepherd could see the tension in his jaw.

Lin passed the aerials over the briefcase. The buzzing continued, and grew louder as the aerials reached the handle. That was where the bug was hidden. As the aerials passed directly over the handle, the buzzing reached a crescendo.

Shepherd smiled. 'Croissants,' he said. The SOS word had been Amar Singh's idea. The bug was his, and he was monitoring transmissions in an Openreach van around the corner. Singh had figured that 'croissant' wasn't a word that could be used by mistake in a Chinese restaurant.

Lin barked at the heavies and all three began to reach inside their jackets.

'Croissants!' shouted Shepherd again, getting to his feet. He grabbed the teapot and threw it at the heavy who was furthest away. It hit him in the chest and hot tea sprayed over him. He yelped and staggered backwards. Shepherd was already moving around the table towards the man standing next to Lin. His hand was emerging from his jacket. Shepherd kicked him in between his legs and the man roared in pain. He pulled the gun clear of his jacket and started to point it at Shepherd, but Shepherd was too quick. He sidestepped, grabbed the gun and twisted it out of the man's hands, then slammed the butt against the side of the man's head. The man fell back and crashed into a wall.

Shepherd heard footsteps on the stairs, hopefully his back-up. If it was back-up, he just hoped they wouldn't shoot anyone holding a gun. The heavy he'd hit growled and moved forward but Shepherd kicked him between the legs again and he went down howling in pain.

The heavy by the door was pulling his gun out, but he stopped when the door flew open and a woman in a grey suit and a blue scarf appeared in the doorway brandishing a Glock. 'Armed police!' she shouted. 'Drop your weapon!'

Shepherd didn't drop his gun but he held both his hands up above his head to show that he wasn't a threat.

The heavy seemed to be weighing up his options so the woman pointed her gun at his face and screamed louder. 'Armed police, drop it now!'

She stepped into the room and a second armed cop appeared. She was wearing a blue dress and had her blonde hair tied back with a blue ribbon, and she pointed her Glock at Shepherd. 'Drop the weapon!' she shouted. Shepherd didn't argue. Sometimes in the heat of the moment, an armed officer might well forget the colour of the day. He held the gun between his finger and thumb and placed it on the chair in front of him.

The heavy that Shepherd had hit with the teapot reached inside his jacket, but both cops pointed their guns at him and screamed for him to get down on the ground. He put his hands in the air and dropped to his knees.

Lin's eyes had gone cold. He picked up his bowl and sipped his tea.

The two cops covered the room with their guns. Shepherd caught the eye of the one in the blue dress. He opened his mouth to speak but before he could say anything she screamed at him to shut up. The adrenaline was obviously coursing through her system so Shepherd just put his hands behind his head. Sharpe followed Shepherd's example.

All the heavies were now on their knees with their hands in the air.

Almost a minute had passed since the cops had burst into the room. There were screams outside in the street and Shepherd pictured the rest of the armed cops running around from the nearby fire station, probably causing all sorts of confusion among the tourists and shoppers. There were thumps on the stairs and uniformed cops with Kevlar helmets and vests appeared, holding Heckler & Koch carbines with laser sights. Green dots whipped around the room as the armed officers piled in. Shepherd shrugged at Sharpe. Sharpe shrugged back and wrinkled his nose. Shepherd knew what he was thinking. The operation hadn't gone the way they had hoped. The plan was to take the notes for analysis, and to track the briefcase to see where it went. They weren't intending to bust Lin for several months; in fact they hoped to prove that the Chinese government was behind the fraud. But it was a good bust, there was no question of that, and no one had been shot. Swings and roundabouts.

Shepherd and Sharpe walked out of Chinatown and headed south. It was half an hour's walk to Thames House and Shepherd was in no hurry to get back. 'Fancy a drink?' asked Sharpe. He was based at The National Crime Agency's HQ, across the river from Thames House at One Citadel Place in Tinworth Street.

'Yeah, but I'm going to have to brief Giles Pritchard so best I don't smell of alcohol.'

'Yeah, I guess,' said Sharpe. He shrugged. 'Maybe I should have done more of the talking back there.'

'What?'

'I'm just saying, people tend to trust the Scottish accent. That's why so many call centres use Scots. We inspire trust and confidence.'

'Razor, you don't have a Scottish accent. You have a Glasgow growl.'

'I'm just stating a fact. The Scots accent is the most trusted.'

'And the least trusted would be . . .?'

'Scousers, of course. Followed by Brummies. And Northern Irish. Here's a funny thing, no one trusts anyone with a Northern Irish accent, but everyone loves the Southern Irish. Yet as we both know, it's the Paddies south of the border that tell the most porkies. You look like you don't believe me. These are facts, Spider. Written in stone.'

'And where do Geordies fit into this equation?'

'Ah, the Geordies. People trust the accent, fair enough, but no one can ever understand a word they're saying.'

Shepherd laughed and shook his head. 'I think you must be due for another diversity course,' he said. 'Anyway, I think he was going to check the case out no matter what we said. We were lucky he didn't give it the once over before allowing us in. Then we'd have nothing.'

'True,' said Sharpe. He looked at his watch. 'I really can't face going back to the office. They'll only find me something to do.'

'Busy?'

'Worked off our feet,' said Sharpe. 'The whole system is broken, you know that. From the top down. We're trying to put ordinary decent criminals behind bars while the government and its friends are trousering billions.' He grinned. 'Still, can't complain.'

Shepherd was about to reply when his phone rang. It was

Pritchard. 'I gather things didn't go as planned,' said his boss.

'Well, it was always a possibility they would twig,' said Shepherd. 'There was something wrong with the bug in the case. Amar's trying to work out what the problem is. It's supposed to be untraceable.'

'Well, they said the Titanic was unsinkable,' said Pritchard. 'Anyway, we can talk about it in the office.'

'I was just about to . . .'

'Sooner rather than later,' said Pritchard.

'I'm on my way.'

Pritchard ended the call and Shepherd put the phone away. 'I've got to go,' he said. 'The boss wants me.'

'Are you getting a bollocking?'

'I can't see why I would. But I will run your theory about trustworthy accents by him. Do you want a lift? We can get a cab and it can drop me at Thames House.'

Sharpe looked at his watch. 'I'm gonna grab a drink,' he said.

'Catch you later,' said Shepherd.

He held out his fist but Sharpe snorted contemptuously. Shepherd grinned and opened his fist to shake hands. They shook, then Sharpe grabbed him and hugged him. 'Don't let the bastards grind you down,' he growled. He patted him on the back and walked away.

Shepherd flagged down a black cab and told the driver to take him to Pizza Express on Thorney Street. The restaurant was opposite Thames House, but he knew from experience that by giving it as his destination he would avoid any conversation about spies or espionage. He was just a guy going for a pizza. As it happened, the driver had no interest in him. He was deep in conversation on hands-free for the entire journey, talking to his accountant about his latest tax demand.

The driver was still talking when Shepherd got out of the cab and paid him. Shepherd jogged across the road and around to the front entrance of Thames House.

Amy Miller smiled when he walked into the office. She was wearing a grey wool cardigan over a pale blue dress and there was a string of large pearls around her neck. She looked as if she had dropped in from a local fete. 'He's on a call, if you don't mind waiting,' she said. A light blinked off on her desk phone and she gestured at the door. 'He's free now.'

Shepherd thanked her and opened the door to Pritchard's office. He was at his desk, tapping his fingers on his phone. His tie was fully up and his jacket was on, which was usually a good sign. He looked at Shepherd over the top of his glasses and waved for him to sit on one of the two wooden chairs facing his desk. 'The cash is on its way back, so at least that's good news,' said Pritchard. 'The accounts department were never happy at the idea of Charlie Lin hanging on to two hundred and fifty thousand pounds of taxpayers' money.'

'It's an ill wind . . .'

'That's what they say. We can obviously get Lin on counterfeiting charges, and probably conspiracy, and of course there's the guns. In the normal course of events that would be enough leverage for some sort of cooperation deal, but Lin knows what his bosses will do if he does that. He still has family in China, so . . .' He shrugged and left the sentence unfinished.

'Sammy Kwok will sing like a canary, but I don't think he's even aware that the Ministry of State Security is involved.'

'We're looking into the three heavies as we speak,' said

Pritchard. 'We might get lucky there.' He sat back in his chair and took off his glasses. 'Anyway, remember that Afghan translator, the one who was working with Tony Docherty?'

'Of course. Sayyid Habibi.'

Pritchard grinned. 'I know, you and your perfect memory, it was a stupid question. Well there turns out to have been more to him than we thought. He might not be the hero we assumed he was.'

'That's not good.'

'You got him out with his wife and kids. His wife came forward yesterday and is claiming that he's an Islamic State wolf in sheep's clothing and that he and a few like-minded jihadists are planning a terrorist atrocity in the UK.'

'What sort of atrocity?'

'That she doesn't know. But she's claiming that all the time he was working as an MI6 translator in Kabul, he was passing information to Islamic State.'

Shepherd frowned. 'What does Tony have to say about this?'

'He's in shock. He worked with the guy for the best part of three months. Says he'd trust him with his life. But the wife is adamant. They've got her in a safe house in Wimbledon. I'd like you to pop down and assist in the debriefing.'

'I don't remember her English being especially good.'

'It isn't. One of our Pashto speakers has been assisting in the debrief, she'll take you there and do any translating that's necessary. Her name's Farah Nuri.' He looked at his watch. 'She should be here at any moment. Tony Docherty will be waiting for you at the safe house. Once you've heard what the wife has to say, we can take it from there.' Amy Miller appeared in the doorway. 'Ms Nuri is here,' she said, and stepped to the side to reveal an Asian girl in her mid-twenties. She was wearing a grey suit over a dark blue shirt and her jet black hair hung down to her shoulders. She was only a little over five foot three but she had a confident look about her and had her chin up as she walked into Pritchard's office.

'Ah, Farah, excellent. I was just talking about you. This is Dan Shepherd, he'll be heading to Wimbledon with you.'

Farah immediately stuck out her hand, 'Pleasure to meet you, Dan,' she said. 'We've never met but obviously I've heard of you.'

Shepherd stood up and shook her hand. It was small and almost got lost in his, but she had a firm grip and she looked him in the eye as they shook.

'Farah works on our Afghanistan Desk. She did an excellent job of getting Laila Habibi to open up yesterday.'

'Thank you, sir, but she was clearly eager to talk.' She looked at Shepherd and smiled, showing perfect even teeth. 'There's a car waiting for us outside, so whenever you're ready.'

Shepherd looked over at Pritchard, who nodded. 'When you're done, come back here and we'll plan a course of action.' He turned his attention to one of his monitors, his way of letting Shepherd know that the meeting was over.

Shepherd and Farah walked along the corridor to the lift. 'How long have you been with Five?' asked Shepherd.

'Two years,' she said. 'I'm still a newbie.'

'People tend to learn fast here.'

'You can say that again.'

'And you're fluent in Pashto?'

Farah nodded. 'I was born in Afghanistan. I moved to the UK with my family just as the Americans invaded. I was three.'

'Do you remember much about it?'

'Afghanistan? Not really. I was too young.'

'But you kept the language skills?'

They reached the lifts and she pressed the button to go down. 'We spoke Pashto at home. At least my mother did. Her English was never great. My dad speaks perfect English, though. He was put on a Taliban death list for teaching girls, that's why we had to leave. He was a teacher in Kabul.' She forced a smile. 'He could never get a job as a teacher in England.'

The lift doors opened. There were two young men in suits inside. They both recognised Farah and there were smiles and nods. She kept smiling but made no attempt to continue the conversation with Shepherd. She didn't start speaking again until they were out of the lift and walking towards the main entrance. 'He started working as a minicab driver, and then during the pandemic he signed on as an Amazon delivery driver. He loves it. No drunken passengers throwing up over his back seat or refusing to pay or getting into an argument about immigration.'

'And why Five?'

'As opposed to Six? Or as opposed to becoming a pharmacist, which is what my father wanted?'

'Just why.'

'It was the London bombings in 2005. I was just a kid but I remember being really angry about what they did. And again in 2013, when they killed Lee Rigby. I just couldn't understand why people could do something like that. And I guess I wanted to stop them.' She wrinkled her nose. 'I sound like I'm being interviewed for a job.'

'No, not at all. I totally get what you're saying. I'm pretty much the same. Somebody has to stop terrorists and I'd rather be doing that than reading about the latest atrocity or seeing it on the TV.'

'Job satisfaction, right?'

Shepherd laughed. 'Well, it has its ups and downs, that's for sure. But there's nothing that matches the feeling you get after you've taken some seriously bad guys off the streets.'

'Have you always been with Five?'

'No, I was in law enforcement before that.'

They left the building and walked along the pavement towards a waiting black Lexus.

'Cops and robbers?'

'Something like that. So, tell me about the translator's wife.'

'About what she said?'

Shepherd shook his head. 'No, about her. Do you believe her? She's been in the UK for almost a year, why has she only just come forward?

'Oh, I believe her one hundred per cent,' she said. 'No question. You'll see for yourself. There's no evasiveness, no confusion, and she speaks from the heart. As to why she's only now telling us what she knows, well, she could hardly say anything in Kabul, could she? Then when she first moved here she wouldn't have known the way things work, that husbands can't beat or kill their wives just because they don't agree with them. She was scared of him when she was in Afghanistan. She's still scared of him, but I think now she understands that the police – and MI5 – will protect her.'

'Does she love him?'

Farah snorted. 'Heck no. She fears him, and that's about it. It was a forced marriage or arranged marriage, whichever way you want to describe it. She was fifteen, he was almost thirty. They had a third child but it was a girl and Sayyid always made it clear he only wanted sons. Laila found the baby dead in her cot when she was just two months old. She's certain that Sayyid killed her. Smothered her, probably.'

Shepherd stopped in his tracks. 'That's awful.'

Farah stopped and turned to face him. 'He's a nasty piece of work. He as good as raped her on their honeymoon and he used to beat her if she didn't do exactly what he wanted, and he broke her wrist once when she answered back. So yes, I believe her. Every word.' She forced a smile. 'But that's just my opinion. I get that you've got a lot more experience than me so I'd be interested to know what you think.'

'Sounds as if you've done a great job so far,' he said. 'What about her children? The two boys?'

'They're in the safe house, too. Most of the time they're upstairs with some comics we gave them and they seem happy enough.'

The Lexus was just a few feet away and Farah opened the door for him, which Shepherd thought was a nice touch. He couldn't help but smile as he thanked her and climbed inside.

She got in beside him and pulled the door closed. The driver put the car in gear and pulled into the traffic. Farah smiled at Shepherd but again didn't start a conversation. She'd obviously been taught never to discuss office business in front of others, even if they worked for MI5. Shepherd actually knew the driver, Dyfed Morgan. He was a former sergeant major with the Welsh Guards who had worked surveillance for MI5 for a decade before switching to general transport.

'How's it going then, Spider?' asked Morgan as they headed towards Chelsea Bridge.

'Same as always, Dyfed. How's your grandson getting on?'

Morgan's grandson was in 2 Para and was gearing up to

attempt SAS selection. Shepherd had spoken to the lad on the phone a couple of times, and they chatted via email whenever he needed guidance. 'He's getting there. He followed your advice about the bricks in a rucksack and he says it's done wonders for his stamina. I thought you were winding him up, to be honest.'

'No, it works. And the first stage of selection is all about stamina. Once he's worked on that I'll talk him through the jungle phase. That's where they really separate the men from the boys.'

They continued to chat as they headed across the river to Wimbledon. Farah listened but didn't say anything, though several times she smiled at their banter and covered her mouth with her hand.

The safe house was a detached stone cottage on the edge of Wimbledon Common, surrounded by a high wall with wrought-iron gates. Morgan pulled up outside. He twisted around in his seat. 'I'm to wait for you and run you back to Thames House,' he said.

Shepherd nodded. 'That's okay, but I'll be a couple of hours. Why don't you take a break, I've got your number so I'll text you when I need you.'

'You're a gentleman and a scholar,' said Morgan.

Farah and Shepherd climbed out of the Lexus and it drove away.

'So you were in the SAS?' asked Farah.

'A long time ago,' said Shepherd. He opened the gate and let her go through first. She stiffened a little at the gesture. Shepherd was never sure what the rule was about opening doors and gates for women. He did it out of habit, even though from time to time he'd get sneered at or snapped at. Farah just looked a little uncomfortable and mumbled her thanks as she walked past him.

'That must have been interesting,' she said as they walked together to the front door.

'It had its moments.'

'I thought you guys were supposed to never talk about it. Same as we're never supposed to discuss what we do with anyone outside the service.'

'That's a good rule,' said Shepherd. 'But Dyfed and I go back a long way and as you heard, I'm advising his grandson on SAS selection. But yes, you're absolutely right, as a general rule you say nothing to outsiders.'

They reached the front door. There was a CCTV camera looking down at them and another aimed at the gate. Shepherd didn't bother knocking, they would have seen the car arrive. Sure enough he heard footsteps and the door opened. It was Tony Docherty. If anything he looked even more stressed than when Shepherd had seen him emerge from the basement in Afghanistan. His hair was dishevelled and he was wearing a rumpled suit with a sprinkling of dandruff on the shoulders. He forced a smile as he opened the door wider. 'Spider, hi. Sorry about this, obviously.'

'How about we have a quick chat, you can bring me up to speed.'

'Let's go into the garden, I could do with a cigarette.' He smiled at Farah. 'Do you want to wait in the kitchen, Farah? I'm letting Laila have some time with the kids in the front room, just to get her relaxed. Help yourself to a tea or coffee or a soft drink, whatever.'

Farah headed down the hall towards the kitchen. Docherty

stepped outside and pulled the front door closed. He was holding a pack of Marlboro and a cheap disposable lighter. He lit a cigarette as they walked around the side of the house to the rear garden. It was a good size with a clump of apple trees, an ornamental pond and a barbecue area. Docherty blew smoke up into the sky as Shepherd looked up at the rear of the house. There was a man watching them from a bedroom window. Shepherd only caught a glimpse but he saw the man's binoculars and an earpiece in his left ear.

'I'm still in shock about all this,' said Docherty.

'Farah believes her,' said Shepherd. 'What about you?'

'I wish I didn't. I wish I could put it down to a woman scorned. But everything she said seems kosher. We had her tell her story four or five times and she never put a foot wrong. She never hesitates, she maintains eye contact, she never embellishes.'

'She could have been well rehearsed.'

'Sure. Yes. But why? I could understand why she would lie to protect her husband, but why lie to hurt him?'

'Farah said it was a forced marriage. And that maybe Sayyid had murdered their daughter. So plenty of reasons there for her to lash out.'

'Okay. But where's he gone? There's no trace of him.'

'Maybe he left her and that made her angry.' He saw Docherty open his mouth to speak and raised his hand to stop him. 'I'm just playing devil's advocate, Tony. If she's telling the truth there's a big pile of shit going to hit the fan so we need to be sure, one way or the other.'

Docherty nodded and took another pull on his cigarette.

'Give me the gist of what she's claiming.'

Docherty blew smoke at the grass. 'First off, she says that

Sayyid has always been on the Taliban's side. From day one. Everything he learned while he was working for me, he passed to them.'

'Is that possible?'

Docherty looked pained. 'Anything's possible.'

'Tony, mate, I know this is awkward, but you're going to have to bite the bullet on this. If Sayyid is bad, we need to know now.'

'I get it, Spider. Obviously I get it. But if he is bad, how the hell did I miss it? I hired him. I took him into pretty much all the briefings I attended. He was in my office on a daily basis. I risked my life to get him and his family to the UK. If he truly is a Taliban agent, how does that make me look?'

'Do you think he was? Looking back, could he have been working for the Taliban?'

Docherty grimaced. 'On the basis of twenty-twenty hindsight, maybe.' He sighed. 'Don't get me wrong, he never put a foot wrong. He didn't once give me any reason to believe that he wasn't exactly what he said he was.'

'Which was what?'

'A guy who hated the Taliban and everything they stood for. Who wanted to live in a free Afghanistan, who wanted to help us to bring that about.' He took a long pull on his cigarette, held the smoke deep in his lungs, then blew a tight plume of smoke towards the apple trees. 'But . . .' He hesitated, then grimaced again. 'There was one time, six weeks before we pulled out. Another translator had gone AWOL – now he was a bad one, no question – and it put an operation in jeopardy. We were sending a patrol out to pay funds to a local head man in a village about twenty miles outside Kabul and they needed a translator. I agreed that they could borrow Sayyid.

He was fine about it, we'd done it before. Then the night before he was due to go out, he got food poisoning. A serious case of the shits. I saw him, he wasn't faking it. Anyway, long and the short of it was that he couldn't go. They found another translator.' He took another pull on his cigarette, and then flicked it towards a flower bed. 'The patrol was ambushed, a huge IED followed by RPGs and gunfire. They were all killed. The money was taken. At the time it looked like Sayyid had had a lucky escape. Now, with hindsight . . .' He shrugged.

'How did you do the interview yesterday?'

'Slow and gentle. We sat down with her in the sitting room. Just her and me and Farah. We had tea and sandwiches while her kids watched TV in the kitchen. We had full sound and video with two MI6 staffers watching the link.'

Shepherd nodded. 'I'll do the same. You can watch on the link today.'

'You don't want me with you? I know her, she trusts me.'

'No, I need you to take a step back, to be more objective. It'll be easier if you're watching on a monitor. I need you to watch her and see if she's any different today. Not just what she says, but the way she behaves. The way she holds herself.'

'Active listening?'

'Exactly.'

Docherty nodded. 'I'm on it.'

Shepherd patted him on the back. 'This isn't as bad as you think, Tony. At least we're on it now. Whatever Sayyid is planning, we can stop it.'

Docherty forced a smile. 'I hope you're right.'

Laila Habibi looked as if she was wearing the same blue pullover she'd had on when Shepherd first saw her, in the shophouse outside Charikar, but the jeans were different and she wasn't wearing a hijab. She looked tired and there were dark patches under her eyes. She was sitting at one end of a floral-patterned sofa. Farah sat at the other end. There was a coffee table in front of them. Laila was holding a glass of orange juice with both hands as if she was scared it would try to get away from her.

Laila spoke to Shepherd in Pashto, then Farah translated. 'She said she never really thanked you, for helping to get them out of Afghanistan. If you and your friends hadn't rescued them, she doesn't know what would have happened.'

'I hope your boys weren't too scared,' said Shepherd.

Farah translated and Laila spoke again. This time she was smiling.

'The boys were excited,' said Farah. 'First time ever on a helicopter and the next day they had their first trip on an aeroplane. And they love England. They love their school and they love playing in the park. So thank you. From the bottom of my heart, thank you.'

'You're very welcome,' said Shepherd. He sipped his mug of coffee. He had made it himself in the kitchen while he briefed Farah on how he planned to proceed. He wanted Laila to tell her story again, from start to finish, and he wanted Farah to translate in a continuous stream, rather than doing the interview as a Q&A. It was always easier to lie to direct questions – it was much harder to alter a continuing narrative.

Shepherd had spotted two cameras in the room – one in a smoke detector in the ceiling, another in a clock on the side-board – but he was sure there were more. Docherty was upstairs in the back bedroom, watching the feeds with two MI6 officers.

Shepherd smiled at Farah. 'Okay, ask her to tell me everything. From the start. Even if it sounds irrelevant, just let her talk.'

Farah nodded and spoke to Laila in Pashto. Laila began to speak and Farah translated. Shepherd looked at Laila, nodding from time to time as he listened. It was a little disconcerting hearing Farah's voice in English while Laila spoke in her own language, but after a minute or so he got into the rhythm.

Laila had met Sayyid for the first time on her wedding day. There had been no dates, no courtship, just a ceremony followed by what could only be described as rape in the bedroom of his house while his parents sat in the kitchen below them. Sayyid had been a devout Muslim and had made her wear the full burkha whenever she left the house. She was supposed to clean the house, to cook, and to take care of his parents. She did as she was told, because he would beat her if she didn't do exactly as he said.

Sayyid hated the Americans and the British. He called them infidels and kafirs and he rejoiced whenever the Taliban killed a foreign soldier. He ran a small construction company, mainly repairing houses and workshops, always working for locals and refusing to have anything to do with what he referred to as the occupying powers. But that all changed one day, about two years before the Americans left. A man came to their house. He was an old man with a long grey beard and a black patch over one eye. He arrived with two younger men who both carried rifles. Sayyid told Laila to prepare tea and cakes and once she had served them she was banished to the bedroom. The men stayed for more than an hour and only after they had left was Laila allowed out of the bedroom.

Not long after the visit, Sayyid began doing construction

jobs for the British. He repaired a school, then a medical centre that had been damaged by a Taliban bomb, and then he started working inside the British Embassy. Sayyid had always spoken good English, languages came naturally to him, and he made a point of speaking to as many members of staff as he could. Eventually he was called in to talk to one of the embassy officials who offered him a full-time job as a translator.

'Did he say who offered him the job?' asked Shepherd.

Farah translated. 'Spies, he said. Stupid spies, he called them. They had no idea what they were doing. They didn't understand Afghanistan or its people. But he knew how to make them like him. He said all he had to do was to smile and laugh at their jokes. When he came home he always said his face was hurting from smiling so much.'

Shepherd listened as Laila continued her story. Her husband had worked with different people at the embassy, all of them spies. Sayyid began travelling around the country, often away for days at a time. Once the Americans announced that they were pulling out of Afghanistan, Sayyid became even more busy. His hatred of the British also grew. They were cowards, he had said. The British and the Americans were scared of the Taliban and now they were running away with their tails between their legs, like dogs.

The following year, the man with the eyepatch came back to their village to talk to Sayyid. Again Laila was told to serve tea and cakes and then she was sent out of the house with her sons. When she returned the man with the eyepatch had gone and Sayyid told her that they would be moving to England. Laila said that she didn't want to leave Afghanistan but he said that she had no choice, they had to move as a family. She had argued and Sayyid had beaten her. That was the only reason she had agreed to go with him. She didn't want to be beaten again.

After Shepherd had helped to rescue the family they were flown to a military airfield in the UK and then taken to a hotel by the sea. Laila had trouble saying the name of the town and it took her several goes before Farah understood and translated. Scarborough. They were given two rooms in the hotel with a view of the sea.

Farah asked Laila a question and Laila replied. Farah began translating again. While they were in the hotel, Sayyid met with two other Afghans, both men. One was another refugee who was staying at the hotel. He used to walk on the beach with Sayyid and Laila would watch from the window. One day the man disappeared from the hotel and Laila didn't know what had happened to him. She had asked Sayyid who the man was and he had snapped at her and told her to mind her own business. The other man wasn't staying at the hotel but visited Sayyid several times. Sayyid never said who he was or what they talked about, and Laila knew better than to ask any more questions.

After almost three months in the hotel, the family were moved to a permanent house in Birmingham. Sayyid had said that he wanted to live in London but he hadn't been given the choice. Sayyid had begun attending several local mosques and he would leave the house five times a day to pray. He told Laila that she was to stay indoors and to only go out to buy food or to take the children to and from school. She wasn't allowed to have a phone and he took control of any money they had. At this point Laila began to cry. Farah gave her a tissue and put her arm around her.

'Ask her if she knows which mosque he went to.'

Farah nodded and asked. Laila wiped her nose and answered.

'The Makki Masjid, it's about a mile from their house,' said Farah. 'He went to others but that was his local.'

Shepherd put down his coffee mug and smiled at Laila. He thanked her and told her how much he respected her for coming forward. He waited for Farah to translate. 'This man who came to talk to your husband, the man with the eyepatch, if I showed you a photograph of him, would you recognise him?'

Farah translated and Laila nodded. 'Yes,' she said.

'And what about the men that Sayyid was friendly with in Scarborough? At the hotel?'

Farah spoke and Laila nodded again.

'Tell Laila we'll come back with some photographs to look at.'

Farah translated and Laila spoke for some time, looking earnestly at Shepherd. Eventually she finished and continued to look anxiously at Shepherd as Farah spoke. 'Yes, she's happy to help. She'll do whatever you want. She just wants reassurance that she and her sons will be okay. She's terrified that she'll be sent back to Afghanistan. She says the only reason she is in the UK is because she is Sayyid's wife and now that you know he is your enemy, she's worried that she will be punished, too.'

Shepherd smiled at Laila and shook his head. 'Tell her that she's fine, we'll help her and no matter what happens to her husband, she will stay in this country. She's safe now, she can stop worrying.'

'And she wants to know how long she has to stay here. She wants to go back home.' Farah saw that Shepherd was about to speak so she added hurriedly: 'I know, I've already told her that it's not safe for her to go home, at least not until this is resolved. I've explained that she needs to stay here until we've decided what to do next.'

'Exactly,' said Shepherd. 'Tell her she needs to stay here for the next few days. We can buy her anything she and her boys need, and we can send out for whatever food she wants. If the lads need a PlayStation I'm sure we can spring for that. And then once it's resolved, we can see about rehousing her.'

'She seemed very keen to stay in the same house. Her boys really like the school and they've made friends there.'

'If it's safe, of course. We'll have to see what happens regarding her husband. The priority is to deal with her husband, then we'll sort out her situation. But make sure she understands that we will take care of her and her family.'

'She was also asking about her mother.'

'Her mother?'

'Her mother is still in Afghanistan. She wanted to know if we can bring her mother to the UK.'

Shepherd's smile became a little more forced. 'Obviously we'll do what we can,' he said. 'Tell her that we'll certainly speak to the Home Office about her mother. But our priority right now is to stop her husband from doing whatever he has planned.'

'I'll make sure she understands.'

'I'm sure you will.'

Docherty lit a cigarette and took a long drag on it. 'How did she look this time?' asked Shepherd. They were standing by the clump of apple trees, looking back at the house. Shepherd had sent a text message to Morgan, who had replied saying he'd be there in ten minutes.

'If anything, even more believable,' said the MI6 officer. 'Everything pretty much the same as yesterday. Actually a bit more detail. But nothing that contradicted what she said the first time. Her body language, the way she told the story, it all seemed just right. And when you looked away, her face stayed the same. She wanted you to believe her, I could see it. Not because she was lying but because she was telling you the truth.'

Shepherd nodded. 'She felt right to me. Not a single red flag.'

Docherty took another pull on his cigarette. 'So I brought a jihadist into this country. That's me fucked.'

'All we can do is take it one step at a time. We know Sayyid is bad, now we need to stop him doing whatever he's planned.'

'Except we have no idea what that is.'

'It's up to us to work that out,' said Shepherd. 'What progress have you made, investigation-wise?'

'There is no MI6 investigation, so far as I know. Laila called me and said she needed to talk to me. I had a brief chat on the phone and once it became clear what was happening I drove up to Birmingham and brought her and the kids here. I contacted Penniston-Hill and he said he'd talk to your mob and then I was told to expect you.'

'Which means there's no corroboration for anything that she says?'

'Well Sayyid wasn't at her house, that's for sure.'

'Did you check to see if he'd taken clothes with him, toiletries, stuff like that?'

'I just collected her and the kids, I didn't even go into the house. Just pulled up outside and they piled in.'

Shepherd's jaw tightened. If Docherty hadn't gone into the

house there was no way he could know if Sayyid was there or not. For all they knew, he could have been upstairs watching them leave. It showed a lack of professionalism, and that was a worry. 'Did Sayyid have a car?'

Docherty shook his head. 'No. No vehicle, not even a bike.'

'Did someone pick Sayyid up?'

'She said two Asian guys came in a white van. He went with them.'

'And did he take a bag with him?'

'She didn't say.'

More likely, thought Shepherd, Docherty hadn't asked.

'Spider, I was just told to go and get her and bring her here. I was told the priority was to get her interviewed as quickly as possible. We did that yesterday. In fact we were still going at one o'clock this morning by which time she was exhausted and we had to let her sleep. I briefed Penniston-Hill first thing this morning and he said to hang fire until someone from Five got here.'

'Did you keep in touch with Sayyid?'

'No. He and his family came back about a week before I did. By the time I got back to the UK, Border Force had processed them and they were in the hotel in Scarborough.'

'So you didn't even speak to him?'

'I did talk to him, yes. On the phone. I was given his number and I called him a few times to check that he was settling in. The usual grumbles, not enough money, when could he have a house, all that guff.'

'And no clue that he was up to something?'

'He didn't seem interested in talking, to be honest. I suggested I go up to meet him and he said he'd get back to me and he never did. They moved him to Birmingham and I called him again and he said things were fine. Again he wasn't really interested in chatting. I just assumed that he'd got what he wanted – i.e. out of Afghanistan – and that he just wanted to get on with his new life.'

'Give me his number,' said Shepherd. Docherty took out his phone, scrolled through his address book and read out the number. He frowned when Shepherd didn't write the number down or put it into his phone. 'Aren't you going to write it down?' Docherty asked. 'Or were you just checking if I had it?'

'I've got a trick memory,' said Shepherd. 'I can remember pretty much everything I see or hear.'

'Seriously?'

Shepherd repeated the number without hesitating. Docherty had to check on his phone but he nodded when he saw that Shepherd had been right.

'Tony, do you want to work with me on this? You know the guy.'

'I thought I did,' said Docherty, his voice loaded with bitterness. 'But yeah. I want to be in on it.'

'Okay, I'll clear it with my boss. So, first things first. It would be handy to know who the Taliban guy was who came to see Sayyid. The one who obviously persuaded him to start working for the British. It could well be that he's running the UK operation. I can think of a couple of Taliban leaders with eyepatches but I'll check our database and run it by the Americans. Then we need to find out who Sayyid has linked up with here in the UK. I'd like to think that the hotel in Scarborough has CCTV but even if it does I can't see them hanging on to the files for this long.' He rubbed his chin. 'If they came out during the Kabul airlift, we could run pictures of the evacuees past her, but there would be thousands of faces.'

'You're going to check his phone records?'

'Sure, and hopefully his GPS,' said Shepherd. 'I guess it comes down to how well Sayyid was trained. If he's on the ball then it will be burner phones and call boxes and draft email files all the way.' He looked at his watch. 'Okay, I'll head back to Thames House. Give me your number and I'll call you once I know what's happening.'

Docherty told Shepherd his number. 'That's a neat trick, never having to write anything down,' he said.

'Yeah, it comes in useful.'

'And you can remember everything you're told?'

'Pretty much. Names, dates, faces, conversations.'

'And your brain doesn't get full?'

Shepherd laughed. 'It hasn't so far,' he said. 'It's not as if all that information is buzzing around all the time, I have to consciously access it. In fact most people don't actually forget things, the information is still in their brain somewhere, they just lose the ability to access it. That's why hypnotism can help people recover the memories they don't realise they have. The information is in there, you just need to find it. But for me, that's never a problem.'

The two men bumped fists and Shepherd walked around the side of the house. He could see Morgan through the gates, standing by the Lexus. As he reached the path, the front door opened. It was Farah. She had obviously been waiting for him. 'Dan, can I have a word?'

'Sure, What's up?'

She pulled the door closed behind her and went over to him. 'I'd really like to be involved in this investigation.'

'You are. And you're doing a great job.'

She shook her head. 'I'm translating, that's all.' She sighed. 'I spend most of my life in a windowless room wearing headphones and listening to muffled conversations. More often than not it's teenage boys trying to impress their friends. Every now and again I'm allowed out to talk to a human being. But then I'm sent back to the headphones. I want to be involved in a real investigation. You're obviously going after Sayyid and I can help you.'

'The problem is, the communities that Sayyid hangs out in don't tend to respond to questions from . . .' He shrugged and left the sentence unfinished.

'From women?' She folded her arms defensively.

'I know it's not what you want to hear, but it's the truth.'

'It's not fair, and if you really think about it, you'll realise it's not fair. If I was in Kabul, of course I wouldn't be allowed to do this job. Women there can't even go to university, they're sure as hell not allowed to work for the intelligence agencies. But this is England. And you can't tell me that I can't do the job because I'm a woman. If we start thinking that way, then the terrorists have won.' She stopped speaking and glared at him.

Shepherd looked at her, trying not to smile at her enthusiasm. 'I hear what you're saying.'

'But you're not going to change your mind?'

This time he couldn't help but smile and he saw from the way her eyes hardened that she thought he was laughing at her so he spoke quickly. 'No, you've convinced me.'

'Seriously?'

He nodded. 'Seriously. We'll need a team on this and I'll ask Giles Pritchard for you to be on that team. You've got skills that we could make use of.'

She beamed. 'You won't regret this,' she said. 'I will work so bloody hard for you.'

'I'm sure you will,' said Shepherd. 'Now you need to stay with her this afternoon, see if you can get any more information out of her, and I'll phone you from Thames House.' He gave her his phone and she tapped in her number.

'Thank you, thank you so much,' she said as she gave him back the phone. She was still thanking him as he let himself out of the gate.

The Lexus was waiting for him, the engine running. 'Change of venue,' said Morgan as Shepherd climbed into the back. 'Tamesis Dock. You know what that means?'

Shepherd nodded. Yes, he knew.

The Russian reached slowly into his rucksack and took out an energy bar. He had already opened the packet and wrapped the bar in tissue paper so it made no noise as he put it to his mouth and chewed. He was in the middle of a bush, lying on a groundsheet with camouflage netting covering his head and body. The trail was about fifty yards ahead of him, passing from left to right. It was a muddy track that wove its way through the trees, pockmarked with horseshoe prints.

It was the Russian's third day on surveillance and he planned to do at least another two. He had arrived two hours before dawn. His driver had dropped him at the side of the road, and then returned to the Holiday Inn they were using as their base. Once he had left the road he had slipped on night vision goggles which allowed him to move confidently in the darkness, across the fields and through the woods to his hiding place. He had chosen a different bush each time so that he would have a different view of the rider.

The rider appeared each day at between five and ten minutes past eight. He varied his clothing but it was the same horse. And he didn't wear a riding hat. He would keep the horse at a trot and the rider was clearly experienced, every movement was smooth and controlled. The rider would follow the track out to the far side of the woods, where he would take the horse around the adjoining field to an area laid out with jumps. When the rider returned, about an hour later, the horse would be cantering and occasionally breaking into a full gallop.

The Russian watched the rider carefully. Every little thing he noticed could be helpful. It was the gallop he was especially interested in. The rider sat high in the saddle, the reins lose, letting the horse have its head. Presumably the horse was rushing to get back to its stable and its food.

The Russian had to remain in his hiding place until night fell. He couldn't afford to be seen walking around. People would remember. Once it was dark he would head back to the road and his driver would pick him up and drive him to the Holiday Inn where he would grab some food and a few hours' sleep. The driver rarely spoke. His English was good enough but he was smart enough to know that the Russian didn't appreciate chit chat. They had a job to do and that was all that mattered.

The Russian wasn't thrilled at having to work with the Afghans, but he had been given the job and the people he worked for didn't react well to refusal. You either did as you were told, or you were let go, which in his line of work could mean ending up buried in a field somewhere. The Russian once had to deal with two men who had refused a job in Chechnya because it meant children would die. The two men were shot in the head and buried while they were still warm.

The children died the following week, along with their parents.

The problem with the Afghans was that they were fanatics, in the true sense of the word. The Russian had studied English at an advanced level, and he knew that the word fanatics came from the Latin word *fanaticus*, which meant inspired by a god. The Russian didn't believe in god, in any god, and that made his life much simpler. But the Afghans truly believed that if they died for their cause they would go to heaven and sit next to their god, with seventy-two virgins at their beck and call. It was nonsense, the Russian knew, it was a story you told to children, but these were grown men and they believed every word. It was annoying that they insisted on praying five times a day, and they never touched alcohol. The Russian would never trust a man who did not take a drink. Men drank and fucked, that's what they did. The Afghans sipped fruit juice and dreamed of virgins in heaven. Fanatics.

It was their fanaticism that meant they were keen to claim credit for their actions. When they killed, they wanted the world to know what they had done and why they did it. The Russian never wanted anyone to know what he had done. The perfect murder was one where no one even knew that a murder had been committed. A heart attack, a car crash, an accidental overdose – they were the killings that the Russian was proud of. The killings that no one knew about, other than his employers. They knew, and they valued his discretion. But these Afghans, these fanatics, when they did what they were planning to do, the whole world would know. They were welcome to the credit, and the notoriety. All the Russian wanted was to get the job done and to get back to Russia.

He finished his energy bar and took a sip of water. He was

drinking as little as possible because if he needed to empty his bladder or bowels he would have to do it into a plastic bottle.

He began to tense and relax his various muscle groups. Lying in one position for hours on end wasn't good for the body. But it had to be done.

Tamesis Dock was a former 1930s Dutch barge that had been converted into a pub, which sometimes floated and sometimes rested on the river bed, moored between Lambeth and Vauxhall Bridge. It was a night-time live jazz venue and a place where hipsters flocked for brunch at the weekend. It was also almost exactly midway between Thames House in Millbank and the SIS Building at Vauxhall Cross, so was often used as a meeting place when operatives from the two agencies needed to share intel face to face. The barge had been painted a garish red and yellow and the deck had been lined with trellis tables that offered stunning views of the Houses of Parliament, the London Eye and Battersea Power Station. During the day it was quiet and there was a clear view of anyone going on board, so it was the perfect venue for a quiet chat. Shepherd had used it several times for business and was a fan of their fish and chips.

Morgan parked and as soon as Shepherd climbed out of the Lexus he saw Giles Pritchard sitting at one of the tables near the bow. The man he was sitting with had his back to the road but Shepherd knew who it was. Julian Penniston-Hill, the head of MI6. Tongues would wag if Penniston-Hill was seen at Thames House, ditto if Pritchard visited the SIS Building, so it made sense to meet on neutral territory. There were only two other people sitting on the deck, big men in dark suits who both casually scrutinised Shepherd as he walked to the barge. They were minders, and as Shepherd had never seen

Pritchard with security that meant they were there to watch over Penniston-Hill.

Shepherd walked across the gangplank and on to the deck. The two minders were drinking Coke and nibbling on olives. They pretended to ignore Shepherd as he walked over to Pritchard's table. Pritchard smiled and waved at the seat next to him. 'Dan, thanks for coming. Please, sit.'

Shepherd sat down and nodded at Penniston-Hill. 'Sir,' he said. He was wearing a dark blue suit, a crisp white shirt and an MCC tie.

'No need to stand on ceremony, Dan,' said the MI6 head. 'Julian is fine. Do you want a drink?'

'I'm okay, thank you,' said Shepherd. Pritchard and Penniston-Hill were sharing a bottle of white wine and a platter of hummus with bread. The wine was half gone but the food appeared to be untouched.

'How did it go?' asked Pritchard.

'She's telling the truth,' said Shepherd. 'Her husband is a committed jihadist and is clearly up to something.'

Penniston-Hill groaned. 'How the hell does this happen?'

'He slipped through the net,' said Pritchard. 'Positive vetting is all well and good here at home, but out in Afghanistan there were limits to what checks could be made.'

'If it helps, I met Sayyid in Kabul and he seemed right to me,' said Shepherd.

Penniston-Hill flashed him a thin smile. 'Your loyalty is to be commended. But a cock-up like this led to the untimely death of my predecessor and I'm damned if I'm going to see history repeat itself.'

'The question is, where do we go from here?' said Pritchard. 'Do we have any idea where he is and who he's working with?'

'He met with two Afghans in Scarborough but we haven't ID'd them yet.'

'Scarborough?' said Penniston-Hill.

'The family was put up in the Grand Hotel there,' said Shepherd. 'They stayed there for going on three months before they were rehoused in Birmingham. His wife remembers him talking to the men about a month after they arrived in the UK.'

'Why does she remember that specifically?' asked Pritchard.

'Because she asked him who they were and he slapped her and told her to mind her own business. Once they moved to Birmingham he started going to one of the local mosques. He never brought anyone home and she was pretty much a prisoner in the house. She was only allowed out to take the kids to and from school and to visit the local shops.'

'These guys he met in Scarborough, were they staying in the hotel too?' said Pritchard.

'The wife says one of them was, but that he left a day or two later.'

'Absconded? That means we might be able to identify him.'

Shepherd nodded. 'I hope so.'

'And which mosque in Birmingham?'

'The Makki Masjid. I haven't heard of it but I'll run a check.'

'What about possible targets?' asked Penniston-Hill.

'I think he was careful what he said around her, when it came to specifics.'

Penniston-Hill nodded thoughtfully. 'Obviously we can't go public on this.'

'Obviously,' said Pritchard. 'But the threat level is going to have to be raised.'

Penniston-Hill's jaw clenched. The threat level was set by

the Joint Terrorism Analysis Centre based on intelligence supplied by MI5, MI6 and GCHQ. The level could vary from 'low', which meant an attack was highly unlikely, up to 'critical', which meant an attack was highly likely in the near future. The current level was 'substantial', meaning that the JTAC considered an attack was likely. Knowing what they now knew, the threat would probably need to be raised to 'severe' or even 'critical'. But if that happened, journalists might start asking some very awkward questions.

'Does the threat level need to be raised though?' said Penniston-Hill. 'Would extra vigilance help in any way? It's not as if we're releasing his photograph, is it?'

'We're going to have to brief JTAC and Number 10,' said Pritchard.

'At some point, yes, obviously. But let's not rush into anything prematurely. All we know is that a potential jihadist has gone AWOL. For all we know he might turn up again next week. He might not even be in the country. I would counsel against spreading alarm until we know for sure what we're up against.'

Pritchard nodded. 'We can certainly hold off informing JTAC until we've carried out a preliminary investigation.'

'Agreed. As things stand, it's just the word of one woman against her husband. She has a lot to gain if we mark him down as a terrorist. And for all we know, she has another man lined up.'

The two men looked at Shepherd, waiting for him to speak. Shepherd didn't think for one moment that Laila was lying, and there was zero chance of her having another man. Penniston-Hill was more worried about damage control, and Pritchard was happy enough to go along with it. If nothing else, the head of MI6 would be indebted to Pritchard and that was always a useful card for him to have in his hand. 'I'm ready to start right now,' Shepherd said. 'My first thought was to see if I could ID the Taliban leader Sayyid met, the one who got him started working for the Brits. If I can get a handle on him, then we might have an idea what's being planned. Then we need to ID the two men in Scarborough who met with Sayyid. I'll check our databases and Border Force's and run any likely suspects by Laila. And I'll talk to any of our people who have had dealings with the mosque in Birmingham.'

'Phone records?' said Penniston-Hill.

'It's in hand,' said Shepherd. 'We have Sayyid's mobile number, but if he's been well trained then he won't have used it for anything sensitive. But if the GPS works we'll be able to see where he's been, and if we cross-reference that with CCTV we might get lucky.'

'And you've got the wife's phone?' asked Penniston-Hill. 'That needs to be given a going over.'

'I'll get that organised, of course, I just wanted to check I was being put on the case first.'

'Oh, you're definitely on the case,' said Pritchard.

Pritchard looked at Penniston-Hill who nodded enthusiastically. 'Best man for the job, no question.'

'Right then, full steam ahead,' said Shepherd. 'Obviously our first priority is to find out where he is, who he's with, and what his plans are.'

'What do you need, team-wise?' asked Pritchard.

'It'd be a big help if Tony Docherty could work with me.'

Penniston-Hill snorted. 'He might not even have a job tomorrow.'

'He knows Sayyid. Yes, Sayyid lied to him, but he will know

things that could come in useful. Small stuff, stuff that's particular to Sayyid. His interests, what he eats. Intel that could tip the balance.'

'Fine,' said Penniston-Hill curtly. 'I suppose we should give him the chance to redeem himself.'

'And the translator. Farah. I think she'll be useful.'

'She's never worked on an operation before,' said Pritchard.

'No, but she's gotten to know Laila. And she's familiar with the culture.'

'She's very young.'

Shepherd shrugged. 'She's keen. And we were all young once.'

'You can keep an eye on her? Take her under your wing?'

'She's very capable. But yes, I'll watch her.'

'Okay then. Anyone else?'

'I think at this stage the three of us will be enough. Obviously we'll be drawing on Thames House resources but until we know where he is there's no need for surveillance or technical support.'

'What about giving their house a going over?' said Pritchard. 'On the off chance he left something behind.'

'I thought we could do that first thing tomorrow. I can liaise with our guys in Birmingham while I'm there.'

Pritchard nodded. 'Sue Johnson is our senior operative in Brum. I'll let her know you're coming. Right, it looks as if we're on track. You report to me, obviously. Docherty and Farah Nuri report to you but I'd suggest that Docherty also keeps Julian in the loop.'

'That's fine,' said Shepherd. He would have expected Docherty to report back to his boss even if he was seconded to MI5, but at least now the arrangement would be formalised.

Pritchard looked at his watch. 'Maybe you should be heading back to Thames House. Julian and I have a few things to talk through so I'll see you later.'

Shepherd nodded and smiled at them both, studiously ignored the two minders, and walked off the barge. Morgan was waiting for him by the Lexus. 'Back to the office,' said Shepherd. 'Actually, tell you what, I'll walk back.'

'You're sure, Spider? I'm yours for the rest of the day.'

'Nah, I need some fresh air.'

'Tough day?'

'And getting tougher.'

Shepherd walked along Albert Embankment, the wind from the river ruffling his hair. As he walked on to Lambeth Bridge he phoned Farah and told her that Giles Pritchard had agreed for her to join the investigation. She immediately began to thank him effusively. He grinned and waited for her to run out of steam. 'I need you to bring me Laila's phone,' he said when she stopped talking. 'Come to Thames House about five and I'll brief you on what we're doing.'

'I'll get her fixed up with a temporary pay-as-you-go.'

'How will she be with you not around?'

'Her English is okay for asking for things. She has the basics. And I'll give her my number so that she can call me if there's a problem. Worst possible scenario, I can get another translator assigned to her, but I don't think that'll be necessary.'

'Make sure she's happy, we don't want any problems with her.'

'I'm on it, Dan.'

Shepherd ended the call and phoned Docherty. 'So do I still have a job?' asked the MI6 officer.

'You're on the team, Tony. Julian said it would be a chance to redeem yourself.'

'I bet he said that through gritted teeth.'

'This isn't your fault, Tony, you need to stop beating yourself up. Swing by Thames House when you're ready. Ask for me at reception. Bring any photos of Sayyid you have and any biometric data. Plus anything you have on file that might be useful. I don't want us to keep asking for data from Vauxhall Cross, so let's do it in one full sweep.'

'Will do.'

'Farah's on the team if you want to liaise with her. You could come in together.'

'And what's the game plan?'

'We'll take a run up to Birmingham. See what we can turn up.' Shepherd ended the call and walked the rest of the way to Thames House deep in thought. He had a lot to do and he wanted to make sure he used his time as efficiently as possible.

Once he'd passed through security he went up to the third floor and along to the office that was nicknamed Carphone Warehouse. It was tasked with liaising with the various phone companies to arrange data dumps or phone tapping. It was one of the most boring jobs within MI5, but one of the most vital, and usually given to new entrants who were still fired up and eager to prove themselves. The work was so repetitive that management usually made sure that no one stayed for more than six months, unless they were there as a punishment. All requests for data from mobile phones and landlines had to go through the office, there was no shortcut. But they were in competition with all the police forces around the country who needed phone data as part of their criminal investigations. The limiting factor was the number of people employed by the phone companies to deal with the data requests. When the police first realised how helpful phone data was, enquiries were usually dealt with in a few days. But there was now such a tsunami of requests that it could take weeks or months just to check a customer's name and address.

There were two men and a woman sitting in the office pods, all in their early twenties and probably straight out of university. They were wearing headsets and had their eyes glued to their screens as their fingers tapped away at their keyboards. There was a table to the left of the door with two wire baskets on it. One was labelled 'PHONE REQUESTS' and the other 'URGENT PHONE REQUESTS'. The first was empty, the second had about a dozen sheets of paper in it.

Shepherd waved at the man nearest to him. He was wearing a grey suit but had hung the jacket over his chair, rolled up his sleeves and had flicked his tie over his shoulder. Shepherd finally caught the man's attention. He had black hair and was wearing glasses with wire frames and an Apple watch with a bright red strap. The man pointed at the baskets, then looked back at his screen. Shepherd walked over and stood next to the man's pod. The man looked up and was about to point at the baskets again but Shepherd interrupted him. 'I've a number that needs checking and it's a priority,' said Shepherd.

'They're all priorities,' said the man. 'We've had more than two dozen requests come in this morning and they're all marked urgent.'

Shepherd smiled. 'I understand that,' he said. 'What's your name?'

The man frowned. 'Alastair.'

'I get that they're all priorities, Alastair, but this number is being used by an active threat, and while I know it's a cliché, the clock really is ticking.'

'I'll need a chit to authorise a fast track,' said Alastair.

'And I'll get you one. From Giles Pritchard's office. I'll call him now.'

Alastair frowned. 'Sorry, your name is?'

His nails were bitten to the quick. The work was monotonous but it was also extremely stressful. 'Dan Shepherd. I'm—'

'Oh, shit. Sorry. Yes, I know who you are. Okay, yes, I'll put this request through myself right now, Mr Shepherd. No need to bother Mr Pritchard.'

'You're a star, Alastair. Much appreciated. And call me Dan. All I have is the number, and I need to know everything connected with it.' He gave Alastair the number and he scribbled it down on a notepad. 'I need to know how the bill was paid, what calls and messages he made and received, and I need names and billing addresses of all his contacts.'

Alastair's smile tightened. He was clearly under a lot of pressure and Shepherd was asking for a lot. 'Not a problem,' said Alastair, which was clearly not true.

'I'm going to be on the move so could you do me another favour and send me a text whenever you have anything? Send the data through the system as usual but just text me that it's on the way.'

'I will do.'

Shepherd gave him his mobile number, Alastair scribbled it down and repeated it back to him. He was already tapping on his keyboard, his cheeks flushed, as Shepherd left the office.

Shepherd's second call was to the Afghan Desk, on the fourth floor. It was run by Janice Warren, a twenty-year veteran of MI5 who had previously worked on the Libya Desk when

Gaddafi had been overthrown and on the Iraq Desk when Saddam Hussein had been executed. She had the knack of remaining calm no matter how stressful the situation, an ability that she put down to the large amounts of chocolate she ate on a daily basis. He knocked on the door and opened it. There was a large screen on one wall showing BBC rolling news, with the sound off, and several maps on the other walls. Shepherd spotted Warren immediately, sitting in one of the dozen or so pods scattered around the room, and he waved.

She grinned and waved back. 'Spider, long time no see,' said Warren. 'Take a pew.' She had her chestnut hair pulled back with a scrunchie and was wearing an over-sized white pullover over baggy brown trousers and black Crocs. She was tied to her screens for more than twelve hours a day so he understood her desire to dress for comfort. Shepherd pulled a chair from an empty pod and sat down. 'Right, I'm looking for a high-ranking Taliban, with an eyepatch and a straggly beard. In his sixties but let's look at anyone between fifty and seventy. He would have been in the Kabul area around 2020. Off the top of my head I thought of Amrullah Fazi and Amir Khan Massoud.'

'Fazi has been in Pakistan since 2018. He's got kidney problems and they're looking for a donor.'

'Good to know.'

'But Massoud was definitely in Afghanistan at that time. And what about Malik Salam Mukhlis?'

'He's got an eyepatch?'

'As of 2019. An IED went off in his face but he tells people it was the result of a firefight with American troops. So how soon do you need this?'

Shepherd grinned. 'Yesterday.'

'Okay, give me a few minutes to tie up what I'm doing and I'll have a look.'

'Any intel would be gratefully received, and photographs.'

'No problem. Do you want to wait for me in the canteen? I'll be needing a caffeine injection. I shouldn't be more than half an hour.'

'Sure,' said Shepherd. He took the stairs to the canteen and got himself a coffee and a cheese and ham toastie. He was taking the last bite when Warren appeared, carrying a Manila envelope. She got a coffee and chocolate brownie and sat down opposite him. 'I used a time frame of start of 2019 until end of 2020 and came up with three possibilities,' she said. She opened her envelope and took out three photographs. She slid one of them across the table. 'As you thought, Amir Khan Massoud was definitely in Afghanistan over that period.'

Shepherd picked up the picture. Massoud was in his late sixties with a hooked nose, long grey beard and a black patch over his right eye.

She passed over the second photograph. This man had an eyepatch on his left eye and there was a thin scar running across his cheek. His thinning hair was swept back and his greying beard was almost a foot long. 'Mohammad Hassan Baloch, AKA the Butcher. Old-school Taliban but he thought they were getting soft so moved over to ISIS-K. He's a really nasty piece of work. Fathered three children with underage girls. One of the girls was eleven and she died in childbirth.'

The man in the third photograph also had a patch on his left eye. He was the youngest of the three, or at least his face was less lined and there were patches of black in his grey beard. 'Malik Salam Mukhlis. Taliban bombmaker. Lost his eye when an IED he was working on went off prematurely.

He was lucky in that it was a small one, in a phone. Only an ounce or so of explosive, but he lost the eye and is deaf in his left ear.'

'Shame,' said Shepherd.

'Mukhlis was based on the Pakistan border for most of the time that the US-led forces were in Afghanistan, but he's in Kabul now.'

'I'll show the pictures to the translator's wife, see if she recognises anyone.'

'I've put the basic details on the back of each photograph, but if you need any more, let me know.'

'Are you okay to wait for a few minutes?'

'Sure, I've earned this coffee.' She picked up the brownie. 'And I'm not going anywhere until I've eaten this big boy.'

Shepherd put the three photographs on the table, then took out his phone. He took a picture of each one, then he opened WhatsApp and sent the images to Farah, with a short message: 'RUN THESE BY LAILA.'

He sipped his coffee and smiled over at Warren. 'So how's it going on the Afghan Desk?'

Janice grimaced. 'Under-resourced and over-worked,' she said. 'You would have thought the bosses would have seen this coming, but we're staffed as if it was still 2001. Back then we had fewer than fifteen thousand Afghans in this country, and they were generally a well-behaved bunch. By 2011 we were up to sixty-five thousand and as of today, who knows? Because the government clearly doesn't. In 2019 the Office for National Statistics said there were about eighty thousand Afghans in the country, half of them with British passports. If you were to ask me – and nobody ever has – I'd say that the true figure is closer to a hundred and twenty thousand and three-quarters of them are in London. They were flooding in even when the Taliban were under control, but once the Americans pulled out the flood became a . . .' She frowned. 'What's bigger than a flood?'

'A torrent. A deluge, maybe.'

'Yeah. We've been deluged with Afghans. The vast majority are men of fighting age. And the checks we're doing are minimal. Well, I say "we" but obviously I mean Border Force and the Home Office.' She leaned across the table towards him and lowered her voice. 'It's a nightmare, Spider, and nobody seems to care. I know the vast majority of these Afghan refugees are good guys. Same as there are plenty of good Libyans and Somalians and Iranians. But you're always going to get a percentage that are bad, either trained jihadist bad or lone wolf bad, but bad nonetheless. Me, I reckon about five per cent are bad. But even suppose I'm wrong by a factor of ten, that means five out of every thousand are bad, then that means we have six hundred potential Afghan terrorists in the UK. How am I supposed to deal with that? You could increase my staff ten-fold and we still couldn't come close.' She sat back in her chair. 'Sorry, I didn't mean to vent.'

'I understand the pressure you're under,' he said.

'Which is what my bosses say. But then they talk about resources and funding and priorities and nothing gets done.' She sipped her coffee.

'The operation I'm working on involves one of the translators that was brought out. Have you had many problems with them?'

'A few. You know the story, right? Pretty much all of the translators who were working for the army were taken out once it became clear that the Taliban were taking over. Them and their families. That was four and a half thousand people, give or take, and that was before the airport fell into Taliban hands. But then every Tom, Dick and Abdul who had ever worked for the army started screaming that they needed to be taken out as well. Thousands of people in total, including their families. My best estimate is that we've taken another four thousand since the Taliban took over, and the number is still going up. The thing is, most of them had either quit because they couldn't do the job, or were sacked. And a fair number were sacked because they'd been dealing with the Taliban. They couldn't be trusted. But then the media got hold of the story and the next thing we hear is that they're all being granted fast-track asylum. Then Kabul fell and the government told them to make their own way to another country and we'll repatriate them from there. You couldn't make it up. We block those that we can but the dyke is way too big and we don't have enough fingers.' She sipped her coffee again.

'My guy is a bit different,' said Shepherd. 'He was an MI6 translator and I helped get him and his family out last year. But now he's gone AWOL and his wife thinks he's planning a terrorist attack. We think the guy with the eyepatch was his handler, at least in Afghanistan. And that there are several other jihadists involved.'

'Any idea what they have planned?'

'No. None at all. He and his family were put up in a hotel in Scarborough and his wife said he met a couple of guys there.'

'The Grand?'

'You know it?'

She nodded. 'A lot of the Afghans were put up there. Very bizarre because there were regular holidaymakers there and they couldn't understand why there were so many Afghan kids running around. It became a media-fest for a while.'

'Anyone there you red-flagged?'

'I'm sure there would be. Do you want me to check?'

'That would be awesome. What I'd like is photographs of anyone you were worried about and then I can run them by the translator's wife.'

'That's easy enough,' she said. 'Just give me the dates he was there.'

'August through to the end of October last year.' Shepherd's phone beeped to let him know he'd received a message. It was from Farah. She'd sent him back the photograph of Mohammad Hassan Baloch, along with two words: 'THIS ONE'.

Shepherd pushed the other two photographs back to Warren. 'It's Baloch,' he said.

She put the pictures into the envelope. 'Baloch's bad news,' she said.

'None of them are a barrel of laughs,' said Shepherd.

'Yes, but Baloch hates the British, hates us with a vengeance. He might well have big plans for your translator.'

'Why do you say that?'

'He blames the Brits for his eye. He was with a Taliban group that attacked a patrol up near Mazar-e-Sharif, some fifteen years ago. The patrol were Paras protecting a crew working for the Provincial Reconstruction Team. Baloch and his jihadists went in guns blazing and they'd bitten off more than they could chew. Within minutes the Paras had killed half a dozen of the Taliban and captured Baloch and another fighter. The Paras were a bit rough with the prisoners and Baloch lost an eye.'

'Why was he still on the loose, then?'

'They were transferring him to Kabul for questioning and en route his convoy was attacked and he was freed. And ever since he's had it in for the Brits.'

Shepherd looked at the photograph. The man was sneering, head slightly back and nostrils flared, and the single eye blazed hatred. 'And now with ISIS-K, you said?'

'Indeed. ISIS-Khorasan. He's been with them almost right from the time they were formed in 2015. The relationship between them and ISIS proper has always been a strange one. They have a similar ideology and use the same tactics, but ISIS-K has always been regarded as the more dangerous of the two. The Americans have targeted the emirs who run the organisation, usually with drone airstrikes. They took out the founding emir, Hafiz Saeed Khan, in 2016, Malik Hasin and Abu Sayed in 2017 and Abu Saad Orakzai in 2018. It's not a job title with prospects, obviously.' She forced a smile. 'There have been rumours over the last year that Baloch would head up ISIS-K but he always managed to duck the poisoned chalice. Remember that massive car bomb at Kabul Airport during the evacuation?'

Shepherd nodded. 'I do.'

'Well, we're pretty sure that Baloch was behind it. The Americans claimed that they killed the planner in a drone strike in Nangarhar Province in late August but that was PR BS. It was Baloch who planned it, holed up in a villa in the north of Kabul.' She looked at her watch, a slim Cartier. 'Okay, I've got to get my nose back to the grindstone. Good luck with your hunt.' She got up and headed out.

Shepherd sighed, swung his feet up on to his desk and leaned back in his chair as he ticked off all the items on his mental checklist. He had requisitioned an operations room with two plain desks and two pods. There was a television mounted on the wall by the door. He had installed two whiteboards on easels and had put a photograph of Sayyid on one and Baloch on the other. Above Baloch's picture he had written the man's name and 'POSSIBLE HANDLER'. The check on Sayyid's phone was in progress, and Warren and her team were working their way through the Afghans who had been sent to Scarborough. He had made a call to the search team hoping to speak to John Weston, one of MI5's top search experts, but he was away on leave. Instead he'd arranged for another searcher, Mick Leach, to drive up to Birmingham with him, along with Lyn Burns, a locks and alarms specialist. He hadn't worked with either before but they both came highly recommended. They were due to meet him in Battersea at seven o'clock in the morning. He'd touched base with Sue Johnson in Birmingham, explaining who Sayyid was and giving her the details they had. Johnson assured him she would give him any assistance he needed. Finally he'd gone up for a quick briefing with Giles Pritchard to bring him up to speed. It had been a productive afternoon, though he was still no closer to locating Sayyid or finding out what he was up to.

There was a soft knock on the door and it opened. It was Farah. Docherty was close behind her and they walked into the room. They were both carrying coffees and Farah had one for Shepherd. He thanked her and sipped it. It was just the way he liked it, which meant that she had been paying attention when she was with him in the kitchen of the house in Wimbledon.

Docherty went over to the whiteboards. 'Baloch's a nasty piece of work,' he said, tapping the photograph.

'Laila was sure it was him?' Shepherd asked Farah.

'A thousand per cent.'

'Do you think he's still running Sayyid?' asked Docherty.

'That's the sixty-four thousand dollar question, isn't it?' said Shepherd. 'He might have had a long-term plan for Sayyid when he first approached him. But equally he might have just been looking for short-term intel. Can you get everything MI6 has on Baloch? Obviously I'd love to get proof of phone calls between Kabul and Scarborough, but that's probably too much to hope for.'

'I will do,' said Docherty.

'We also need to know who else Baloch was running in Kabul. I doubt that Sayyid was the only man he approached. There'd be no point in putting all his eggs in one basket, so there could well be others out there. Also see if your guys have any leads on rogue Afghans in Birmingham. I realise that's not MI6's brief but you never know. Just ask around and see if any names pop up. And I need you to rethink everything you and Sayyid did, everything you ever talked about. With the benefit of hindsight something might spring to mind.'

'I don't have your trick memory, but sure, I'll give it a go.'

'Trick memory?' said Farah.

'He remembers everything he sees or hears. There's a name for it, right?'

'Photographic?' said Farah.

'Eidetic,' said Shepherd.

'That's it,' said Docherty. He grinned. 'I almost remembered it.'

'We're going to take a run up to Birmingham tomorrow,' said Shepherd. 'We'll turn over Sayyid's house and see if the local MI5 team have anything on him.'

'Shall I get the keys from Laila?' asked Farah.

'No, I don't want her to know we're searching her place. We'll have a locksmith with us. I'll travel up with her in my car. Can you two fix up a car and travel together? I'll be leaving at seven and I'm assuming a three-hour drive but let's say four to be on the safe side. We'll RV at the Hopwood Park services on the M42, about ten miles south of the city, at eleven a.m. at the latest.'

'What do you need me to do?' asked Farah.

'Did you bring Laila's phone with you?'

'I did.' She took a Samsung phone from her bag.

'Have you come across Amar Singh?'

She shook her head. 'I haven't, no.'

Shepherd grinned. 'Then you're in for a treat.' He took her down to Amar Singh's office and knocked on the door. Singh opened it and he grinned when he saw Shepherd. 'Spider, how the hell are you?'

'All the better for catching you in the office, Amar.'

Singh opened the door wider and smiled when he saw Farah. 'And you're not alone.'

'This is Farah, she's helping with a little job we're doing.'

'Nice to meet you, Farah.' He waved for them to walk into his office. He was wearing one of his Hugo Boss suits and a blue silk tie. His jet black hair was slicked back and as always his skin looked as if it had benefited from some very expensive grooming aids.

'Amar is one of our best dressed officers, and the best tech guy in the building by far.'

'You'll make me blush, Spider.' Singh closed the door. The blinds were down and the lights were on. There were two desks in the office, side by side, with matching three-monitor workstations. One wall was lined with shelves that were piled high with electrical equipment, some of it boxed or covered in bubble wrap, but most of it loose or in clear plastic boxes.

'How's the family?' asked Shepherd.

'I'm wondering that myself,' said Singh. 'With the hours I'm working at the moment I leave the house before the kids wake up and they're tucked up in bed by the time I get home. The workload has gone crazy.'

'Everyone says the same.'

'They need to start doing some serious recruiting,' said Singh. 'We're holding the fort at the moment but one slip and the whole house of cards is going to come crashing down.' He forced a smile. 'I'm guessing you want me to drop everything and do something for you?'

'You're a mind reader,' said Shepherd. He nodded at Farah and she produced Laila Habibi's phone.

She gave it to Singh. 'The password is six-four-two-seven-five-three,' she said.

'The phone belongs to the wife of a potential jihadist,' said Shepherd. 'Can you give us a breakdown of calls made, messages sent, let us see any pictures she's taken and get the GPS to tell us everywhere she's been?'

Singh laughed. 'I thought you were going to give me something challenging,' he said. He reached for a lead and connected the phone to one of his computers. 'It won't take long.'

'And when you're done, can you do your magic and set the phone up so we can monitor all calls and messages? Plus GPS tracking.' He saw the look of confusion on Farah's face. 'We'll give her the phone back and we'll know if Sayyid makes contact with her.'

'You don't trust her?'

Shepherd laughed. 'I don't trust anybody,' he said. He grinned at Singh. 'I'll leave Farah with you,' said Shepherd, then gave her a thumbs-up. 'See you back at the ops room.'

Shepherd's mobile rang. It was Janice Warren. She told him she had come across two Afghan asylum seekers who had stayed at the Grand Hotel at the same time as Sayyid, and who had both been red-flagged by Border Force. 'There'll be more, I'm sure,' she said. 'The Border Force top brass want to cover their arses so the edict sent down was: "If in doubt, red flag." There were so many coming over from Kabul that their staff were overwhelmed, plus they have to deal with hundreds a day crossing the Channel in dinghies.'

'What sort of processing did Border Force do?'

'For the Kabul flights? They took DNA, a picture and fingerprints. And they checked the paperwork they had with them.'

'That's all?'

'That's why there are so many red flags. They were able to check the biometrics against the Border Force database, but not all the data had been transferred from Kabul to the UK. The ambassador and his staff had moved out of the embassy and into offices at the airport, and my understanding is that they were working with paper files and laptops. So a lot of the arrivals from Kabul weren't in the system. But they couldn't really be refused entry if they had the correct paperwork and the approval of the ambassador, so they were waved through, albeit with a red flag.'

'And is anyone working their way through these red flags?'

'In theory it's on our to-do list, but as I said before, we just don't have the manpower.'

'Personpower,' said Shepherd.

'What?'

'Didn't you see the Mission Critical document? The one written by Sir Stephen Lovegrove, the national security adviser? It was referred to as a diversity toolkit. We were all supposed to read it. Inclusivity, diversity, cultural awareness and the rest. He actually highlighted manpower as an offensive term.' Warren went quiet for a few seconds and eventually Shepherd laughed. 'Sorry, Janice, I was trying to lighten the moment.'

'Ah, right. Good one. Anyway, I've sent the two possibles to you on the system. And there'll be more to follow.'

'Great, thanks. I'll be out of Thames House all day tomorrow but send me a text when there's something I need to look at.'

'Will do, Spider. Stay safe.'

As she ended the call, there was a knock on the door and Farah opened it. Shepherd smiled. 'You don't need to knock,' said Shepherd.

'Sorry.' She was carrying an A4 Manila envelope.

'Or apologise. This is your office so long as the op is running. How did it go?'

'Amar's brilliant.' She closed the door and went over to Shepherd's desk.

'Isn't he just? One of a kind.'

She opened the envelope and spread out several printed sheets in front of Shepherd. Docherty got up from his work-station and went over to get a look. 'We have a list of all the calls she made and received. Most are from her husband. All very short. He was probably just checking up on her or giving her instructions. There are calls to and from a school in Birmingham, a doctor's surgery and a dentist's. There are calls from another mobile number, three in total, each call just lasting a few seconds. She never called the number back. I wondered if it might be Sayyid using a different phone.'

'Excellent. When we're done here, pop down to Carphone Warehouse and give that number to Alastair. Tell him it's for me.' He grinned. 'He'll moan and groan but his heart is in the right place. Tell him if it's a pay-as-you-go we'll need a full call and message list and GPS data. What about the GPS for Laila's phone?'

'Yes, it was on. She got the phone when she moved to Birmingham so it's all post-Scarborough. She was either at home, the kids' school, the doctor and the dentist, or going to the local shops. There a few trips to the Bullring shopping centre. He kept her on a very tight leash.' She shook her head. 'I can't believe he'd treat her like that. Not in England.'

'What about photographs?' asked Shepherd.

'Lots,' she said. She spread out four sheets of paper, each of which had fifty or so thumbnails on them. 'Mostly of her and the kids.'

'Any of Sayyid?' asked Docherty.

'Some. Always with the kids. And always in the house.'

'Never any other Asian men?' asked Shepherd.

Farah shook her head. 'No.' She sat down at a workstation. 'And in the pictures she took of him, he never looked happy. They'd all been deleted, by the way. Amar had to recover them.'

'Did she use the phone to browse the internet?' asked Shepherd.

'Just to check what was happening in Afghanistan. Afghan news websites.'

'And what about bugging her phone?'

'He says he'll have it done by this evening.'

Shepherd looked up at Docherty, who had picked up one

of the thumbnail sheets and was squinting at the photographs. 'Is Sayyid still on MI6's payroll?' Shepherd asked.

'Not as far as I know. We haven't used him outside of Afghanistan.'

'So who pays him? I can't imagine that he just signs on at the local Jobcentre.'

'It's handled by the Home Office,' said Farah. 'Border Force puts them into the hotels initially and then the Home Office takes over the funding and disperses them around the country. Councils are given extra funding to bump them up the housing lists. That's why Sayyid and his family got a house so quickly.'

'And what about money for day-to-day living?'

'Generally asylum seekers get about £40 a week, that's per family member. The money gets loaded on to an Aspen card every week and can be withdrawn at any cash machine.'

'Aspen card?' repeated Shepherd.

'It's a Visa debit card supplied by the Home Office. Works just like a regular card. They're issued with one per family unit.'

'That means Laila has it?'

Farah shook her head. 'No, Sayyid handled all the money. Usually he went with her to the shops but if she went alone he would give her some cash. The Home Office will also hand out things like Tesco vouchers in cases of hardship.'

'Are the cards monitored?'

'Big time,' said Farah. 'It's one of the ways the Home Office keeps track of them. They can see if they are where they're supposed to be, if they're feeding their kids. If they don't use the card it might suggest they're working, which of course they shouldn't be while their cases are being heard.'

'I'm liking the sound of this card,' said Shepherd. 'It could help us a lot.'

'You think he'll be stupid enough to keep using the card?' asked Docherty.

'People get blind spots,' said Shepherd. 'You'd be surprised at the number of people who will conscientiously wipe a gun clean but will forget that their prints are all over the cartridges. Or go to the trouble of getting a burner phone but then using it to phone their wife.' He shrugged. 'People make mistakes. And we have to thank God for that. Sometimes the only difference between dozens dead and bad guys behind bars is a simple cock-up.' He looked over at Farah. 'Can you talk to our Home Office liaison people and get us a breakdown of what the card has been used for and where? If there are any cash withdrawals then we'll need any CCTV footage from the machines.'

'Definitely,' she said. She gestured at the call records. 'I'll leave those with you,' she said. 'I'll talk to Alastair and then I'll look into the Aspen card.'

'Who's doing the driving tomorrow?' asked Shepherd.

'I'll pick Farah up,' said Docherty. 'Do you think we'll be overnighting?'

'Depends on what we get from the locals,' said Shepherd. 'We'll play it by ear.'

Farah headed out and closed the door behind her.

'She's very keen,' said Docherty. 'I can just about remember when I was keen.'

'I like her enthusiasm,' said Shepherd. 'And she did a good job with Laila. By the way, did you ever meet Laila in Kabul? Before the evacuation?'

'First time was when I went to pick them up. Sayyid didn't mention his family much when we were working together.'

'She wasn't wearing a burkha when we evacuated them, she was wearing a hijab,' said Shepherd.

'Yeah, I wondered about that,' said Docherty. 'Maybe he was pulling the wool over our eyes. Making it look like they were Westernised so we'd be more likely to get them out of the country. If that's true, then he's a devious bastard.'

'I think that ship has sailed,' said Shepherd. 'So did MI6 use any other translators?'

'There was one before Sayyid, but he disappeared one day. I was told that he just never turned up for work.' He narrowed his eyes. 'You think that was arranged? They made sure there was a vacancy?'

'I was actually wondering if there were any other translators we should be looking at.'

'There were a few at the embassy. The ambassador had a couple in his office. And there were quite a few bilingual workers dealing with visa applications and the like.'

'Can you put together a list?'

Docherty nodded. 'Sure.'

Shepherd gestured at the photograph of Baloch. 'If he got one in, there could have been others.'

'It doesn't have to be translators, though,' said Docherty. 'All sorts of contractors were getting visas. Pretty much anyone who did any work for the embassy was covered. That included gardeners, painters, the guy who cleaned the drains. The argument was that anyone who had any dealings at all with the embassy would be targets when the Taliban took over. So if Baloch wanted to get his own people into the UK, he'd be spoiled for choice. There were hundreds of embassy workers and their families jostling to get out.'

Shepherd rubbed the back of his neck. He could feel the

muscles there knotting up. Docherty was right. It had never been about translators, it was about getting jihadists into the UK. 'It's interesting that he didn't ask you or MI6 for money,' said Shepherd. 'The family left Kabul with nothing. Literally just the clothes they had on their backs. They fly halfway around the world and are put into a hotel, and he doesn't ask for money. Not a penny. That just seems a little off. Unless he knew that he was going to be looked after by someone else.'

'He was fairly well paid when he worked for us. And we paid him with cash. US dollars.'

'He could have brought money with him?'

Docherty nodded. 'Easily.'

'Okay, but I would've still expected him to have asked you for more money once he got here. He's a refugee with a wife and two kids, he was getting some money from the state but not much.'

'So you think that maybe someone wanted Sayyid to cut all links with MI6 once he was in the country?' Docherty nodded. 'That makes sense.'

'Do you think you could get photographs of the Afghans connected to the embassy who were given visas? We could run them by Laila, see if she recognises anyone. Ideally we need to know where they are now.'

'Pictures won't be a problem. But their locations will be down to the Home Office. They would have been dispersed around the country.'

'Okay, so get me the details and I'll have Farah run them by our Home Office liaison.' He sat back in his chair and swung his feet up on to the desk. 'I never asked you what you were doing in Kabul,' he said. 'You've got a wife and kids, I'd have thought you'd have been the last person they'd send.'

'It was only meant to be temporary,' said Docherty. 'They were short-handed in Kabul and I was sent out to help for a couple of months. But then it all went tits-up. Back in February 2020 Trump signed the Doha Agreement which slashed the number of US troops in Afghanistan and promised a complete withdrawal by May the first, 2021. That was conditional on the Taliban keeping up their end of the deal. But of course they didn't, and anyway no one really thought Trump was serious. Biden got into office and in the middle of April he moved the goalposts and said he would aim to have all troops out by September the eleventh. Then it became real, so the embassy started getting its people out. The workload went through the roof so they sent me to Kabul. The wife wasn't happy but I was assured I'd just be there for a couple of months. I was supposed to man the phones and emails while the staff who were already there were reassuring our assets that they'd be okay under the new regime.' He snorted. 'Of course they didn't believe it, they wanted out.'

'What sort of assets?'

'We had agents in the police, the army, the government. And obviously we wanted them to stay put, even though they'd be in danger. We wanted to make sure we'd still be getting intel once we'd pulled out. Anyway, the Taliban smelled blood and started their final offensive in May and they moved so quickly that Biden changed his deadline to the thirty-first of August. And you know how that went.'

'It was a disaster,' said Shepherd.

'Yeah, we were all hands to the pumps but the end result

was that I had to stay on. There were five of us working flat out right until the last moment.'

'So you didn't get to Kabul until May?'

'Start of June, actually.'

Shepherd frowned. 'Well why are you getting the flack for Sayyid? You didn't have anything to do with hiring him. He was in place long before you even arrived.'

Docherty shrugged. 'I was the last one to work with him. And I got him out of the country. I guess the feeling is that if it wasn't for me, he'd still be in Afghanistan.'

'That's not fair.'

Docherty snorted. 'Yeah, because the intelligence agencies are all about fairness.'

'I hear you. But it seems to me that whoever hired Sayyid is the one who should be carrying the can.' Shepherd sighed. 'We might be lucky. He might have just walked out on the wife and moved on to pastures new.' He stared at the photograph of Baloch and gritted his teeth. He wanted to make Docherty feel better, but his gut told him that Sayyid was involved with something much, much worse than a sexual adventure.

Shepherd's iPhone alarm woke him at six-thirty. He made himself a mug of coffee, then shaved and showered and pulled on a shirt, jeans and leather jacket. It was always difficult to know what to wear for a breaking and entering operation. Too shabby and he'd look like a drug addict on the rob, too smart and people would wonder what he was doing in the area. Smart casual was always his preferred choice, with trainers just in case things went wrong and he had to run for it.

He finished his coffee, took the lift down to the building's

car park and collected his black BMW X5. Mick Leach and
Lyn Burns were waiting for him on a bench close to the
building entrance. Leach was in his forties, bearded with a flat
cap and wearing a tweed jacket with leather patches on the
elbows. His job was to turn over a home and discover anything
that had been hidden, so he didn't need much in the way of
equipment – most searchers made do with a Swiss Army knife
and a small torch. In the old days searchers had used a Polaroid
camera to take photographs of the rooms they worked on, so
that they could put things back the way they were. These days
a smartphone did the trick.

Burns had a large black case at her feet, the type used by
airline pilots, and a black holdall. She was about the same age
as Leach, with tousled blonde hair and bright red lipstick. She
was laughing at something Leach had said, then she saw the
SUV and waved at Shepherd. He waved back.

Burns picked up her case and bag and they walked over to
the car. Leach climbed into the front and Burns got into the
back with her bag. Shepherd introduced himself, fist-bumped
Leach and twisted around to flash Burns a smile.

He headed across the Thames on Chelsea Bridge and
headed west to Chiswick and the M4. He gave them a quick
briefing as he drove. There was no need to tell them too much
about Sayyid, just that he was a potential jihadist and they
needed to turn his house over. Burns and Leach had worked
together several times and they chatted away, which suited
Shepherd as he wasn't really in a talking mood. He found
working on an investigation more stressful than combat. When
you were fighting an enemy who was trying to kill you, you
were constantly reacting, choosing from whatever options
presented themselves so that you had the best chance of

survival. And if you made a mistake you still had the chance to correct it immediately and get back on the right track. But with an investigation, he was always second guessing himself. Had he missed something? Was there any way he could get things done quicker? Even deciding whether or not he should go to Birmingham had required thought. He wasn't a lock-smith or a searcher, so he wouldn't add anything to the search of Sayyid's house. He could talk to Sue Johnson face to face but he could just as easily talk to her over Zoom. Everything he did, every decision he made, could easily come back to haunt him. He dreaded the thought that any minute he'd learn of a massive terrorist attack and find out that Sayyid was behind it.

They hit heavy traffic on the M40 north of Oxford and slowed to a crawl for almost half an hour. They never did see what caused the hold up and the rest of the journey was uneventful. They reached the service station at a quarter to eleven.

Burns took her bag and case with her – she was clearly reluctant to let them out of her sight. Leach headed straight for the toilets while Shepherd and Burns grabbed a table. They sat down and Burns put her bag and case under her chair. 'I'll watch them,' said Shepherd. 'You grab yourself some breakfast.'

'Do you want anything?'

'Just a coffee. And maybe a bacon roll.'

'Maybe?'

Shepherd laughed. 'Definitely a bacon roll.'

Burns went over to one of the food counters. Shepherd took out his mobile and called Docherty. The MI6 officer was driving so he took the call on hands-free. He and Farah were five minutes away.

'We've got a table on the left, by the windows,' said Shepherd, and ended the call.

Leach returned from the men's room and headed to get some breakfast. Burns came over to the table. She had a bacon roll and a coffee for Shepherd, and a full English for herself plus two slices of toast. Shepherd took his roll from the tray. She had brought a sachet of brown sauce and one of tomato ketchup, which he thought was damn decent of her. She caught him looking at them and smiled. 'I know the purists insist on ketchup but I'm a bit of a rebel and go for HP. I wasn't sure which you were?'

Shepherd grinned and took the brown sauce.

'Yeah, that's what I thought,' said Burns.

Leach came over with a bowl of muesli and a pot of low-fat yoghurt. He sat down next to Burns. 'Doc says I have to eat healthy,' he said. He looked down at the muesli and sighed.

'Mine too,' said Burns, spearing a sausage with her fork and taking a bite out of it.

Farah and Docherty appeared at the entrance. Docherty gestured that they were going to get food first and Shepherd flashed him a thumbs-up. They joined one of the queues and after a few minutes came over with trays.

Shepherd wolfed down his bacon roll and then sipped his coffee as he waited for the others to finish. When they were done he took two printed sheets from his jacket pocket. One was a screenshot from Google Maps, showing the street where Sayyid and his family lived, the other was a screenshot from Street View, showing the front of the house and the houses either side. Google had revolutionised operations planning. Gone were the days of Ordnance Survey maps and A–Z street guides. All it took now was a few clicks and you had an overhead satellite view of the house and the surrounding area, as well as an image of the house itself.

Docherty moved their plates and trays on to another table. Shepherd put down the map of the street. 'It's a quiet street, semi-detached houses with gardens front and back, with a parking space to the side.' He tapped Sayyid's house. 'The target house is number seventy-one. So far as we know it's empty. The husband is the target and he's AWOL and the wife is in London with the kids. I figure I'll do a drive by, west to east with Farah and Mick.' He tapped the map. 'There's a parade of shops here with parking so we can pull up there. I suggest Tony waits there with Lyn. Once we arrive and it's all clear, you drive Lyn to the house and drop her off. How will you be playing it, Lyn?'

'Good old British Gas,' she said. 'Can't go wrong with a suspected gas leak.'

'Excellent. Tony can drop you and drive straight ahead, then turn first left.' He pointed at the side road on the map. 'There are parking spaces there. We all wait until Lyn tells us she's in and then we walk to the house. Farah, I need you to stay outside and keep watch, just in case. We're not expecting visitors, but better safe than sorry.'

Farah nodded.

Shepherd put down the second sheet, the one showing the front view of the house. 'It looks like getting around to the back is easy enough,' he said to Lyn.

She looked at the picture, then back at the satellite photo. 'No sign of an alarm and the back doesn't appear to be overlooked,' she said. 'I'll try the back first. The front door is visible from the pavement and that's never ideal.'

'Any questions?' Shepherd asked. He was faced with shaking

heads. Briefing MI5 personnel was very different from the SAS's Chinese Parliament. Whereas the SAS guys would chip in with ideas, opinions and criticisms, the MI5 staff tended to listen and nod. So far as they were concerned it was his operation and the details were up to him. Often he had to read body language to gauge people's feelings, but in this case they all genuinely seemed to be on board. 'Right,' he said, gathering up the print-outs. 'Let's do this.'

Burns gained access to Sayyid's house through a sliding patio door at the rear, a simple matter of inserting a screwdriver and lifting. Leach organised the search, starting at the top of the house – a dusty attic which clearly hadn't been used in years – down to the kitchen and the back garden, a small square of grass with a rusting child's swing set in the middle and a rotary washing line at the end close to a large unkempt hedge. Farah stayed on the front pavement as lookout.

They found a large machete under the sofa, which they bagged to be examined back in London. Something had been hidden behind the bath panel judging by the marks in the dust, but there was no way of knowing what it had been. There was no razor or shaving foam in the bathroom, and most of Sayyid's clothes were missing. There were bank statements in a kitchen drawer which Shepherd photographed with his phone.

They had more luck in the garden. Someone had lit a fire behind a small rockery. All that remained were ashes and a few scraps of unburnt paper which went into another evidence bag. Leach was dubious about the value of the ashes. 'If he was going to the trouble of burning the stuff in the garden, why not burn the bank statements as well?' he said. 'Generally when people are worried enough to burn stuff, they bury the

ashes or flush them down the toilet. They don't just leave the
fire to burn out and they definitely don't leave unburned paper
behind.'

Once they had finished the search, they left by the patio
door and Burns used her screwdriver to relock it. Shepherd
called Farah to check that everything was clear then they made
their way back to their vehicles. It had taken less than an hour.

MI5's Birmingham office was one of eight regional bases
around the United Kingdom. The Security Service had opened
up offices outside London in 2005 to spearhead its fight against
Islamic extremism. The Birmingham office took up the whole
of a nondescript block in the city centre, having outgrown the
much smaller Viceroy House office block in Water Street a few
years back. Shepherd parked his SUV in a multi-storey car
park and walked with Docherty and Farah to the entrance of
the building. There was no sign at the entrance, just an intercom
and two CCTV cameras. Shepherd pressed the button and
gave his name and a six-digit number he had been given. The
lock buzzed and he pushed the door open.

The reception area was small with a line of red plastic seats
facing a counter to the right, and a metal detector arch and a
uniformed security guard to the left. There were two more
cameras covering the reception area. There was a young man
behind the counter with a ledger in front of him. He asked
the three visitors to show their IDs and sign in. He gave them
plastic badges to clip to their chests before waving them to
the chairs. 'Ms Johnson will be down shortly,' he said.

Shepherd nodded. Even though he was an MI5 officer,
guests had to be escorted at all times. He sat down and Farah
and Docherty joined him. In the event it wasn't Sue Johnson

who came down to meet them, it was one of her officers, an Asian guy in his twenties who introduced himself as Adam. He was wearing a tight navy suit, a crisp white shirt and a dark blue tie, and had the disarming smile of an estate agent on commission. He shook their hands, checked their badges and took them through the metal-detecting arch. There was a small notice stuck to it: 'PLEASE DECLARE ALL FIREARMS'.

The lifts were opposite the arch and they went straight up to the fifth floor and along to a meeting room. Adam knocked and opened the door, then stepped to the side to let them go in first. There were two women and a man waiting inside, sitting at a large table in the centre of the room. The man was sitting in front of a laptop. Unlike Adam he was casually dressed, in a yellow polo shirt and cargo trousers. He had slicked-back hair and a neatly trimmed beard, and a wedding ring that gleamed as if it was new. His face broke into a grin when he saw Farah. 'OMG,' said. 'Long time no see.'

He stood up, hurried over and air-kissed Farah on both cheeks.

'Kamran and I were on induction together,' Farah explained to Shepherd. 'We were paired up on a couple of exercises.'

'Fun days,' said Kamran. He realised his colleagues were all looking at him and he raised his hand by way of apology and sat down. The older of the two women, a brunette, smiled at Shepherd. 'Sue Johnson,' she said. 'We spoke on the phone. Welcome to Birmingham.' She held out her fist and Shepherd bumped his against hers. One of the few good things to have come out of the Covid pandemic was that he was no longer faced with a decision whether to shake hands or air-kiss colleagues of the opposite sex. He had never felt comfortable with the air-kiss and the handshake had always felt too formal. Fist-bumping – and the occasional elbow bump – was a lot less stressful.

Johnson was in her early forties, with chestnut hair and black-framed glasses. Shepherd knew that she had been with the Birmingham office since it had opened and had been in charge of several successful operations, including taking down a planned assault on Birmingham Airport that would have left hundreds dead. She introduced the third member of her team as Tina Taylor, who was in charge of the surveillance teams. Taylor smiled, nodded and fist-bumped Shepherd. 'Good to meet you,' she said, and he realised she had an Australian accent.

Johnson nodded at Adam. 'Adam is responsible for six mosques here in Birmingham,' she said. 'Including the Makki Masjid.'

Shepherd gestured at Docherty. 'This is Tony, on loan from MI6. He worked with Sayyid in Kabul for a few months.'

'And helped get him and his family out, I'm told,' said Johnson.

'Well to be fair, I was also on the team that evacuated Sayyid and his family,' said Shepherd. 'I'm as much to blame as anyone.'

'I wasn't being facetious,' said Johnson curtly. 'And I'm certainly not in the business of pointing fingers. I was just demonstrating that I know who Tony is. And that he'll be an asset to the operation. Anyway, please sit down and we'll show you what we have so far.'

Farah, Shepherd and Docherty sat down together. It meant that they were all facing the Birmingham team, which immediately felt adversarial, but they were all smiling so Shepherd tried not to read too much into the seating arrangements. There were two large screens on one wall and between them a white-board, on to which had been fixed four head-and-shoulder shots of Sayyid.

Johnson nodded at Adam. He typed on his laptop and a picture of Sayyid appeared on the left-hand screen. It was one that Shepherd had seen before. 'So, Sayyid Habibi. Former translator working out of the British Embassy, flown to the UK late August as part of the evacuation operation.'

She nodded at Adam and another picture appeared on the second screen, this one a surveillance photograph of Sayyid walking past a mosque. 'Once you passed on his details we checked and yes, he is known to us. But to date he hasn't been a person of interest.' Several more pictures of Sayyid appeared on the screen. They had clearly been taken at different times. His clothing was different in each, and in some pictures he was wearing a mask while in others he wasn't. 'He is a regular at the Makki Masjid, as you said, but so far we have seen him at three other mosques. He always arrives alone but he seems very sociable. And several of the men he meets are on our watch list.'

'What about the Makki Masjid? Is there any significance there?'

Johnson looked over at Adam, letting him know the question was for him to answer. 'It's not a hotbed of jihadism, no,' said Adam. 'The principal imam is very much one of the good guys. He's always one of the first to condemn terrorism and he's built relationships with leaders of many other faiths in the area. But there is one imam at the mosque who is on our watch list . . .' He bent down over his keyboard and typed. A picture appeared on the right-hand screen: a young bearded man dressed in a thobe and wearing a skullcap. 'Mohammed

Choudhury,' said Adam. 'One of the firebrands, a poppy-burner every November, keeps putting up jihadists videos as quickly as YouTube takes them down. He's had several tweets that border on race hatred but the general feeling is we don't want to make a martyr of him. Most of the worshippers at the Makki Masjid are middle-of-the-road Muslims and they treat him with contempt, pretty much. But Choudhury has, we think, helped several guys travel over to Pakistan for training. It's hard to prove for sure. Anyway, so far we have no evidence that Sayyid has met Choudhury, but we're still looking.' He tapped on the laptop keyboard again and two more photographs appeared on the left-hand screen. 'We do know that he has met with a fundamentalist preacher at one of the other mosques.' They all looked at the photographs. They were of Sayyid and a middle-aged man in a thobe, balding with a grey-streaked beard that almost reached his pot belly. They were taken on different occasions. One was inside, the other was in the street outside a mosque.

'This is Malik Ahad Kamali, and he is a problem,' said Adam. 'He used to be down in London, hanging out with Mustafa Kamel Mustafa, AKA Abu Hamza, at the Finsbury Park Mosque. He was also tight with Abu Qatada, and Omar Bakri Mohammed. Unlike Abu Hamza, now buried in an American supermax, Kamali seemed to know that there was about to be a backlash, so in 2004 he went to Pakistan, stayed there for five years and in 2009 he reappeared in Birmingham. He's kept his head down, no rants on social media, no public outbursts, but he does hold a lot of private meetings where we believe he makes his true feelings known. We've tried infiltrating his meetings but to no avail.'

'Obviously Sayyid meeting Kamali isn't a red flag in and of

itself,' said Johnson. 'But once you brought him to our attention, it's probably not a coincidence. What we're doing now is
checking all the surveillance video we have to see who else he
might have met. And Adam will be checking with his agents
to see if they remember seeing him.'

'Do you have a lot of agents here?' asked Docherty.

Johnson nodded. 'An awful lot,' she said. 'It's surprisingly
easy to get Muslims to work for us here. The vast majority
abhor the jihadists and the fundamentalists. Birmingham's
Muslim community has been established for decades, long
before 9/11 and 7/7. There are thousands of third-generation
Muslims in the city and they're very different from the ones
that are coming in from the Middle East now. They see or
hear anything that sounds like trouble and they're on to our
terrorism hotline straight away.'

'We've got active agents in most of the city's mosques,' said
Adam. 'The problem is that the likes of Kamali have started
playing their cards close to their chests. It can take a long time
to get near them. But we're on it. I'll be putting feelers out
tomorrow to see if anyone recognises Sayyid. And if anyone
knows where he is.'

'What about this Kamali's phone?' asked Docherty. 'Do you
have it tapped?'

'We do,' said Johnson. 'But he's crafty. He has a mobile and
he uses it to call his wives, the council, the mosque. Everyday
stuff. But he's always on the landlines at the mosque, which
we're not allowed to tap, and he uses public pay phones when
he's out and about. We've seen him borrow mobiles at the
mosque. He knows we're watching him and he's careful.' She
looked across at Shepherd. 'Did you find anything at his house
today that might help?'

Shepherd frowned. He hadn't told her that they were searching Sayyid's home.

Johnson smiled, then nodded at Adam. The picture of Sayyid disappeared from the screen on the left and was replaced by four photographs – Lyn Burns getting out of Docherty's car, Burns walking to the side of the house, Shepherd and Leach walking to the front door of the house, and Leach and Burns leaving. Shepherd raised his eyebrows. 'Now that is impressive.'

'Tina has some first-class surveillance people,' said Johnson.

Taylor grinned. 'We couldn't get a view of the rear of the house,' she said. 'We still don't know how she got inside so quickly.'

'Patio door,' said Shepherd.

'Ah, that explains it,' said Taylor.

Shepherd looked at the four photographs. The watchers must have been good because he hadn't had any inkling that the house was under surveillance. He looked at Johnson and smiled. 'Nice job.'

'Well, as I said, it's down to Tina and her team. So did you turn up anything useful?'

'He's definitely cleared out,' said Shepherd. 'He took clothes and toiletries with him. He had a hiding place under the bath where we think he kept a bag. No way of knowing what was in it. He burned some papers in the back garden and we'll get them checked but it's possible he did that to throw us off the trail.'

'And no idea what he's planning?'

Shepherd shook his head.

Johnson looked across at Docherty. 'Anything in his past that might indicate what he was up to?'

'He was involved in construction before he became a translator. He never carried a gun while he was with us so I don't know what, if any, weapons training he's had.'

'That means he could be planning anything. A remote bombing, a suicide bombing, marauding terrorist attack, firearms, who knows. Or even a lone wolf attack?'

'We're thinking not a lone wolf attack because this has been planned,' said Shepherd. 'It looks as if he was persuaded to become a translator by a Taliban chief named Mohammad Hassan Baloch. We're trying to see if there has been any contact since Sayyid came to the UK.'

Johnson smiled at Adam and nodded. Adam typed on his laptop and after a few seconds the four surveillance photographs were replaced by a photograph of Baloch. Adam gave a brief rundown on the man and Johnson listened and nodded.

'Right, let's see if we can find any links between this Baloch and anyone at our mosques,' she said once Adam had finished. 'Any connections at all.'

'I'm on it,' said Adam.

'Sayyid could have a totally different handler now that he's in the UK,' said Shepherd.

'We'll put Sayyid under the microscope now,' said Johnson. 'If he has a handler and he met him at a mosque here, we should be able to find him. What we're doing at the moment is going back through all our surveillance footage and seeing who Sayyid was in contact with. It's taking time, unfortunately. And Adam will start talking to his agents tomorrow.'

'Sounds like a plan,' said Shepherd.

'But after that, I'm not sure how much more we can do,' said Johnson. 'We're pretty stretched at the moment. The government is sending a lot of its new arrivals to the Midlands and our hotline is ringing non-stop. I can put the resources into checking the surveillance footage and talking to our agents, but beyond that . . .' She shrugged. 'The problem is, we don't have any evidence of a direct threat from Sayyid, but I do have four ongoing plots that are nearing fruition. We have a group that have filled a storage locker with ANFO explosives, a group of six wannabe jihadists who have twice cased out the Bullring for a machete attack, a group of Muslim students who are spending a lot of time researching airborne anthrax attacks, and two guys who are asking a Croatian criminal group to sell them high-powered rifles. Plus we have another two dozen operations involving possible major terrorism incidents. I'll help as much as I can, obviously, but priorities are priorities.'

'I understand,' said Shepherd. 'Would you mind if I watched some of the footage with Adam? I have quite a good memory and it might be useful down the line if I saw video of the people that Sayyid met, and any other radicals that you're watching.'

'Be my guest,' she said. She brought the meeting to a close, and Adam took Shepherd, Docherty and Farah down the corridor to a small windowless room with five work pods and two large screens on the wall. Adam took off his jacket, draped it over the back of one of the chairs. He sat down and logged on to the terminal. 'Grab a seat, guys, and I'll show you what we've got.'

Shepherd woke early, pulled back the curtains and looked out of his bedroom window. The sky was bright blue and cloudless so he decided he'd walk from Battersea to Thames House. He showered and shaved and put on a dark blue suit. He couldn't be bothered making himself coffee so he bought one from a cafe across the road from his apartment block, along with a bacon roll. He finished eating his roll as he walked across Vauxhall Bridge and drank the last of his coffee as he walked into the building. He took the lift up to the fourth floor and headed to the Afghan Desk. The large screen on the wall was still showing BBC rolling news with the sound off. Janice Warren was standing in front of another screen watching a slow-motion video of four Asian men walking along a pavement. She smiled when she saw him. 'You're in bright and early,' she said. She was wearing a hoodie with 'Oxford University' across the front, and fluorescent green Crocs. She pressed a remote and the video froze.

'You too,' he said.

She laughed. 'I didn't actually go home last night,' she said. 'We've had some urgent requests come in from the FBI's Washington office and Pritchard has said we need to give them priority.' She gestured at the screen she'd been looking at. 'The guy on the left is a Brit who has just turned up in Chicago, but according to the Department of Homeland Security he didn't arrive by plane.'

'Rubber dinghy?'

She laughed again. 'More likely by road from Canada or Mexico, but either way they wouldn't have issued him with an ESTA. He's been in Belmarsh twice on terrorism charges.'

'Have they arrested him?'

She shook her head. 'They're watching him at the moment. The worry is, if he got under the radar, others could. Bit like your problem with the Afghan boys. Speaking of which . . .' She went over to one of the pods and opened a drawer. 'I've come up with another nine possible red flags from the hotel in Scarborough, in addition to the other two I gave you.'

'Our woman didn't recognise either of them.'

'Well try these on her. Some we had red-flagged, five of them went AWOL from the hotel during the time that Sayyid was there.' She gave him a stack of sheets with photographs and names. 'If any of them ring a bell with Sayyid's wife, let me know and I'll give you the details.'

Shepherd looked over at her screen. 'Where is that?'

'Leeds, last year,' she said. 'The guy they're looking at is on the left. I'm trying to ID the guys he's with.'

'I know the one on the far right. His name's Hasib Tanweer. Or Mohammed Hasib Tanweer in full.'

'Oh you lifesaver, thank you.'

'He's in prison, got sent down six months ago. He was part of a cell planning to shoot up a local shopping mall. Luckily the guy they approached for weapons called the anti-terrorism hotline and they were shut down.'

'I wish I had your memory,' said Warren.

'Tanweer was close to an imam in Leeds Grand Mosque. Guy by the name of Mustafa Sharjeel. They were never able to charge Sharjeel, but he was almost certainly involved. And Sharjeel has contacts in the US. He's on their no-fly list, so he can't travel there, but he has made several trips to Mexico. I wouldn't be surprised if he's been getting people into the US from there.'

'Spider, you've just saved me a week's work.'

Shepherd grinned. 'Happy to be of service.' He held up the printed sheets. 'And thanks for these.'

Docherty and Farah were already in the operations room, drinking coffee and looking at a large screen on the wall. It was showing a map of the UK and on it were hundreds of red dots. Shepherd went over to join them. 'It's from the

Carphone Warehouse,' said Farah. 'Sayyid's phone has been offline since he left home, but prior to that his GPS was on for a few weeks in December and January so they were able to track his movements then.'

'Which phone? He had two numbers, right?'

'This is his regular phone. It was given to him by the Home Office when he first arrived. The GPS was on when he first had it.' She went over to a keyboard and tapped on it. The screen went blank and then was replaced with another UK map. This one had no red dots. 'This is the burner phone, the one he used to call Laila a couple of times, probably by mistake. The GPS was never on for this phone. And it was only ever used to call one other number. Another pay-as-you-go.' She tapped on the keyboard again and the first map reappeared. 'The burner phone hasn't been used for the last three months. We're assuming the SIM card was destroyed. Ditto for the pay-as-you-go number that Sayyid called.'

'And what about the Home Office phone?'

'Sayyid was using it until the day he disappeared. But the GPS was switched off at the end of January.'

'So we're assuming that the number Sayyid called on his burner phone is someone he's working with?' said Docherty.

'Probably,' said Shepherd. 'Another jihadist, maybe. Or his handler.'

'You think someone's running him? He's not following his own agenda?'

'He was certainly being handled by Baloch the Butcher in Afghanistan,' said Shepherd. 'I don't think he's smart enough to be doing this on his own.' He stared at the map. 'Lots of hits around Scarborough, obviously when he was in the hotel with his family. Then a lot of hits around Birmingham. But what's this?' He pointed at a small cluster of dots to the north-west of Oxford.

'Chipping Norton,' said Farah. 'The Cotswolds. He was just there for one day. That was in January.'

'Maybe visiting Jeremy Clarkson's farm shop,' said Docherty.

'Lots of high-profile residents,' said Farah. 'David Cameron. Elisabeth Murdoch. The Beckhams have a place there. Several members of the House of Lords.'

'High profile, but they don't spring to mind as jihadist targets,' said Shepherd. 'I know Cameron's a former prime minister but most jihadists probably wouldn't even know the name. Tony Blair would be a more obvious target. Or the current prime minister, obviously.' He stared at the dots around Chipping Norton. Sayyid had criss-crossed the area as if he was lost. Or looking for something. 'He drove from Birmingham, spent what, three hours driving around, and then went back to Birmingham?'

'That's what it looks like, yes.'

Shepherd pointed at the cluster of red dots in London. 'When was he in London?'

Farah went over to the keyboard and tapped on it. The map changed to a view of London, peppered with red dots. 'He was there for two days at the end of January, shortly before the GPS was switched off. After he'd been to Chipping Norton. He travelled all over. Houses of Parliament, Downing Street, Buckingham Palace. Lots of targets.'

'Or tourism,' said Shepherd. 'Looks like he might well have been on an open-topped tourist bus at some point, that looks like the route they take. They go right by Downing Street, the Houses of Parliament, all the touristy places. Where did he stay?'

'According to the GPS data he spent two nights in a hotel in Bayswater. Should we get it checked out?'

'Let's find out who owns it and who works there,' said Shepherd. 'And can you get me a large-scale print-out of the GPS map and put it on the wall?'

'I'm on it,' said Farah.

'So far as the hotel goes, if it's a jihadist hangout then we'll need a softly-softly approach, but if it's a regular hotel we can see if there was anyone with him. And what about the number that Sayyid called from his burner?'

Farah nodded. 'The guys in Carphone Warehouse are on the case.'

'Okay, all good,' said Shepherd. He handed her the papers that Warren had given him. 'Can you pop down to Wimbledon and show these to Laila? See if she recognises anybody.'

'No problem. And Amar has finished with Laila's phone, so are you okay if we give it back to her?'

'Absolutely. And bring back the pay-as-you-go she was using for Amar to have a look at. How are you getting on with that Aspen debit card thing that Sayyid was using?'

'I have a list of all transactions made on the card – mostly cash withdrawals from ATMs in Scarborough and Birmingham. It hasn't been used since Sayyid went AWOL. There are just under fifty withdrawals and I'm reaching out to the banks to see what they have in the way of ATM footage. If we're lucky we might catch Sayyid with someone else. It's going to take time though. I've marked them priority but the banks are snowed under with requests. These days if any suspected criminal even walks past an ATM there's a chance a detective is going to request the footage.'

'We'll give them forty-eight hours and if we haven't got anything back I'll see what pressure we can apply.'

'There are about a dozen times when the card was used as a debit card to buy items the family needed. Most of them were in Scarborough. Clothing at TK Maxx and Sports Direct. Toiletries at Boots. There were three in Birmingham but I think by then he was using mainly cash. One was a Pizza Hut.'

'He doesn't seem the type to take his family out for pizza,' said Shepherd.

'That's what I thought. So I'll see if there's any CCTV footage. Also he bought petrol on two occasions.'

'He doesn't own a car so far as we know. Though he did travel to London and to Chipping Norton. That's a point, Tony, can Sayyid drive?'

'I'm not sure.' He frowned. 'I never saw him at the wheel of a vehicle.'

'If he can't drive, then he must have been with someone who could when he went to the Cotswolds. Can you check with DVLA and see if he has a UK licence?'

'Will do. Also, I've pulled everything that Six has on Baloch. Not much, to be honest. The Americans have him on their most-wanted list but he's a Scarlet Pimpernel type. They seek him here, they seek him there . . .'

'And no phone calls to the UK?'

'Not on any phone that we know about.'

'Any thoughts as to who else he might have encouraged to move to the UK?'

Docherty shook his head. 'Sorry.'

Farah grabbed her coat and headed out.

Shepherd took out his phone, uploaded a picture of Malik

Ahad Kamali and the photographs he had taken of Sayyid's Santander bank account on to his computer and printed them. He moved the picture of Baloch to the left and put Kamali's picture next to it. He picked up the marker and added an 'S' to 'POSSIBLE HANDLER'. Then he spread the bank statements out on a table. Docherty came over to look at them. There were statements for three months, with a balance of just over a thousand pounds on the final pages. The only transactions were ATM withdrawals, twenty or thirty pounds each time.

'Like you said, he could have brought cash with him from Afghanistan,' said Shepherd.

'We paid him in US dollars. So yes, he probably squirrelled some away. He could have brought the cash to the UK, changed it into sterling and opened the bank account.'

'He's messing with us. As Mick Leach said, it doesn't make sense that he would burn those other papers but leave these in a drawer. Nor does it make sense that he didn't completely destroy the ashes. He wants us wasting our time checking this account and the burnt papers. It's misdirection. He wants us to take our eye off the ball.'

'The ball being whatever he's planning.'

'Exactly. It's like the machete he'd hidden under the sofa. Did he really forget it or did he want us to find it? We find a machete so we start thinking that's what he's planning. I'll bet good money that our tech boys will discover maps or something in the ashes that will suggest where he might be planning to attack. Except it'll be misdirection.'

Shepherd was in the canteen eating an early lunch of fish and chips when his phone beeped. He put down his knife and fork and picked up the phone. It was a message from Farah: 'LAILA SAW THIS GUY', underneath an image of one of the photos Warren had given them. The photo was of an Asian man in his twenties. His name was at the bottom of the picture: Javid Hakim. Shepherd called Farah and she answered immediately. 'How sure is she?' asked Shepherd.

'Very sure,' said Farah. 'She says she got a good look at him.'

'Well done,' said Shepherd. 'Can you head back to Thames House? We'll start looking at this Hakim in more detail.'

'I'm on my way,' she said, and ended the call.

Shepherd forwarded the picture to Warren, along with a note: 'THIS ONE'. He was just finishing his fish and chips when his mobile rang. This time it was Janice Warren. 'He's one of yours, Spider,' said Warren.

'One of mine?'

'Well, one of your old mob's. Javid Hakim was a translator for the SAS, started working for them in Kabul in 2016 and left in August last year, on one of the British evacuation flights.'

'And who in the SAS signed his ARAP application?'

'Let me see. Okay, here it is. Captain Stephen Harvey. Do you want a copy of this file?'

'I do.'

'I'll email it to you right now.'

'Nah, that's okay, I'll come along and pick it up. I'm in the canteen, what can I bring you?'

'I'd kill for a latte. And anything with chocolate in it. Croissant, muffin, biscuit, anything.'

'I'm on my way,' said Shepherd.

Shepherd bought a latte and a chocolate brownie and took them to Warren's office. Her eyes widened when she saw the brownie. 'Oh my, you certainly know the way to a girl's heart,' she said.

She took the coffee and brownie and put them on her desk, then gave him a print-out of Hakim's ARAP application. 'Do you know this Captain Harvey?' she asked.

'No, officers come and go. I'll drive to Hereford and have a chat with him.'

'How's the investigation going?'

'Truth be told, we're not making much progress. Even if we ID them, we're still no closer to knowing where they are or what they're doing.'

She flashed him a thin smile. 'Welcome to my world.'

Shepherd nodded grimly. 'I'd like to think that this was only temporary, but part of me thinks we could be like this for a long time to come. And it's like the IRA said all those years ago when they almost killed Margaret Thatcher: "you have to be lucky all the time, we only need to be lucky once".'

'You know what might help?'

'What?'

She pointed at her brownie. 'Chocolate,' she said.

It took Shepherd three and a half hours to drive from Battersea to Hereford. He had gone home first and changed out of his suit into a leather jacket and jeans before collecting his car from the underground car park. He could have talked to the captain on the phone or over Zoom but the matter was sensitive and the questions needed to be asked face to face. The suit would have put a barrier between them, whereas the jacket and jeans would be reassuringly familiar. He needed to be seen as a former member of the Regiment on a fact-finding mission, rather than an MI5 officer looking for somebody to blame.

Shepherd brought his SUV to a halt in front of the barrier and showed his ID to a uniformed guard as another guard ran a mirror under the vehicle. The guard checked Shepherd's name against a list on his clipboard, nodded, and began to give him directions. Shepherd grinned and silenced him with a wave of his hand. 'It's okay, I know where to go,' he said. 'I used to live here.' The barrier came up and Shepherd drove through.

The Stirling Lines base in Hereford encompassed almost a thousand acres, with state-of-the-art training facilities and massive beige hangars containing all the equipment the SAS needed to conduct operations around the world. It was home to the four SAS squadrons – A, B, D and G – along with the 18 Signal Regiment, who looked after communications, and the Special Reconnaissance Regiment, who were tasked with intelligence gathering and undercover operations. The Army Air Corps kept Gazelle and Dauphin helicopters at the base so that the troopers could be flown out at short notice. The buildings were set well apart and linked by a network of roads and walkways, and the camp had been cleverly landscaped with trees and sloping banks so that visitors often had trouble finding their way around.

Shepherd drove to the main admin block and parked. Captain Harvey's office was on the ground floor and his door was open. He was sitting in a high-backed chair with his boots up on the desk and he scrambled to his feet when Shepherd appeared in the doorway. Harvey was in his mid-twenties, tanned, with sandy brown hair and a decent beard that suggested he wasn't long back from the Middle East. He was wearing desert fatigues and had a holstered Glock on his hip. 'Dan Shepherd?' he said.

Shepherd nodded. 'Guilty as charged.'

Harvey stuck out his hand. 'Pleasure to meet you,' he said. 'You're a bit of a legend around here.' They shook. Harvey had a strong grip and perfectly manicured nails. He waved Shepherd to a chair and sat down.

Troopers and sergeants could stay in the Regiment for as long as they wanted to – or at least for as long as they could perform the job – but officers were transient. Generally they were attached for between two and three years and usually it was simply a step on their career ladder. There were good officers and bad officers, but they were never taken too seriously as everyone knew they were only temporary. The smart ones listened and learned and let the troopers get on with doing what they did best. Officers would plan the missions and oversee them, but the Chinese Parliament system meant that any wrinkles were ironed out by the men who would be doing the job. 'I'm here about an interpreter you used out in Afghanistan.'

Harvey nodded. 'We had quite a few terps. They came and went.'

'This guy's name was Javid Hakim.'

'Ah, yes. Javid. He was one of the good guys. He started assisting the Regiment in 2016 and I met him in early 2020. We had about a hundred guys out there, running hunt and kill ops and training the Afghan commandos. We didn't use interpreters for the ops, obviously, but we definitely needed them for the training. The Afghans didn't even know their left from their right.'

'And you signed off on his ARAP application?'

'Sure. Happy to. He was well known in the area and his life wouldn't have been worth anything once the Taliban had taken over. Is he okay? Has something happened?'

'That's what we're trying to find out. But he made it to the UK in August last year, during the mad scramble out.'

'Yeah, that was a nightmare. They almost sent me there to help with the evacuation but we had an urgent job in Syria. I'm glad to hear he got out.'

'Yeah, they sent him to a hotel in Scarborough but then he went AWOL. No one is sure where he is now.'

'Scarborough? Why would they send him there?' He leaned back and swung his boots up on to the desk.

'They were dispersing them around the country. Luck of the draw.'

'He always said he wanted to go to London. He really did believe that the streets were paved with gold. I tried to tell him about places like Southall and Tower Hamlets but he wasn't having any of it.'

'Did he have friends or relatives in London? Anyone he might have stayed with?'

'I can't really remember, sorry. Maybe. I think he might have mentioned that he had a cousin who had a kebab shop in Ealing. You think he ran off to work or something?'

'We're not sure. He just upped and left.'

'But that doesn't make sense. Under ARAP he'd have been fast-tracked to citizenship. He knew that. He was going to be a teacher again and his wife wanted to train as a nurse.'

Shepherd frowned. 'Wife? He was married?'

'Yes. I never met her but he'd been married five years or so.'

'That wasn't mentioned in his ARAP application.'

'I'm sure it was. I filled it in myself.'

'Yes, I know,' said Shepherd. 'I have a copy.' He took three folded sheets of paper from his jacket and passed it to the captain.

Harvey took his feet off the desk and reached for the papers.

He shook his head as soon as he saw the photograph on the front page. 'No, no, no, there's some mistake. That's not him.'

Shepherd frowned. 'Correct name, though?'

Harvey nodded. 'Yes. Javid Hakim. But it must be another Javid Hakim. This guy is younger and heavier. And Javid had a mole on his chin. A big mole.' He waved the papers in the air. 'And the date of birth's wrong. Javid is in his forties. This guy is what, twenty-six? No, I'm sorry, different guy.'

'Have a look at the reference section, the part you completed.'

Harvey frowned and flicked through the sheets. He found what he was looking for and his jaw dropped as he read it. 'This is what I wrote. For Javid. Word for word.' He took out his phone and flicked through his photos. 'There you go,' he said. 'That's Javid.' He showed the photograph to Shepherd. In the picture, Harvey was wearing desert fatigues and had a black-and-white keffiyeh scarf around his neck. He was surrounded by a dozen Afghan soldiers carrying American carbines. 'That's Javid, on my left,' said Harvey.

Shepherd squinted at the screen. The Javid in the picture was a wiry middle-aged man with a greying beard. He was grinning at the camera as he held up a Heckler & Koch 417 and there was a large mole on his chin. It most definitely wasn't the man on the MoD's database. 'Chalk and cheese,' said Shepherd, giving the phone back to Harvey.

'What's going on?' asked the captain. 'Is Javid okay, do you think?'

'Hand on heart, no,' said Shepherd. 'I don't think he is.'

'But how could the wrong information get on to the ARAP application?'

'That, Captain Harvey, is a very good question.'

★

The Russian saw Sayyid driving down the road towards them in a grey Skoda Octavia. He looked across at the Afghan. 'Get the door up.' The Afghan's name was Jafri, a quiet, determined man who rarely spoke.

Jafri nodded and raised the metal door of the lock-up so that Sayyid could drive in. There were several large cardboard bags stacked at the far end, and two old barrels. Sayyid reversed in, switched the engine off and climbed out. 'Let me see the paperwork,' said the Russian. Sayyid gave him the rental document and the Russian examined it, then nodded. 'Good man.'

'What now?' asked Sayyid.

'Now we leave it here until it's needed.'

'When will that be?'

'Soon,' said the Russian. He put the paperwork in the glove compartment and closed the door. 'You should go back and wait at the house.' The Afghans were staying together in a rented house in the Sparkbrook district. There were more than twenty-five thousand people living in the area and nearly 70 per cent were of Asian ethnicity, so it was easy for the Afghans to blend in. The Russian stayed alone, in a warehouse conversion in the city centre.

'Okay,' said Sayyid. He looked over at Jafri. 'Are you coming?'

'He's staying with me,' said the Russian. 'We have something to do. You can wait at the house until I call you.'

'I have to pray.'

'Then pray.'

Sayyid nodded and walked away, his hands in his pockets. The Russian stared after him with a look of contempt on his face. 'Do you want me to install the bomb now?' asked Jafri quietly.

'Yes,' said the Russian.

'Do you want to help? It's a two-man job.'

'Of course I'll help,' said the Russian. 'Just be careful.'

Jafri laughed dryly. 'Do not worry, I am a professional.'

'I know you are. That's why you were chosen.' The Russian switched on the single fluorescent light hanging from the ceiling and pulled the door down so that they couldn't be seen.

'Amar, mate, this is one nice car,' said Shepherd, as he climbed out of the Tesla Model S. It was ten o'clock in the morning and Singh had driven them from Thames House to a B&Q store in north London.

'If you're asking how I can afford it, one word,' said Singh. 'Overtime.' He was wearing a dark blue Hugo Boss suit and black shoes that had been polished to a shine. 'I've been working non-stop for the past two years. Plus there's all the money we saved by not travelling or eating out during Covid.' He pressed the key fob to lock the doors.

'I guess working from home was never an option, was it?' said Shepherd.

'Not for me, no.'

They walked towards the store and through the main entrance. A grey-haired man in a black polo shirt with the B&Q logo beamed at them and asked if he could help.

Shepherd returned the man's smile. 'It's okay, we know what we want.' He and Singh turned left and then headed down an aisle filled with paint brushes and sprayers. Craig McKillop was standing by a large paint-mixing machine that was vibrating a large can of paint. Like the greeter at the entrance he was wearing a black polo shirt and black trousers, protected by a bright orange apron. The machine came to a stop and McKillop unfastened the can and handed it to the customer, a middle-aged woman in a raincoat, with a tired smile. 'Have a great day,' he said in a dull monotone. As the woman walked towards the checkout, he saw Shepherd and his smile froze.

'How are you doing, Craig?' asked Shepherd.

'How does it look like I'm doing?' replied McKillop. 'I'm mixing paint in a B&Q, that's how I'm doing.'

'Yeah, I heard you left the MoD.'

'Left? I was kicked out,' said McKillop. 'As soon as I was no use any more, I was shown the door. You must have known that?'

Shepherd grimaced. 'Actually I didn't. Sorry. I've been busy.'

McKillop shrugged. 'It probably wouldn't have made any difference, it came from the top.' He rubbed the back of his neck. 'Everything was ticking over just fine until about two months after Kabul fell.' He forced a smile. 'In fact I followed your advice and had her sleep with me.'

'I'm not sure that was my advice.'

'No, you were right. I made a move one evening and she didn't hesitate. The sex was good. Better than good. It was great. She made me feel like . . .' He shuddered. 'I know it was all an act. But she played the part perfectly.' He forced a smile. 'It was the best sex I've had. Probably the best sex I'll ever have.'

'Well at least you got something out of it.'

'That's one way of looking at it. But she was using me, right from the start. I should have seen that.'

'It's easy to get blindsided by a pretty girl. And she was very pretty.'

McKillop shrugged. 'Yeah. She was pretty. Anyway, one day her phone was disconnected. I went around to her flat and she'd gone. Like she'd never been there. I went to her office and they denied that she'd ever worked there. I was gaslighted. Totally gaslighted. Ciara said she'd gone to Italy. Rome. She was using a different name, probably had another guy in her sights.' His jaw clenched. 'Bitch. If I ever see her again . . .'

'You won't,' said Shepherd. 'And if you do, just remember the great sex you had.'

McKillop shook his head. 'She ruined my life.' He waved his hands around. 'Do you think I'd be working here if I had a choice? I've got a PhD for fuck's sake. I speak fluent German. But the MoD wouldn't give me a reference after five years so everyone assumes the worst.'

'To be fair, you did break the Official Secrets Act. And you passed confidential information to the Russians.'

'You know that the data I gave her wasn't sensitive. And I thought she was German. I mean, she was German, I just didn't know that she was working for the Russians. And I did everything you asked of me after you told me what was happening. And they still sacked me.'

'Sure, but on the plus side you didn't go to prison.'

'I helped you. I should have got some credit for that.'

'You'll bounce back. Why not go to Germany? Use your language skills?'

'Brexit has put paid to that,' said McKillop. 'And even in Germany they'd want to know why I left the MoD.' He ran a hand through his receding hair. 'So what are you here for? To gloat?'

'Actually we need your help,' said Shepherd. 'This is Raj, he's a colleague of mine.' MI5 officers rarely used their real names when interacting with the public.

'He likes abducting cyclists, does he?' said McKillop, glaring at Singh.

'He's not that sort of colleague,' said Shepherd.

'I'm more on the IT side,' said Singh. 'I just want to ask you a few questions about what happened last year.'

McKillop frowned and looked at Shepherd. 'Am I in trouble again? Because this time I want a lawyer. Which is what should have happened last time.'

'You're not in any trouble,' said Shepherd. 'What's done is done. But Raj here needs to fill in the details.'

'It's just for the record,' said Singh. 'There's just a few details we need. Mainly about the flash drives you used to pass on the intel.'

'Again with the intel,' snapped McKillop. 'It was data I gave her.'

Singh put up his hands to placate him. 'I just want to know where the flash drives came from.'

'Came from? Currys, I think. Bog-standard USB flash drives. Big memories because there was a lot of data, so two hundred and fifty-six gigabytes and up.'

'What make?'

'SanDisk usually.'

'And you always bought them? You bought them, you downloaded the intel – the data – and you gave them to your handler?'

'She wasn't my . . .' McKillop shook his head sadly. 'What's the use? You never listen.'

'You always bought the flash drives? From Currys?'

McKillop nodded. 'Yes.'

'And you passed them to your . . . contact?'

'Yes.'

Singh frowned. 'Always? She never gave you a flash drive to use?'

'No. They were mine.' His eyebrows shot up as he **remembered** something. 'No, wait. The first time I gave her a thumb drive she gave it back to me the next time.'

'Why did she do that?'

McKillop shrugged. 'I don't know. She just did. So I used it again and gave it back the next time I saw her. She only did that the once. The rest of the times I used a new one.'

'And the one she gave you, was there anything on it?'

'No. It was blank. She'd deleted the data I'd given her.'

'And there was nothing else on the drive?'

McKillop frowned. 'Like what?'

'I don't know,' said Singh. 'Anything.'

'No, it was blank.'

Singh looked across at Shepherd. 'Okay, I think we're good.'

Shepherd smiled at McKillop. 'That's all we need, Craig, thank you.'

'Whatever.' A customer appeared by the paint-mixing machine and McKillop went over to speak with him, his plastic smile already in place.

Shepherd and Singh left. 'Raj?' said Singh as they walked away from the building. 'Is that the best you could come up with for a cover name?'

'What's wrong with it?'

'It always makes me think of "days of the Raj", that's all. The colonial days.'

'I've come across loads of Asian guys called Raj,' said Shepherd. 'But yeah, duly noted. So for future reference, what name would you prefer I use?'

'Brad,' said Singh. 'I've always liked Brad.'

'Brad it is,' said Shepherd. 'What do you think was on the thumb drive? Some sort of Trojan virus?'

'Almost certainly.'

'But McKillop didn't see anything.'

'No, he wouldn't, not if they were pros. It'll be in the hardware. Same as when we put stuff on to mobiles. We fiddle with the chips rather than the software. If it's in the software, a decent programmer can find anything that shouldn't be there. But if it's in the hardware, you'll need some very sophisticated equipment to find it. She only gave him the one thumb drive back, so I'd guess it installed a backdoor that they used to access the system as and when they wanted.'

'Is it that easy?'

Singh grinned. 'No, it's not easy. Especially with a system as secure as the MoD's. But it's possible. And doable.'

They reached Singh's car. 'But if they had a backdoor, why not use that to take the information they needed from the database? Why keep using McKillop if they had their own way in?'

'Because downloading data outside the building would be an automatic red flag,' said Singh. 'McKillop could sit there all day looking at stuff and no one would bat an eyelid, but once files are examined remotely, there'd be security notifications.' He took out his key fob and unlocked the Tesla. 'The way I see it, she gave your guy the thumb drive early on and got their software loaded. Then they carried on using him to get the files they wanted. Then, and only then, did they use the backdoor to manipulate the files.'

'Would that backdoor still be there?'

Singh wrinkled his nose. 'Maybe, maybe not. If it was me, I'd use the backdoor once and then once I've done what needed to be done I'd delete it and log off. Hopefully no one would be the wiser. But a backdoor into the MoD mainframe, that'd be a big thing to give up.'

'Could you take a look?'

'I'd need the assistance of the MoD IT people.'

'We'll need to get it done,' said Shepherd. 'Last thing we need is for them to get back into the system in six months or six years.'

They got into the car. 'Back to the office?' asked Singh.

Shepherd nodded. 'Yeah, I'm afraid so,' he said.

Singh dropped Shepherd at the entrance to Thames House and went off to park his car. Shepherd went through the metal detector and up to the operations room. Docherty looked up from his terminal as the door opened. 'It seems that Sayyid does indeed have a UK driving licence. He passed his test in December.'

'That's good to know,' said Shepherd. 'That means he could well have been driving when he visited Chipping Norton.' Farah had obtained a large print-out of the GPS tracking they had done on Sayyid's phone and stuck it to the wall. Shepherd pointed at it. 'How easy do you think it would be to see if he rented a car over those days?'

'I can try,' said Docherty. 'I can call around the local car rental places.'

'Give it a go,' said Shepherd.

'How did you get on at Hereford?'

'Yeah, we have another wolf in sheep's clothing.' Shepherd printed out pictures of the man passing himself off as Javid Hakim. 'Grab another whiteboard, Tony, and set it up for this guy,' said Shepherd. He spelled out the name.

Docherty stuck the photograph on to a whiteboard and wrote 'AKA JAVID HAKIM' above it.

The door opened and Shepherd looked up to see Pritchard.

He was in harassed mode, his shirtsleeves rolled up and his tie at half mast. He walked into the room, looked at the whiteboards and put his hands on his hips. Shepherd and Docherty joined him. 'Please give me some good news,' he said.

'Well, we know how they did it,' said Shepherd. 'They gave McKillop a thumb drive with a Trojan virus on it that let them get into the MoD to rewrite the ARAP applications. They were able to change the biometric details, so when their guys appeared they matched.'

'Their guys? How many?'

'We don't know.'

'We don't know yet or we'll never know?'

'Amar is on the case. The thing is, it's obviously a very sophisticated hack, so if they're that good they will probably have wiped all their traces.'

Pritchard ran a hand through his hair. 'This is a nightmare.'

'It's not good,' said Shepherd. 'If they are as good as Amar thinks they might be, then the only thing to do would be to run a check on every single person who came in under ARAP. We'd need a current photograph, and then to run that by the person who sponsored the application.'

Pritchard nodded. 'I get it. And if we had ten teams on it, and they managed two a day, it would still take more than a year to check them all. And we don't have ten teams.'

'We could get the police involved,' said Docherty. 'Spread the workload.'

'We could,' agreed Pritchard. 'But what about the ones who are flying below the radar?' He shook his head. 'That means we have one suspect at the moment.' He pointed at the photograph of Javid Hakim. 'Do we know where this guy is?'

'No,' said Shepherd.

'Do we have a phone number? Anything?'

'Nothing.'

Pritchard's jaw tightened. 'Can we use facial recognition?'

'We can and we are doing it as we speak. But needle in a haystack doesn't come close.' He shrugged. 'We might get lucky.'

'I really don't want to be depending on luck,' said Pritchard. He pointed at the whiteboards. 'All we know is that Javid Hakim met Sayyid Habibi in Scarborough. Then Sayyid went to Birmingham and Javid went where?'

'AWOL,' said Shepherd. 'Off the grid. He was due to be rehoused but left the hotel with all his belongings.'

'He's been off the grid for almost a year?' Pritchard frowned. 'Somebody must be taking care of him.'

Shepherd nodded. 'Almost certainly.'

'Does he have family in the UK?'

'The real Javid, no. His family is all in Kabul. So far as the fake Javid goes, who knows?'

'And what about the real Javid? Where is he?'

'No way of knowing,' said Docherty. 'We have a mobile for him but there's no answer. The way things are in Kabul right now it'll take time to check.'

'Do MI6 still have agents in place?' asked Pritchard.

'In theory, quite a few,' said Docherty. 'But most of them are keeping their heads down for understandable reasons. I managed to get in touch with one – a former teacher – but she says she's scared to leave the house.'

'The fact that they sent a substitute suggests that the real Javid isn't in a position to identify himself,' said Shepherd. 'I would put money on him being dead. His family, too.'

'Yes, that sounds about right,' said Pritchard. 'We know that the Taliban were using the data McKillop supplied as a death list. What we didn't know was that they were using the data to get their own people into the UK.' He rubbed his chin. 'But who the hell is behind this?' He pointed at the photograph of Kamali. 'Who's this?'

'A pro-jihadist imam that Sayyid met with at a mosque in Birmingham. It's only circumstantial at the moment. But it's possible that he's Sayyid's handler.'

Pritchard nodded. 'Okay, so the Butcher approached Sayyid and convinced him by whatever means to start working for the British. I guess the big question is, when he did that, was his ultimate aim to get Sayyid to the UK? Or was it simply a way of getting intel about what the British were doing?'

'At the time Baloch knew that the Americans were preparing to pull out and that the rest of the troops would be going with them,' said Docherty. 'And he must have known that we would take as many of our people as we could with us.'

Pritchard nodded. 'Right. But if that's the case, what was his long-term plan? He's stuck in Afghanistan, why does he think he can get something started in the UK?'

'Bin Laden brought down the twin towers and attacked the Pentagon from a cave in Afghanistan,' said Shepherd.

'But Bin Laden was a master strategist,' said Pritchard. 'He played terrorism like a game of chess. They don't call Baloch "the Butcher" because he's subtle.' He pointed at the picture of Javid. 'And Javid got into the UK because the Russians hacked the MoD database. So are the Russians running him? He couldn't have got into the UK without them. Then he meets with Sayyid in Scarborough. So did the Russians get Javid into the UK for Baloch? Are they helping him? Or is it just a coincidence and this whole investigation is a waste of time?'

Shepherd shrugged. He wasn't sure if the question was rhetorical, but either way he didn't have an answer.

'And if this is jointly planned, what on earth are they up to and why is it taking so long? It's been almost a year. If they planned on a bomb attack, that's not going to take more than a few months to put together. A marauding terrorist attack – well you just buy your knives and you're good to go. What could they be doing that takes this long?'

'Well whatever it is, it's getting ready to go, obviously,' said Docherty. 'The fact that Sayyid has left his family is proof of that.'

'Are there any major events coming up? Party conferences, G7 meetings, that sort of thing? There's nothing I'm aware of.'

'Maybe it's not an event. Maybe it's a person or people they were waiting for,' said Shepherd.

Pritchard looked at him inquisitively. 'Explain?'

'Well, we got Sayyid and his family out before the airport closed. And Javid got out not long after. But what if there were others who weren't so lucky? Getting men out using fake ARAP profiles wouldn't be easy. First they'd have to track down the genuine applicant and take him out. Then they'd have to change the details on the MoD database. Some might have been done quickly but others would have taken time. And of course time ran out, didn't it? When Biden became president he set a departure deadline of September the eleventh and everyone was working to that. Except the Taliban surge from the north caught everyone by surprise and the US were out by the thirtieth of August.'

Pritchard nodded. 'Some of the men being smuggled out with the fake ARAP profiles got trapped in Afghanistan, is that what you're suggesting?'

'Exactly. There were thousands of people still outside the airport as the final Americans flew out. The last few days were a logistical nightmare. As you know, we left hundreds of genuine translators behind. It makes sense that the fake ones were also blocked from flying. With no obvious way for them to get out, HM Government's advice was to get to a neighbouring country and arrange to fly to the UK from there, which was obviously a lot easier said than done. Pakistan, for instance, closed its borders within days. Anyway, the only option for them was to make their way to Pakistan, Iran, Turkmenistan, Uzbekistan or Tajikistan. Most of them were refusing to allow in refugees, but with the right paperwork and big enough bribes they might have been able to persuade the border guards to let them through. If they managed to clear that hurdle they'd then have to get to the British Embassy and get them to arrange a flight to the UK. All that would take time. A lot of time.'

'They've been waiting for the whole team to get here, is that what you think?'

'I think it's possible,' said Shepherd. 'And if that's the case, we don't have to look at every single Afghan who came over under ARAP. The final one probably came over during the last few days, a couple of weeks at most. And there probably won't be more than a dozen or so.'

Pritchard nodded. 'I can't fault your logic.'

'I'll get on it straight away,' said Shepherd.

'What about bringing in the Russia Desk, see if they have any thoughts on who might be involved?'

'I'll do that,' said Shepherd. 'I can take a look at new faces they've spotted.'

'What's your gut feeling on this?'

'I think it's big. I think a lot of planning has gone into this, they wouldn't put that amount of time and effort into a machete attack or a single suicide bomber or anything like that. It'll be what the IRA used to call a spectacular.'

'But whatever it is, it's not time dependent, right?'

'It could be an event that happens every year, I suppose. They missed it last year but it's coming around again. But as you said, there's nothing obvious in the calendar. On that point, do you think you could get me a list of the prime minister's forthcoming appointments, anything that would take him outside Downing Street? Also any venues that members of his Cabinet will be attending.' He shrugged. 'Maybe the Royal Family, and the likes of Tony Blair. Anyone who might be a jihadist target.'

'You're casting your net widely, aren't you?'

'Whatever they're planning is big, I'm sure of that. Now it might well be a major civilian target – a shopping centre, train station, airport – but it could also be a specific target, so I'd like to know what their options are.'

'I'll get someone to get you that information,' said Pritchard. 'Okay, well full steam ahead, obviously. I'll leave you to it, but keep me in the loop.' He headed out and closed the door behind him.

'He looks worried,' said Docherty.

'Yeah. It was MI5 that brought Sayyid out of Afghanistan, so if he's behind a major terrorist attack then he'll have a lot of flak to deal with.'

'It's not his fault, is it? If anything it was MI6 that did the damage by hiring Sayyid in the first place.'

'The press won't see it that way. Whenever there's a terrorist incident the papers take great delight in pointing out when a perp was known to the security services.' Shepherd shrugged. 'Let's just make sure it doesn't come to that, shall we?'

MI5's Russia Desk was overseen by a former Oxford don by the name of Gilbert Nicholson, but he was on a six-month sabbatical and his place had been taken by his number two, Robert Elliott. Elliott had joined MI5 straight from university and his fluency in Russian and Polish meant he had spent almost all of his career on the Russia Desk. He was in his late forties, his hair was greying but he was still trim and fit and could often be found arriving at Thames House in running gear with his suit and brogues in a backpack.

Elliott had moved into Nicholson's office, a glass cubicle in the centre of a large open-plan room that contained more than twenty pods and a hotdesking section with spaces for up to a dozen officers. Nicholson had left his personal photographs and mementos in the office as if trying to show that his absence was only temporary. When he had applied for his sabbatical, Nicholson had claimed he was going to research Russian military techniques of the early twentieth century, but the office gossip was that he was on an extended narrowboat holiday, exploring the country's canal network with his wife and two red setters, Lenin and Trotsky.

Shepherd introduced Docherty and Elliott waved them to a low L-shaped sofa in the corner of the office. 'We think we've got a jihadist cell about to get very busy,' said Shepherd as they sat down. 'Two Afghan jihadists that we've identified, but almost certainly more. The thing is, we know that the Russians have been instrumental in getting at least one of the jihadists into the country. Which means there's the possibility that they have a Russian handler, or at the very least a facilitator.'

'The Russians and the Taliban working together on a terrorist operation?' said Elliott. 'That's dangerous.'

'Would it make sense?'

'From the Russians' point of view, yes it would,' said Elliott. 'There's nothing they like more than causing mischief here in the UK. Their agents have carried out a fair number of assassinations on British soil, as you know. And obviously it would win them brownie points with the Taliban at a time when the country is looking at divvying up its mineral rights. Putin is a devious bugger. The Russians had already been helping the Taliban by supplying them with weapons and intel right throughout most of the war. But as always Putin has been playing all sides against each other.'

'How so?' asked Shepherd.

'It's his nature,' said Elliott. 'Former KGB, he can't help himself. So on the one hand he's cosying up to the Taliban, but at the same time he's working with the Pakistanis to strengthen their border with Afghanistan. He's also increased his security cooperation with India, ostensibly to counteract terrorism and narcotics trafficking. That's a laugh because Putin is doing everything he can to push illicit drugs into Europe and the States. He's carried out military exercises with Uzbekistan and Tajikistan and he's ordered Rosoboronexport to sell Central Asian countries bordering Afghanistan whatever arms and equipment they want.'

'Rosoboronexport?' Shepherd repeated.

'Putin set it up to handle all defence-related sales,' said Elliott. 'Now it's one of the biggest arms dealers in the world. So he's selling – or more likely giving – weapons to the Taliban, and at the same time he's arming Afghanistan's neighbours.' He grinned. 'Not that the Taliban need much

Russian equipment at the moment, the Yanks left behind billions of dollars of state-of-the-art weaponry.' He smiled. 'I sometimes wonder if Putin has a big wall chart somewhere with all his devious plans scrawled on it. I can't see how he can keep track of all his double-dealing. Anyway, you think the Russians are helping the Taliban to pull off a terrorist attack in the UK?'

'It's a theory we have, but we're a bit short on hard evidence at the moment,' said Shepherd. 'Is there a precedent?'

'Well yes, now you come to mention it, there is,' said Elliott. 'Yuri Andropov was head of the KGB back in 1972 and he was behind a shipment of machine guns, rifles, pistols and ammunition for the IRA. He sent it on a ship named Reduktor. He submitted a paper to the Central Committee of the Communist Party entitled "Plan for the Operation of a Shipment of Weapons to the Irish Friends". And he arranged for members of the IRA to fly to the Soviet Union for training. More recently we've seen the Russians trying to fan sectarian violence in Northern Ireland through social media. It's small scale but persistent. But helping the Taliban to carry out a terrorist attack on British soil . . .' He grimaced. 'That would be major, obviously. And a first.'

'Presumably the Russians wouldn't want it known that they were helping Taliban terrorists, right?' said Shepherd.

'They'd have nothing to gain and everything to lose if it became known,' said Elliott. 'Putin's quite content for it to be known that assassinations of his enemies abroad are at Moscow's behest. Poisonings, so-called suicides, the radiation hits – he knows that fingers are going to be pointed at him and he relishes it, because he knows it puts the fear of god into his enemies. If he can get to you in a Mayfair hotel bar or a cafe in Salisbury then he can get to you anywhere. But to be caught planning terrorism in the UK, well that's a whole different ballgame.' Elliott shrugged. 'Mind you, after what he did in the Ukraine, he clearly doesn't care what the world thinks. And he's already said that he regards the British as being at war with Russia because of the help they gave the Ukraine.'

'If it is the Russians, it's unlikely to be anyone from the embassy who's running it, right?'

'I'd say that's a fair assumption,' said Elliott.

'How about I tell you what we have so far and you can tell me if you can think of anyone who fits the bill.'

Elliott nodded and leaned back. 'I'm all ears.'

'One of the jihadists was an MI6 interpreter out in Kabul. We brought him and his family back to the UK in August last year. Shortly afterwards another interpreter was brought into this country. But he turned out to be an imposter. The Russians had used a honey trap on an MoD data analyst and got access to the mainframe.'

'Ah, yes, I remember that honey trap,' said Elliott. 'Gilbert oversaw the case but I saw all the files. Elly Weigel, using the name Anna Schneider. One of FSS's hottest babes. She's back in Berlin now.'

Shepherd nodded. 'At the time we thought she was just taking intel on ARAP applications which the Russians were passing on to the Taliban. But it's become clear now that they used a Trojan virus to get into the mainframe and rewrite the data to allow jihadists to get into the UK.'

'Now that is impressive,' said Elliott, raising his eyebrows.

'They got one guy in that we know of and he met the MI6 interpreter, then vanished. That was last year. We've no idea how many others came in under false names but the MI6 interpreter has just gone dark so we think they're now ready to complete their mission.'

'But no link between your MI6 interpreter and the Russians?'

'None that we know of. He was being run by a Taliban warlord. It's possible the warlord had a Russian connection but we don't have the specifics and the way things are going in Afghanistan we're not likely to make any progress on that front.'

'So we'd be looking at a Russian who was here last August and who is still here?'

'He could have gone back and forth.'

'It's unlikely they'd use anyone from the FSS or the Foreign Intelligence Service because if they were blown that's a direct link to the Kremlin. The heads of both the FSS and the FIS report directly to Putin. I suppose it's possible that they might use the Main Intelligence Directorate, GRU – that's Russia's largest foreign intelligence agency. Their director reports to the chief of the general staff and the minister of defence. That would give Putin a measure of plausible deniability.' He rubbed his chin. 'I can give you details of any possibilities, but where will that get you?'

'How many possibilities do you think there might be?' asked Shepherd.

'At any one time there can be up to two hundred case officers operating out of the Russian Embassy. Obviously they're not listed as case agents – they'll be press officers, consular officers, diplomats, security, trade officials, anything but what they really are. We reckon about half of all the diplomatic staff are engaged in intelligence work. We'll have them all on file; we photograph everyone going in and out, twenty-four seven. Plus we have various things in play inside the embassy.'

'You bug the Russian Embassy?' asked Docherty.

'I couldn't possibly say that,' said Elliott. 'But it's fair to say that they bug our embassies, all around the world. The problem is, while I can show you photographs of likely personnel and give you the CVs they've registered with the Home Office, they're obviously not going to admit to their intelligence backgrounds. Now, in many cases we do know exactly who they report to, but there are others where it's guesswork. The thing is though, if Putin really wants to keep some distance between his office and the operation, then as you say he'll probably make sure they stay well away from the embassy.'

'Which means what?' said Shepherd.

'Well, we generally consider that there are a hundred and fifty thousand Russian expats living in London, and that as many as half are Russian intelligence assets.'

'What?'

Elliott held up his hands. 'Not agents, assets. People who will give information to the Russian security services if asked. Or are on a watching brief for them. It's very different for us in Russia, of course. If we ask a Brit banker or salesman or academic to help us, the chances are he – or she – will tell us to go fuck ourselves. But if an FSS officer asks for help from a Russian here in London, it's difficult for them to say no. They'll have relatives back in Russia and if they don't cooperate then bad things will happen to them. The Chinese are even worse. You can assume that pretty much every Chinese expat in London has been spoken to by their intelligence agencies at some point.'

'You're saying any one of those tens of thousands of Russian expats could be handling the jihadists?'

'Can you think of a reason why that couldn't be the case?'
Shepherd sighed. 'I guess not.'

'I'm sorry, I don't want to take the wind out of your sails,
I just want to point out that identifying the handler isn't going
to be easy. And that's before we consider the deep cover operatives they use.'

'I'm listening.'

'For the really black ops they need operatives who absolutely
cannot be traced back to the president. So what they do is
keep an eye out for likely candidates during the initial phase
of training. More often than not they're former Spetsnaz who
want to change careers. When they spot candidates with the
right skill set, they let them finish basic intelligence training,
then they pull them out and build them a whole new legend.
They change their name, their history, everything. They're
issued with a new birth certificate, new passport, educational
qualifications, and a work history that will pass any investigation. They're rebranded as bankers, salesmen, journalists, pretty
much anything that would allow them to travel and work
overseas.'

'They're sleepers, is that what you mean?'

'Some are sleepers, they stay in place and wait to be used,
others travel around as and when needed. We know of half a
dozen who are ostensibly employed by Rosoboronexport. That
gives them carte blanche to fly into the world's trouble spots.
Ditto the people they have on Pravda's books. Or RT UK. All
of them with valid visas and work histories.'

'And you have their details?'

'Some. Not all. It's an ongoing battle. We spot them, they're
withdrawn and placed elsewhere, they send in new faces. But
you see the problem, right?'

Shepherd nodded. 'Yes, unfortunately I do.'

'If you give me a name, or a face, there's every possibility that we can identify them. But if you're asking us to come up with names of potential handlers, there'll be hundreds.'

Shepherd looked over at Docherty. The MI6 officer grimaced. It wasn't what they wanted to hear, but it was the truth.

They went back to the operations room. Farah was there and she had brought them coffees and muffins. 'I spoke to the Pizza Hut where Sayyid used his card,' she said. 'They have CCTV but it gets wiped after ten days. I've had more luck with his ATM withdrawals. Santander and Halifax have been helpful, the others have said my applications are working their way through their systems.'

'If you get any pushback let me know and we can apply pressure through Pritchard's office.'

Farah nodded. 'I called them all again this morning and explained the urgency, so I'll give them until this evening to come through. In the meantime, I have four videos, all from Birmingham.'

'Excellent, show me,' said Shepherd.

She sat down at a terminal and logged on, tapped on her keyboard and sat back. 'This was a month ago, in the city centre.' A video began to play. It showed Sayyid, dressed in a black puffer jacket and a white skullcap, walking towards the ATM and making a withdrawal. As he walked away from the machine, he took out his phone.

'This is the same machine, six weeks ago.' She played a second video. Sayyid was wearing a long tunic and the same skullcap. Shepherd looked carefully at the background as the video played, but he didn't see a vehicle or anyone waiting for Sayyid.

The third video was a different ATM, in a shopping centre

by the look of it. 'In this one, you can make out somebody standing next to the machine,' said Farah. 'Of course it could just be somebody waiting.'

Shepherd watched the video. This time Sayyid was wearing a sweatshirt and jeans and an Aston Villa cap. Farah was right, there was a figure standing close to the machine, but all that could be seen was a vague shape. When Sayyid walked away, the shape vanished. 'I thought I'd contact the centre management and see what CCTV they have, if any. We know the date and time he used the ATM so we might be able to catch him on the centre's CCTV. Then we'd know for sure if there was anyone with him. And this one is interesting.'

She played a fourth video. This one was the view from an ATM in a Birmingham street. She tapped the side of the screen. 'There's a car parked here, a Prius, I think. You can't see for sure, but it looks to me as if there is somebody in the driving seat and that Sayyid exits from the passenger side. You can see the car move, just a bit.'

Shepherd watched the screen carefully. Sure enough, the bonnet of the car wobbled and a few seconds later Sayyid appeared. He stood in front of the ATM and made a withdrawal. 'Now you'll see him walk away, and shortly afterwards the car drives off. I can't be sure it's him in the front passenger seat, there are too many reflections off the window.'

They all watched carefully as Sayyid left the ATM and moved out of view. Farah was right, there was no way of seeing who was in the vehicle. 'So again I have the time and the date so I'm going to look for CCTV possibilities in the street, traffic lights and so on. Hopefully I'll be able to get a better view of the car and its occupants.'

'Really good work, Farah,' said Shepherd.

Farah beamed at the compliment. 'Thank you,' she said. Shepherd was fairly sure she was blushing.

Shepherd woke at seven-thirty and was in Thames House within an hour. He sat down in a pod and logged on to the MI5 system. There were half a dozen messages from Pritchard. Attached to the emails were a diary for the PM, diaries for four members of his Cabinet, and a list of all venues which would be visited by senior members of the Royal Family. 'More to come,' he said in the final email.

The door opened and Farah walked in. She greeted him, took off her coat, and placed it on the back of her chair. 'I've been promised council CCTV footage today.'

'That's good.' He opened the PM's diary and began looking through it. Most of his meetings were at Number 10.

The door opened again. It was Docherty. He grinned. 'Last man in gets the coffees, right?'

'Camomile tea for me,' said Farah.

'Your wish is my command,' said Docherty. He headed for the canteen.

Shepherd went through the PM's diary. Meetings, a conference, a cheese and wine party, a COBRA meeting, a phone call to the French president, a visit to a factory in Leicester. Busy, busy, busy. The next day was just as busy. He frowned when he recognised a place name. Enstone. The prime minister was attending a funeral there, in three days' time. Enstone was close to Chipping Norton, and Sayyid had driven by there on his visit to the Cotswolds in January. The prime minister was going to the funeral of Baron Heysham. Shepherd knew the name. He had been an MP and for a while had been Speaker of the House of Commons.

He opened up Google and tapped in 'Baron Heysham death'. Most of the top hits were newspaper websites. He clicked through to the *Daily Mail*. Baron Heysham – former MP and Speaker Ronald Heysham – had died in hospital after falling from a horse. He had been badly injured in the fall and had been taken to hospital in Oxford where he had suffered a heart attack. Heysham was seventy-eight years old, an experienced rider. He had fallen off his horse while riding on his estate and had been taken by ambulance to the hospital where he had later died. There were several photographs of him riding a horse and it was clear he was good at it, jumping over high fences and ditches. There were several pictures of him riding to hounds with a local hunt. There were also photographs of him sitting in the 13-foot-high Speaker's Chair in the House of Commons. One had been taken at the opening of Parliament and he was wearing a black satin robe trimmed with gold lace and a ceremonial wig.

Shepherd clicked through to the BBC's website. Their report from two weeks earlier had a satellite photograph of where the Baron had lived, and there was a red cross in the nearby woods where the accident had happened. Shepherd frowned as he stared at the map. He stood up and went over to the map on the wall that showed Sayyid's GPS movements. 'Something wrong?' asked Farah.

'No, not at all. I've just read that the PM will be visiting a village that Sayyid went to in January. Enstone. There's a funeral there.'

'Coincidence?'

'I'm not a great believer in coincidences.'

'Whose funeral is it?'

'Baron Heysham, a former MP.'

'How did he die?'

'He fell off a horse.'

'Are you thinking he was murdered? It doesn't sound like a jihadist attack. And if they had killed him, wouldn't they have claimed responsibility?'

Shepherd grimaced. 'It doesn't make sense, does it?' He went back to his pod and spent another ten minutes reading about the death. Then he Googled 'Baron Heysham funeral' and read through the details. He was to be buried at a local church in Enstone and the PM was expected to be there, along with former prime ministers Tony Blair, David Cameron and Theresa May.

He called Giles Pritchard and told him about the funeral, and that Sayyid had visited the area in January. 'Look, I don't believe that Sayyid's visit to Chipping Norton was a coincidence,' said Shepherd.

'I remember reading about the death at the time,' said Pritchard. 'It was an accident. And if it wasn't, if Sayyid had somehow managed to kill him, wouldn't the Taliban be falling over themselves to be taking the credit? And Ronnie Heysham wasn't an obvious target, was he? He hadn't been an MP for ten years or so. It seems to me that you're overthinking this.'

'It just feels wrong to me.'

'You think the visit in January was a recce and that he went back two weeks ago to carry out the killing?'

'When you say it like that I know it sounds crazy. But Enstone is a tiny speck on the map. I really don't buy that it's a coincidence.'

Pritchard didn't say anything for a few seconds, then he sighed. 'Do you want to go to Chipping Norton and take a look around?'

'I do.'

'Then I think you should. I trust your instincts.'

'I might take some back-up.'

'Whatever you need.'

Pritchard ended the call and Shepherd phoned Jimmy Sharpe. 'How are you fixed today, Razor?' asked Shepherd.

'Infiltration,' said Sharpe in his Glaswegian burr. 'Long-term penetration of a supposed right-wing terror group. It's early days so basically I'm sitting in pubs looking shifty.'

'Do you think your bosses would let me use you for a day? Today, that is?'

'I wouldn't even have to tell them,' said Sharpe. 'We've pencilled in a month for this and I'm owed days, so all good. What do you have in mind?'

'I need to go to Chipping Norton. I'm looking into the death of Baron Heysham. He fell off his horse and died in hospital the week before last.'

'MI5 is investigating riding accidents now?'

'I want to check that it was an accident,' said Shepherd. 'Can you have a quick word with the local cops and see who was on the scene? See if we can meet them for a chat.'

'Will do. How are we getting there?'

'I'll drive. Where are you?'

'Fulham.'

'Fulham's good. I've got to go back to Battersea to get my car. It's a two-hour drive on the M40 and I can pick you up on the way.'

Sharpe gave him the address and Shepherd ended the call. 'I'm going out for a while,' he told Farah.

'Enstone?'

'Yeah, it's just nagging at me.'

'I guess you have to go with your instincts.'

'They've never let me down in the past.'

'I get it,' said Farah. 'Look, I've checked the ownership of the hotel in Bayswater that Sayyid stayed at. It's owned by a Greek guy, has been for more than thirty years, so I think I'm okay to go and ask a few questions,' she said.

'Go for it,' said Shepherd. 'And tell Tony that I'll be in later. Tell him he can have my coffee.'

Shepherd took the lift downstairs, then hurried on foot to Battersea to collect his BMW. He sent Sharpe a text message to say that he would pick him up outside Fulham Broadway tube station and received an 'OK' back.

Sharpe was wearing a sheepskin jacket over a dark brown suit and had the look of a racetrack bookie. 'Nice jacket,' said Shepherd as Sharpe climbed into the passenger seat.

'It's what the best-dressed fascist racist is wearing these days.'

'Well it suits you.' Shepherd pulled away from the kerb and headed for the M40. 'So how's the operation going?'

Sharpe snorted softly. 'It's bollocks and everybody but the top brass knows it. It's just so that they can say that they're being even-handed and that terrorism isn't an Islamic thing. At one of the briefings I asked for a list of previous right-wing terror attacks and everyone looked at me like I'd farted. Islamic terrorists bomb tube trains and buses, decapitate squaddies in the street and slash civilians with machetes. To balance that we're infiltrating groups of middle-aged white guys who moan about the way the country is going to the dogs and who might, just might, nail a pig's head to a mosque door. It's racist trouble-making but it's hardly terrorism.

Unless of course you're a senior officer with his eye on a chief constableship.'

'Is that a word?'

'It is now.' Sharpe sighed. 'Seriously, these guys are all talk. They get a few drinks inside them and they vent. I'm supposed to record it and at some point they'll be charged with conspiracy to do something or other.'

'Racism is racism. It needs to be stopped. You know as well as I do that terrorist threats come from many sources, including the ones you're tracking.'

'OK, I hear you.' He grimaced. 'The problem is that now they're asking me to be an agent provocateur. I'm to start suggesting stuff they could do. Telling them how to get explosives. Guns. Whatever.'

Shepherd frowned. 'That's not good.'

'Tell me about it. You can see where it's headed, can't you? I gee them up, then point them in the direction of someone who can supply them with what they need. We film the buy and they all get sent down for twenty years, ten if they plead guilty. And the top brass can take the credit for thwarting a right-wing terrorist outrage, skipping over the fact that they initiated it.' He shrugged. 'That's why I'm in no rush.'

'Sorry, mate.'

Sharpe shrugged again. 'It is what it is. Anyway, I put in a call to the Chipping Norton cops, part of Thames Valley. They've no record of any investigation. He died in hospital in Oxford, and again there was no police investigation. Cause of death was heart failure brought on by a bad fall.'

'No police involvement at all?'

'He fell off a horse. Quite badly. Broke his hip and his leg and an arm. Somebody at the house called 999 but they only needed an ambulance. The next day he died in hospital of heart failure. Death certificate, signed, sealed and delivered. Police aren't interested, end of. So do you want to tell me why your Spidey sense is tingling?'

'It's complicated, and yes, it is a hunch. We're looking for a potential jihadist who has been in the country for a year or so. Guy by the name of Sayyid. We tracked a pay-as-you-go phone of his to the Chipping Norton area.' He grinned. 'And before you say anything, we've no evidence that he was a Jeremy Clarkson fan.'

'You think this Sayyid is behind Baron Heysham's death? Why? Was this baron a target?'

'He was an MP for twenty-five years, and he was Speaker of the House of Commons when the invasion of Iraq and Afghanistan was discussed in parliament, which might have made him a target. But you know as well as I do, just being an MP puts you in the firing line these days.'

'With a knife, yes,' said Sharpe. 'But who uses a horse to assassinate someone?'

'I know, I know. But if it isn't a killing then it's one hell of a coincidence.'

'Well, yes, but coincidences happen.'

'Which is fine,' said Shepherd. 'We take a run out, we satisfy ourselves that it is a coincidence, and then we can pop into the Diddly Squat Farm Shop and buy some Jeremy Clarkson home brew.'

'That works.'

Shepherd had met Sharpe more than twenty years ago when they both worked for an undercover unit run by the Met but operating country-wide. They had come from completely different backgrounds – Shepherd had been in the Paras and the SAS while Sharpe had walked a beat in Glasgow – but had clicked immediately. They had worked literally hundreds of undercover jobs together, first for the Met and then for the Serious Organised Crime Agency. They had instinctively understood each other's rhythms and idiosyncrasies and had played off each other in dozens of guises – hired killers, drug dealers, arms salesmen, terrorists, whatever was necessary. Shepherd had eventually moved on to work for MI5, Sharpe had stayed with SOCA until it had imploded under the weight of its own bureaucracy and was reborn as the National Crime Agency.

They chatted about old times during the two-hour drive, and caught up on their news, then got into a good-natured argument about the merits of football teams north of the border.

They reached the gates leading to the Heysham estate just before midday. They were close to the village of Enstone, about four miles east of Chipping Norton and fifteen miles north-west of Oxford. There was a tarmac drive that wound its way through landscaped gardens to the main house, a two-storey stone cube with tall chimneys and steps leading up to a double-height door. There was a terrace of four single-storey cottages to the left, and behind them a couple of stone barns. Shepherd brought the SUV to a stop, just outside the entrance to the driveway. There was a stone gatehouse to the left but it was unoccupied and the gates were open. There was a CCTV camera fixed to the top of the guardhouse, pointing at the approach to the gates. 'How do we play it, good cop, bad cop?' asked Sharpe.

'They'll be grieving for him and getting ready for the funeral, so I think sympathetic cop, caring cop will probably work best. Let's see who's in.'

'There's a widow, right?'

'Yeah, and three kids. Including a son who's now the sitting MP and rumoured to be in line for a Cabinet post. So we need to tread carefully.'

'Got you.'

They drove up to the house. There were a dozen cars parked in two rows, including two Land Rovers, a black Bentley, an Aston Martin and a Porsche. Shepherd parked some distance away, close to a Honda Civic that presumably belonged to a member of staff. As they climbed out of the SUV, a woman in her thirties opened the front door and peered at them. She was tall and thin and wearing a baggy pullover and tight jeans. 'Can I help you?' she called, in a voice that suggested they were trespassing and the dogs were about to be set loose.

Sharpe took his warrant card from his pocket and held it up as he walked towards her. 'Sorry to bother you, ma'am,' he said. 'Inspector James Sharpe, with the National Crime Agency. We're here about Baron Heysham's death.'

'Police?' She frowned. 'It was an accident.'

Sharpe stopped a few feet from her and put his warrant card away. Shepherd joined him. 'That's what we've been told, ma'am, but as Baron Heysham is a peer of the realm, there's a few extra checks we need to carry out. But we are absolutely not here to bother you, we just want to confirm what happened.'

'He fell off his horse and died in hospital,' said the woman. 'That's what happened.'

'Are you his daughter?' asked Sharpe.

'Daughter-in-law,' she said. 'I'm married to Gerald Heysham.'

Shepherd nodded. Gerald Heysham was the baron's son and the local MP. 'Were you here when it happened?' he asked.

'No. We were at home. Look, my mother-in-law is still very distraught and I need to be with her. Can you please come back some other time? Everyone is very upset, obviously, with the funeral fast approaching.'

'I absolutely understand, Mrs Heysham,' said Shepherd. 'We really don't want to bother you or your mother-in-law, but is there someone who could maybe talk Inspector Sharpe and me through what happened?'

The woman's jaw tightened, so Shepherd gave her his most reassuring smile. She gritted her teeth, and then pointed off to the side of the house. 'You can talk to Jo Hardy, she's our head groom. The stables are that way.'

'Thank you so much,' said Shepherd. 'And we are so very sorry about your loss.'

Mrs Heysham nodded, then closed the door. Shepherd and Sharpe walked in the direction she had pointed. 'How would you like to live in a house where you had a head groom?' asked Sharpe.

'I'm not a big fan of horses.'

'Me neither.' He looked around. 'How many gardeners do you think they employ?'

'I've no idea.'

'It would take one guy full-time just to cut the grass. Another two to keep the hedges neat. Did you see the topiary?'

'I did. Nice work.'

'And how many cleaners would you need inside?' He shook his head. 'I could never live in a place this big. How much do you think it's worth? Ten million? Fifteen?'

'Maybe. I guess it depends on much land it comes with.'

They smelled the stables before they saw them. It was a single-storey building with a flat roof and a cobbled yard in front of it. There were half a dozen stalls and three horses looked at them and snorted as they walked over. There was a Land Rover Defender parked at the side of the stables and an old Triumph motorcycle. They looked around but didn't see anyone.

'Hello!' shouted Sharpe. 'Jo Hardy?'

'Yes?' called a girl. 'Who's that?'

'Police.'

A girl with long chestnut hair appeared at one of the split doors. 'Police?'

'We just need a quick chat about the accident,' said Sharpe.

She undid the door and stepped out. She was wearing a tweed jacket over beige jodhpurs and her riding boots were smeared with mud.

'Jo, Mrs Heysham said we could talk to you,' said Sharpe. He showed her his warrant card. 'I'm Inspector Sharpe, and this is my colleague, Dan. We just wanted to ask you a few questions about Baron Heysham's accident.'

'Sure, okay,' she said, brushing a stray lock of hair from her eyes. A white horse stuck its head through the gap above the door and snorted at them. 'What is it you want to know?' she asked.

'Where exactly did it happen?'

'The North Wood,' she said. She pointed off to the left, towards an undulating field. 'About a half a mile that way.'

'Was anybody with him when it happened?'

She shook her head. 'No, Ronnie always rode on his own in the morning.' She saw the look of confusion on Sharpe's face and smiled. 'Sorry, we always called him Ronnie. He never used the title and didn't even like it when the staff called him Mr Heysham. He was Ronnie to everyone.'

'And do you have any idea why he fell off his horse?' Shepherd asked. 'Was he a good rider?'

'He was brilliant,' said Jo. 'He'd been riding for more than sixty years. And the horse was his regular mount. Jasper.'

'Could something have spooked Jasper?'

Jo shrugged. 'It's possible. Any horse can be spooked under the right circumstances. There are rabbits and foxes in the woods, adders and vipers sometimes. Stray cats. If something ran out and startled Jasper, then maybe. But Ronnie was such an experienced rider I can't see that he'd have been thrown.'

'Except he was,' said Sharpe.

'Yes,' said Jo. 'He was.'

'Can you show us where it happened?' asked Shepherd.

'Sure, of course,' said Jo. 'Now?'

'Yes, if you don't mind.'

The white horse tossed his head and snorted. 'Don't worry, I'll take you out soon,' said Jo, patting him on the nose. She checked that the door was bolted, patted the horse again, then walked across the yard. She pointed over at a wooded area to the north. 'He usually goes from here at a walk, then trots over the field there. There's a trail through the woods and Ronnie always liked to canter. Then he'd ride east to the stream and walk Jasper over it into the next field. We'd set up some jumps there and depending on how he felt he'd give Jasper a work out. Then he'd cross back over the stream and through the woods again. Jasper knew he'd be going home so he'd often gallop the last stretch.'

'And always the same time?'

'Eight o'clock sharp,' said Jo. 'Back between nine and ninethirty. Barbara is a late riser and they would usually have breakfast together at ten.'

'Barbara would be his wife?' said Sharpe. He winced and corrected himself. 'Ex-wife.'

'I think widow is the word you're looking for,' said Shepherd.

'Yes, Barbara is Lady Heysham. She's distraught, obviously. They had been married for more than fifty years.'

They were following a path that had been formed from years of horses being ridden back and forth. Jo was striding towards the woods. Shepherd could just about keep up with her but Sharpe was soon falling behind. The path wasn't wide enough for them to walk together so they had to stick to single file.

'He always rode on his own? He didn't like company?'

'Ronnie always said it helped him get ready for his day. Just him and Jasper. He said it cleared his mind. Do you ride?'

'I can ride, but I wouldn't say I was good in the saddle,' said Shepherd. 'I wouldn't feel safe jumping, that's for sure.'

'It's the best feeling in the world,' said Jo. 'When the horse understands you and you understand the horse, it's as if the two of you become one. When you gallop, it's as if you're the one galloping, you can almost feel the ground under your feet.'

'You get to ride a lot?'

'Every day,' she said. 'There are six horses in the stable and they all need exercising, so we take them out in the afternoons and evenings.'

'Over the last few weeks, did you ever see strangers on the land? Someone who shouldn't be here?'

'Not really,' said Jo.

'Not really?'

'Well, there's always people stopping for a picnic at the weekends. It's really pretty around here and they don't realise that it's private land. Or they know and they don't care. And we get dog walkers. We're a fair walk from the village but if it's a nice day sometimes you'll get people letting their dogs play in the woods.'

'And Ronnie didn't mind?'

'He was fine so long as they didn't do any damage. He was a lovely man, live and let live he'd always say.'

'And what about security?'

She stopped and turned to look at him. 'Security?'

'Bodyguards? Police?'

She smiled and shook her head. 'You clearly don't know the first thing about him.' She started walking again and Shepherd followed her. 'Everybody loved Ronnie,' she said. 'He didn't have an enemy in the world.'

'He used to be an MP, and these days MPs are targets for anyone with a grudge and a knife.'

'Not Ronnie,' she said. 'My dad never voted for him, but he respected him. Liked him, even. Once my dad had a problem with the council, they wouldn't give his shop a licence he needed, so he went to one of Ronnie's surgeries. He took me with him, I was only six. I always remember Ronnie in his green tweed suit and his big moustache and the way he made a point of standing up and shaking my dad's hand. Then my dad started off by saying, "I've never voted for you, Mr Heysham, but I need your help," and Ronnie listened and then promised to get it sorted, which he did.'

'I get it,' said Shepherd.

'He was a great MP, same as his father before him, and his grandfather too. It's in the blood. So no, Ronnie never needed security, he'd have laughed at the idea.'

They reached the edge of the woods and they stopped to let Sharpe catch up. There was sweat on his brow and he was breathing heavily. He grinned ruefully at Shepherd. 'Are we nearly there yet?'

Shepherd laughed. 'You need to get out more, Razor.'

'Razor?' repeated Jo.

'Razor Sharpe,' said Shepherd. 'Jimmy really, but his friends call him Razor.'

'That's funny,' she said.

They stood and looked back at the house. 'So that's, what, half a mile?' said Sharpe.

'Pretty much,' said Jo.

'And he'd always come this way?' said Shepherd.

'Regular as clockwork.'

'Okay, so show us where it happened.'

Jo took them into the woods. It was a mixture of oak, horse chestnut and sycamore. It looked like wilderness but Shepherd could see that it had been expertly managed. The mature trees were well apart so that there were gaps in the canopy overhead to allow plenty of light for the bushes and flowers at ground level. Saplings had been planted and there were plenty of grassy glades. Shepherd could understand the attraction to picnickers.

The track was about five feet wide, peppered with horseshoe tracks, so there was enough room for Shepherd to walk alongside Jo.

'It's beautiful,' said Shepherd.

'Isn't it? And it's an awesome ride. The horses love it. You can come down here at a canter easily, and as I said, on the way back Jasper would be galloping home.'

They walked a couple of hundred yards into the wood and then Jo began looking around, getting her bearings. Eventually she stopped. 'Here,' she said. She pointed at the ground. There were dozens of shoe and boot prints. Four people. Maybe five.

'Were you the first person here?'

Jo nodded. 'Yes. And when I saw he was hurt, I called 999.'

'But the house is a long way from here, how did you know he'd fallen?'

'Oh, I wasn't at the house.' She pointed to the north-east, through the trees. 'I was over there, mending a gate with Jack.'

'Jack?'

'Another of the grooms. Well, he's more of a handyman, he does odd jobs as and when needed, and helps me with the horses.'

'Can you show me where you were?'

'Of course.' She led him through the undergrowth, threading her way around bushes until they emerged from the wood on to a rutted track wide enough for a vehicle. The track ran alongside a wooden rail fence that was bordering a pasture. To the left was a five-bar wooden gate. She took them over to it. 'A hinge had rusted and the catch wasn't holding so we put on a new hinge and new catch.'

'And what happened?' asked Shepherd.

'It was just after nine. We heard Ronnie galloping and then Jasper snorting and then Ronnie shouted and we heard a thud. We weren't sure what had happened and then Jasper came running out of the wood. I shouted to Jack to get Jasper and I ran to the track. Jack got hold of Jasper and tied him to the fence and he joined me.'

'Show me where you went.'

'Okay.' Jo went back into the woods to the path. Shepherd and Sharpe followed her.

'And where was he?' asked Shepherd when they reached the track.

'Here,' said Jo, pointing.

Shepherd looked around, and then back to where she was pointing. 'Then what did you do?'

'I knelt down to see if he was okay, but he was unconscious. He was breathing so his airway was clear. But his left leg was obviously broken, I could see the bone sticking out.'

'And which way was he lying?'

She frowned. 'What do you mean?'

'Where was his head? And where were his feet?'

'Ah, I see.' She pointed at the track. 'His head was here. His feet were there.'

'That must mean that he fell backwards, right?'

'I see what you mean. Yes. He must have. So, Jasper must have reared up?'

'That's what I was thinking,' said Shepherd. 'If the horse had stopped sharply then he would have gone over the top. And if the horse had swerved off the track then he would have fallen to the side. He was lying in the middle of the track, right?'

'Yes. He was.'

'So Jasper must have reared up and he fell back. Was he wearing a helmet?'

'Yes. He always had a helmet.'

Shepherd nodded. 'Okay. And you called 999, you said?'

'Straight away. As soon as I saw the broken bone. Because of where we are they said they'd send an air ambulance, but there'd be a delay as their helicopter was busy. So I told them they could drive down the track from the main road, and that's what they did. They were here within fifteen minutes. Ronnie was unconscious the whole time. The paramedics couldn't wake him up and they took him to North Cotswolds Hospital in Moreton-in-Marsh. They did some X-rays and scans there before deciding he should be moved to the JR.'

'JR?' repeated Shepherd.

'The John Radcliffe Hospital in Oxford,' she said. 'It's the main hospital in the county, about twenty-five miles away.'

'And did you go with him, in the ambulance?'

She shook her head. 'They said only family could travel in the ambulance. I went back to the house with Jasper.'

'And Jack went with you?'

'Yes.'

'And at any point did you see anyone else, in the wood or the field? Or a vehicle of any sort?'

'No, why?'

'Just trying to put a picture together of what happened,' said Shepherd. 'Look, you've been very helpful, thank you so much. We won't take up any more of your time.'

'I'll take you back to the house.'

'No, that's okay. Razor and I will take a look around. Just to get the lie of the land.'

Jo looked confused but she forced a smile and headed along the track.

'Your Spidey sense still tingling?' said Sharpe as they watched her go.

'Humour me,' said Shepherd. He walked off the track and looked at a towering sycamore tree. There was a thick branch about eight feet above the ground, running parallel to the track. He narrowed his eyes as he stared at the branch. Sharpe stood next to him, trying to work out what he was looking at. Shepherd walked over to the tree and slowly walked around it, looking up at the branch and down at the ground. Sharpe followed him, still bemused.

Shepherd peered at the other side of the track. There was another tree there, this one a spreading horse chestnut tree, directly opposite the sycamore. He walked over to it and Sharpe followed. Shepherd walked around the tree slowly, staring at the trunk, then looked up at a branch a few feet above his head. 'Give me a leg up, Razor,' he said.

'Say what now?'

Shepherd pointed up at the branch. 'I need a closer look.'

'Have you seen the state of your shoes?' He shook his head disdainfully. 'Now I see why you asked me to come.'

'Bloody hell, Razor. Fine. You go up and tell me what you see.' He linked his fingers together and bent down. Razor put his right foot on to Shepherd's hands, put his own hands against the trunk to steady himself and then let Shepherd boost him up the tree. After a few seconds, Shepherd grunted. 'What do you see?'

'A squirrel,' said Sharpe. 'Staring at me like he wants to steal my nuts.'

'Razor, mate, I'm not doing this for fun. Am I right or not?'

'Yeah, you're right. Something has been tied around the trunk and over the branch. A rope, probably. Lots of abrasions, some broken bark.'

Shepherd lowered him down and wiped his hands on his trousers as he went back to the track.

'Someone tied a rope to that tree, and ran it across the track and looped it over the branch of the other tree,' said Sharpe. 'Probably placed it on the ground and either covered it with soil or leaves. As the horse approaches they pull harder on the rope and the rider fell off.'

'You ought to be a detective,' said Shepherd with a grin.

'Great plan, but it didn't work,' said Sharpe. 'Not if the plan was to make it look like he'd died in a riding accident. Death was never guaranteed, was it, not if he always wore a helmet?'

'They – assuming it was more than one person – didn't have time to follow through,' said Shepherd. 'They knocked him off the horse, then they could have broken his neck or whatever, to finish him off, but it would still look like an accident, as if the fall had killed him. But first things first, they have to take down the rope. That's why I'm thinking more than one, because I don't see them bringing a ladder with them. The rope is a dead giveaway so they start taking that down, then they hear Jo and Jack so they have to get the hell out of Dodge. If they're seen then the whole operation is blown.'

'And they didn't get the chance to finish the job? They had to leave him lying there, still alive.'

'Exactly.'

'Now what?' said Sharpe.

'They must have come here early in the morning. Before dawn maybe. There'd always be a chance that he wouldn't ride so I think they'd stay hidden until they saw him ride out. Then they'd set the rope and wait for him to gallop back. The rope was tied to that tree and looped over that branch, so I'd say they stayed this side of the track.' He began to walk through the bushes, his eyes scanning left and right.

'And they must have been watching him before they set the trap,' said Sharpe. 'For days. Weeks maybe. To make sure that there was a pattern. If Ronnie came with another rider, for instance, or if he changed his route.'

'Yeah, that sounds right.'

'That means they must have parked not too far away.'

'Not necessarily. They could have been dropped at the road and walked along the track. Then been picked up later. Hello, here we go.' He pulled at a spreading rhododendron bush with purple flowers. The inside of the bush had been hollowed out and the ground flattened. There was enough space for two men to lie side by side. Shepherd looked back at the track. It could be seen clearly enough. 'Okay, they stake out the wood for days or even weeks until they know there's a pattern. One guy could have done that initially. Once they know when Ronnie's vulnerable, two of them come back before dawn. They hide here and wait for him to ride by. They set up the rope trap and wait for him to come back. They spring the trap, they start to untie the rope but then Jo comes charging through the wood so they have to hide. I'm guessing they hid here until the paramedics came and took Ronnie away with them. Once it had all calmed down they get picked up and they're out of here.'

'Then they go to the hospital, is that what you think? So he didn't die from natural causes?'

'The hospital is our next stop,' said Shepherd. 'But yeah, this doesn't look like an accident to me.'

The John Radcliffe Hospital was a collection of six and seven-storey buildings – some covered with blue tiles, others white – on Headington Hill, on the outskirts of Oxford. It was the area's main teaching hospital and the major trauma centre for Thames Valley, and Oxford Children's Hospital and Oxford Eye Hospital were also on the site.

Shepherd parked and walked into the main building with Jimmy Sharpe. Shepherd let Sharpe do the talking. Sharpe showed a receptionist his warrant card and asked to speak to the doctor who had dealt with Baron Heysham after his accident. The receptionist tapped on her computer and shook her head. Sharpe asked her to try Ronnie Heysham.

'There was a Ronald Heysham,' she said. 'I'm afraid he passed away.'

'We know,' said Sharpe. 'That's why we need to talk to the doctor who treated him.'

The receptionist nodded and tapped on her computer again. 'It was Dr Gupta who treated him in the emergency department.' She tapped on the keyboard again. 'He's there today, it might be best if you go over there.'

'We'll do that, thank you. What is Dr Gupta's first name?'

'Chandra. If you turn right out of the main entrance and then right again at the end of the building, you'll see the emergency department. Just look for the line of ambulances.'

They thanked her and headed out. She was right about the ambulances, there were half a dozen lined up, their engines running. There was another reception desk and another receptionist, this one slightly more stressed than the first. Sharpe showed her his warrant card and said they needed to talk to Dr Gupta. 'He's very busy,' she said curtly.

'I'm sure he is,' said Sharpe. 'We only need a couple of minutes of his time.'

The receptionist sighed. 'Take a seat and I'll let him know you're here. But I can't promise anything.'

'You're an angel,' said Sharpe, without a trace of sarcasm in his voice.

They sat down with their backs to a wall festooned with NHS notices. There were a dozen people waiting but nobody seemed in distress. Most people were staring at their phones. A woman was comforting a small boy who had a bloodstained bandage on his hand and within minutes a nurse took them away down a corridor.

'I really don't like hospitals,' Sharpe whispered.

'No one does, Razor.'

'No, I really feel uncomfortable. You can pick all sorts up in a hospital. Stuff that can kill you.'

'We won't be here long,' said Shepherd.

In fact they had to wait almost half an hour before Dr Gupta appeared. He came down the corridor, looked around, then strode over to where they were sitting. He was in his thirties, slightly overweight, and his tight green scrubs emphasised his paunch. He had a bright red stethoscope around his neck. 'You wanted to see me?' he asked.

Sharpe and Shepherd stood up. The doctor kept his hands on his hips so there was no question of whether or not they should shake hands. 'We just need to ask you about a patient you treated ten days ago,' said Sharpe, producing his warrant card. 'He fell off his horse. Broke his hip and his leg. And his arm.'

'Yes, Mr Heysham. Or Baron Heysham I suppose we should call him. My first peer of the realm.' He frowned. 'He took his fall in Chipping Norton. You're from London?'

'It's just for the record,' said Sharpe. 'It's a House of Lords thing.'

'It was a straightforward accident,' said Dr Gupta. 'I got him stabilised here and then we had Mr FitzGerald from the orthopaedic department down to take a look at him.'

'The injuries were bad?' said Shepherd.

'Yes, he'd fallen badly, and given his age the damage was quite severe. Mr FitzGerald wanted to transfer him to the Nuffield Orthopaedic Centre, just down the road. But they didn't have a bed available so we had to move him to the JR's own orthopaedic department. They had a bed in ward 6b so we sent him there. The plan was to manage his pain and keep him under observation at the JR until a bed became available at the Nuffield and they would operate there. The following day there was still no bed available. We were still trying to move him but then he passed away.'

'What state was he in?'

'When he came in? He was badly injured, obviously. He had a major break in his left femur and we had to reset the leg as a matter of urgency, and then there was a fair amount of stitching to do. He lost a pint or so of blood so we had him on plasma. His hip was broken in two places, and there was damage to several of the discs in his back. As you say, his arm was fractured but that was relatively minor. Anyway, we patched him up and stabilised him but he was going to need major surgery. Mr FitzGerald said we were looking at a plate with four bolts in the hip and a rod with eight bolts in the femur.'

'I suppose if he was a horse you'd have had to put him down,' said Sharpe.

Shepherd winced at the black humour, but the doctor just smiled. 'You're not far off the truth,' he said. 'Falls like that when you're in your seventies are a serious business. We can fix it, we have the technology, but seventy-eight-year-old bones are brittle and they take a long time to heal. Apparently he was galloping when it happened?' He shook his head. 'Someone that age shouldn't even have been on a horse, but if he had wanted to ride, a slow walk would have been the limit.'

'But were the injuries life-threatening?' asked Sharpe.

'You know he died, right?' said the doctor, his voice loaded with sarcasm.

'That's why we're here.'

'Well, doesn't that answer your question?'

Sharpe grimaced. 'Well, not really, no. He was alive when

you worked on his leg, and when you sent him to the ward. Was he conscious at that time?'

'He was regaining consciousness when we had him in the emergency room, but he was in a lot of pain. We treated the pain and that pretty much put him to sleep.'

'And the cause of death was heart failure?' said Shepherd.

'Yes, during the second night he was here. He'd undergone major trauma, he was on a high dose of painkillers, there was some blood loss, it was just too much of a strain for his heart. But it was the fall that killed him. Or more accurately, the damage caused by the fall.' His phone started to ring and he reached into his pocket and answered it. 'Right,' he said on to the phone. 'Yes. Now.' He ended the call and nodded at the two of them. 'I have to go,' he said.

'No problem,' said Sharpe. 'And thank you.'

The doctor was already hurrying away.

'What do you think?' Sharpe asked Shepherd.

Shepherd looked up at a security camera in the corner of the room. Its red light was blinking. 'We need to talk to hospital security,' he said.

As luck would have it, Jimmy Sharpe knew the deputy head of security for the NHS trust that managed the hospital. He made a call to the security office and was told that the deputy, Bob Tracey, would come down and talk to them.

'Not Spencer Tracey?' Sharpe had said but the woman on the other end of the line just repeated that his name was Bob. When Tracey came out of the lift and saw Sharpe his face broke into a grin. 'Well there's a blast from the past,' said Tracey. He walked over and hugged Sharpe. 'You're a sight for sore eyes, Razor. How many years has it been?' He was just over six feet tall with receding hair and square-framed glasses, wearing a dark blue pinstripe suit that looked as if it had been made to measure.

'Ten? Eleven,' said Sharpe. He nodded at Shepherd. 'This is my wingman, Dan.'

'Pleased to meet you, Dan.' He bumped fists with Shepherd.

'Spencer and I used to work on the Met a lifetime ago,' said Sharpe. 'He climbed the slippery pole and retired as a Chief Super.'

Tracey nodded. 'Left as soon as I had the pension locked in and walked straight into the job here.' He patted Sharpe on the back. 'And no one here calls me Spencer, but I'm guessing you're still Razor. You're not still with the Met are you?'

'NCA,' said Sharpe.

'How's that working out for you?'

'It's better than SOCA, but that's not saying much.'

'And what brings you on to Thames Valley's turf?'

'There was a death here the week before last. Baron Heysham. Peer of the realm.'

'That's right. Horse riding accident. I remember reading about it in the papers. So what's your interest?'

Sharpe looked around. 'Is there somewhere quiet we can talk?'

'Sure, let's go up to my office.' He took them to the lift and up to the top floor, then along a corridor to a large office with three young men in dark uniforms looking at a row of screens, each of which was divided into sixteen CCTV views.

'Nice set-up,' said Sharpe.

'Should be for what it cost,' said Tracey. 'We have cameras in all the public areas and the corridors. Not the rooms or treatment areas, there are privacy issues. The car parks are covered, obviously. And the lifts and stairwells. Close to four hundred cameras in all. And we have this state-of-the-art AI system that pulls up anything that might be of interest. It can pick up if a person is carrying a knife or a gun and flag it. It red-flags anyone running, signs of a struggle, someone loitering. That way our guys aren't always flicking between screens, the AI does the hard work.'

'Impressive,' said Sharpe.

'Coming to a street near you, sooner or later,' said Tracey. He took them through to his office, a twenty-foot cube with a window overlooking one of the car parks. There was a desk with a computer on it, and two small sofas set at a right angle around a glass-topped coffee table. He closed the door, sat on one sofa and waved for them to sit on the other. 'Anyway, how can I help you?'

'We have reason to believe that Baron Heysham's death wasn't accidental,' said Shepherd. 'And we'd like anything we say to you to stay within these four walls.'

'You're not a cop, are you?' said Tracey.

'Not now, no. But I was. Undercover mainly.'

'He's still one of the good guys,' said Sharpe.

'Okay, I can fill in the blanks. And of course, discretion etcetera etcetera.'

'He was brought in to the emergency room after a riding accident,' said Shepherd. 'We've been out to the scene and we think it was deliberate. We think someone tried to kill him while he was out riding, and when that didn't work they came here to finish the job. We've spoken to the emergency room doctor who treated him, and he says that Heysham was hurt but basically okay when he was taken to an orthopaedics ward. They were planning to transfer him to the Nuffield once a bed became available. And he obviously wasn't too bad or he'd have been in the ICU.'

'Okay,' said Tracey. 'Did he say which ward?'

'6b. Obviously what we'd like to do is take a look at any CCTV footage that you have.'

'And you seriously think someone came into the hospital and killed him?'

'I'm afraid so.'

'I don't see how they could get to the orthopaedics ward without being stopped.'

'We're assuming it was professional.'

'And how do you think they killed him?'

'The doctor said it was heart failure. There are plenty of drugs around that can mimic a heart attack. Are you able to access his records to see what time his death was reported?'

'Yes, I can do that.'

'Then we can work back from there to see who, if anyone, went into his room prior to his death.'

Tracey stood and went over to his desk. He sat down and tapped on his keyboard. 'The time of death was noted as five past one in the morning. That's when his alarm went off and by the time the nurses got to his bed he was dead.'

'Can you call up the video here?' asked Shepherd.

'Of course,' said Tracey. 'Give me a minute.' He tapped on the keyboard, peered at the screen, and then tapped again. 'Okay, here's the nurse.'

Shepherd and Sharpe got up and walked to stand behind Tracey's chair. He leaned back to give them an unobstructed view of the screen. It was showing a view of a hospital corridor. The camera was at an angle to three doors, all of them closed. There was a date and time code across the bottom. 01.04.00.

He pressed a key and the time code began to move forward. A male nurse in pale blue scrubs ran down the corridor. More female nurses followed, then a doctor in a white coat. They all ran into the room on the right of the screen. He stopped the video. 'Right, so at that point, Mr Heysham had just passed away,' said Tracey. 'I'll play it backwards from that point.'

He tapped on the keyboard again and the footage began to play in reverse. The doctor walked out backwards, then the nurses, then the male nurse. Then the corridor was empty for several minutes. When the time clicked to 00.57.06, two nurses walked backwards down the corridor, deep in conversation. Then at 00.55.22 the door to Heysham's room opened. Tracey stopped the video just as a man in a white coat appeared in the doorway, his back to the camera. 'This guy left Heysham's room at just after five minutes to one.'

'Can you show me him entering the room?' asked Shepherd.

'Sure,' said Tracey. He went back two minutes and then restarted the video. A man in a white coat walked purposefully towards Heysham's room. He was wearing a surgical mask and kept his face turned away from the camera. Tracey stopped the video as the man reached the door.

'Do you recognise him?' Shepherd asked.

'I don't, but then I don't know every member of staff. Plus we have doctors and specialists visiting all the time.'

'How long was he in the ward for?' asked Shepherd.

Tracey played the footage forwards at double speed as the man went inside and closed the door. Nothing happened for a while and then the door opened again. Tracey paused the video and peered at the time code. 'Ninety seconds,' he said.

'Clearly a pro,' said Shepherd.

'But the alarm didn't sound until ten minutes after he left,' said Tracey.

'Heysham was on a drip,' said Shepherd. 'He could easily have injected something into the IV bag or the tube, giving him plenty of time to get away. Can you show him walking down the corridor and going into the room again?'

'Sure.' He tapped on the keyboard, and the video played, showing the man walking down the corridor. He was wearing a white coat and had a stethoscope around his neck. He was completely bald and the lower part of his face was hidden by his surgical mask. He was heavy-set with slightly bowed legs that meant he swayed as he strode down the corridor. Shepherd frowned. There was something familiar about the man.

He reached the door to Heysham's room and put his hand out to grab the handle. As soon as Shepherd saw the rope-like scar on the man's hand he remembered where he had seen him before.

The man opened the door and stepped inside. The door closed and Tracey paused the video. 'Can you play it again and let me record it?' asked Shepherd.

'I shouldn't,' said Tracey. He grinned. 'But any friend of Razor's.'

Tracey rewound the footage and played it again. This time Shepherd recorded the man on his iPhone. Tracey let it play until the man emerged from the room and walked away.

'He knows exactly where the camera is,' said Sharpe. 'Definitely a pro.'

When Shepherd had finished recording he put his phone away. He and Sharpe walked around the desk. 'I think we're good, thanks for your help,' said Shepherd. 'And as I said, I'd be grateful if you could keep this to yourself.'

'Secret squirrel,' said Tracey, tapping the side of his nose. He took them back downstairs to reception, then fist-bumped them both. He stayed to watch them leave as if he wanted to make sure that they were no longer in the building.

'Nice guy,' said Shepherd as they walked to the car park.

'Yeah, a real straight arrow,' said Sharpe. 'He was in uniform for almost his entire career.'

'He'll keep quiet, will he?'

'Oh, sure. If he had any problems with that he'd have told us to our faces.'

'I get the feeling he didn't like being called Spencer,' said Shepherd.

'He's got no reason to complain,' said Sharpe. 'When he first started there were moves to call him Dick so really he got off lightly.' They reached the car. 'It looks as if they killed Baron Heysham. Why though? Because he was a peer of the realm? A member of the establishment? Because he used to be an MP?'

'Maybe all of the above.'

'But this isn't a jihadist thing, is it? No one has taken the credit and it's all being kept below the radar. This was an assassination. And the guy in the white coat, he's not Afghan. Even with the mask on, I could see that.'

'He's Russian.'

'Russian? How would you know that?'

'I've seen him before.'

'You and your memory. But why would the Russians want to kill a peer of the realm?'

'That, Razor, is a very good question.'

Shepherd dropped Sharpe in Fulham and drove back to his flat in Battersea. Parking near Thames House was always a nightmare and he knew from experience that his best option was to leave the car at home and catch an Uber to the office, or walk. He phoned Docherty when he was in the taxi and confirmed that he was in the operations room, and when Shepherd finally arrived it was with coffees and muffins. Docherty was sitting in front of a terminal looking at a CCTV recording that had obviously come from an ATM. He paused the video and took the offered coffee. 'Help yourself to a muffin,' said Shepherd, putting the bag on to Docherty's desk. He gestured at the screen. 'How's it going?' he asked as he sat down at the neighbouring terminal.

'Slowly but surely,' said Docherty. 'The banks are coming through. I've had twelve in so far. You can see Sayyid but that's all. Well, his wife was in one of the early ones when he withdrew money in Scarborough but once he was in Birmingham it's only him in view. But in some of them you can tell there's somebody with him, standing just out of view. Farah's still waiting on the council CCTV footage.'

Shepherd sipped his coffee. 'Remember those Russians we saw in the embassy in Kabul?'

'Sure.'

'What did you do with the pictures you took?'

'I put them in my report when I got back.'

'Was there any interest?'

'In the Russians? Not that I remember. I copied the Russia Desk in but I never heard anything back. Everyone was snowed under at the time.'

'Can I see the pictures?'

'We'd have to access the file and I can't do that remotely. We'll have to go across the river.'

'Let's do that,' said Shepherd.

'What's the story?'

Shepherd took out his phone and played the video from the hospital CCTV. Docherty watched the man in the white coat go into the room and leave shortly afterwards. 'This guy went in to Heysham's room, not long before he died of what they're referring to as natural causes.' He called up a screenshot of the man's scarred hand and showed it to Docherty. 'I thought I recognised the scar on his hand.'

Docherty frowned. 'Your memory's better than mine. But yes, we can go and check. Are the cops involved?'

'No, we're keeping a lid on it. I'll have to talk to Giles Pritchard, obviously.'

'It opens up a whole can of worms, doesn't it?'

'And some. But let's take it one step at a time.' He picked up his coffee and stood. 'We can drink as we go.' He grabbed a chocolate muffin from the bag.

It was a fifteen-minute walk from Thames House to the SIS Building in Vauxhall. There were two routes – north of the river along Millbank and then across the Vauxhall Bridge, or walking across the Lambeth Bridge and following the river along Albert Embankment. They went along the south route, passing the Tamesis Dock on the way. There was an underground tunnel running under the Thames from Whitehall to the SIS Building, but access was strictly controlled and Shepherd had never used it.

When MI6 had first announced they were moving to the green and cream building bordering the Thames, Shepherd had assumed it was some sort of false flag operation, that the garish building would be used as a decoy and the real work would be done in a secret location elsewhere. But no, the powers that be had decided that the Secret Intelligence Service would indeed be based in a landmark building that was so prominent that just six years after it opened the IRA were able to hit it with a rocket-propelled grenade.

The building – which had cost 150 million pounds, plus another 135 million for the land – was supposed to represent an ancient temple but had ended up looking more like a chunky wedding cake. The architects had given it sixty separate roof areas, a ridiculous extravagance in a building where business was supposed to be carried out behind closed doors and drawn blinds. Because it was such a high-profile target, the building was equipped with bomb-blast protection including triple-glazed security windows and emergency back-up systems, none of which had protected it against the IRA's RPG attack.

Docherty had to sign Shepherd in, then they passed through a metal detector arch. It was similar to the one in Thames House but without the note warning that firearms had to be declared. They went up in the lift to the sixth floor and along a corridor to a door which opened into a large open-plan office, with two dozen hotdesk workstations and a view across the river.

There was no one in the office, though there were bags on the chairs of two of the workstations and a half-eaten sandwich in front of another. Docherty sat down at a terminal and logged on, then tapped on the keyboard for a few seconds before sitting back and waving at the screen. 'There you go,' he said.

Shepherd pulled up a chair and sat down next to Docherty. There were two pictures on the screen. The one on the left was of the two Russians standing together in the British embassy corridor. They weren't looking at the phone; Docherty had been standing at the side and the men had been looking at Shepherd. The second picture was of the heavy-set Russian with the scar. He had his hand up and was turning his face away from the phone, and in doing so was revealing more of the scar on his hand. Shepherd nodded. 'Bingo,' he said.

'That's definitely him?'

Shepherd took out his phone, called up the screenshot of the scarred hand and showed it to Docherty. Docherty held it up next to the screen, compared the two, and nodded. 'Your memory is quite something,' he said.

Shepherd took back the phone and slipped it into his pocket. 'Did your Russia people identify him?'

Docherty tapped on his keyboard, studied the screen for a few seconds, then shook his head. 'The contents of my report were noted, but nothing was actioned.'

'Why wouldn't they at least check?'

'I guess because we were pulling out of Afghanistan, they'd be more concerned about our own people than a couple of Russians. And you've got to remember, most of our people were working from home at the time under the Covid restrictions. And the Foreign Office mandarin in charge was on holiday, as was our beloved foreign secretary.'

'Nobody was working?'

'You must have seen the stories in the papers. There were thousands of people in Afghanistan emailing for help and one junior civil servant at the Foreign Office reading them. He opened them all so that the prime minister could say they were all read, but nothing was done.'

'So your report didn't fall through a crack so much as into a bloody chasm,' said Shepherd.

'Do you want me to talk to them again, see if they can ID him?'

'No, let me run it by our Russia Desk,' said Shepherd. 'Let me see the photographs again.'

Docherty put them back on the screen and Shepherd took a picture with his phone.

'I'm sure that breaks the Data Protection Act and the Official Secrets Act,' said Docherty.

'Yeah, well I won't tell if you won't,' said Shepherd. He sent the picture to Janice Warren with a note: 'THIS GUY WAS IN OUR EMBASSY IN KABUL LAST AUGUST. RUSSIAN. MAYBE ROBERT ELLIOTT CAN HELP?'

After a few seconds she replied. 'URGENT?'

Shepherd sent her a smiley face and put his phone away.

Farah was tapping on a keyboard when Shepherd and Docherty got back to the operations room. She looked over at Shepherd, her eyes shining with enthusiasm. 'I was in Bayswater checking out the hotel that Sayyid stayed in. I think I might have something.' Her face broke into a grin. 'Actually I'm sure I have something.'

'Don't keep us in suspense,' said Shepherd, leaning against one of the tables.

'I spoke to the nephew of the owner and he was very helpful. They have CCTV but it's an old system and doesn't upload to the cloud, so everything is recorded over. There's nothing older than three weeks on their system. But he checked the booking records and as it happens the nephew was working the day they checked in, and he remembers them. I showed him a picture of Sayyid and he was a hundred per cent sure he checked in with two other Asian men. He remembers them because they wanted to stay in one room and he only had doubles. They had a bit of an argument but eventually they

agreed to pay for a double and a single. Then they wanted to
pay cash and the nephew said they had to pay by credit or
debit card. They've had problems with guests causing damage
or running up huge phone bills and then disappearing without
paying. Anyway, long story short they used a debit card and
I have the details. It was an Aspen card under the name of
Wajid Yasin. Almost certainly a refugee from Afghanistan but
I haven't checked with the Home Office yet.'

'That's good work, Farah, well done.'

She grinned. 'There's more. Down the road from the hotel
there's a Middle Eastern restaurant, Kimo's. I thought there
might be a chance they'd eaten there so I popped in for a late
lunch. Met a really nice Afghan waiter there. Young guy, he's
only been in the UK for three years, he's putting himself
through university. Anyway, I showed him Sayyid's picture and
he didn't recognise him, but they do have CCTV linked to
the cloud so he let me look at the footage for the time that
Sayyid was in London.'

Shepherd frowned. 'That's very amenable of him?'

'I told him that I was Sayyid's probation officer and I was
checking that he hadn't fallen back into bad habits.'

'Nice.'

'Anyway, Ali – that's his name – showed me the CCTV
footage and Sayyid was there, the evening of the day they
checked in. All three of them, in fact.' She opened her briefcase
and took out three printed sheets. 'I've got video of the footage
but Ali did these for me.' She passed them to Shepherd. 'The
quality isn't great, I'm afraid. They paid in cash so there's no
credit card receipt.'

Shepherd looked through the photographs. They were in colour
but they were grainy and blurred. One was a shot of three Asian

men walking into the restaurant. One was Sayyid, the other two were dark-skinned and bearded and wearing skullcaps. Another shot showed them sitting at a table. The camera angle meant he could see Sayyid and one of the men, and the back of the third man's head. The third photograph showed the three men leaving the restaurant. Shepherd passed them to Docherty. 'What do you think, Tony? Will facial recognition ID them?'

Docherty grimaced. 'Touch and go,' he said.

'I'll see what Janice Warren says,' said Shepherd. He flashed Farah a thumbs-up. 'You did really well, Farah. Really, really well.'

Farah beamed with pride. 'Thank you.'

'Set up two more whiteboards and put the new guys up. Hopefully Janice will be able to tell us which if either is Yasin.'

Shepherd used his phone to take pictures of the two men with Sayyid and sent them to Warren. 'QUALITY NOT GREAT BUT THESE TWO WERE WITH SAYYID. ONE MAY BE CALLED WAJID YASIN'.

She replied after a few seconds. 'OK'. And a sad face.

Five minutes later she called him back. 'Wajid Yasin was an easy find,' she said. 'He worked security for the British Embassy from 2009 until 2021. He left in March but was allowed on to the ARAP programme. He wasn't able to make it to the Kabul airlift but he managed to get into Pakistan. He arrived here in January this year.'

'Did any family come with him?'

Farah finished putting up the two whiteboards and used tape to stick the photographs to them.

'No, just him.'

'Can you send everything through to me? There's every chance that he's another ringer.'

'Of course. I'm doing it as we speak. We're still looking for a match for the other man at the table.'

'And any joy with the Russian?'

'I've spoken to Robert Elliott and he's working on it. I'll call you as soon as I hear anything.'

'Thanks, Janice.'

Shepherd ended the call and waved at Farah. He pointed at the picture on the first whiteboard that she had assembled. 'That's the one claiming to be Wajid Yasin,' he said.

'Excellent,' she said. She used a marker to write 'AKA WAJID YASIN' under the picture.

Shepherd logged on to the system and checked his messages. Warren had sent him a copy of the Yasin ARAP file, along with a note that the diplomat who had signed off on the application and supplied a reference for Yasin was in London on an intensive three-month language course at the Foreign Office's language centre, a fifteen-minute walk from Thames House. Shepherd printed off a copy of the ARAP form.

'Fancy a walk?' he asked Farah.

Shepherd and Farah walked by Westminster Abbey and the Houses of Parliament to get to the Foreign, Commonwealth and Development Office in King Charles Street, just around the corner from Downing Street. The massive classical building had been built in 1868 when Britannia truly did rule the waves. The building was later added to, first with the India Office and then with the Colonial and Home Offices. Britain no longer had an empire but the Foreign Office had more civil servants than ever before – more than 14,000 staffers working in London and overseas.

The diplomat they needed to talk to was Liz Maguire, and

according to the receptionist she was downstairs in the language centre. Shepherd and Farah were given visitor name badges and told that they could take the lift down to the basement where she would be waiting for them.

Maguire had shoulder-length chestnut hair and black-framed glasses and was wearing a dark blue suit. She smiled as the lift doors opened and introduced herself. 'Sorry if I seem a bit stressed, I'm in the middle of four hours of Mandarin teaching and the tones are making my head hurt,' she said. 'I'm due in Beijing in six weeks and I'm still far from proficient.'

'Huge difference between Beijing and Kabul,' said Shepherd.

Maguire shrugged. 'Pros and cons to both,' she said. 'How can I help you?'

Two young men in rolled-up shirtsleeves walked by, talking earnestly in an Eastern European language.

'Is there somewhere we can have a quick talk?' said Shepherd. 'Where we won't be overheard.'

'Of course.' She took them down a corridor and peeked through a glass panel in a door. A middle-aged man in a grey suit was sitting at a desk while a young woman with a blonde ponytail wrote in Russian on a whiteboard.

There were four students wearing headphones in the second office but the third wasn't being used, and Maguire ushered them in. There were two large whiteboards covered in what looked like Japanese writing and half a dozen chairs. Maguire closed the door behind them. She sat down and looked at them expectantly. Shepherd and Farah pulled up chairs and sat down in front of her. 'When you were in Kabul, you signed an ARAP form for one of the embassy's security guards.'

'I signed dozens of ARAP forms,' she said. 'Probably close

to fifty. Every man and his dog was trying to get out. In fact, joking apart, we did help get a number of dogs out. And cats.'

'It's one form in particular we're interested in,' said Shepherd. Farah opened her briefcase, took out Wajid Yasin's form and handed it to the diplomat.

Maguire frowned as she looked at the first sheet. 'Well I have to say, he doesn't look familiar,' she said. She looked at the second sheet. 'But I definitely filled in the form. Those are my details.' She looked back at the photograph on the first sheet. 'Wajid Yasin?' she said. 'The name is definitely familiar.' She looked up at Shepherd. 'Is there something wrong?'

'Yes, we think there is a problem. But not with anything you did. Try to forget about the photograph, just try to remember the name. Wajid Yasin. He was a security guard at the embassy between 2009 and March 2021. He left but then applied for the ARAP scheme.'

She nodded. 'There were a lot like that. Anyone who could come up with any sort of link to the embassy or the armed forces was knocking on our door.' She frowned as she looked at the first sheet. 'But yes, I do remember a Wajid. He was a sweet guy, always saluted me when he saw me. And he had such a big smile. But that's not him in the photograph.' She lowered the papers and looked at Shepherd. 'Yes, Wajid. His wife got ill and he said he had to nurse her. Leukaemia, I think. March? Yes, it was March 2021. Then of course the shit hit the fan and he asked the embassy if we could get him and his family out. The fact that he'd left made it a little difficult, but by August we were allowing pretty much anyone to come to the UK under ARAP. I remember one chap who only painted the embassy's outside wall, a two-week job back in 2010; we let him and his entire extended family in. So Wajid was a certainty.'

'He had children?'

'Oh, a big family. Six kids, I think. And we let his mother in as well. We couldn't have her left alone, could we?'

'Have a look at the reference on the last page.'

She flicked through the sheets and started to read. 'Oh, no, no, no,' she muttered. 'I didn't write this.' She started to shake her head as she read. 'That's not what I wrote. There's no mention of his wife. Or his children. Or his mother.' She looked up at Shepherd again. 'What's going on?'

He held out his hand and she passed him the papers. Shepherd gave them to Farah, who put them into her briefcase. 'It's complicated, but basically the MoD database was hacked and a number of ARAP files were altered.'

'But why would . . .?' Realisation dawned and her jaw dropped. 'Oh my goodness. They sent someone in Wajid's place?'

'We think so, yes.'

Her hand moved to cover her mouth. 'But what about Wajid and his family? Are they still stuck in Kabul?'

'Possibly.'

The colour drained from Maguire's face. 'Possibly? You mean something might have happened to them?'

'We really don't know. But if they were okay we would have expected them to have been in touch.'

'And they haven't have they?' She gritted her teeth. 'Sometimes I wonder if what we do makes any difference at all.'

'I hear you,' said Shepherd.

She looked up at him, blinking away tears. 'Whoever came in Wajid's place, you're looking for him?'

'Oh yes.'

'Make him pay for what he's done,' said Maguire.

'I intend to,' said Shepherd.

Sayyid brought the Skoda to a halt at the side of the road and looked at the hand-drawn map that the Russian had given him. The Russian had told him to keep his phone switched off and only to switch it on again when he had arrived at his destination. Now he was there but he couldn't see the men who were supposed to be collecting the car from him. He was to look for two Asian men, and one of them would be wearing a dark blue shalwar kameez. But there were no men nearby. In fact the road was empty. It had been a long drive, almost two hours. He had taken the M5 south out of Birmingham, driven past Cheltenham down to the M48 and then crossed the Severn Bridge to Beachley. The idea was that the men would drive him to a train station and he would take the train back to Birmingham. He didn't understand why the men hadn't come to Birmingham to collect the vehicle, but Sayyid knew better than to argue with the Russian.

He took out his phone, switched it on and called the Russian. He answered immediately. 'Where are you?' he snapped.

'I'm here, where I am supposed to be,' said Sayyid. 'On Beachley Road. The bus stop is on the right but there's nobody there.' There was a pole with a sign and a bus timetable on it, and a few yards behind it was a brick shelter with a red tiled roof.

'Yes, there's been a change of plan. You have to drive a bit further. There's an estate on the right and you drive into it and they'll be there to meet you. It's about a hundred yards. Stay on the line and I'll talk you through it if there's a problem.'

'Okay,' said Sayyid. He put the phone on speaker and

placed it on the seat next to him. 'Okay, I'm driving forward,' he said.

He saw the turn-off ahead of him so he kept the speed down. He frowned as he saw a policeman standing on the grass next to a sign but then realised it was a cardboard figure, presumably to stop motorists from speeding. He smiled to himself. Why would anyone use a cardboard policeman? Why not put a real one there?

He slowed as he reached the turn. 'Okay, I'm about to turn right,' he said.

'That's it,' said the Russian. 'You'll soon be there.'

Sayyid could see a sign next to the turn. It was like a flag, with green, black and pink stripes, and in the middle was a logo. There was writing on it. '1ST BATTALION THE RIFLES'. Sayyid frowned. It was an army sign.

'Are you there yet?' asked the Russian.

As the car turned, Sayyid saw a single-storey brick building just inside a fence. Ahead of him was a barrier, blocking his way. 'What is this place?' he asked.

'It's just a camp, don't worry,' said the Russian. 'Are you at the gate?'

A soldier in camouflage fatigues stepped out of the building. He was holding a black assault rifle, the barrel pointing at the ground.

'There's a soldier here,' said Sayyid, picking up the phone with his left hand. 'What's happening?'

A second soldier appeared, also carrying a rifle. Both soldiers stared at Sayyid. One of them started shouting. Both men were pointing their guns at the car.

Sayyid opened his mouth to say that he wasn't there to hurt them but he didn't get the chance to speak. He never heard the explosion that killed him. One moment he was alive and gripping the phone in frustration, the next his body was atomised into a red mist as the bomb in the boot exploded and turned the car into deadly shrapnel. Both soldiers died in the blast, and three more inside the guardhouse were badly injured. One of them would die later that night in hospital.

The Russian used an opened paper clip to eject the SIM card from the phone. He snapped it in half then went to the bathroom and flushed it down the toilet. He went back to the sitting room and switched on the TV. He looked at his watch and wondered how long it would be before the explosion was reported.

He had no regrets about killing Sayyid. The man was an idiot. He had signed his own death warrant when he had left his phone GPS switched on not long after they had met. And he had continued to use the debit card the Home Office had given him. The Russian had told him not to because the government could use it to track him, but the man was greedy and continued to use it to withdraw cash. The Russian had pointed out the errors and the Afghan had just laughed and said it wasn't important, that nobody knew what he was doing and that the British police were stupid. But it was important and the British police weren't stupid. If they started to look for Sayyid the first thing they would do would be to check his phone records. And they would see that he had been to Chipping Norton, and to London. He'd been in the car the first time they had visited Chipping Norton, to check out the routes and to take a look at the Heysham home. Then he'd gone with his friends on a sightseeing trip to London. It was only when he got back from London that the Russian had checked his mobile and realised that the GPS had been on the whole time. Sayyid had lied and said it was because he needed to use his phone to navigate around London, but the Russian hadn't argued, he had made sure that the GPS was off and that it stayed off. From that point on, the Russian had decided that Sayyid would be more use dead than alive.

All eyes would now be on the bombing in Beachley. They would identify Sayyid almost immediately because he had used his own credit card and driving licence to rent the car. But it would be a literal dead end. The Taliban would claim the credit for the bombing and Sayyid would be in heaven with his god and seventy-two virgins. And while the police and the security services had all their attention focused on the car bomb at the army base, the real attack would take place – one that would destroy the British government and teach them a lesson they would never forget. The Taliban would take credit for that, too, which was fine by the Russian. He never cared about getting the credit for a kill. So long as his bosses knew, that was all that mattered.

Shepherd was in the operations room going through ATM video footage with Farah when his mobile rang. He took it out of his pocket and looked at the screen. It was Pritchard. 'Have you heard?' said Pritchard as soon as Shepherd took the call.

'Heard what?'

'Do you have a TV there?'

'Sure.' Shepherd clicked his fingers to get Docherty's attention, then jabbed his finger at the TV on the wall. Docherty looked around for the remote.

'Look at a news channel.'

'Which one?'

'Any one.'

Docherty found the remote and switched the TV on. It was showing Sky News. The picture was a live transmission of a badly damaged car. There was a headline running along the bottom of the screen. 'SUICIDE CAR BOMB AT ARMY BASE. 3 DEAD'.

'Where was this?' Shepherd asked Pritchard.

'Beachley Barracks.'

Shepherd knew that Beachley Barracks was a British Army base in Gloucestershire, close to the border with Wales and home of 1st Battalion, The Rifles.

'Has anyone claimed responsibility?'

'The Taliban. It's all over the internet. They say that The Rifles had committed war crimes in Afghanistan and Iraq. And we know who the bomber was.'

'Who?'

'The translator. Sayyid Habibi.'

'You're sure? There's no doubt?'

'I need you in my office, now. Bring Farah with you.'

'On my way.'

Shepherd put his phone away. Docherty was staring at the screen. 'Is this our guys?' he asked.

'Pritchard says it's Sayyid.'

'Oh shit.'

'Farah, come with me. Pritchard wants to see us both.'

'Why me?'

'If Sayyid's dead, I'm guessing he wants you to break the bad news to his wife.' Her face fell. 'Sorry,' he said.

Shepherd hurried out of the operations room with Farah following and they took the stairs to Pritchard's office. Amy motioned for them to go straight in. Pritchard was sitting on his sofa watching BBC news on his wall-mounted TV. Shepherd scratched the back of his head as he stared at the screen. Farah stood next to him, her hand over her mouth. The explosion had reduced the car to a scorched hulk, the roof had erupted and the doors had blown off. 'How do you know it was Sayyid, there can't be anything left of the driver?' said Shepherd.

'The rear number plate was untouched. The car was a rental from Birmingham. Sayyid used his credit card and driving licence.'

'That doesn't prove that it's him.'

'Fair point. But it's likely, you have to admit that. We'll see what CCTV we can get between Beachley and Birmingham.' He grimaced. 'To be fair, it could have been worse.'

'I suppose so. If he'd detonated a bomb that big in the centre of Birmingham, he could have killed hundreds.' He shook his head. 'But this isn't what it was about, surely? All that planning? All the hassle of bringing jihadists in from Afghanistan? For one opportunistic bomb outside an army base?'

'Sometimes it is what it is,' said Pritchard.

Shepherd's mobile rang. He pulled it out and looked at the screen. It was Janice Warren. He took the call. 'I'm just in with Robert,' she said. 'Can you join us?'

'Absolutely,' said Shepherd. He ended the call and flashed Pritchard an apologetic smile. 'I've been summoned to the Russia Desk.'

'Why?'

'I'm trying to ID the man who killed Baron Heysham.'

'You're still on that?'

'He's working with the Taliban, whoever he is.'

'You're chasing shadows,' said Pritchard.

'Maybe,' said Shepherd. 'But I won't know until I've caught him.'

'Go,' said Pritchard, his eyes still fixed on the TV.

'What about me, sir?' said Farah. 'You asked to see me.'

'Oh, right,' said Pritchard, frowning as if seeing her for the first time. 'Yes, right. At some point you'll need to go and talk to Sayyid's wife. Are you okay to do that? To break the bad news?'

'Yes, sir. No problem.'

'Wait until we have confirmation, though. At the moment we only know for sure that he rented the car. But once we've confirmed that it was him, you'll need to sit down with her.'

'I will do, sir,' said Farah, but Pritchard was already looking at the TV again.

Shepherd and Farah hurried to the Russia Desk. Warren was sitting on the sofa and Elliott was behind his desk. Shepherd introduced Farah and Elliott waved for them to join Warren on the sofa, then he stood up, walked around his desk and leaned against it.

'The man you saw in the British Embassy in Kabul is Andrei Sokolov, at least that's the name we have on file,' said Elliott.

He picked up a remote and pointed it at a large monitor on the wall by the door. A head-and-shoulders shot of the Russian filled the screen. 'It is almost certainly not his real name, however. He has travelled to the UK twice that we know about, most recently on October the third last year. We have no record of him leaving, but of course Border Force don't record departures any more.'

'I think the CCTV photograph of him at the JR Hospital shows that he's still very much here,' said Shepherd.

Elliott nodded. 'We've done a computerised visual check

on the scar and there's a ninety-seven per cent chance it's him.'

'I can assure you it's definitely him,' said Shepherd. 'One hundred per cent. So is he FSS?'

'Almost certainly yes, and probably Spetsnaz before that. But we'll probably never know for sure. He has a valid working visa under the name Andrei Sokolov and his CV checks out, but of course it would do if it was manufactured by the FSS. According to his CV he attended school in Tomsk and went on to study economics at Tomsk State University. He worked for several companies in Tomsk and then in Moscow, and then last year he came to work for a think tank in London.' He grinned when he saw Shepherd's eyes widen. 'Yes, the very same think tank that employed your honey trap girl, Elly Weigel, AKA Anna Schneider.'

He pressed the remote again and another photograph filled the screen. It was Sokolov sitting at a table with Anna Schneider. They were both smoking and had glasses of wine in front of them. 'This was taken during the time Craig McKillop was passing her the data that we had manipulated,' said Elliott. 'She would meet McKillop, take the thumb drive that we had prepared, then at some time within the following twenty-four hours she would meet Sokolov.' He grinned and pressed the remote again. A new surveillance photograph showed Sokolov and Schneider walking into a hotel together. 'Not all their meetings were for business, from the look of it.'

'Well, that's interesting,' said Shepherd. 'The connection, not the hotel visit. This pretty much ties this Sokolov to our jihadists. Do we have any intel at all on what he was doing in Afghanistan or how long he was there?'

'Not our remit,' said Elliott. 'As long as he's overseas, he's not on our radar.'

'Yeah, well unfortunately MI6's Russia Desk dropped the ball on that front. They had the photographs but didn't follow up.'

'To be fair, I doubt they'd get much more than we've got,' said Elliott. 'The FSS will have destroyed all of his old records. When a government issues a new identity it's usually faultless.' He sat down and crossed his legs at the ankles. 'I have to ask, why would they send Sokolov to kill Baron Heysham? What would the Russians have to gain by killing a former Speaker of the House of Commons?'

'The Russians did it to help out the Taliban,' said Shepherd. 'They've got the skills that the jihadists don't have.'

'Okay, then I'll rephrase the question,' said Elliott, punctuating his words with jabs of the remote. 'Why would the Taliban want to kill a former Speaker of the House of Commons?'

Shepherd flashed him a tight smile. 'Bait.'

'Bait?' said Pritchard, peering at Shepherd over the top of his glasses. 'What do you mean, bait?'

Shepherd and Farah were sitting on the two chairs facing Pritchard's desk. They had gone straight back to his office as soon as he had left the Russia Desk and Pritchard had seen them immediately. 'There's no way that Heysham was a serious jihadist target, and there's no reason for the Russians to have wanted to kill him,' said Shepherd. 'Not because of anything he might have done in the past, anyway. This is less about who he was and more about who will attend his funeral.'

Pritchard frowned and removed his glasses. 'Ah, yes. I see.'

'David Cameron is a neighbour and friend. His main house

is in London but he spends a lot of time in Chipping Norton. He's a definite target. In 2014 his government ordered British planes to bomb Islamic State targets in Iraq and a year later authorised attacks against Islamic State in Syria. For the rest of his life he's going to be on the jihadist hit list. Cameron went to Eton and Oxford, as did Heysham. And who else went to Eton and Oxford? Boris Johnson. And all three were in the Bullingdon Club. Along with George Osborne, the former chancellor of the exchequer. At different times, obviously. Plus the Oxford connection alone puts him in some very high-powered company. Tony Blair? Oxford. Theresa May? Oxford. By my reckoning there will be at least three former prime ministers and one sitting PM at the funeral. Plus several present and former Cabinet ministers and a lot of very high-ranking civil servants.'

'And this will be in London, right?'

Shepherd shook his head. 'Chipping Norton. There's a family plot in the local churchyard. Heysham's parents are buried there, as are his paternal grandfather and grandmother and several aunts, uncles and cousins. The family have lived in the area for generations.'

Pritchard put on his glasses and blinked through the lenses. 'What's the name of the church?'

'St Peter's. It's on the outskirts of Enstone. Not far from Chipping Norton.'

Pritchard's fingers played over his keyboard and then he peered at one of his screens. 'A two-hour drive from London?'

'Quicker by helicopter.'

'The press is always looking to see who's trying to minimise their carbon footprint,' said Pritchard. 'I can't see the prime minister flying in.'

'I drove by the church on the way back,' said Shepherd. 'It's a traditional village church, probably holds a couple of hundred at the most.'

'And you think this has all been planned to get high-profile targets into the church?'

'Into the area, at least,' said Shepherd. 'We've now identified the Russian who is helping them: Andrei Sokolov. Tony and I saw him in the British Embassy in Kabul when we were getting Sayyid out. Sayyid visited Chipping Norton earlier this year, which we assume was a recce, and we have CCTV footage of Sokolov entering and leaving Heysham's hospital room shortly before his death.'

Pritchard took off his glasses again and leaned back in his chair. 'When is the funeral?'

'In three days.'

'Well then we cancel the funeral. Or hold it somewhere where we'd have more control over the situation.'

'I'm not sure the family would go for that,' said Shepherd.

'They could hold the service elsewhere and then the coffin could be taken to Chipping Norton for burial.'

'If we did that, it's a dead giveaway that we know something's wrong. And if we scare them off, they'll just go back to planning something else. If we had Sokolov under surveillance it'd be different, but we don't know where he is. At least at the moment we know where and when they plan to attack.'

'And if they're successful and if it gets out that we knew about it in advance . . .?' Pritchard showed his palms.

'I hear you,' said Shepherd. 'But nothing can happen until the day of the funeral and that's still some time away. We can use that time to track them down. And if that proves to be impossible then we can revisit cancellation.'

'But Number 10 needs to be informed, obviously.'

'I disagree. The Russian involvement adds a whole new dimension. If it was simply a jihadist plot then there's little or no risk attached to letting more people know what's going on. But with the Russians we have state-sponsored espionage and they have eyes and ears everywhere. Plus most of the members of the Cabinet brief against their counterparts all the time. The fewer people who know, the better. Though I thought I should talk to someone at the top of Royalty and Specialist Protection.'

'What about Six?'

'I haven't told Tony that we've identified the Russian. By name, anyway. But he knows that he was in the hospital. It was our Russia Desk that did the ID.'

'Let me talk to Julian first,' said Pritchard. 'I'd rather tell him face to face and ideally keep it between the two of us. Maybe you and Farah could spend some time in the canteen? Grab a coffee, maybe?'

'No problem,' said Shepherd.

'It would be helpful if we had a mourners list for the funeral and a list of RSVPs. Leave that with me. So, as things stand, Heysham died from heart complications caused by a bad fall. There is no police interest, which is good. Do you happen to know where we stand on a post mortem?'

'There shouldn't be one. There are only three instances where a hospital death is reported to the coroner: negligence regarding the treatment, if the patient dies before a prognosis is made, or a death under anaesthetic. The medical staff are all of the opinion that the death was the result of a heart attack brought on by the fall and that's what's on the death certificate.'

'And who else knows that there is more to the death?'

'The only outsider in the loop is the head of hospital security.'

'Is he a former cop?'

Shepherd nodded. 'Yes, with the Met.'

'They're always leaking stuff to the press.'

'This guy's sound, I think. Jimmy Sharpe vouches for him. To be honest, I think he has the hospital's interests at heart so wouldn't want it getting out that there had been a breach of security.'

Pritchard forced a smile. 'Well let's hope that's the case. So, the priority now is to track down Sokolov and anyone else he's working with. Any thoughts on that?'

'We have our thinking caps on,' said Shepherd.

'Caps or not, we need to come up with something, and soon,' said Pritchard. 'I really don't want a prime minister – retired or not – assassinated on my watch.'

Shepherd and Farah went to the canteen. Shepherd collected a coffee and a ham salad sandwich and Farah took a yoghurt and a camomile tea. Shepherd paid for them both, despite her protests, and they went over to a table by the window.

'So Mr Pritchard wants to get to Mr Penniston-Hill before we've told Tony what's happening?' said Farah.

'I know it sounds ridiculous, but he wants to make sure he has control over the narrative,' said Shepherd. 'It's fair enough, he has the big picture and Tony will only know what we tell him. This way, he makes sure that MI6 is in step and there are no nasty surprises down the line.'

'Nasty surprises?' She sipped her tea.

'Sayyid was an MI6 translator and they brought him out of Afghanistan. But equally, MI5 is responsible for identifying and apprehending terrorists, so what we don't want is the two agencies blaming each other for what has just happened.'

'A united front?'

'Exactly.' He took a bite of his sandwich, chewed and swallowed, as Farah tucked into her yoghurt. 'I just want to say what a great job you're doing,' said Shepherd. 'Getting the CCTV of Sayyid from that restaurant was inspired, and you're putting in a lot of hours, that's clear.'

'I love it,' she said. 'It's why I joined MI5, not to act as a translator or to sit in a dark room with headphones on.'

'You can understand why they'd want to utilise your language skills,' said Shepherd.

'Of course, but I'm more than that, Dan. I could work undercover, that's what I should be doing. Put me into the jihadist mosques, let me get close to the terrorists.'

'Working undercover isn't as much fun as you might think.'

'It's not about fun, it's about doing a job that matters. Catching Sokolov matters. Catching the bad guys before they detonate a suicide vest or go on a rampage with machetes, that matters.'

Shepherd couldn't help but smile at her enthusiasm.

'You're laughing at me,' she said, and pouted.

Shepherd shook his head. 'No, I'm not, really I'm not. I'm just remembering how I used to feel when I worked undercover. I wasn't much older than you.'

'For MI5?'

'No, the police. I was assigned to an undercover unit that worked anywhere in the country. We were called in when they wanted new faces.'

'And how did you feel?'

'How did I feel? That's a difficult question. It was exhilarating. Exciting. A bit scary.'

'You're really trying not to say fun, aren't you?'

Shepherd laughed. 'Farah, seriously, it often means putting your life on the line. You don't always have back-up next door ready to charge in with guns to pull your nuts out of the fire.'

'My nuts?'

'It's an expression. Metaphorical nuts.' He grinned. 'I hear what you're saying. And I think you'd be great working under-cover. Any time you want any help or advice, I'm your man.'

'Thank you, Dan. I appreciate that.' She finished off her yoghurt. 'What's the worst bit about working undercover?'

'The worst? That's a good question.'

'Well, it'll counterbalance the fun aspect.'

Shepherd popped his last bit of sandwich into his mouth and chewed as he thought how best to answer her.

'That's a clever trick,' she said. 'Giving yourself time to think?'

He swallowed and chuckled. 'You got me,' he said. He sipped his coffee. 'The worst thing that can happen is to get too close to the target. It tends not to happen so much with MI5 because more often than not we're up against terrorists and empathy tends not to come into play. But as a cop, often I'd be up against what they call ordinary decent criminals and they're much more of a spectrum. There are some right bastards who'd kill you for your Rolex, but most of them have wives and kids and they're nice to animals. They might be great fun on a night out and you have a real laugh with them, but at the end of the day if they're arms dealers or drug dealers then they're breaking the law and they deserve to be sent down. But some-times the good seems to outweigh the bad.'

'They become friends?'

He nodded. 'That's the problem, Farah. You're introduced

to them as targets. You know everything about them, who their contacts are, what their record is if any, the things they have done and the people they've hurt. So you go in knowing that they are bad guys and have it coming, but then you find out what they're like as human beings. And often they can be genuinely nice people. And that only comes out over time. If it's a short job, in and out, a drug deal, say, or an arms buy, then it's all business. But sometimes you get given a long-term penetration job that could take weeks or even months. You insinuate yourself into their group and gradually become their friend. That's when you start to connect with them.'

'Stockholm syndrome?'

Shepherd nodded. 'Yeah, it's a thing. Even though you're aware of it, it still happens. And that's a very dangerous situation to be in because if you genuinely like the target there's a chance that your subconscious will start to look for ways to help them.'

Her eyebrows shot up. 'Are you serious?'

'Very,' he said. 'I've seen it happen. It was years ago, not long after I'd joined the Met. There were two of us trying to get close to a big-time cocaine importer. Big time as in tons. Tons and tons. He was a Scouser who spent most of his time in Galway. He was bringing cocaine over from Colombia in yachts, which would be met out in the Atlantic by local trawlers who would bring the drugs into port. Then they'd transport it by truck into the UK. He'd been doing it for years and was very clever. Never went near the drugs, never went near the money. The Liverpool cops had been watching him and tried putting their own guys in with no joy, so they asked the Met for help. They gave the job to me and a DI by the name of Jamie Constable.'

'That means he was Inspector Constable?'

'I know, I know, crazy right? Anyway, Jamie liked a drink and that was good because to get close we had to spend hundreds of hours in Liverpool nightclubs whenever the Scouser was in town. Terry Hughes his name was. They called him Tel. Anyway, we eventually work our way into his inner circle and Tel and Jamie really hit it off. Both had Irish fathers, both big Everton fans, they actually looked similar, big guys going bald, sleeve tattoos and a habit of farting in public.'

'Lovely.'

'Yeah, I was never that drawn to Tel but Jamie started talking about him as if he was a pal. A real pal. "Tel this" and "Tel that". And it got so bad that I tried to talk to him about it, but I was the young gun still and he'd been working undercover for fifteen years so he basically told me to watch and learn. Eventually Tel trusts us so much that he invites us over to Miami. We figure that at some point he'd be meeting his Colombian contact so we get confirmation that we can go. Turns out that Tel owns a couple of nightclubs in Miami so that was useful, investigation-wise. We were VIPs obviously, magnums of champagne, cocaine for everybody, it was mad.'

'You took cocaine?'

'You can only fake so much, Farah. If you're passing your-self off as a drug dealer but don't use the product, it can be a red flag. You can use an excuse, heart condition or whatever, but it's still a red flag. But Jamie, he was well up for it. Line after line. Which was great for our cover but not so good for his state of mind. Anyway, the third night we're out, we still haven't met Tel's contact but Tel's been on the phone a lot so we're pretty sure something's happening. Then out of the blue, Jamie goes all weird. Starts hugging Tel and telling him what a great guy he is, how they're brothers for ever, how Jamie would step in front of a bullet for him. Weird stuff. And then he starts making jokes about intel. In-Tel. Best intel in Miami. Stuff that didn't make any sense. I tried to interrupt but he didn't react. I called him Davie two or three times and he didn't look at me. Davie was his cover name. Davie O'Brien. But when I called him Davie he didn't turn to look at me. Tel noticed that. He didn't say anything but he looked at me and I saw it in his eyes. Jamie wasn't reacting to his cover name. Eventually I said "Fuck you, Davie, you deaf bastard" and only then did he react, but it was too late.'

'Your cover was blown?'

'No question. But Jamie wouldn't have it. He said I was being over-sensitive. Here's the thing, Farah. Sometimes you have to go with your gut instinct. If you have a feeling that something is wrong then nine times out of ten you're right. Yes, you can be nervous and maybe overthink a situation, but if the hairs on the back of your neck start to stand up, you need to have a good look at what's going on around you. I told my bosses I thought we should pull out but Jamie said otherwise and he had seniority so they backed him. Also, they'd put a lot of time and money into the investigation and if we pulled out we'd have wasted most of it. We'd gotten some intel but we were nowhere near putting a case together.' He sipped his coffee. 'Anyway, the next day we get a call from Tel. He wants to take us out on his boat. Now, for me alarm bells really start ringing. It's going to be shirts and shorts so we're not going to be able to wear a wire or carry guns. We'll be out at sea so we'll be on our own. Jamie is all gung-ho, he says Tel is being sociable. He persuades our bosses to let us go. We have back-up on a sports fishing boat but they're going to be half a mile away.' Shepherd shook his head. 'Madness, but no one was listening to me. So we board the boat, it was a big one, with half a dozen heavies trying to look casual. Again, it just feels wrong to me but Jamie is hugging Tel and chatting away nineteen to the dozen. We go about a mile offshore and then Tel stops smiling and accuses us both of being cops. We deny it, of course we do, and Tel says he's got a way of finding out for sure. He's going to throw us into the sea. If we're cops, somebody will come and rescue us. If we're not . . .' He shrugged.

'You'll drown?'

'Yeah. We'll drown but he'll know we weren't cops.' He grinned. 'Bit like the way they used to check for witches. Looking back, it was funny. But at the time, not so much. Tel made a big thing of it. He'd even bought a plank and made us walk it. Me first and then Jamie. As we're splashing around, he sails away. To be honest, I could have probably made it to the shore but Jamie was hungover and exhausted from all the coke and booze. He couldn't have managed a length of the hotel pool.'

'So what happened?'

'Well, we didn't drown, obviously. Tel continued to sail away and eventually our back-up came over to fish us out. Thereby proving to Tel that we were what he thought we were. We were on the next plane back to the UK.'

'And did Jamie ever admit that he'd screwed up?'

Shepherd shook his head. 'No. He told our bosses that somebody must have tipped off Tel. Nobody ever asked my opinion. But that was the last time I worked with Jamie.'

'And Tel?'

'Retired now, by all accounts. Lives on a huge estate in

Costa Rica. Lives like a king. I always think of Tel when people say that crime doesn't pay. But the point I'm making is that you can't afford to get too close to the target.'

'Well, yes. Sure. But in that case, it probably saved your life.'

Shepherd frowned. 'How so?'

'Because Tel was obviously attached to Jamie. If he hadn't been, he'd have just had you both killed. He knew you'd be rescued.'

'Maybe.'

'No, if you think about it, Jamie had bonded to Tel, and it was reciprocated. If that bond hadn't been there, it could have ended very differently.'

Shepherd nodded. 'I'd never thought of that,' he said.

'Jamie still screwed up, but at least you're alive to tell the story.'

Shepherd sipped his coffee as he considered what she had said. His phone rang and he took it out of his pocket. It was Jimmy Sharpe. 'Hey, Spencer has just been in touch. He went back through the timeline and found your Russian arriving in a car.'

'Please tell me he got the registration number.'

'He did. I told you he's one of the good guys. Have you got a pen?'

'I don't need a pen, Razor.'

Sharpe laughed and gave him the number. 'I've already run it through DVLA and it's a rental. Small place in Birmingham, not far from the airport.' He told Shepherd the name and address.

'Razor, that's brilliant.'

'I'm assuming you're going to be wanting licence and credit card details and any CCTV footage they have.'

'Razor, you really ought to be a detective.'

Sharpe laughed. 'Yeah, you said. No, the reason I'm asking is that I've a couple of good NCA mates in Brum and I'm sure one of them would swing by.'

'I appreciate the offer but we've got good people up there. Let's keep it in-house at the moment.'

'No problem.'

'And tell Spencer that I owe him one.'

'Oh, I think he knows that,' said Sharpe.

Shepherd ended the call and phoned Sue Johnson in Birmingham. He ran through what had happened to Heysham, and gave her Sokolov's details, then told her about the car that Sokolov had arrived in. She promised to get someone around to the car rental place and that she would call him back. 'So Sayyid was behind the car bomb at Beachley,' she said.

'I'm told he rented the car but the body was blown to smithereens.'

'We've got a decent picture of him behind the wheel in Birmingham about two hours before it went off,' said Johnson. 'The Severn Bridge has cameras at both ends and we're checking on them as we speak. But it looks pretty certain it was him.'

'Was he alone in the car?'

'In the picture we have, yes. So that's what all this was about, trying to blow up an army camp?'

'He didn't get past the guardhouse,' said Shepherd. 'He killed three squaddies. I know every death's a tragedy, but it seems overkill to go to all that trouble to kill three people.'

'Well, The Rifles have served in Iraq and Afghanistan. There's PR value in hitting their HQ, I suppose.'

Shepherd ended the call and turned to look at Farah. 'It was

Sayyid at the wheel. There's a picture of him in the car leaving Birmingham.'

'I'll go and talk to Laila this evening,' she said. She sipped her tea as Shepherd quickly brought her up to speed on his conversation with Sue Johnson. 'That's good news,' she said. 'Big mistake for them to hold on to the car they used at the hospital.'

'We haven't confirmed that they still have it, but they've no reason to suspect that we're on to them,' said Shepherd. 'And the car's not in Sokolov's name. But I'm sure they'll change cars soon. Anyway, once we're back in the office, can you run the registration number through ANPR?' The Home Office's automatic number plate recognition system used a network of more than 11,000 cameras to collect more than 100 million number plate reads every day. The ANPR computers were at a data centre in Hendon, North London, and they stored number plate photographs for two years along with a note of the time, date and place. ANPR data, along with CCTV and mobile phone records, now accounted for the vast majority of cases solved by the police. 'I need you to put together a map of everywhere the car went. Ideally from that we'll get an idea of where they're holed up. And what other targets, if any, that they're looking at.'

'Will do,' she said. 'Do we know how long they've had the car?'

'Hopefully we'll get a copy of the rental agreement ASAP. But get all sightings for the past month and we can take it from there.' He finished his coffee and looked at his watch. 'I'm going to have another coffee,' he said. 'And a chocolate brownie. Do you want one?'

Farah grinned. 'I shouldn't, but yes, please.'

Shepherd and Farah walked into the operations room. Docherty wasn't there. Shepherd had brought him a coffee and he placed it on one of the tables. Farah sat down and phoned the ANPR centre. Shepherd went over to the map that showed the GPS route of Sayyid's pay-as-you-go phone. He rubbed his chin as he stared at the black lines and red dots. Hopefully Farah would be able to compile a similar map from the ANPR data for the car that Sokolov had been using. But as useful as the information was, it didn't tell them anything about the occupants of the vehicles.

He took a whiteboard from the stack leaning against the wall and placed it on an easel. He logged on to a terminal and printed out photographs of Andrei Sokolov and put them on to the board. Above the pictures he wrote the man's name and 'THE RUSSIAN CONNECTION?'

His mobile rang and he fished it out of his pocket. It was Sue Johnson. 'That was easy, the car rental place is just down the road,' she said. 'The driving licence they used is in the name of Sakeb Nazir but he can't have rented the car because he's in HMP Birmingham as we speak.'

'Terrorism-related?' said Shepherd.

'Underage girl related. Part of a large grooming gang that the cops put away two years ago.'

'That means someone's using his ID?'

'And his credit card,' said Johnson. 'We've had a look at the CCTV footage and the guy using the card is fairly similar to Nazir, a bearded Asian man wearing round glasses.'

'Do you have a decent shot of his face?'

'Fair, but I've run it through facial recognition and didn't get any hits.'

'He might well have only just arrived from Afghanistan, so

I'll ask Janice Warren to check with the Border Force database. And the Russian?'

'He wasn't in the rental office. Whoever was posing as Nazir was alone when they did the paperwork and collected the car. But we have CCTV footage of the car down the road, stopping to let a big bald guy get into the front passenger seat.'

'Do they still have the car?'

'They do.'

'Well that's the first good news I've had in a while,' said Shepherd. 'We're checking with ANPR as we speak. Just a thought, this Nazir didn't leave any fingerprints, did he?'

'I thought of that,' said Johnson. 'It was all done on computer and he signed on a tablet. No prints.'

'And what about checking for Nazir as a potential contact of Sayyid?'

'Adam is checking as we speak. But he's not a familiar face.'

'And you have his mobile phone number?'

'I do, yes. It's all in the email that I just sent to you.'

'That's brilliant, Sue, thanks so much. Let me run some checks and if I need anything else I'll give you a call.'

'Happy to be of service,' she said. 'One other thing. Adam hasn't come up with any links at all between Mohammad Hassan Baloch and anyone at the Makki Masjid mosque or the three other mosques that Sayyid visited. So far as we can tell, Baloch isn't in communication with anyone here in Birmingham. But we're still looking.'

Shepherd thanked her again and ended the call before sitting down at a terminal. He logged on and opened the message from Johnson. She had included the footage from the car rental office and what looked like a feed from a traffic light camera. In the first, an Asian man in his thirties wearing a black anorak was standing at a counter while a young woman with a blonde ponytail tapped his details into a computer. He stood looking at her until she handed him a tablet and he signed with his finger, then she gave him a small folder and the keys. Shepherd froze the footage when he had a clear view of the man's face and took a picture with his iPhone. He sent the picture to Janice Warren. 'POSSIBLE RECENT ARRIVAL FROM KABUL'.

After a few seconds he received a reply. 'I'M ON IT'.

The second video showed a silver Prius pulling up at the side of the road. A bald man in a dark blue fleece walked quickly over to the car and pulled open the passenger door. It was Sokolov. The Russian climbed into the Prius, pulled the door shut, and it sped off down the street.

Shepherd read through Johnson's message. She had included the registration number of the Prius, a copy of the rental agreement, a copy of Sakeb Nazir's driving licence, Nazir's credit card details and Nazir's mobile phone number. There was also a head-and-shoulders shot that she had taken from the video. Shepherd pressed the button to print the picture and the copy of the rental agreement.

As the sheets began to print, he put another whiteboard on to an easel and wrote 'AKA SAKEB NAZIR' at the top.

Farah finished her phone call and went over to stand next to him. 'Is that the driver?' she asked, pointing at Nazir's name.

'It's the name he used to rent the car. The real Sakeb Nazir is in prison.'

The door opened and Docherty walked in, carrying a stack of files. He dropped them on a table and spotted the coffee. 'Is that for me?' he asked.

'It is,' said Shepherd.

'You're a star,' said Docherty. He picked up the cup, sipped the coffee and then walked over to stand next to Farah as Shepherd began sticking sheets of paper on to the board. 'Sakeb Nazir?' he said. He frowned when he saw the board with the Russian on it. 'Is that the guy from the embassy in Kabul?'

'It is,' said Shepherd. 'Courtesy of MI5's Russia Desk. And Nazir's ID was used to rent a Prius that Sokolov used to get to and from the hospital.' He showed Docherty the rental agreement, then passed it to Farah. 'There's a mobile number that they gave to the car rental company. I need you to get Carphone Warehouse on the case as a matter of urgency. If you get any pushback at all let me know and I'll get Giles Pritchard on the case. We need all texts and calls and GPS information and we need it yesterday. I'm assuming the phone belongs to Nazir but it could be the Russian's.'

Farah nodded. She took out her phone and took a picture of the agreement.

'He's using the name of Sakeb Nazir but as I said the real Sakeb Nazir is in a cell in Birmingham nick. I've got Janice trying to ID him. But whoever he is, he's been driving Sokolov around. If we find him, we find the Russian.'

'I'll go see them now,' she said. 'I think Alastair has the hots for me so I'm sure he'll treat me as a priority.'

'Whatever works, carrot or stick,' said Shepherd. 'Once you've done that, can you go and see Laila and show her pictures of Yasin and Nazir. See if she saw either of them in Scarborough.'

'Will do.'

'And I think you should tell her that Sayyid is dead. It's only a matter of time before the press get hold of it so she needs to hear it from you otherwise it'll blow any trust.' She nodded but he could see the hesitation in her eyes. 'Are you okay?'

She forced a smile. 'Oh, I'm fine. I'm just wondering, do I ask for her help with the pictures first, or do I tell her about Sayyid first? If she's upset, she might not want to help.'

'Oh, you have to give her the bad news first. Definitely. Even if it means you have to wait for her help with the ID.'

'Okay, brilliant, thanks.' She picked up her bag. 'I'll call you after I've spoken to her,' she said, and hurried out of the door. Shepherd looked over at Docherty. 'Just so you know, Giles Pritchard has reached out to Penniston-Hill to bring him up to speed.'

'Best he gets it from the horse's mouth? No problem.' He surveyed the six whiteboards. 'We're getting there, aren't we?'

'Slowly but surely,' said Shepherd. He moved the whiteboard featuring Baloch and Kamali to the left of the group, then placed Sokolov's whiteboard next to it. He placed the whiteboards featuring the four jihadists – Sayyid, Hakim, Yasin and Nazir to the right. He used the marker to write 'DECEASED' at the top of Sayyid's whiteboard.

'But we've still no idea what they're planning?'

'I think it's to do with Heysham's funeral,' said Shepherd. 'Heyshams are always buried in a local churchyard in Chipping Norton. Some very high-profile people will be there, including the PM and several members of the government.'

Docherty's jaw dropped. 'You think they're planning to attack the church?'

'The church, or any one of the VIPs en route to the funeral. There's only one main road running through the village.'

'But the PM's protection team will be all over it, surely?'

'Sure, but I'm planning to have a chat with them, see what options are being considered.'

'Okay, but following the bomb at Beachley, it's all moot, isn't it? They have video footage now of Sayyid at the wheel of the car. There's no doubt, it was definitely him.'

'But it doesn't make any sense, what happened. All that trouble, all that planning, to attack a guardhouse?

'It makes sense to them,' said Docherty. 'It's jihad. Kill the infidel.'

'But there was no clear target. He was parked at the side of the guardhouse. He was never going to take out more than a few squaddies. And look at the timing. Sokolov would have needed help at Enstone. It would have taken two of them to fix up the rope to knock Heysham off his horse plus they'd need a driver. But once Heysham was dead, Sayyid would be surplus to requirements. And what better way of getting rid of him than by using him as a distraction?'

'A distraction?'

'That's what this is, Tony. I'm sure of it. Sokolov wants us focused on the car bomb so that we miss what's coming next.'

'Which is what?'

'That I don't know,' said Shepherd.

Shepherd was back in his apartment wondering whether to scramble some eggs or microwave a Marks and Spencer frozen meal when his phone rang. It was Farah. 'Sorry to bother you so late, I'm just checking in with you,' she said.

'It's fine, I'm always on the clock,' he said. 'How did it go with Laila?'

'She was surprisingly calm,' said Farah. 'No tears, just a

shrug. She said she'd tell the kids in the morning. I had tissues ready and everything but she was fine.'

'He treated her pretty badly, she probably thinks she's better off without him.'

'The one thing she was worried about was losing her right to live in the UK with her sons. I assured her she'll be okay. That's right, isn't it? There's no chance they'll deport her?'

'If they try, it'll be over my dead body,' said Shepherd. 'After all the help she's given us, she deserves a medal.'

'That's what I told her, I just wanted to hear it from you.'

'Well you can take that as given,' said Shepherd.

'Laila remembers seeing Wajid Yasin with her husband in Scarborough. At least she's fairly certain. He was some distance away and she was looking through a window. But she says it was him.'

'That's great, Farah.' He looked at his watch. It was just after eight. 'Are you still working?'

'I thought I'd keep her company for a while,' said Farah. 'She's going a bit stir crazy and I think she just wants someone to talk to.'

'That's good of you, thank you.'

'She's a nice lady, I want to help. She keeps asking when she can go back to Birmingham. She really wants to stay in the same house and for her kids to continue at their school.'

'I hear you, and that's a definite possibility. Obviously with Sayyid's death there's no chance of him coming back for revenge. But if word does get out that she turned her husband in, there could well be repercussions and we might have to look at some sort of witness protection programme. But obviously that's just between us, we don't want her fretting.'

'No problem.'

Shepherd ended the call. He decided on the microwaveable chicken dumpling casserole, paired with a bottle of lager. He was just chewing on the last mouthful when his phone rang again. It was Pritchard. 'Just calling to see what progress you've made.'

'Some,' said Shepherd. 'We've got the names and photographs of three jihadists that Sayyid was working with, phone records of at least one of them, and the registration number of a rental car that the Russian assassin used. I think the prospects are good.'

'But not definite?'

'We don't have eyes on them, no. But we're working on it.'

'How sure are you that the funeral will be targeted?'

'It's still just a hunch. But Heysham was assassinated, and there has to be a reason for that. And I'm sure that today's car bomb was a distraction.'

Pritchard sighed. 'I'm tempted to inform the PM direct and get him to avoid the funeral. Blair, Cameron and May, too.'

'But if we remove the most likely targets, the danger is they'll drop below the radar and regroup. Then we'll have no idea where they're going to strike.'

'I get that, but if the shit hits the fan and the PM is assassinated, I doubt that argument will carry any weight.'

'I guess the question is, how secure is the Chipping Norton area? And how secure could we make it?'

'That was my thought exactly,' said Pritchard. 'I've just spoken to the head of Protection Command and he's given the okay for you to be on a recce of the area with a team leader tomorrow. His name is Inspector Simon Cookson. He'll pick you up in Battersea and drive you there. I'll text you his number.'

'How much did you tell them?'

'That we suspect there is a probability of a terrorist attack in the Chipping Norton area but we are light on specifics. I explained that Sayyid visited the area some time ago, but didn't mention Sokolov or his involvement in Heysham's death. I said we were still gathering intel but we wanted to check the security arrangements for the funeral. He did ask if I thought the funeral should be moved and I said we weren't yet at that stage but we were constantly reviewing the situation. Once you've had a look around, call me and give me your thoughts. We still have a couple of days.'

Pritchard ended the call and a few seconds later Cookson's contact details arrived in a text.

There were two branches in the Met's Protection Command – Royalty and Specialist Protection, who provided protection to the Royal Family and top government officials, and Parliamentary and Diplomatic Protection, who took care of diplomats, government buildings and less important officials. All of those with close protection duties were authorised firearms officers and were routinely armed. Shepherd phoned Cookson and introduced himself. The conversation was short and to the point. Shepherd gave him his address, and Cookson said he'd pick him up outside at seven-thirty, prompt. The inspector had actually said 'prompt', which made Shepherd smile. He wondered how much trouble he would be in if he was a few minutes late. He was still smiling as he took his empty plate to the kitchen.

Shepherd was outside his building at seven-thirty, prompt. The inspector arrived in a black Range Rover at a quarter to eight, with no apology, just a fist-bump and a muttered 'nice to meet you.'

Cookson was in his late forties, with a shaved head and wire-framed glasses. He was wearing a dark blue suit and a light blue tie with what looked like eagles' heads on it. Shepherd was also wearing a suit and tie. He'd run into RaSP officers before and they tended to be well dressed – unless they were tramping after members of the Royal Family on the Sandringham or Balmoral estates, in which case Barbour jackets and green wellington boots were the norm.

Cookson edged the Range Rover into traffic and headed north over Albert Bridge. Police officers were generally suspicious of the intelligence agencies, and with good reason. They were bound by the Police and Criminal Evidence Act and any infringement could lead to demotion or outright dismissal. The intelligence agencies on the other hand appeared to operate with impunity and there seemed to be no repercussions when things went wrong. So far as most police officers were concerned, MI5 and MI6 officers just muddied the waters. Or worse: they killed investigations where national security was at risk. So for the first fifteen minutes, Shepherd kept the conversation light, chatting about policing in general and how the job had changed over the years. Most cops who had done ten years or more were unhappy at the state of modern policing, but Cookson appeared to be less bitter than most. Shepherd brought up the fact that he'd worked for the Met as an undercover cop and that he'd spent time in SOCA, hoping that his police credentials would cut him some slack. It was hard to get a read on the man; he was quiet and thoughtful and spoke without emotion.

'Have you been to Chipping Norton before?' asked Cookson as they reached the M4 and headed west. Shepherd was about to say that he had been there a couple of days earlier but that would have required an explanation, so the simple option was to lie and say no, he hadn't.

'It's a nice place, very genteel,' said Cookson. 'Pretty as a chocolate box, as my old mum used to say. Lots of lovely little villages, cute cottages, beautiful manor houses.'

'You know the area well?'

'I was on Cameron's protection team when he was PM, so I was out there a lot. To be honest, it's one of the safest places on earth. Outsiders stick out, so I was a bit surprised to hear that there was a possibility of a jihadist attack.'

'Did you ever meet the chap who died? Baron Heysham?'

Cookson chuckled. '"Call me Ronnie", he always said. We never did, of course. It was always "sir". He was a real gent, I was so sorry to hear about his accident. In the days that I looked after Cameron he was often around at his house and vice versa.'

'What are Cameron's security arrangements these days?'

'Generally he's not considered a high-risk target, but of course these days who knows, right? Who would have thought a common-or-garden MP like Sir David Amess would get macheted to death in his surgery in Leigh-on-Sea of all places?. I heard that the kid responsible had been reported to Prevent, right?'

'Not my case,' said Shepherd. Prevent was a government scheme which was supposed to nip radicalisation in the bud, but it wasn't well regarded by the men and women at the sharp end of the fight against terrorism.

'He did well to choose a soft target like Sir David. If he'd tried it with Cameron or the PM he'd have been shot the moment he pulled out his knife. In fact he wouldn't have got in the same room as the PM, he'd have been identified as a possible threat and searched.'

'And what about Tony Blair's protection team?'

Cookson chuckled. 'Ah, that's a whole different ball game, you can never let your guard down when you're protecting Blair. He's going to have a target on his chest for the rest of his life. I mean, he invaded Afghanistan and Iraq and he'll never be forgiven for that. And he's not the sort to keep a low profile, is he? He pops up everywhere.'

'What about his arrangements at the funeral?'

'His head of security is meeting us in Chipping Norton, we can talk it through there. I'm assuming he'll have six, the same as the prime minister. Plus drivers.'

'They'll all be driven to the funeral, do you think?'

'Blair's country place is in Buckinghamshire, less than an hour's drive from Chipping Norton. It'll take the PM a little over two hours from Downing Street. I'm sure he'd prefer to use a helicopter but the public never likes to see that.'

'And the funeral is at eleven?'

'Right. So the PM will be leaving just before nine and Blair at about ten. Cameron is local, of course. Then there's Theresa May who has confirmed she'll be coming, and George Osborne, though he doesn't have RaSP protection.'

'Any other dignitaries with bodyguards?'

'Not with RaSP close protection officers, no. But Heysham did have some very wealthy friends who might well have their own private security.'

'Armed?'

'Definitely not. So, let me ask you a question. How hard is your intel that there'll be an attack on the funeral?'

'It's a possibility,' said Shepherd. He was reluctant to lie to the inspector, but Pritchard had made it clear he wasn't to mention that Heysham had been murdered. 'We're tracking a small jihadist group and one of them – maybe more – went to Chipping Norton for a few hours. We were tracking the GPS on his phone. But he also made a trip to London and was there for a couple of days. All we're doing is covering the bases.'

'But why the sudden interest in the funeral?' asked Cookson. He asked the question casually and he was looking at the traffic ahead of them, but Shepherd could sense that his suspicions had been aroused.

'It's my boss's idea,' said Shepherd. 'If they had been in the area and then heard about the funeral, it might give them ideas. Me, I said they were probably visiting the Diddly Squat Farm Shop but he didn't seem to think that was funny.'

Cookson chuckled. 'Yeah, the locals are really pissed off at Jeremy Clarkson. Traffic jams for miles at the weekend. And Amazon are doing a second series of his show, which will only make things worse.'

They chatted about the TV presenter and cars and moved on to football. Shepherd was fairly sure that he had deflected the inspector's suspicions about the funeral, but he couldn't be sure. The officer clearly had a sharp mind and it was standard interrogation protocol to drop a line of questioning and then return to it later. Time would tell.

Cookson parked off the main road running through Chipping Norton and walked with Shepherd to a cafe that appeared to be in two terraced cottages that had been knocked into one. Two officers in dark blue suits were sitting at a circular table in one corner and they both stood up when Cookson walked in. One was a tall black man with wide shoulders and a chunky gold wedding ring, the other was a slightly overweight white man with receding ginger hair.

'The early birds,' said Cookson. He nodded at the black officer. 'This is Glen Howard, he helps take care of Tony Blair. Guys, this is Dan. He's with our friends in Thames House.'

Howard fist-bumped Shepherd and nodded.

'And this is Roger Clarke. He's with Cameron's team.'

Clarke also fist-bumped Shepherd. A waitress came over with two menus to match the ones that Howard and Clarke had in front of them.

'We're going for the full English and coffee,' said Howard as he and Clarke sat down.

'Sounds like a plan,' said Shepherd. He sat down opposite Howard.

'Brown or white toast?' asked the waitress.

'Actually no toast for me,' said Shepherd. 'I'm trying to cut down on carbs.'

'It's included,' said Clarke. He winked at the waitress. 'I'll have his toast, Debbie.'

'Full English for me,' said Clarke. 'And tea. White toast.'

'Why is Thames House interested in a funeral in Chipping Norton?' asked Clarke as the waitress walked away.

'As I was telling Simon, we've nothing concrete but a known jihadist was here a few months ago. When my boss heard that Baron Heysham's funeral would be here, he decided to send me to have a look around. More of a box-ticking exercise than anything.'

'Well Simon has probably already told you, there's no safer place for the PM than Chipping Norton,' said Clarke. 'Everyone here is civil. There are a fair number of shotguns around but they're almost never used in anger. And outsiders stick out like the proverbial sore thumbs.'

'By outsiders you mean Asians?'

'Let's just say three Asians in a souped-up Nissan Micra would be noticed. Phone calls would be made. So far as the locals go, even if one of them were to vehemently disagree with Tony Blair, or the prime minister, the worst that would happen is a disapproving look or a disdainful shake of the head. This isn't the sort of place where eggs get thrown, let alone explosive devices.'

All three officers nodded. 'If the whole of the country was like Chipping Norton, we'd be out of a job,' said Howard.

'They keep out the riff-raff, is that it?' said Shepherd.

'The price of houses does that,' said Cookson. 'I couldn't afford to live here. Cameron's house here is nothing special and it's worth two million. You saw the Heysham place, that's got to be ten million quid, right?'

Their drinks arrived and Cookson smiled up at the waitress. Shepherd's thoughts went into overdrive. The question had been casually asked, almost a throwaway remark, and there was no indication that the inspector was expecting an answer. But Shepherd had never said that he had been to the Heysham house, so was it a test? The waitress put Cookson's tea down in front of him and he thanked her. Shepherd couldn't admit to visiting the house so he would have to try being evasive. He didn't want to tell an absolute lie. Evasion could always be passed off as a memory lapse or a misunderstanding, but a lie was a lie. 'I don't know, is it big?'

Cookson turned to look at him and Shepherd smiled up at the waitress. She gave him his coffee and he thanked her. When he looked back at the inspector, Cookson was still watching him, a slight smile on his lips. 'It's a fair size. And there's a lot of land. Cottages for the workers. Stables.'

'That's right, he fell off a horse, didn't he? I've never been a fan.'

'Of horses?'

Shepherd nodded. 'Never seen the attraction. I've only ridden a couple of times but the horses were always farting.'

Howard laughed. 'That's right, blame the horse, why don't you?'

They all laughed as the waitress finished placing their drinks on the table. Shepherd sipped his coffee. Cookson was concentrating on his tea, adding sugar and stirring it. Maybe it had been a slip of the tongue, but somehow Shepherd doubted it. He was sure that the inspector had been testing him. But had Shepherd passed? 'Can you talk me through the arrangements for the day of the funeral?' Shepherd asked, changing the subject.

It was a question aimed at no one in particular, but it was Cookson who answered. 'Actually we'll be starting the day before,' he said. 'We'll run a dog through the church and the churchyard looking for explosives and weapons. And we'll be checking all parked vehicles in the area. Then Thames Valley will put a uniform, maybe two, outside the church overnight. We always try to keep the local police involved, it makes them feel loved.'

Clarke chuckled. 'Even though you wouldn't trust them as far as you could throw them. Not where VIP protection is concerned.'

'Early morning we'll have two ANPR vehicles east and west of the church on the A44, and Thames Valley will have a patrol car checking on anyone who shouldn't be there, including the press,' continued Cookson. 'There'll be press at the church, papers and TV, but they'll be tightly controlled. Any freelancers or paparazzi will be told to move on. Enstone is a small village so we'll leave it up to Thames Valley to contain the area. We've asked them to have two armed response vehicles within a minute's drive of the church from nine a.m. onwards and they've agreed to that.

'Also at nine a.m., a dozen Thames Valley uniforms will take up position around the perimeter of the churchyard, in dress uniform. No high-vis jackets or stab vests. At eight-forty-five the PM will leave Downing Street. So far as we know his wife won't be going, but George Osborne will be travelling with the PM.' He smiled thinly. 'I think he's embarrassed at not having security. We'll have three vehicles: two Range Rovers for the protection staff and the PM's Jaguar.'

The PM had a fleet of custom-built armoured V8 Jaguar XJ Sentinels at his disposal, with run-flat tyres, a bomb-proof floor plate and bulletproof windows. The cars had gun ports for his close protection officers to fire through, an independent air supply and a tear gas release system. Once he was safely inside his Jaguar, he was pretty much unreachable.

'Now, the route. We'll take the A4 to the M4, then along the M40 to junction 8 where we'll take the A40 to North Way and then the A44 to Enstone. I'll be in the front Range Rover with one other close protection officer and a driver, there'll be another of our people in the front seat of the Jag, and three more and a driver in the tail-end Range Rover.'

'Motorcycle outriders?'

Cookson shook his head. 'We can get them but generally the view from Number 10 is that the public don't want to see blatant trappings of power. But we'll have an NPAS helicopter following us all the way and it'll take up position over the church, but not so close that there'll be a noise problem.'

Shepherd nodded. Due to cutbacks, police forces no longer had their own helicopters. Since 2012, individual forces had access to the National Police Air Service, and there were always two helicopters based at Lippitts Hill in north-east London.

'We'll deliver the PM and Osborne to the church and four of us will go inside with him,' said Cookson. He looked at Howard. 'Can you tell us about your plans for Sir Tony, Glen?' Shepherd thought he detected a slight sense of irony in the reference to Blair's knighthood, but there was no hint of a smile on the inspector's face.

'Pretty much the same, except we'll leave the house at ten o'clock and we won't have a helicopter. He has an identical Jag and we'll be in two Range Rovers.' He grinned at Shepherd. 'Before you ask, he paid for the Jag himself. He wasn't allowed one of the PM's.'

'Good to know,' said Shepherd.

'We'll come in on the A44. I'll be in the front vehicle with a driver and one other, there'll be one officer in the Jag with the principals and three in the final Range Rover. Four of us will go into the church and two will remain outside.'

'Cherie will be with him?'

Howard nodded. 'She knew him quite well.'

'And you, Rog?' said Cookson, looking at Clarke.

'We'll have a driver and I was going to be in the front seat of the family vehicle – a Tesla. There'll be Cameron and his wife. To be honest, that's all we were going to do. We did a risk assessment and well, it's a funeral in Chipping Norton.' He shrugged. 'I get that the presence of so many VIPs ups the ante, but with the PM's protection staff there I don't see I need to do more.' He looked at Shepherd. 'Unless there's something you're not telling us.'

Shepherd held up his hands. 'If I knew of a credible threat, I'd tell you,' he said. 'As I said, I'm just ticking boxes.'

The waitress returned with breakfasts for Howard and Clarke. Clarke's came with four slices of toast and he began to butter one.

'I think with Glen's team and mine we'll be well covered,' said Cookson. 'The service should be about an hour, followed by the burial, another thirty minutes. Then the plan is to drive to the Heysham house for the reception. The PM has pencilled in half an hour for that. I'm going to suggest we go in one convoy, along with Theresa May's group.'

'What protection does she have?'

'Just one personal protection officer and a driver. She'll be coming alone. So we'll have four groups driving from the church to the house. I'd suggest you first Roger as you're local, followed by Glen, then my team, then Theresa May's team.'

The two men nodded as they tucked into their breakfasts.

'The PM will leave after half an hour, Osborne will go with him, and we'll drive back to London the same way we came. We'll take the helicopter with us. You two guys stay as long as your principals want. How does that sound?'

'Sounds good to me,' said Howard.

'It's almost as if you've done this before,' said Clarke, buttering a second slice of toast.

The waitress reappeared with breakfasts for Shepherd and Cookson. They thanked her and waited for her to walk away before continuing. 'So it all seems straightforward,' said Shepherd.

'We're a well-oiled machine,' said Cookson. 'The PM's on the go from eight in the morning often until ten or eleven at night, and he travels all over the country. After the funeral he's got back-to-back meetings at Number 10 then he's in to the City for a presentation at six followed by a seven o'clock dinner with some big Tory fundraisers. Then the following morning he's up in Newcastle for a factory visit. He keeps us on our toes.'

'Yeah, but he's not a patch on Blair,' said Howard. 'He's flying around the world and we have to go with him. I mean the overtime is great but the ulcers and hypertension aren't fun.' He shrugged. 'At least here we can relax a bit.'

'What's Blair's house like?' asked Shepherd.

'It's lovely. Really lovely. It's a Grade-1 listed mansion. Sir John Gielgud used to live there. They bought it for four million quid in 2008 and it's probably worth double that now.' He grimaced. 'I'd have to work a dozen lifetimes to even come close to affording a place like that.'

'Yeah, and you won't be getting a knighthood anytime soon either,' said Clarke. 'Anyway, look on the bright side.'

Howard looked across at him. 'What bright side?'

'You don't have to climb into bed with Cherie every night.' Clarke faked a shudder.

Shepherd smiled. 'Is it okay to laugh at the people you're protecting?'

'We don't have to like them or admire them,' said Clarke. 'All we've got to do is make sure that nobody kills them.'

'Ah you see, that's the question,' said Howard. 'Would you take a bullet for David Cameron?'

'It depends on what you mean by "take", doesn't it?' said Clarke.

'I mean would you throw yourself in front of a bullet that was heading for Cameron?'

'Maybe, if I was wearing a Kevlar vest.'

They all chuckled and tucked into their breakfasts.

The Range Rover came to a halt in front of the church. There was a waist-high stone wall running around the churchyard and an arched stone entrance with a wooden gate. Shepherd was in the front passenger seat and Clarke and Howard were sitting in the back. There was a wooden sign to the left of the lychgate with the name of the church – St Peter's – and underneath the names of two churchwardens and the vicar, along with their phone numbers and email addresses. The vicar's name was Reverend Emily Battersby. To the right of the gate was a wooden glass-fronted noticeboard with a list of service times and public notices. The lychgate looked to be hundreds of years old, a sturdy wooden gate with an arched roof above it. The church was built of stone with a weathered, square-turreted tower to the left and a main building with a steeply pitched roof and stained-glass windows along the side to the right.

Cookson switched off the engine and they all climbed out. 'This is the main entrance, obviously,' he said. 'There'll be two Thames Valley officers on the lychgate, checking people as they go in. There's no guest list as such, but a lot of locals will want to be there because he was well liked in the area so they'll be asking for ID from anyone they don't recognise.'

He turned and pointed to a grassy field on the other side of the road. 'We'll be corralling the press over there. We'll have half a dozen Thames Valley uniforms there but generally the press play by the rules. And from there they'll get a good view of everybody entering and leaving, which is all they want.'

'And what about the public?' asked Shepherd.

'There are just over a thousand residents in the village, but it's a work day and a school day so we're not expecting more than a hundred. The vicar will be at the lychgate and she will be able to identify the regulars. Anyone else will be asked for ID and if they are local they'll be allowed in. There will be people coming in from Chipping Norton and the surrounding area, but it's been made clear that the funeral is for family and friends and hopefully people will respect that. People out here generally do as the police suggest.' He pointed down the road to the left. 'There will be an ANPR van about half a mile down the road, and a Thames Valley patrol car about two hundred yards away that will stop any suspect vehicles.' He turned to the right. 'Ditto in that direction.'

Directly opposite the church was a line of stone cottages. Most were clearly homes but there was a small shop that doubled as a post office and there was an osteopath surgery next to it. 'We've checked out all the occupants and on the morning of the funeral we'll run a dog through. Three of the cottages are second homes and are currently empty, the rest are long-term residents. We'll have two uniforms on the pavement outside the cottages and one stationed outside the post office.' He pointed to the right. 'There's a small car park at the end of the cottages. The locals tend to park outside and run in but we'll be moving people on and get them to use the car park. There'll be an officer there monitoring any vehicles.'

Shepherd nodded and looked around. There were houses on either side of the road, mostly one or two-storey cottages. The land was flat so there were no vantage points overlooking the church. Cookson smiled. 'You're thinking snipers?'

'Force of habit,' said Shepherd.

'One of the lovely things about the Cotswolds is that there

are very few places for snipers to work from,' said Cookson. Shepherd couldn't tell if the man was being sarcastic or not.

'It's probably why property values are so high,' said Clarke.

Shepherd smiled. They were clearly professionals and had everything covered. The only places where a gunman could get a clear shot would be from the cottages facing the church, and provided the uniforms did their job properly there was no possibility of that. The VIPs were arriving in armoured cars and would be taken through the gate by armed officers. Shepherd couldn't see any openings for an attack. 'Looks good to me,' he said.

Cookson took them through the gate into the churchyard. A wide tarmac path led to the entrance to the church, where there was an arched stone porch over a large weathered oak door. There were stained-glass windows set into the wall of the main building. Many city centre churches had been forced to protect their windows with wire shields but there were few vandals in Chipping Norton and the St Peter's windows were there for all to see. To the left was a grassy area dotted with yew trees, to the right there was more grass and then the graveyard, dotted with gravestones and small crypts that had obviously been there for decades. 'The vicar should be inside as there's a service today,' said Cookson. 'They only have services on Sunday and Thursday. The rest of the time the church is open for private prayer but the vicar isn't here.'

'Where does she stay?'

Cookson pointed off to the east. 'The vicarage is about a quarter of a mile that way. She's been here almost twelve years, she's very well liked.'

'That's okay, I didn't have her down as a suspect,' said Shepherd.

Cookson walked to the door and pushed it open. Shepherd, Howard and Clarke followed him inside. The four men looked around the nave. There were two columns of pews, separated by a walkway, with aisles either side. The floors were of flagged stone and there were thick oak rafters overhead. There were stained-glass windows either side casting blue, green and red light over the dark oak pews. Shepherd did a quick count. If pushed, as many as three hundred people could probably pack into the pews.

They heard footsteps and looked across the pews to the transept. The vicar walked towards them, her shoes whispering on the stone flags. She was a blonde lady in her forties, with piercing blue eyes, wearing a long, black cassock and a gleaming white dog collar.

'Good morning, vicar, I'm Simon Cookson with the PM's protection team. I spoke to you yesterday.'

'Welcome to my church.' She flashed Clarke a smile. 'Good to see you again, Roger.'

'And you, Reverend,' said Clarke.

'Roger you know, and this is Dan and Glen. We're here to have a look around to make sure everything is ready for the funeral. Obviously you've had VIPs here before, so you know the drill. This time it's a different PM but basically nothing has changed.'

'No uniforms inside the church, I hope?'

'Absolutely not. Though we would like to have some officers in dress uniform in the graveyard.'

'But not those awful high-vis jackets.'

'No, they will be very presentable. And the close protection officers will all be in dark suits and will be very low key. The officers in the road will be wearing high-vis vests, though.'

'How many will there be actually inside the church?'

'I think eight: four from my team and four from Glen's. Roger will stay outside, and so will Theresa May's personal protection officer.'

'Oh, Theresa May is coming?' said the vicar. 'She's lovely.'

'I'm sure she is. Like Mr Cameron, she'll just have the one protection officer and I think he, or she, will wait outside. Now, what we'd like you to do is to stand at the lychgate while the mourners arrive. We know all the VIPs, obviously, but we need to know if there is somebody there who shouldn't be there.'

The vicar's eyes narrowed, just a fraction. 'I'm not sure I'd want to be involved in stopping people coming to worship. Usually we try very hard to get them to come.'

Cookson flashed her a reassuring smile. 'Absolutely, of course. And we certainly wouldn't want to inconvenience any of your parishioners. But if there was someone you didn't recognise, someone you thought might be out of place, just a nod would be enough and we would very quietly ask them for ID.'

'I just wouldn't want anyone to feel that I was acting like a bouncer at a seedy nightclub.'

Cookson laughed and threw up his hands. 'It absolutely won't be like that,' he said. 'We're very professional at this.'

The vicar nodded but she didn't look happy at the prospect.

'It's a lovely church,' said Shepherd, figuring he should try to get her thinking about something else. 'How old is it?'

'Oh, there's been a church on this site since the thirteenth century,' she said. 'The original tower was built some time in the fifteenth century and it was incorporated into the building when it was rebuilt in the Perpendicular style in 1847. Our pulpit is eighteenth century and we are especially proud of our font, which dates back to the thirteenth century. And our bells are something special. They were installed in 1847 and still ring true.'

'What we'd like to do is give the church a thorough checking over the day before the funeral and then have two men stay here overnight,' said Cookson.

'What exactly are you worried about?' asked the vicar.

'We're not really worried, it's just the protocol for when the prime minister visits,' said Cookson.

'I really don't think he'll be in any danger here.'

'And neither do I, Reverend. But I have to do my job and I'd be in trouble if I didn't do it properly.'

'It's very easy to secure,' said Clarke. 'Just two entrances, the main one and one at the back, near the office.'

'Don't forget the devil's door,' said the vicar, with a sly smile.

'The what now?' said Cookson.

'The devil's door,' repeated the vicar. 'It's in the north wall of the church. They were traditionally left open during baptisms so that any evil spirits within the child could escape. Most were blocked up during the Reformation, but ours can still be opened. In theory, anyway. It has been locked all the time I've been here and I wouldn't know where the key was.'

'Is it all right with you if Roger shows us around?' Cookson asked the vicar. 'He's familiar with the building so it might save time.'

'Of course. I'll be in my office if you need me.' She walked away towards the transept, the bottom of her cassock swinging from side to side.

Cookson looked around the nave. 'I'm thinking two men at the main doors, two at the rear entrance, the rest standing in the aisles at the side. What do you think, Roger?'

'I think that'll be fine. Viewpoints are good all around the church. Having said that, I know the vicar isn't happy to have anyone in the transept, she thinks it detracts from the service.'

'What am I missing?' said Glen. 'What's the transept?'

Clarke pointed towards the altar. 'The bit that crosses the nave, where the vicar stands during the service.'

'Got you.'

Cookson nodded at Shepherd. 'Are you happy?'

'I think so,' said Shepherd. 'I suppose somebody could parachute on to the tower and come down the stairs, but that's probably unlikely.'

Cookson opened his mouth to reply but then realised that Shepherd was joking. 'Yes, it probably is. Let's have a walk around just so we can all get our bearings.' They walked all around the nave, then to the transept. There was a pulpit and off to the left an old stone font. Behind the font was an opening which led to a stone stairway. To the right of the nave was a short corridor with two oak doors, one of which had 'OFFICE' on it, and then the corridor turned to the left.

'Have you been up the tower?' Cookson asked Clarke.

'Several times. Do you want a look?'

'Why not?'

Clarke led them up a winding stone staircase, the steps of which had been worn down over the centuries so that each one was slightly concave. It was quite a climb, and while Shepherd managed it with no trouble, Howard was panting for breath when they finally reached the top. The stairs opened into the bell tower, with two large bells hanging from thick beams. More beams criss-crossed the roof and there were square glassless windows on all four sides. Shepherd looked out of the window to his left. He had a clear view of the road, the graveyard and the fields beyond. He walked around to the window on the other side. Again there was a clear view of the road and the churchyard. Cookson joined him. 'You're thinking we should station someone here?' the inspector asked. 'One of our people?'

'I was actually thinking sniper,' said Shepherd.

'In Chipping Norton? My bosses would think I was crazy. Unless there's something you're not telling me.'

'I meant that if there was a bad guy here with a gun he'd have a clear view of the VIPs as they arrive.'

'As I said before the church will be searched the day before and then Thames Valley will have a couple of uniforms here. But if it makes you feel any better, I can station a guy here.'

'I guess it wouldn't hurt,' said Shepherd. He walked around to a window which had a clear view of the entrance to the church and the terraced cottages on the far side of the road. 'I can't see it'd do any harm. There's a good view of the road both ways.'

'I'll make sure that's done,' said Cookson.

'We never bothered when we brought Cameron here,' said Clarke.

'The world has changed a fair bit since the days when he was PM,' said Shepherd.

'That's true enough,' said Clarke. 'And it's rare to get so many PMs together, outside of the Houses of Parliament.'

'A bit less of the negativity, please,' said Cookson. 'Are we all satisfied so far?'

His three colleagues nodded. Cookson looked pointedly at Shepherd. Shepherd smiled. 'All good,' he said.

'Terrific,' he said. 'Let's go and have a look at the graveyard.'

Clarke led the way down the stone steps and across the nave

to the office. Cookson knocked on the door. 'Come in!' said the vicar.

Cookson opened the door. She was sitting behind a large Apple computer terminal and was now wearing dark-framed spectacles. The office had thick beams across the ceiling and an ancient stone-flagged floor, but all the equipment was ultra modern, with a large photocopier in one corner, sleek brushed-steel filing cabinets against one wall, a map of the parish dotted with multicoloured pins on another, and behind her desk a large planner marked off with the days of the month. It had the look of a Thames House operations room.

'Reverend, would you mind showing us where the burial will take place?' asked Cookson.

'Of course,' she said, removing her glasses and placing them next to her keyboard. She stood up and Cookson held the door open for her.

'If we could perhaps start in the church and you could show us how the coffin will be moved.'

She nodded and took them along to the transept. 'The coffin will be here, in front of the altar, and once the service is over it will be carried through the nave to the church entrance.'

'Do we know who will be carrying the coffin?' Shepherd asked.

'I think that is still to be finalised, but I am assuming it will be family members,' said the vicar.

'I'm sure Blair will be jostling for the photo opportunity,' whispered Howard.

If the vicar heard, she didn't react. She walked through the nave to the entrance. 'Both doors will be opened, we'll go outside and then we'll turn left to the graveyard.'

'I'm surprised that the church still carries out burials here,' said Shepherd.

'Oh, generally we don't. Only for long-established family plots and there are only six of those. There just isn't room. The graveyard was full years ago.'

They stood outside the church on the tarmac pathway that ran around the building and looked about. Shepherd could see that the VIPs would be vulnerable as they left the church but there were no vantage points overlooking the area. Providing the perimeter remained secure, the risks of an attack were minimal.

'We will walk along the path, this way,' said the vicar. She began to walk and the men followed her. Her cassock was swinging from side to side again, and her hair was moving gently in a soft wind that blew over the stone wall to their right.

Shepherd looked at the dates carved into the gravestones and crypts that seemed to have been placed haphazardly around the graveyard. Most were hundreds of years old, the stonework weathered and dotted with moss and lichen. Some of the taller monuments were leaning as the soil had shifted over the decades.

She took them to the end of the church. The path turned to the left but she walked on to the grass between two spreading yew trees. There were some newer gravestones around, made of gleaming marble with gilt lettering. Some had marble edging, others had marble vases of flowers in front of them. They passed a stone angel with its hands clasped in prayer. John Crawley, who died in 1862. Loving husband and father. There was a cluster of tall stone crosses that were so old the lettering had all but been obliterated.

'This is the Heysham plot,' said the vicar, pointing to a waist-high crypt with a horizontal cross on the top. There were eight gravestones of different designs around the crypt. 'The crypt is Baron Heysham's grandfather and grandmother. They died twenty years apart but they are interred together.' She pointed to a large square headstone with two names on it. 'These are his parents. Again they died some time apart but were buried together. In fact the plot for Baron Heysham is a double and in time his wife will be buried next to him.' She pointed to a patch of grass to the right of the crypt. 'This is where he'll be buried.'

'When will you dig the grave?' asked Shepherd.

'I won't be digging it personally,' said the vicar with another sly smile.

Shepherd couldn't help but grin. 'I meant when will it be dug. I'd assumed it would have been done already.'

'In the old days when they were dug by hand, they'd start on it a few days before the funeral, but we use a machine these days so we can do it the day before. You really don't want them standing empty for too long. They fill up with rain or the rats get in.'

'So in the morning? Or the afternoon?'

'Probably morning.'

'The Thames Valley cops will be here first thing,' said Cookson. 'They can keep an eye on things. Plus they'll bring the dog early afternoon.' He smiled at the vicar. 'Thank you so much for your time today, Reverend, and for your patience. We'll try to keep any inconvenience to an absolute minimum.'

'That would be best for everyone, obviously,' she said. 'Funerals can be distressing enough at the best of times.'

'I do understand, and thank you again for all your help. We'll see you again, on the day.'

The vicar nodded, flashed them all individual smiles, then

turned and walked back to the church. Shepherd did a slow three-sixty of the area. The wall ran around the entire grave-yard. There were houses and cottages dotted around but none were high enough to offer any sort of vantage point for a sniper. Someone could walk across the fields to the wall, but they'd be seen, and there was no cover – just grass and the occasional tree.

'All the teams from the church will be out here during the burial,' said Cookson. 'One each close by the principals, the rest can spread out around the perimeter.'

'But keep the guy in the tower, right?'

'Yes, of course.'

Shepherd nodded. 'And when the service is finished?'

'Then we go into full close protection mode,' said Cookson. 'We'll move in closer and escort them from the churchyard to the cars.'

'PM first?'

'We'll probably play it by ear. The PM might want to press some flesh, and Blair certainly will. I know from experience that Theresa May will probably go straight to her car, but for the rest we'll have to wait. Generally the PM doesn't take kindly to being told what to do so we'll take our lead from him.'

'Okay, but at the cafe you said the four groups would drive together to the house. Roger first, followed by Glen, then your team, then Theresa May's team.'

Cookson nodded. 'That's right.'

'But that will mean the early leavers having to wait outside the church, in their cars?'

'They'll be well protected. And the press will be corralled across the road.'

'But presumably there'll be civilians stopping by to see what all the fuss is about. Taking pictures with their phones.'

'I shouldn't think there'd be many. It's Chipping Norton, not central London. And most of the locals will be in the churchyard.'

Shepherd grimaced. 'I don't know. If it was me, I'd keep all the principals in the churchyard until they are ready to leave, then take them out together.'

For a moment Shepherd thought that Cookson was going to reject the suggestion out of hand, but after a few seconds the inspector nodded. 'That makes sense. We'll try it.' He looked at Clarke and Howard. 'Does that work for you?'

'It's probably going to be like herding cats, but we'll give it a go,' said Clarke.

'Theresa will be fine, but there might be a power struggle between the PM and Blair,' said Howard. 'You just know that Blair is going to want a picture of himself standing next to the vicar and looking grim.'

'I really want to stick with the convoy to the house, that way the helicopter can keep an eye on everyone,' said Cookson. 'When they're ready to leave, bring them to the gate and hold them there. The PM has meetings later in the day so I don't expect him to hang around. Once he's moving, maybe nudge anyone else who's still around.' Everyone was nodding so Cookson smiled. 'Excellent,' he said. 'Let's go and check the house.'

The three police officers chatted as Cookson drove to the Heysham house, giving Shepherd time to collect his thoughts. He had assumed that they would only be checking the church, but obviously as the VIPs would be attending the reception it made sense to include it in the inspection. The problem was that he had lied to Cookson about not having visited the house and if he was caught in the lie their relationship would suffer. On the plus side, he had only spoken to two people at the house – Baron Heysham's daughter-in-law and Jo Hardy, the head groom – so if he could avoid them, he'd be in the clear.

They drove by a large manor house surrounded by several acres of land. It really was a beautiful part of the country and he could see that outsiders would stick out. There was no graffiti, no gangs prowling around with knives or youngsters standing on street corners selling drugs. Shepherd had always considered himself a city person, but he could see the attraction of living in a place like Chipping Norton. But as Howard had said, most of the houses would be out of his price range.

The house was a ten-minute drive from the church, mainly along a narrow two-lane road flanked by hedges. 'You're worried about the route?' asked Cookson.

Shepherd realised the inspector was talking to him. 'Sorry, what?'

'You were frowning, do you have reservations about the route?'

'No, not at all. I'm guessing your options are limited.'

There was a large red tractor ahead of them and Cookson slowed. 'Unfortunately, yes. And we can't block the roads so we're stuck with any traffic there is.' He gestured at the tractor. 'Case in point.'

'Do you worry about ambushes?'

Cookson flashed him a tight smile. 'You really do always look on the bright side, don't you?'

'Just considering my options.'

'If this was taking place during the bad old IRA days, then

yes, it might be an issue. You could have a roadside car bomb, a bunch of guys with AK-47s hiding in a ditch, maybe even an RPG or two. But those days are gone. The only serious threats these days are Islamic fundamentalists and generally they don't have the equipment to mount an ambush against a protected convoy. Knives and homemade explosives are about their limit. That doesn't mean we're complacent, but the threat level is relatively low.' They had slowed to below 10 mph but the inspector made no move to overtake the tractor. 'Besides, the PM is as safe as safe can be while he's in the car. Plus I'll be in front and more armed officers directly behind him. As far as the route goes, we'll have a Thames Valley squad car in front, about a hundred yards ahead, and another bringing up the rear. And the two Thames Valley ARVs will only be a minute away. We won't be using blues and twos, it is a funeral after all. And the chopper will be our eye in the sky. They'll be able to flag any potential problems.'

'I'm guessing there aren't many alternative routes?'

'From the church to the house? This is it, unless you really want to go the long way around.'

The tractor pulled into a field and the inspector accelerated. He drove for about half a mile and then turned left. Shepherd recognised the road – it led directly to the Heysham house. Sure enough, after a few hundred yards the gate came into view. Cookson stopped and gestured at the house in the distance. 'Chez Heysham,' he said. 'On the day we'll have a Thames Valley car here checking anyone who arrives. The grounds are huge so there's no question of trying to maintain a perimeter.'

'What about people already in the house?'

'I was here yesterday,' said Clarke. 'I have a list of family members and staff and I've checked out the catering company they'll be using. They're local and they checked out.'

Cookson turned into the driveway and drove slowly towards the house. 'The plan is for the PM to stay for thirty minutes or so, and then we'll take him straight back to London.'

'What about the helicopter?' said Shepherd. 'It's going to have to refuel, right?'

'Once the PM has been delivered to the church they'll head off and refuel,' said Cookson. 'Then once he's in the house, they'll refuel again. There's an airfield just two miles north of Enstone so it'll take fifteen to twenty minutes each time. They'll check in with me when they leave and when they return.'

They reached the front of the house and Cookson turned to the left and parked. Shepherd recognised the two Land Rovers and the Bentley from his previous visit, along with the Honda Civic and two other saloons. 'Who are you here to see?' asked Shepherd as they climbed out of the Range Rover.

'The deceased's son, Gerald Heysham. He's been the local MP for the past ten years. He'll be at the church to meet the PM and the VIPs. I asked him if he'd meet us there but he said he was too busy.'

'He's an arrogant prick,' muttered Clarke. 'Nothing like his father.'

'That may well be, but it's his father's funeral so we need to cut him some slack.' Cookson locked the car and turned towards the house.

'Actually I'll just have a walk around outside,' said Shepherd. 'Snipers?'

Shepherd grinned. 'I think once he's in the house the VIPs are secure. I just want to get the lay of the land.'

'I won't be long, I'll just explain to Mr Heysham what we'll be doing on the day and see if there have been any additions to the guest list.'

Cookson headed for the front door, followed by Howard and Clarke. Shepherd walked to the side of the house but kept away from the stables. He heard the officers go inside, then he took out his phone and called Docherty. 'Just checking in,' said Shepherd. 'I'm in Chipping Norton now and won't be back until later this afternoon.'

'All good here,' said Docherty. 'We've got more CCTV coming through, from ATMs and from council cameras. I'll help Farah go through them.'

Shepherd ended the call and was putting his phone away when an Aston Martin drove down the driveway to the house. Shepherd turned his back on the car and took out his phone to fake a call but his heart sank when the car came to a stop and he heard the window wind down. 'Excuse me!' His heart sank further as he realised it was Mrs Heysham, the woman he had spoken to when he had visited the house. 'Excuse me, can I help you?' It was the same aggressive tone she had used last time, suggesting that helping him was the last thing on her mind. He forced a smile and turned to face the car. 'Oh, it's you,' she said. 'That policeman.'

'Yes Mrs Heysham, so sorry to bother you again. I'm here with the protection team to check the arrangements for the funeral. My boss is in the house with your husband.'

'I really don't understand this nonsense,' she snapped. 'Policemen at a funeral. It's ridiculous.'

'There will be some very important people attending, so we need to make sure that everyone is safe,' said Shepherd.

'That's as maybe, but funerals are stressful enough as it is.

You can't seriously think that anyone would be evil enough to do something at a funeral?'

'There are some very sick people around,' he said.

'Not in Chipping Norton there aren't,' she said coldly. 'Anyway, why aren't you inside? Why are you slinking around the grounds?'

Shepherd tried to keep smiling but the woman was seriously hard work. 'I'm just checking that the grounds are secure,' he said.

'Secure?' she said. 'Have you any idea how much land we have here? Of course it's not secure, it's the countryside, people walk across our land all the time.'

'I meant for the vehicles that will be coming here after the funeral,' he said.

'This is nonsense,' she said. 'I told my husband as such. If it's this much trouble it would be better if these so-called VIPs just stayed away and we were allowed to bury Ronnie in peace. Have you any idea what Lady Heysham is going through? It was bad enough when you turned up asking questions, but turning our house into a fortress is just not on, it really isn't.'

Shepherd's face was aching from smiling so hard. 'I really do apologise, Mrs Heysham . . .' She had already turned away from him and the window was closing. She gunned the engine unnecessarily, and roared off towards the house. 'Three bags full, Mrs Heysham,' he muttered, under his breath.

He watched her park the car and could hear her high heels clicking as she walked across the tarmac and into the house. She clearly wasn't happy and he just hoped that she wouldn't mention her earlier meeting with him and Jimmy Sharpe to Cookson. He took a deep breath and sighed. There was no point in worrying about it because it was out of his control.

He walked slowly back to the parked cars. Just as he reached the Range Rover, Cookson and his colleagues walked out of the front door. Shepherd tried to get a read on the man as he walked to the car, but he was deep in conversation with Clarke. When he reached the Range Rover he nodded at Shepherd. 'Get the lie of the land, did you?' he asked.

Shepherd didn't think it was a loaded question. 'It's a big place, that's for sure,' he said. 'I spoke to Mrs Heysham when she drove up, she said there were always people walking across her land.'

He watched Cookson's face closely for any reaction. 'You spoke to her, did you?'

'When she drove in just now. She didn't seem a happy bunny.'

'Yes, she made that clear to us all. She's not happy at having uniforms at the house and her husband agreed with her, so I've said that we'll use our people. I'll send out a car with three of our guys first thing and they can do a sweep, and two of them can be at the gate to monitor arrivals.' He forced a smile. 'Mrs Heysham said I should make sure they are wearing black suits.'

Shepherd was pretty sure that Mrs Heysham hadn't said anything about him to Cookson, so he was in the clear. He relaxed a little. 'It can't be easy for them, the family,' said Shepherd.

Cookson unlocked the Range Rover and they all climbed in. 'Don't you believe it,' said Cookson as he started the engine. 'The son is nothing like the father. He's as hard as nails. He'll be in the Cabinet before long and I can see him in the top job in a few years. He knows exactly what we have to do, he just likes throwing his weight around. But if using our guys in black suits makes him and his wife happy, we can give him what he wants. No point in antagonising a man who might well be a future prime minister.'

Cookson dropped Shepherd outside Thames House. 'Thanks for that,' said Shepherd. 'I know it can't be fun having someone tagging along when you're working.' He opened the door and climbed out on to the pavement.

'Promise me one thing,' said Cookson.

'Sure.'

'If you do have any inkling that there's a credible threat, let me know.'

'I will.'

Cookson stared at him with unblinking eyes. 'Me personally. You have my number. I really don't want anything to happen to the PM on my watch.'

'I hear you,' said Shepherd. He closed the door and entered Thames House as the Range Rover drove away.

Shepherd went straight to Pritchard's office. He waited under the watchful eye of Amy Miller until Pritchard had finished a phone call, and then she ushered him in.

'How did it go?' asked Pritchard as he waved Shepherd to a seat.

Shepherd sat down. 'They're a very professional team,' he said. 'All bases covered. It's hard to see how anyone could even get close to the PM or the rest of the VIPs. The PM and Blair will be in armoured Jags with close protection cars front and back. There'll be a helicopter shadowing the PM all the way. When they get to the church there'll be more than a dozen armed CPOs in plain clothes and two armed response vehicles one minute away. There are no sniper vantage points over-looking the church and there'll be uniformed officers everywhere.' He shrugged. 'If it was me, I wouldn't know where to even start to mount an attack.'

Pritchard smiled. 'I'm sure that's not true.'

'Even if I had an SAS unit, the options are very limited. Okay, maybe you could go in with helicopters and full body armour, guns blazing. But the jihadists aren't going to have access to equipment like that. Knives, guns and explosives is pretty much it.'

'Remember 9-11,' said Pritchard. 'Al-Qaeda achieved that with a few box-cutters.'

'The world has changed since then,' said Shepherd. 'I doubt that they're planning to hijack a plane and crash it into the church.'

'Suicide bombers?'

'They wouldn't get close. It's Chipping Norton, there won't be crowds. And if they were to drive car bombs into the area, the helicopter would see them and there'll be road blocks on the ways in.'

'What, you think we're worrying about nothing?'

'I think RaSP has it all under control. Cookson is slightly suspicious of our interest, it has to be said.'

'He's a good copper, he's very highly regarded.'

'Yeah, I didn't like lying to him.'

'Nobody likes lying,' said Pritchard. 'But I'm afraid it comes with the turf.'

'I said I'd call him immediately we know of a credible threat.'

'And at the moment, we don't.'

'No, we don't. But Sokolov killed Heysham, there's no doubt about that. He must have done that for a reason.'

'Maybe Heysham was the target, pure and simple. Maybe he'd done something to offend the Russians.'

'Is that likely?' said Shepherd.

'I'm not aware of anything, but then we haven't been looking. I'll talk to Bob Elliott, maybe give Gilbert a call. See if they've any ideas. It would make our life a lot easier if Heysham was the target. We can call it a murder investigation and track down and arrest Sokolov.'

'But if it was a straightforward Russian hit, why involve the Taliban?'

'That's a very good question,' said Pritchard. 'Unfortunately that's all we have at the moment – a lot of good questions and no real answers.'

'And how do we move forward?'

'Keep looking for Sokolov and the jihadists. We've got two days before the funeral, let's make the most of what time we have. If we can find them, that might go some way to answering our questions.'

Shepherd spent the rest of the afternoon looking through CCTV footage with Docherty. In all the videos Sayyid was alone, except for the withdrawals he made in Scarborough when sometimes he would be accompanied by Laila, covered from head to foot with a black burkha.

His mobile rang as he was leaving the office. It was Sue Johnson. 'Couple of things for you,' she said. 'Adam has a source who recognised the man who has been using Sakeb Nazir's driving licence. The source is sure that he saw him at the Makki Masjid mosque with Malik Ahad Kamali.'

'When was this?'

'On a few occasions. Latterly about two months ago.'

'That's helpful, thank you.'

'I've something that might be even more helpful,' she said. 'We've been looking for any connections between Baloch the

Butcher and the mosque and we're pretty sure we have something. Adam has an agent working in a foreign exchange shop
in Birmingham city centre. It's used as a hawala shop with a
lot of traffic between the UK and Afghanistan.'

Hawala was a Muslim money transfer system which enabled
funds to be transferred internationally without money actually
moving between countries. Hawala dealers kept details of their
credit and debit transactions in a book, never online. A customer
would hand over cash or assets to a hawala dealer in one
country, and someone else would pick up the equivalent
amount in their own country. Migrant workers often used the
system to send money home to their friends and family, but
it was also the perfect untraceable system for terrorist organ-
isations to move money around the world.

'According to Adam's agent, large amounts of money have
been coming in from Afghanistan for Kamali. Thousands of
pounds at a time. The agent doesn't know who the money is
coming from, there's just a code number, but it's definitely
Kamali who's collecting it.'

'Any CCTV?'

'Unfortunately the guys running the shop are rabid fundamentalists and if they even got wind of our agent he'd be dead
before you could say Allahu Akbar. He's taking a big enough
risk even talking to Adam.'

'Understood,' said Shepherd. 'How many payments?'

'Three that our agent is aware of, but he's not on the desk
all the time. He's only allowed to look at the book when he's
noting transactions, and he's always being supervised. That's
a long way of saying that there could well be more.'

'That's really helpful, Sue, thank you.'

'And how's the investigation going?'

'Slowly but surely,' said Shepherd. 'We know who we're dealing with, but at the moment we've no idea where they are or what they're up to.'

'Welcome to my world,' said Johnson. 'Good luck.'

Shepherd ended the call and continued walking towards Battersea, deep in thought. So the Taliban were funding whatever it was that the jihadists were up to. It was their operation, so did that mean that Sokolov was just offering a helping hand? Baloch had managed to get Sayyid into the country, but the rest of the jihadists had been helped in by the Russians. Had the Russians discovered what the Taliban were planning and offered to help? And what were they planning? The Taliban had claimed responsibility for the car bomb in Beachley, promising death to all infidels who invaded Muslim countries, but it made no sense to go to all this trouble to attack a guardhouse. There had to be more. But what?

His mind was still in turmoil when he got back to his flat, so he changed into his running gear and spent an hour running around Battersea Park. By the time he returned to the flat his muscles were aching and he was drenched in sweat, but he was no closer to understanding what the jihadists were up to.

Shepherd sipped his coffee and looked at the spreadsheet on his screen. The coffee was courtesy of Farah, who had been the last to arrive in the operations room. The spreadsheet was courtesy of Giles Pritchard, who had forwarded it from Tony Blair's security team. The former prime minister was almost as busy as the current one, with meetings most days and talks to various institutions in the evening. His current rate for an after-dinner talk or a lecture was in the low six figures, and judging by the spreadsheet he was pulling in millions of pounds every year. He had five overseas trips booked over the next three months, two to the States and three to the Middle East. There was clearly going to be lots of overtime for his security team.

A message popped into Shepherd's inbox and almost immediately his phone rang. It was Janice Warren. 'Good morning, good morning!' she said in a sing-song voice.

'How do you get to be so cheerful first thing in the morning?' he asked, and then answered his own question: 'Chocolate.'

'Exactly,' she said. 'And if you want to show your appreciation, they do have a rather lovely chocolate cake in the canteen at the moment. I've just sent you a file.'

'I see it,' said Shepherd, clicking on the message.

'We managed to get a hit on Sakeb Nazir. And yes, he came in through the ARAP scheme. He arrived in March. He got left behind in the August airlift and made it out through Iran.'

'That's unusual.'

'The Pakistanis were making it difficult for refugees to cross their border. Nazir made it into Iran and flew out through Tehran. Except he wasn't Sakeb Nazir, of course. He was using the name Abdul Qadir Akbari. That's Qadir with a Q.'

The file contained Akbari's ARAP application. The photograph was of the man caught on the Birmingham car rental company's CCTV.

'Nice work, Janice. You're due two slices.'

She giggled. 'I'll hold you to that,' she said. 'Akbari came in alone, no family, and Border Force put him in a hotel in Leicester. He absconded after a couple of days. They gave him an Aspen card and a mobile, but neither seem to have been used. He's been off the radar ever since. He was down as an interpreter with the Paras. I put in a call to the captain who signed off the ARAP and he confirmed that the picture we have isn't the man he knows as Akbari.'

'Janice, I will get you the whole cake,' he said. 'Thank you so much.'

He ended the call and read through the file and then printed the photograph from the ARAP application. He took it over to the 'AKA SAKEB NAZIR' whiteboard and stuck it over the picture they had been using, then he wrote 'AKA ABDUL QADIR AKBARI' across the top.

'We've ID'd another one?' asked Docherty.

'He came in through Iran in March,' said Shepherd. He nodded at Farah who was sitting in her pod. 'Farah, can you do me a favour and give Sue Johnson a call? Tell her we've ID'd the guy who has been using Nazir's driving licence and ask her if she can find any other vehicles he's rented between his arrival in March and the time he drove to the hospital in Oxford.'

'Will do,' said Farah.

'If you do get other vehicles, run the registration numbers through ANPR. Also check the phone numbers on any registration documents.'

Farah reached for a phone.

Docherty studied the whiteboards. 'These are just the ones we know about,' he said. 'There could be dozens more.'

Shepherd nodded. 'Janice on our Afghan Desk thinks that there could be hundreds of jihadists here already, and she only has the resources to scratch the surface.'

'How did we get to this stage?'

'Is that rhetorical? Because I don't have an answer.'

'You'd think that someone would be doing basic checks on the people we're letting in to our country, and not just put them up in a four-star hotel and give them a phone and a credit card.'

'Yeah, well decisions like that are taken well above our pay grade,' said Shepherd. 'We're just here to clear up the mess.'

The door opened and Pritchard walked into the operations room. He was wearing his suit jacket and his tie was done up, which suggested he had either come from a meeting or was about to go to one. 'Just wanted to swing by and see how things were progressing,' he said, walking over to the whiteboards.

'We've found another jihadist who came in using an ARAP identity,' said Shepherd. 'He was the one who drove Sokolov to the hospital. We're just checking to see if he rented any other cars.'

'Is he the one who drove to Chipping Norton?'

'No, that was Sayyid. The guy who died in the bombing.'

'Did the two of them ever meet?'

'Sayyid and the latest guy? We haven't found any evidence of that yet.'

Pritchard rubbed his chin. 'What if there is no big plan? What if they're all working alone? So Sayyid's mission was to blow up the car at the barracks, and this guy is being set up for something else.' He pointed at the other whiteboards. 'Maybe all these guys are somewhere also plotting their own attacks. So basically the Russians have been helping to get lone wolf attackers into the UK. Putin has been looking at ways of getting revenge on the UK after all the sanctions we put in place following the invasion of Ukraine and this fits the bill.'

'But why would Sayyid wait almost a year before carrying out an attack? And this guy, AKA Hakim. He's also been here since last summer. AKA Wajid Yasin, too. If the Russians wanted to hurt the UK, why not start as soon as the jihadists were over here?'

Pritchard sighed. 'Good question. And no, I don't have an answer. Are we any closer to finding out where Sokolov is?'

'He's very good at keeping below the radar,' said Shepherd. 'The only time we caught him on CCTV was at the hospital, and we only identified him then because of the scar on his hand. Look, I thought I might ask for help from the Americans. They might have one or more of these guys on file.'

'What are you thinking? Contact the DIA or the CIA? I'm not sure how cooperative they'll be these days, there isn't much left of the special relationship since Biden became president.'

'I've got a pretty good contact there. I thought I'd ask him for a bit of guidance.'

'Go for it,' said Pritchard. 'At this stage we need all the help we can get.' He looked at his watch. 'Okay, I have somewhere to be. Call me immediately you have anything.'

'I will do,' said Shepherd. Pritchard nodded at Docherty and Farah and hurried out of the room.

Sue Johnson called him after lunch with the news that her team had come up with three more vehicles rented by the man using the Nazir driving licence. She sent him an email with the three rental agreements, one at the end of March, one in April, and another in June. He passed them on to Farah so she could check the number plates against the ANPR system.

Shepherd wasn't sure where in the world Richard Yokely was, but assuming he was in the States he waited until late afternoon before calling him because he didn't want to have to leave a message. When he eventually called Yokely's number, it rang out for a long time but voicemail didn't kick in. Eventually Shepherd gave up. Almost immediately he had an incoming call from a blocked number. He pressed the button to take the call. 'You rang?' It was Yokely.

'I did, sorry to bother you. Where are you?'

'That's classified, but I can tell you that I'm in a country starting with the letter A.'

'Well that narrows it down. Richard, I need a favour.'

'Of course you do. No need to be sorry, our relationship is based on favours. I scratch your back and you scratch mine. Symbiosis. So what do you need?'

'We've got a number of jihadists in the UK that I need to track down. They came in from Afghanistan and all I have is their photographs and the fake IDs they used to get into the country.'

'We've got a similar problem in the US,' said Yokely. 'In the scramble to get people out, they didn't even do basic checks. We've got literally hundreds of potential terrorists in the US and we know next to nothing about them. At some point in the future a lot of shit is going to hit a lot of fans.'

'At least one of the guys in the UK was helped into the country by Mohammad Hassan Baloch AKA the Butcher.'

'Ah, well he might be dead.'

'Might be?'

'The video evidence is inconclusive but we think he was in a vehicle taken out by a drone late last year. Our analysts are giving it a seventy-five per cent chance that it was him. Certainly there have been no sightings of him since then. Time will tell.'

'If I send you the photographs of the guys we're looking

for, can you work your magic and see if they're known to you? It would just be a help if I knew what we're up against.'

'No problem,' said Yokely. He was interrupted by the crack-crack-crack of small arms fire. 'Sorry about that,' said the American.

'Are you okay, Richard?'

'Yeah, sure, I'm just here in an advisory capacity. Send me the pictures and I'll get back to you as soon as I can.'

'Thanks so—' said Shepherd, but the call ended. Shepherd sent photographs of the men passing themselves off as Javid Hakim, Wajid Yasin and Abdul Qadir Akbari. He didn't get a reply, but Yokely was clearly very busy.

Shepherd spent most of the afternoon checking CCTV footage with Docherty, while Farah spent her time cross-checking phone calls made on the jihadists' burner phones. The first of the ANPR results came in at just before six o'clock, just a list of locations, dates and times. In order to make sense of them, Farah wrote down the details on small yellow and orange Post-it notes and then stuck them on a large scale map of the UK. It was slow, methodical work and it was the best part of an hour before she called Shepherd over. 'I tried doing it on screen, but it just doesn't work,' she said. 'I know this is old school but it gets the job done. The yellow ones are the first week, the orange ones the second. And this is his first rental, not long after he arrived in Birmingham.'

Shepherd ran his eyes over the map and the notes. There were probably more than hundred in all, most of them sightings in and around Birmingham. There were no sightings near Chipping Norton or Beachley. There was a trip to Manchester and a trip to Grimsby. Shepherd looked at the details of the drive to and from Grimsby. There were sightings on the M1,

the M18, the M180 and the A180, between 8 p.m. and
11 p.m. Then there were return sightings between 1 a.m. and
3 a.m. Shepherd frowned as he studied the stickers. Why would
they drive to Grimsby in the middle of the night? The Grimsby
stickers were all yellow. The stickers to Manchester were orange.
There were more orange stickers from Birmingham up to
Ashbourne on the edge of the Peak District, returning after
about six hours. 'What do you think he was doing up in the
Peak District?' Shepherd asked Farah.

'No way of knowing,' she said. 'That's the problem with the
ANPR system,' she said. 'In cities and on main roads and
motorways, it's easy to track a vehicle. But as soon as they're
in the countryside or off the beaten track, you've no idea where
they are.'

'What about the other three vehicles he rented?'

'One was the first one we traced, the one he used at the
hospital. There are two more working their way through the
system.'

'What about the phone number he used when he rented?'

'Different number each time. Burner phones, calls made
only to other burner phones and the GPS was never switched
on.'

'Okay, no GPS but presumably the phone company can tell
us which towers the phones pinged off?'

'Alastair thought of that but the phones were all switched
off when they weren't being used. Whoever this guy is, he's a
lot more professional than Sayyid.'

'Which is possibly why Sayyid went up in the car bomb,'
said Shepherd.

Farah frowned. 'You think they killed him because he screwed
up?'

'Sacrificed him, is what I think. If they realised he had jeopardised their mission by leaving his GPS on and telephoning his wife then he'd be the obvious choice to deliver the car bomb.'

He frowned at the map. Manchester, Grimsby and the Peak District. What was the connection?

The morning of Baron Heysham's funeral was bright and sunny so Shepherd decided to walk to Thames House from Battersea. He arrived at the operations room at just after eight o'clock and was surprised to see Farah and Docherty both hard at work. Farah was attaching stickers to a large-scale map of the country and Docherty was looking at CCTV footage. 'Well as last man in, it's beholden on me to do a breakfast run,' he said.

'I could definitely go a bacon roll and a coffee,' said Docherty.

'A man after my own heart,' said Shepherd.

'I would love a camomile tea and a banana or an apple,' said Farah.

'The breakfast of champions,' said Shepherd. He went to the canteen and returned with bacon rolls and coffees for himself and Docherty, and tea and a banana for Farah. He nodded at the map that Farah was working on. 'Which one is that?'

'The second rental. April.'

'Does he rent the same sort of car every time?'

'No. His first rental was a van, a Transit. This one is another van, a Renault. Then for the hospital he had a Prius, and there was another Prius in June.'

'So the trips to Manchester, Grimsby and the Peak District he was in a van.'

She nodded. 'Do you think that's significant?'

Shepherd nodded. 'I do, yes.'

'I've got something here,' said Docherty. He twisted around in his chair. 'We got council CCTV footage for a stretch of road where Sayyid made a cash withdrawal about three months ago.' Shepherd went over, still eating his roll. 'You can see he's with two other guys who look like Afghans.'

Shepherd looked over Docherty's shoulder. The quality of the video wasn't great and the men were walking away from the camera, but the one in the middle was definitely Sayyid. And the man on his right was the one passing himself off as Javid Hakim. Shepherd pointed at the third man. 'Do you think that's Abdul Qadir Akbari?'

'Maybe,' said Docherty. 'He's wearing different clothes, but maybe.'

'Where's the camera?'

'Birmingham, not far from the mosque.'

'Ah, you know what, I think it's Malik Ahad Kamali. The guy that Sayyid was tight with at the mosque.'

The three men walked to a bank ATM. As Sayyid made a withdrawal the two other men stood either side of the ATM, giving Shepherd a clearer view of their faces. It was definitely Kamali and Hakim.

'No sign of a vehicle?'

'Not in the time frame I asked for.' Sayyid took his money. The three men continued to walk away from the ATM until they were out of the frame. 'Not much help, I'm afraid,' said Docherty.

'No, it proves they were working together three months ago,' said Shepherd. 'You didn't see any ATM withdrawals in Grimsby, did you?'

'Grimsby?' He shook his head. 'No.'

Shepherd twisted around in his chair. 'Farah? What about you? Did you see any ATM withdrawals in Grimsby?'

'No, definitely not.'

'Why Grimsby?' asked Docherty.

'They drove a van there in March. At night.'

'That's bizarre,' said Docherty.

'Maybe not,' said Shepherd. 'It's a busy port. They might have gone there to pick someone up. Or something.' He shrugged. 'I guess with no CCTV we'll never know.'

Docherty looked at his watch. 'Your tech department rang up earlier about you wanting a feed from the NPAS helicopter that's shadowing the PM. They said they'll have it running from nine a.m. so it should be up now.' He picked up the remote and pointed it at the TV. He switched it on. It was BBC News. Docherty frowned. 'How did he say I was to do this?' He pressed another button and he had a list of inputs. He selected one but got a blank screen. He pressed again and this time there was a view of central London, St James's Park to the left, the Thames to the right. 'There you go,' said Docherty, tossing the remote on to his desk.

The PM's limousine was just leaving Downing Street, flanked by two black Range Rovers. Shepherd pictured Cookson in the front passenger seat of the leading vehicle, his loaded Glock in its underarm holster.

As the convoy headed west, the helicopter went with them. Shepherd sighed. It was out of his hands now, all he could do was to hope for the best.

The three jihadists looked at Sokolov and grinned. 'What do you think?' asked Curly. 'Do we look like cops?'

Sokolov knew their names but he preferred to think of them as the Three Stooges. Curly, Larry and Moe. Sokolov had watched the American comedians on TV when he was a kid. His father would sit on the plastic sofa drinking vodka and laughing uproariously and Sokolov would sit on the floor laughing along with him. Sokolov was always happy when his father was watching the Three Stooges because it meant he was in a good mood and there was less likelihood of a beating.

'Yes,' said Sokolov, 'you look like cops.'

The three of them were wearing Metropolitan Police uniforms. Harry was a sergeant and Curly and Moe were constables. They had been supplied through the Russian Embassy in London, delivered in a supermarket car park by a woman driving a DHL van. The uniforms were authentic and included dummy radio sets that looked just like the real thing.

Sokolov also thought of the three jihadists as the useful idiots, a term used by Lenin to describe the footsoldiers who did the grunt work in bringing about his revolution. Sokolov had no respect for their ideals, or their beliefs – they were simply tools to be used to carry out his mission.

Moe's tunic was loose-fitting, because the bomb vest had to go underneath it. Curly had built the vest, using explosives and detonators they had brought in from Grimsby, smuggled aboard a freighter from St Petersburg. The explosive was octogen, also known as HMX. No one knew for sure what HMX stood for. Sokolov had heard it called 'high-velocity military explosive' and 'high-melting explosive', and he had once met a Brit who referred to it as 'Her Majesty's explosive'. It was difficult to manufacture but worth the effort – few explosives could match its performance. Curly had used HMX in the bomb in the boot of the car that Sayyid had been driving and even he had been impressed by the results.

The vest was on the roof of the car they were going to use. A Prius. The Prius was the perfect choice because there were so many of them on British roads being used as Uber taxis.

Curly helped Moe take off his tunic, then carefully lifted the vest and put it on him. Moe was grinning. He really did believe that if he died in the service of his god, he would spend eternity in heaven. Sokolov didn't believe in heaven, or hell. He believed only in making good use of the one life you were given.

The vest was made of canvas with eight pockets on the front and eight in the back, each containing a small block of explosive that had been wrapped in nuts, bolts and nails. In all there was just over a kilo of high explosive and half a kilo of metal. There was a detonator in each of the blocks and they were linked to a trigger that Moe would hold in his right hand. The trigger had a safety and it would stay in a pouch on the vest until it was needed. It was an elegant design, as was the bomb that Curly had built to blow up Sayyid's car. The man had a talent for making bombs, and Sokolov respected that.

Once the vest was on, Curly helped Moe put the tunic over it, then buttoned it up. There were a few small bulges, but it would pass muster.

Sokolov nodded his approval. 'Perfect,' he said.

Curly beamed at the compliment.

'What about your guns?' asked Sokolov. 'All checked and ready to go?'

Moe had a Glock, as did Curly. Larry had a Beretta. They had brought the guns and silencers in Manchester from an Asian drug dealer. Sokolov had located the dealer and had put the Three Stooges in touch with him. They had driven to Manchester with Sayyid and paid in cash. Sokolov could easily have supplied the guns but it was important that they did some of the preparation themselves. They took out their weapons and waved them in the air. Moe actually had his finger on the trigger of his Glock and Sokolov winced but didn't want to criticise the man. He was a useful idiot, nothing more. 'Excellent,' he said. 'Keep the guns hidden in the car until you need them. And don't forget the silencers.' Sokolov knew that silencer was an inaccurate way of describing the device – nothing could really silence a gun. Suppression was the best you could hope for, which is why the correct term was suppressor. Sokolov was a stickler for correctness, but most people weren't and when he had called them suppressors the Three Stooges became confused, so he stopped doing it. 'Are you all ready?' he asked.

The Three Stooges nodded. Yes, they were.

'Then let's do it.'

Farah stood up, stretched and then touched her toes. 'My back is aching,' she said. 'I wouldn't have thought that putting stickers on a map would be so tiring.' She touched her toes again, and then linked her fingers behind her back and bent forward. Something clicked in her back and she laughed. 'Did you hear that?'

'Maybe go for a walk,' said Shepherd. 'You've been putting in a lot of hours.'

'I'm fine,' she said, straightening up. She gestured at the map that she had been working on. 'I'm finished with the Renault van,' she said. 'There are two interesting trips.'

Shepherd walked over to her and looked down at the map.

There were more than a hundred Post-it notes, half yellow and half orange. 'It was another two-week rental, a different company to the one that gave them the Transit. I used yellow for the first week and orange for the second.'

The vast majority of the stickers were in and around Birmingham and there were so many it was difficult to see any sort of pattern. But there were two trips outside the city: a yellow one to the Peak District and an orange one to Oxfordshire. Shepherd bent down to get a closer look at the orange trail. The van had been spotted several times along the M40, then on the A429 and then finally on the A44, the road to Enstone. 'We don't know if they went to Heysham's house, do we?' he asked.

'No, we only have the ANPR data. They obviously learned their lesson about GPS. Same with the Peak District. They were spotted in Ashbourne, going to and fro, but we don't know where they went to from there. It's pretty much the gateway to the Peak District, they could have gone anywhere.'

Shepherd looked at the stickers affixed to Ashbourne. The van had been seen arriving at just after seven o'clock in the morning and leaving the town at three o'clock in the afternoon.

Docherty walked over to join them. 'The Peak District again,' he said. 'What's that about?'

'Physical fitness training, maybe,' said Farah. 'Keeping themselves fit.'

'Plenty of gyms in Brum,' said Docherty.

'They could be running checks on whatever equipment they've acquired,' said Shepherd. 'They could be firing guns, RPGs even, or maybe testing explosives. They were in the area for going on eight hours. Most of the Peak District is pretty desolate, they would have all the privacy they needed.'

'It's a pity we don't know exactly where they went,' said Farah. 'We could go looking for signs of what they were up to.'

'It's nearly one and a half thousand square kilometres and we wouldn't know where to start,' said Shepherd. 'A needle in a haystack doesn't come close. But they were definitely up to something, eight hours is a long time.'

'They also spent almost as long in Chipping Norton,' said Farah. 'But that was at night.'

Shepherd looked at the orange Post-it notes in the Oxfordshire area. The last sighting on the outward trip had been at 8.30 p.m. close to Chipping Norton. The return sighting had been at six-thirty in the morning. Just before dawn. So they had arrived after dark and left before the sun had risen. What had they been up to? Watching the Heysham house, perhaps? But why at night? Everyone would have presumably been asleep. And of course there was no way of knowing that they had gone to Enstone. They could have been anywhere in the Chipping Norton area. And this was back in May. He scratched his head, frustrated at his inability to make sense of what he was looking at. His phone beeped to let him know that he'd received a message. He took out his phone. He didn't recognise the number but as soon as he opened the message he recognised the photograph. It was the man passing himself off as Abdul Qadir Akbari and using Sakeb Nazir's driving licence. The message itself was just two words. 'CALL ME'.

Shepherd walked away from Farah and Docherty and pressed the button to call. Yokely answered almost immediately. 'It's a bit easier to talk now,' said the American. 'This guy, he's in the UK?'

'Yes, he got in by passing himself off as a former translator.'

'Then you've got big problems,' said Yokely. 'His name is Mawlawi Jafri and he's been on our hit list for more than five years. No sightings of him over the last twelve months but if he's in the UK, that's understandable.'

'He's ISIS?'

'Very much so. He's one of their top bombmakers. Suicide vests were his speciality and we think he's responsible for the deaths of two dozen Americans and literally hundreds of civilians. He's also been behind some very big roadside IEDs. We got close to catching him a couple of times and there's a bounty on his head. How close are you to finding him?'

'Not close at all,' said Shepherd. 'We know he's in the country and we've had sightings of him, but at the moment he's below the radar.'

'Well if he does pop up on to your radar, be aware that there's a half-million dollar reward on his head, dead or alive. I'd be more than happy to send you a cheque.'

'Let's see how it pans out,' said Shepherd. 'Thanks for this, Richard. I owe you one.'

Yokely chuckled. 'You owe me a lot more than one, Daniel,' he said, and ended the call.

Shepherd put his phone away and walked over to the whiteboard with Jafri's photograph on it. Above 'AKA ABDUL QADIR AKBARI' and 'AKA SAKEB NAZIR' he wrote 'MAWLAWI JAFRI' in large capital letters. Underneath the photograph he wrote 'EXPLOSIVES EXPERT'.

Docherty walked over and nodded at the whiteboard. 'Explosives?'

'Big-time IEDs.'

'Like car bombs?'

'Exactly like car bombs,' said Shepherd. 'He could well have built the one that killed Sayyid.' He went over to the table and looked down at the map that Farah had worked on. 'That could explain the night-time trip to Grimsby in April. They could have been bringing in something by ship, plenty of Russian vessels visiting. Or even a yacht over from the Continent.' He looked over at the television. The PM's convoy had arrived at Enstone and his security team were exiting their Range Rovers. 'I need Pritchard to see this.'

He took out his phone and called his boss, who answered almost immediately. 'I know that generally Mohammed must go to the mountain,' Shepherd said, 'but in this case would you mind coming to the operations room? There's something I need to run by you.'

'You know the funeral is starting?'

'That's what I need to talk to you about.'

'I'm on my way.'

Shepherd put his phone into his pocket and studied the whiteboards. Docherty walked over and joined him. 'You're on to something?'

'Maybe,' said Shepherd. He looked at the television screen. The PM was walking into the church. Shepherd saw Cookson a few steps in front of the PM. A second armoured Jaguar had stopped outside the church. As Tony Blair's security team piled out of their Range Rovers, the former PM and his wife waited until their doors were opened for them before getting out. They moved through the arched gateway where the vicar was waiting to greet them. Shepherd smiled when he saw Blair slightly change his position so that the TV cameras and photographers could get a clearer view of him and his wife. The angle of the helicopter shot meant that he couldn't see the look on the former PM's face, but Shepherd was sure that it would be suitably grim.

As the security team took the Blairs into the church, Pritchard opened the door to the operations room. His shirt-sleeves were rolled up and his tie was loose, and his glasses had been pushed up to the top of his head. 'So are you Mohammed or am I Mohammed in this analogy?' he said.

'Sorry, it's just that there are things here I need you to look at.' He looked over at the television. The vicar was walking into the church now and the gates were closed. Shepherd figured at some point the helicopter would fly off to refuel and they would lose the visual. Shepherd pointed at the Mawlawi Jafri whiteboard. 'This is one of the jihadists who came over as a translator. His real name is Mawlawi Jafri and he's a major IED maker. He's wanted big time by the Americans.'

'Okay,' said Pritchard, folding his arms.

'He entered the UK as Abdul Qadir Akbari, but he was using a driving licence belonging to a guy called Sakeb Nazir. He used the licence to rent a van which they took to Enstone. About four months ago.'

'This wasn't the trip that Sayyid made?'

Shepherd shook his head. 'No, Sayyid's trip was long before that.' He went over to the map with the ANPR details. 'The van was seen approaching Chipping Norton at dusk, and then leaving before dawn. So they – whoever they were – were in the area for more than ten hours.'

'Do you know exactly where they went?'

'Unfortunately, no. There's no GPS data, just the number plates.'

'We don't know if they actually went to Enstone then?'

'That is true.'

'And we don't know who was in the van?'

'No. We only know where it was. Approximately.' He went over to the other map that Farah had drawn up from the second set of data. 'He rented another van and took it to Grimsby in March. He was there for a couple of hours. That was about three weeks before he went to Enstone. And then of course he rented another car which he drove to Enstone and to the hospital in Oxford. And on that occasion we know for sure that he was with Sokolov.'

Pritchard was frowning now as he stared down at the map. 'Jafri drives to Grimsby. Three weeks after that he spends the night at Enstone. Then two weeks ago he drives to Enstone and Baron Heysham dies.' His frown deepened. 'Can you make sense of that?'

'Bear with me,' said Shepherd. 'Jafri is a serious bombmaker. It's very likely that he built the bomb that killed Sayyid. But he's been in the UK for four months and the only bombing is the attack on the Beachley barracks. And even that didn't feel like a real attack. So the trip to Grimsby, what is that about? I'm wondering if it was to pick up explosives, detonators, everything they need. Sokolov could easily bring that sort of gear in. Most British ports leak like sieves.'

'Okay, I'll buy that.'

'They took a Transit van to Grimsby, so they could easily have picked up something big. And then a week later they took another van up to the Peak District. We don't know exactly where they went but they were there for a while. They could have wanted to check that whatever they had acquired would do the job. And if it was anything that went bang, they'd need to be somewhere where they wouldn't be observed. The Peak District would be perfect.' Shepherd frowned. 'They have an expert bombmaker in place, and they have everything they need to build a bomb, so why do they wait four months before attacking the guardhouse? Four whole months?'

Pritchard shrugged. 'I suppose you have a solution to this conundrum?'

Shepherd smiled thinly. 'What if they weren't waiting for someone or something. What if they were just waiting.'

'Waiting?' repeated Pritchard.

'Waiting. Allowing time to pass. Look, as soon as it became clear that the PM and all those VIPs were going to the funeral, the church was pretty much locked down. There's no way terrorists could get anywhere near it. But what if there is a bomb but they put it there four months ago? A big bomb. In the church or the churchyard. Well hidden, and able to be detonated at some point in the future. Not days, not weeks, but months after they'd planted it.'

'Like the Brighton bombing in 1984?'

'Exactly,' said Shepherd. The IRA had planted a bomb in the Grand Hotel in Brighton, intending to kill the then prime minister Margaret Thatcher and her Cabinet who were attending the Conservative Party Conference. They failed to kill the PM but five people did die and thirty-one were injured in the explosion. The bomb had been planted under the bath of a room five floors above the suite where Mrs Thatcher would stay. It contained twenty pounds of gelignite explosive and used a long-delay timer taken from a video recorder. 'But a timer wouldn't work because they couldn't know the precise time or even the day of the funeral. So there has to be some sort of radio detonation. A phone wouldn't work because the battery would die within days, so they'll need to be close by and use some sort of transmitter.'

'This is all guesswork, though.'

'Jafri is an ISIS bombmaker on the US hit list who built large roadside IEDs in Afghanistan. He'd have no trouble building a big bomb in the UK, especially with Sokolov here to source explosives and detonators. And we know he rented the van in May and spent the whole night in the Chipping Norton area.'

Pritchard nodded thoughtfully. 'Okay. So suppose they are planning to attack the funeral. How easy would it be to put a large bomb there?'

'There's nobody around at night, the vicar lives some distance away. And the graveyard isn't really visible from the road. There's a wall around it and no street lighting nearby. They wouldn't have been disturbed. We don't know how many men were in the van. It could easily have been three or four, with everything they needed in the boot. They could have set the bomb under a gravestone or a crypt. The stone would add to the shrapnel. The Brighton bomb was only twenty pounds. They could fit more than ten times that under a tombstone.'

'Wouldn't anyone have noticed what they'd done?'

'They were there on a Monday night. There are no services on Tuesday or Wednesday. But even if someone were to walk by where they'd been, what would they say? They could lift a flat gravestone, dig out a hole a foot or so deep, fill it full of explosives and a detonator, then replace the stone. Or open a crypt. There'd be nothing to see. The explosive could be wrapped in plastic but any odour there was would be gone long before the dog was brought in. After four months there'd be nothing to smell.'

Pritchard rubbed the back of his neck and screwed up his face. 'So they were waiting until they knew the bomb was undetectable, then they killed Heysham? Knowing that the funeral would be at the church?' He frowned. 'But why couldn't the bomb be inside the church and not in the graveyard?'

Shepherd pointed at the television. 'The service has already started, hasn't it? It seems to me that if the bomb was inside, they would have detonated it by now. Also, it's a lot harder to conceal a large bomb inside a church, it's all stone walls and flagged floors. But in the graveyard, all they have to do is lift a gravestone or open a crypt.'

'There are crypts in the graveyard?'

'Quite a few. The above-ground sort. And some of them are close to the Heysham burial plot. If they opened a crypt without doing any damage, it would be almost impossible to spot.'

Pritchard looked at his watch. It was eleven-twenty. 'What do we do, call them and evacuate the church?'

'Not a good idea if they're ready to detonate now. They could set the bomb off as soon as they leave. At the moment the church is probably the safest place to be. The thick stone walls will insulate them from any blast.'

'What do we do?'

'I can get there in half an hour by chopper.'

'You'd have to get to an airport first.'

'Not if you can get one to pick me up at the Victoria Tower Gardens, there's space near the Buxton Memorial Fountain. A police heli, or if not a civilian heli from the Battersea heliport. It's tight but any competent pilot should be able to do it.'

Pritchard nodded and looked at his watch again. 'Okay. Go. I'll see about getting a bomb disposal team there.'

Shepherd hurried over to the door and jogged down the corridor. He had no idea how long the lift would take so he hurtled down the stairs and out into reception. Heads turned as he ran for the front door, his shoes slapping on the marble floor. He ran out on to the pavement and turned left along Millbank, dodging traffic as he ran across the junction with Horseferry Road. Ahead of him were gardens, a triangle of grass with the apex pointing towards Thames House and the base backing on to the Houses of Parliament. He crossed Millbank and ran on to the grass. The Buxton Memorial Fountain was about a third of the way along the open space and Shepherd stopped by it and took out his mobile phone. Cookson would be in the church and almost certainly wouldn't be answering calls, so Shepherd sent him a message: 'CALL ME'. Shepherd scanned the skies but didn't see a helicopter. His phone rang. It was Pritchard. Shepherd answered the call. 'There's a Met chopper en route,' said Pritchard. 'ETA four minutes.'

'Roger that.'

'Call me as soon as you have anything.'

'I will. Listen, if this is going down the way I think it is, Sokolov might well be leaving the country as we speak. And as he doesn't know we're on to him, he might be using his own passport. It might be worth checking flight manifests.'

'Good idea,' said Pritchard. 'I'll get that done.' Pritchard ended the call and almost immediately the phone rang again. This time it was Cookson. 'What's up?' asked the inspector.

'Simon, I've got to tell you that the jihadists we're looking at paid a second visit to Enstone, almost four months ago. They were in the area for almost ten hours.'

'So?'

'They were close to the church. We're thinking they might have planted a bomb.'

'Four months ago? That doesn't make any sense. How could they possibly see into the future? There's no way they could have . . .' Cookson tailed off. 'They killed Heysham,' he said. It was a statement, not a question.

'Yes.'

'And how long have you been keeping that nugget of information from me?'

'Simon, we can rehash the past when this is over, but right now I need you to keep everyone inside the church.'

'You just said there was a bomb in there.'

'No, if the bomb had been in the church it would have gone off already. I think it's in the graveyard.'

Shepherd heard the beat of a helicopter's rotors and he looked up to see a blue-and-yellow NPAS helicopter flying over the Houses of Parliament. 'Look, I'll be there in thirty minutes. I'm flying in. I'll meet you outside.'

'Where the bomb is? Is that what you're saying? What happened to the church being the safest place to be?'

'You're not the target, Simon. Just wait for me, and don't alarm the VIPs. If they come running out they could all die. Just keep them inside.'

Shepherd ended the call and put his phone away. He walked towards the helicopter, waving his hands in the air. The helicopter turned towards him. He stopped walking but continued to wave. It started to descend, the wash from the rotors whipping at the grass and tugging at his suit. It touched down and the rotors slowed but continued to spin. Shepherd bent at the waist and ran forwards. He grabbed at the handle of the rear door and pulled it open, then climbed in. The co-pilot twisted around and pointed at a headset lying on the seat next to Shepherd. Shepherd nodded and put it on.

'I need to ask you your name, sir,' said the pilot through the headset. 'I'd hate to pick up a random stranger.'

'Dan Shepherd.'

'Then we are good to go, Mr Shepherd.' The engine roared and the helicopter lifted off the ground. 'I'm told that Chipping Norton is our destination.'

'It's a village a few miles away,' said Shepherd. 'Enstone. There's a church there. St Peter's. You can drop me in the field behind it. And as fast as you can, please.'

'We'll use the siren, shall we?' said the pilot.

Shepherd was about to reply when he realised the man was joking. He laughed and settled back in his seat.

'There's the cops,' said Jafri. He was sitting in the back of the car, behind the man calling himself Yasin. His real name was Haqqani but he had stuck with the name that he had used to enter the country. Yasin was wearing the suicide vest but the trigger was still tucked away. Jafri's gun was in his right hand, down by the side of his leg. He had screwed a bulbous silencer into the barrel.

'I see them,' said the man calling himself Hakim, who was driving. 'I'm not blind.' Hakim's real name was Omar, but like Haqqani he had continued to use his fake name, the name that had allowed him into the UK.

The car had blue-and-yellow markings and was facing them at the side of the road. Two uniformed policemen wearing hi-vis jackets were standing by the car. One of them stepped into the road and raised his hand for them to stop.

'Everybody ready?' asked Jafri.

'Let's just kill the kafirs,' said Yasin.

'Easy does it,' said Jafri. 'They are not armed. We have all the time in the world.'

Hakim slowed the Prius. The electric motor kicked in and they glided silently to a stop. The constable had realised that they were wearing police uniforms and he frowned and said something to his colleague, who bent down and peered through the side windows. Jafri smiled and wound down his window. He knew better than to speak, the moment he opened his mouth they would realise that he didn't belong in the uniform.

'You guys heading to the funeral?' asked the constable standing on the pavement.

Yasin wound down his window and shot the man in the face. The suppressor kept the sound down but there was still a loud pop, as if a balloon had burst. The constable's face imploded and he took a step back as blood spurted down his hi-vis vest.

The constable standing in the road froze, his eyes opened wide in terror. Jafri moved quickly, opening the door with his left hand, stepping out and shooting the man in the face. Blood and bits of skull splattered across the road and the man fell backwards, dead before he hit the tarmac.

'Quickly,' said Jafri. 'Open the back.'

Hakim pressed the button to open the rear door. Yasin left his gun on the seat and climbed out to help Jafri roll the dead officer into the back of the vehicle. Then they hurried to the front of the car and heaved the second body on top of the first. Jafri slammed the door and banged it with the flat of his hand. Jafri and Yasin scanned the area as Hakim pulled over and parked behind the patrol car. The road was clear.

Jafri and Yasin hurried over to the patrol car. The keys were in the ignition. Yasin got into the front passenger seat and Jafri climbed in behind him. Hakim got out of the Prius, locked it, and jogged over to the patrol car. He climbed in, pulled a tight U-turn, and less than a minute after shooting the two policemen, they were driving towards the church.

Ahead of them they saw a police helicopter coming into land in the field next to the church.

'What's going on over there?' asked Yasin.

'It doesn't matter,' said Jafri. 'They'll all be dead soon enough.'

'Inshallah,' said Hakim.

'Inshallah,' repeated Yasin and Jafri. God willing.

The helicopter landed about a hundred feet from the church. 'Can you guys park up at the far end of this field and wait for me?' Shepherd asked.

'We're on your clock until you say we're done,' said the pilot.

Shepherd thanked him, then he took off his headset, opened the door and climbed out. Two uniformed constables were standing by the waist-high wall looking over at him. He waved as he walked towards them. 'Is Simon Cookson there?'

The helicopter roared behind him and lifted into the air, the downdraft blowing his hair across his face. Cookson appeared at the wall and Shepherd jogged over to him. There didn't appear to be a gate so Shepherd clambered over. 'What's happening?' asked Cookson.

'There's a bomb disposal team on the way,' said Shepherd.

'You think it's a big bomb, not a suicide bomber?'

'What we know is that there was a bombmaker in the area four months ago, and he was here for the best part of ten hours. There's a chance there's a large bomb secreted somewhere in the area.' He rubbed the dust from the legs of his trousers.

'But how are they planning to detonate it? There's no way they could know the day and time that the funeral would take place.'

'They'll probably use a phone. Or a radio transmitter.'

Cookson forced a smile. 'Not possible,' he said. He pointed over at the road where there were four black Range Rovers parked with two black Jaguars. 'The Range Rovers are equipped with a full range of jammers that will kill any signal within a hundred and fifty yards. Normally we keep them off because the PM is always on his phone, but as soon as I got your call I had them switched on.'

'That means no phones in the area will work?'

The helicopter landed at the far end of the field and its twin engines wound down.

'The press pack are bloody unhappy, I can tell you that much,' said Cookson as they walked around the side of the church. 'But if they were planning on using a phone or a transmitter to detonate, they're out of luck.'

'That's good news. But this bombmaker has made roadside bombs out in Afghanistan and they use command wires out there.'

'Shit.'

'I need to check the perimeter. If there is a command wire they'll have run it from the bomb to a place where they can access it. With any luck I'll be able to recognise him.'

'And what do I do?'

'You need to get the press away. And the police in the graveyard, maybe move them inside the church.'

'The church is pretty full.'

'Then move them away from the churchyard.'

'I can tell you now the press won't have it. They'll play the "we've every right to be here" card. Look, do you really think there's a jihadist out here planning to detonate a bomb in the churchyard?'

Shepherd gritted his teeth and nodded. 'I do, yes.'

'Why can't we just get the PM and the VIPs out now, get them into the cars and away?'

'Because I can't guarantee that the guy isn't already out there ready to detonate,' said Shepherd. 'Let me have a quick walk around the perimeter and then we'll talk.' He held out his hand. 'Give me your gun, Simon.'

'No way.'

'Simon, if I do what has to be done, MI5 will protect me. If you shoot and kill, you know what happens.'

Cookson's face tightened. Any armed police officer who fired his weapon was immediately suspended from active duty, and if anyone was killed the officer would likely be treated as a murder suspect until there had been a full investigation by Professional Standards. Most armed police officers went through their whole careers without firing a shot in public and fatalities were rare. But when they did occur the police officer had to prove that he had no choice other than to fire his weapon and there was always the possibility that the investigation might go against him.

Cookson nodded. 'You're right.' He reached into his jacket and brought out a Glock 17. He handed it to Shepherd. 'Good luck.'

Shepherd didn't want to brandish a weapon in front of the press gathered outside the church, so he stuck it into the waistband of his trousers. He walked quickly through the lychgate and looked left and right along the pavement. There were constables in hi-vis jackets standing either side of the gate, facing the press pack. The graveyard was to his left. If there was a command wire it would most likely be running from there to the adjacent field. He started walking in that direction.

Cookson came out of the gate. Clarke was with him and Cookson was saying something to him.

Shepherd saw a police car heading down the road towards the church. A Thames Valley patrol car. He looked over the wall at the graveyard, then back at the car. It was slowing. He frowned. The patrol car was supposed to be further down the road, monitoring traffic that passed through the village.

The car stopped. A rear door opened and a uniformed officer got out. He had his face turned away so all Shepherd saw was the uniform and cap. The man slammed the door shut and started walking away from the church. The car started moving again.

Shepherd narrowed his eyes to try to cut through the glare that was coming off the windscreen. There were two uniforms in the front of the car. That didn't make sense, either. Armed response vehicles usually had three officers on board, but patrol cars generally had two. Or one if they were stretched.

He looked back at the lychgate. The two uniformed cops there were looking over at the car, clearly confused by its approach. One of the cops was talking into his radio.

The car was accelerating. Shepherd's heart raced as he recognised the driver. It was the jihadist using Javid Hakim's ID.

Shepherd pulled the gun from his waistband. The one thought running through his mind was that it was a car bomb and he had to stop it. The driver caught sight of him and his jaw dropped as he saw the gun in Shepherd's hand.

Shepherd brought the gun up and cupped his left hand under his right. He squeezed the trigger and the driver's window exploded into a thousand cubes of glass. He tracked the moving car and squeezed the trigger again. Blood splattered across the windscreen and Hakim slumped over the steering wheel. His foot must have still been on the accelerator, because the engine roared and the car swerved to the left as it accelerated. It crashed into a stone wall and scraped along it with the sound of tearing metal, then swerved to the right, bumped over the pavement and crashed into the wall around the church.

The passenger opened his door and began to run towards the entrance to the churchyard. Shepherd tried to aim at him but the Prius was in the way. He kept both hands on the Glock as he took three quick steps to the side.

Clarke had stepped in front of Cookson and was bringing his gun from its holster. The journalists corralled into the field began shouting and screaming.

Shepherd shouted 'head shot!' at the top of his voice but Clarke was too focused on the running man to hear him. The man wasn't waving a knife or a gun and Jafri was a skilled bombmaker, so there was every chance that he was wearing a suicide vest. Clarke fired but the shot went high.

Shepherd aimed at the running man's head but he was bending forward as he ran and Shepherd knew he had next to no chance of hitting him. He lowered his aim and fired at the man's legs, figuring that if he could bring him down to the ground that would minimise any damage. The first shot went wide and screeched off the tarmac, but the second hit the man in the left calf. He began to stumble and he threw

his arms out in an attempt to regain his balance. Shepherd
saw a trigger in the man's right hand.

The man's head came back. He was wearing a peaked cap
and Shepherd sighted on that. But before he could squeeze
the trigger, Clarke fired twice. There was a flash of light and
Shepherd realised that the vest had detonated. He didn't know
if it was because Clarke's rounds had hit the explosive or if
the jihadist had pressed the trigger but it didn't matter, the
end result was the same. Shepherd threw himself to the side,
trying to get behind the patrol car. He heard the sound then
and the pressure wave caught his left leg as he fell behind the
car, flipping him over on to his back. He heard the rat-tat-tat
of shrapnel slamming into the patrol car and then the screams
of the press pack. The explosion set off all the alarms in the
vehicles parked in the road.

Shepherd lay where he was for a few seconds, moving his
chin to try to equalise the pressure in his ringing ears. He
wriggled his toes and his fingers, then gently moved his neck
from side to side. Only when he was sure that nothing was
broken did he get to his feet. The Glock was on the ground,
he'd dropped it when he fell. As he bent down to pick it up,
his head began to spin and he fought to stay conscious. He
straightened up, gasping for breath.

The windows of the cottages opposite the church had all
been shattered, and the uniformed police were lying on the
ground, their hi-vis jackets turning red. Clarke was sprawled
on his back, blood pooling around him. Cookson was sitting
down, bleeding but still alive. It looked as if Clarke had taken
the brunt of the blast and protected Cookson from much of
the shrapnel.

Shepherd looked over his shoulder. Another man had left

the patrol car and had disappeared around the side of the churchyard. Shepherd realised that he must be heading for the command wire so he turned away from the patrol car and began running. Behind him the car alarms continued to blare.

He reached the end of the churchyard. There was no sign of the man. Shepherd stopped and looked around frantically. Where had he gone? His eyes scanned the surrounding fields as he fought to keep his breathing steady. If he wasn't in the fields then he could only be in the churchyard. He climbed up on to the wall and immediately spotted him, bending over a patch of grass next to the wall at the far end of the graveyard. He was about a hundred yards away, too far to hit with a Glock, so Shepherd jumped down off the wall and began running across the grass. The man was kneeling down next to a grave marked with a small stone cross. He was so engrossed with what he was doing he didn't hear Shepherd's footfall. He was holding a wire in his left hand. He pulled it and more wire emerged from the soil. Shepherd covered twenty yards. The man straightened up. Shepherd slowed. He was seventy yards away now. Still too far away to guarantee a kill shot. The man put the wire down and reached into his tunic. He brought out a small metal box, about the size of a pack of cigarettes. The trigger.

Shepherd ran over a tombstone, then had to swerve around a waist-high crypt of weathered stone. Sixty yards.

The man put down the wire and started fiddling with the metal box. The wires would have to be connected to the box so that the trigger could be pressed and the circuit completed, at which point the bomb would explode.

Shepherd brought the gun up with both hands and slowed

to a walk. The man still hadn't noticed him so Shepherd concentrated on making as little noise as possible as he covered the remaining ground between them.

Shepherd was just forty yards away from the man when he straightened up. Shepherd saw him from side on and recognised him immediately. Mawlawi Jafri. The bombmaker.

Jafri turned towards him, his eyes widening. The metal box was in his right hand. The wire ran from it into the ground by the stone cross. They locked eyes and Shepherd knew immediately that there would be no point in shouting anything, Jafri had already made the decision to press the trigger and detonate the bomb. Shepherd squeezed the Glock's trigger twice. The first shot blew off Jafri's peaked cap, the second smacked into the centre of his face. Jafri didn't fall immediately so Shepherd fired another two shots, one hitting him in the throat and the second smacking into his face again. The trigger was still in Jafri's hand. Shepherd held his breath and said a silent prayer that his thumb wouldn't click down and complete the circuit.

Jafri fell back, his arms outstretched, and he slammed into a gravestone. The metal box fell from his hand and landed in the grass. Shepherd looked over at the church, still holding his breath. There was no explosion. He finally exhaled and took a deep breath. It was over.

'We're preparing for take-off now, sir,' said the stewardess. She was in her early twenties, a natural blonde with what looked like natural breasts under her white silk shirt.

Sokolov smiled at her. He'd been told that the stewardesses on the private 737 would satisfy any and all requests. The jet was owned by a mega-rich oligarch, one of Putin's favoured billionaires, with an empire that encompassed property, mining, manufacturing, electronics, sports teams and health care. The oligarch was also a close friend of several members of the UK government and he was one of the few not to have had his assets confiscated after Russia invaded the Ukraine. The jet was one of three that the oligarch owned, and all were at the beck and call of the president and his friends.

'Let me get that for you,' said the stewardess, reaching down to fasten his seatbelt. Her hand brushed his groin and he was sure that it wasn't an accident. She fastened his belt and flashed him a smile. 'That's you strapped in,' she said. She was close enough that he could smell her perfume. 'I'll be back to release you once we're at our cruising altitude.' She ran her nails along his shoulder as she walked away and he felt himself grow hard.

Sokolov was the only passenger on the jet. He was sitting on a cream leather sofa with a matching footstool. On the bulkhead in front of him was a large-screen television, showing Sky News. He looked at his watch. Unlike state-controlled Russian news, Sky would be reporting the jihadist attack in Chipping Norton within minutes of it happening. He sipped his champagne. It was from the oligarch's personal stock, a 1966 Dom Perignon that would cost upwards of 2,000 dollars a bottle in a restaurant. Sokolov generally preferred beer or vodka, but today was a day for celebration.

There were two newsreaders on screen, a man in his fifties with gunmetal grey hair, and a blonde in her twenties who was pretty but nowhere near as gorgeous as the stewardess. They were reporting on a rumoured Cabinet reshuffle. But then the male newsreader frowned and interrupted his colleague to say that there were reports coming in of an explosion in

Chipping Norton. 'The explosion is believed to have been at a church where the prime minister was attending the funeral of Baron Heysham, a former MP and Speaker of the House of Commons.' The blonde was watching him and nodding with a sombre expression on her face. 'We hope to have a live video feed shortly. In the meantime, there is no word on what has happened to the prime minister. A spokesman for Number 10 said they were trying to get in touch with the PM's security team but to no avail.'

Sokolov smiled to himself. Excellent. Job done. The Three Stooges had come through. He finished his champagne and put the glass down on the table next to him. The stewardess whisked it away.

The jet's engines increased in pitch and the plane rolled forward. Sokolov stretched out and put his feet on the stool. 'Stewardess, how long is the flight time?' he asked. He twisted around so that he could see her.

She smiled at him. The top three buttons of her shirt were undone and he was reasonably sure that only two had been loose when he had boarded the plane.

'Just over three and a half hours,' she said. She gestured at a panelled door behind her. 'There's a bedroom there if you feel like a nap.'

He grinned at her. 'I might take you up on that.'

The plane was picking up speed now as it taxied to the runway. He leaned back and smiled. He was definitely going to use the bed. And the stewardess.

Something blue and yellow flashed by the window to his left. A helicopter. As it disappeared from view the plane braked suddenly and his seat belt bit into his stomach. The jet came to a full stop and the engines powered down. Sokolov unfastened his seat belt and hurried along to the cockpit. The door was open and as he reached it he saw the helicopter land about fifty feet in front of the jet.

The pilot looked over his shoulder. He had the same serious expression and gunmetal grey hair as the TV newsreader. 'I don't know what this prick is doing,' he said in Russian.

'Shall I tell the tower we have a problem?' asked the co-pilot, a young guy with a close-cropped beard.

One of the doors of the helicopter opened and a man in a dark suit climbed out. He was holding a Glock in his right hand. 'It won't do any good,' said Sokolov quietly. He recognised the man. The last time he'd seen him he was in the British Embassy in Kabul, carrying a Heckler & Koch 417 assault rifle and with a Glock 17 strapped to his thigh. The man waved the gun at the pilots and then pointed at the door.

'What do we do?' asked the pilot.

'Do as he says,' said Sokolov. 'It looks as if I won't be going anywhere, for a while at least.'

Shepherd was trying to decide if he should go for a run or watch a Netflix movie when his phone beeped to let him know he had received a text message. It was from Pritchard. One word: 'Tamesis'.

Shepherd looked at his watch. It was just after seven. He pulled on his jacket and headed out. It was a little under two miles to the barge and Shepherd figured that Pritchard had meant sooner rather than later, so he flagged down a black cab.

There was only one reason that Pritchard would want to meet on the Tamesis, and sure enough he was sitting opposite Julian Penniston-Hill when Shepherd walked along the gangplank. There were two minders sitting a few tables away.

Pritchard smiled and waved for Shepherd to sit at the end of the trellis table. Both men were wearing suits and Pritchard had a briefcase at his feet. There was a bottle of white wine and two glasses between them, as well as a bowl of untouched olives. 'Would you like a drink?' Pritchard asked.

'I'm good,' said Shepherd. It clearly wasn't a social visit so he didn't see the point in pretending that it was.

'Sorry to bring you here again, but whenever Julian and I meet in the office, his or mine, minutes have to be taken and tongues start wagging.'

'I get it,' said Shepherd. 'Neutral territory.'

'Exactly,' said Penniston-Hill. 'Anyway, first of all I want to thank you personally for what you did at Chipping Norton. You saved a lot of lives.'

Shepherd nodded. 'Except three police officers died,' he said.

'They did, yes,' said Penniston-Hill. 'And Giles and I will be at their funerals. What happened was awful. But it could have been a lot, lot worse. If they had killed the PM or any of the VIPs there it would have damaged our country immeasurably. As it is the bombing was a major coup for the Taliban and they'll be crowing about it for years, but at the end of the day it won't achieve much.'

Shepherd nodded, but he didn't see it as a victory. Three police officers had died, and one, Roger Clarke, he had met and spoken to. If Shepherd had reacted quicker, then maybe the suicide bomber could have been stopped earlier. But there was no point in thinking about what might have been.

'So we owe you our thanks, and our gratitude,' Penniston-Hill continued. 'And I'm told that your presence will be requested in Number 10 at some point.'

'That's okay,' said Shepherd. 'No need.'

'Just doing your job?' said Pritchard. 'No, Dan, what you did went way beyond that. The PM wants to thank you personally. We don't get medals in our line of work, but you have earned a debt of gratitude in some very high places.'

Shepherd flashed him a tight smile but didn't say anything. Politicians seemed to be the cause of most of the world's problems and the last thing he wanted was their gratitude.

'And we wanted to talk to you about Sokolov, just so you're in the loop,' said Penniston-Hill.

'Your prediction that he'd be on a private plane was inspired,' said Pritchard. 'If he had managed to leave the country, we'd never have seen him again.'

'We were lucky,' said Shepherd. 'A few minutes later and he'd have been in the air.'

'Well he wasn't and now he's in Belmarsh,' said Pritchard. 'Unfortunately he's not talking. At all. Not even to say "no comment". He just sits and listens and says nothing.'

'What's interesting is what he isn't saying,' said Penniston-Hill. 'He hasn't asked what he's being accused of, he hasn't asked for a lawyer, and he hasn't claimed diplomatic immunity. He's obviously feeling us out. He wants to know what we have on him.'

'Which frankly isn't a lot,' said Pritchard.

'We know he killed Baron Heysham,' said Shepherd.

'Yes, but knowing and proving are two very different things,' said Pritchard. 'We've absolutely no evidence that he had him thrown from his horse. And the evidence at the hospital is purely circumstantial. We have someone in a mask who looks like him entering the baron's room, and then leaving shortly before he suffered a cardiac arrest.'

'And he then got into a car driven by one of the jihadists.'

'Circumstantial. And identification is an issue.'

'It was him. I know it was him. I recognised Sokolov.'

'Yes, but we can't put you in the witness box, can we? If we do, we open the door to his defence team asking you how you know him. And what you were doing in Kabul. And why he was of interest in the UK.'

Shepherd frowned. 'I get that we don't want me in court, but Sokolov was organising a terrorist cell here in the UK. A cell that came within a whisker of killing the prime minister.'

'And therein lies our problem,' said Penniston-Hill. 'At the moment, the media is treating the bombing as an ISIS operation. An operation that ended with the deaths of everyone concerned. And frankly we would rather it stayed that way.'

'So no one is going to know about the Russian involvement?' Shepherd asked.

'It's for the best,' said Pritchard. 'The plane that Sokolov was on is owned by a Russian oligarch, a man who is very close to Number 10, much closer than they would care to admit. He's a man who very much stays below the radar, which is one of the reasons that his assets weren't frozen after Putin invaded the Ukraine.'

Shepherd figured that another of the reasons would involve seven-figure donations to whichever party was in power, but he knew that it would be churlish to say so. He just smiled and nodded and waited for them to get to the point.

'Everyone seems happy for the Taliban to take the credit,' said Pritchard. He winced. 'That word never sounds right, does it? Credit. Anyway, it was a Taliban plot, that's the narrative being pushed by the media and we can leave it at that.'

'Except it was a plot that could only have happened with Russia's backing,' said Shepherd. 'The explosives and detonators were Sokolov's, the logistics were his, without him they'd just be group of jihadist nutters. He took them to a whole new level.'

'He did,' said Penniston-Hill, nodding. 'But the Taliban provided the manpower.'

'Manpower which the Russians got into this country.'

'Which is another reason we would prefer that Sokolov's involvement goes unnoticed,' said Pritchard.

'We've got the breach of the MoD's database, we've got terrorists coming in on the translator relocation scheme as a result, and we've got the Home Office losing track of hundreds of these people,' said Penniston-Hill. 'No one comes out of this looking good, and if word gets out that it was a Russian plot then we'll be a laughing stock.'

'And by "we" you mean MI6?' said Shepherd.

Penniston-Hill's eyes hardened. 'I meant British intelligence as a whole,' he said. 'And the government as well.'

'As Julian says, if this looks like a Russian plot, it opens a whole can of worms that we'd rather stay closed,' said Pritchard. 'As it is, Baloch the Butcher is the bogeyman and his henchmen are all dead, thanks in the most part to your good self.'

'So that's what this meeting is about? To ask me to forget about Sokolov?'

'You have the perfect memory, I'm told,' said Penniston-Hill. 'So we don't expect you to forget anything.' He picked up his glass. 'But we would really appreciate it if you didn't contradict our narrative.'

'In my report?'

'In any way,' said Pritchard.

'Not a problem,' said Shepherd. 'I'm not a big fan of paper-work anyway. And I'm not in the habit of chatting about work to outsiders.'

Penniston-Hill raised his glass in salute. 'Then we are on the same page.' He sipped his wine. 'It's for the best.'

'So what happens with Sokolov? You're just going to let him go?'

'On the little evidence we have, we're not going to be able to charge him,' said Pritchard. 'But he possibly doesn't know that. He might well think that we have a lot more on him than we actually have. Hence the silent treatment. He's trying to work out what our case is against him.'

'And at some point he's going to realise that there is no case and that you're going to have to release him,' said Shepherd.

'We're rather hoping that he'll come to understand that getting released isn't actually his best option,' said Penniston-Hill.

'We can hold him for fourteen days under the Terrorism Act,' said Pritchard. 'That should be long enough for him to realise that if he goes back to Russia, there's every chance he'll be punished for his failure. Even if the Russians forgive him for failing, they won't be able to use him overseas ever again. We have his prints, DNA and all the photographs we need. Plus they will always wonder what, if anything, he told us while we had him. His career is over. And a bullet in the head will be cheaper than a pension plan.' Pritchard shrugged. 'Maybe I'm looking on the black side. Maybe they'll throw him a hero's welcome and make him a Hero of the Russian Federation.'

'Or maybe they won't,' said Penniston-Hill. 'It's not a gamble I'd want to take.'

'Exactly,' said Pritchard. He picked up an olive and popped it into his mouth. 'Dan, we'd like you to go in and talk to him at some point. In a few days maybe.'

'Why me?'

'He knows you. You met him in the embassy in Kabul and you took him off the plane. He knows that you're a serious player.'

Shepherd shrugged. 'So what?'

'The thing is, we've tried several combinations. White, black, Asian. Young, old. Male, female, ambiguous. He doesn't react to anyone we put in front of him. He just sits, folds his arms and listens. But if you confront him, maybe you'll get a reaction. At least he might start talking. And once he starts to open up, you can explore his options.'

'Sure, if you think it'll help.'

'It's worth a try,' said Pritchard. 'We'll let you know when.' He looked at his watch, his signal that the meeting was over. 'Anyway, thank you for popping over, I hope you enjoy the rest of your evening.'

Shepherd nodded at the two men, got up and walked away. He was pointedly ignored by the minders as he left the barge and headed back to Battersea, this time on foot. He definitely wanted a run now. A long one.

Sokolov turned off the shower and padded over to collect his towel, his feet slapping on the wet tiles. It was the first time they'd allowed him to visit the shower block. The rest of the time he'd been locked in his cell. He knew that they were supposed to let him out to shower and to exercise, but it was part of the process of grinding him down. That was why they had issued him with threadbare underwear and grey joggers that were so big that they kept sliding down his backside as he walked. They expected him to ask for privileges, maybe even to beg, but there was no way he could do that. Prison was easy, especially a British prison. Russian prisons, now they were tough. Russian prisons sorted out the men from the boys and only the strong survived.

The towel they had given him was dotted with brown stains, and again he was sure that had been deliberate. He grabbed it and began to dry his back. They were trying to show him how unpleasant his life would be if he didn't cooperate. Carrot and stick. So far they had only shown him the stick, but Sokolov knew there was a carrot waiting to be offered. The carrot was a new life under witness protection, the stick was a lifetime behind bars. Neither was particularly attractive and it wasn't how he had planned to live out the rest of his life. He had hoped that he would return to Russia as a hero and be rewarded with a dacha in Plyos and a mistress in Moscow. That wasn't going to happen now. The bomb had gone off but the targets had escaped harm which meant that his mission had been a failure. If he did return to Russia there was a chance – a good chance – that his reward would be a grave and not a dacha. Sokolov knew too much. The British knew that, and so did his masters in Russia. So he would bide his time. He would make the British work for his cooperation, but eventually he would give it. He would tell them everything he knew and in return he'd get a new life. Not the life he'd planned, but a life nonetheless. A house in Chipping Norton, maybe? He smiled. The irony appealed to him.

He heard footsteps behind him and he turned to see an

Asian man big and bearded with lifeless eyes. He was wearing prison sweats, a grubby T-shirt and Nike trainers, and clearly wasn't there for a shower. Sokolov didn't wait for the attack, he threw his towel at the man's face and kicked him between the legs. The man staggered back, pulling the towel from his face. Sokolov punched him in the chest and as he moved closer he hit him with his right elbow, two crunching blows to the chin.

Something hit Sokolov in the back, just below his ribs. Then there were a series of blows across his back and he grunted. He turned around. There were two Asian men standing there, holding homemade knives. The big guy had been a decoy. Sokolov felt suddenly weak, as if all the strength was draining from his body. The knives they were holding were long and thin, like ice picks. Blood was dripping from their knives on to the floor. They would have done a lot of damage to his internal organs, he realised.

He took a step forward and snarled at the two men. 'Fucking stooges,' he grunted. They were wearing prison-issue clothing, scruffy trainers, and grey-knitted skullcaps. He tried to grab the man on the left but there was no strength in his arms. The man grinned and stabbed Sokolov in the chest. The Russian felt the blade go in and then out but there was no pain, just numbness.

Sokolov fell to his knees. He could taste blood in his mouth and he wasn't getting any air into his lungs. He tried to speak but no words came, just bloody froth trickling between his lips.

All three of his attackers were standing in front of him, laughing and sneering. 'Allahu Akbar,' said the big one. He had something in his hand now. A toothbrush with a blade embedded in it. The man slashed at Sokolov's throat and he felt the skin part and blood flow. He toppled forward and hit the tiles face first. As everything turned black he could hear all three men chanting triumphantly. 'Allahu Akbar. Allahu Akbar. Allahu Akbar.'

Want more from Stephen Leather?

Order *STILL STANDING*, the next explosive Matt Standing thriller now.

The SAS are used to deaths during combat – it goes with the turf.

But when one of their own is said to have committed suicide in Thailand, red flags are raised.

Jack Ellis wasn't the sort of soldier who would ever take his own life – and no one is more sure of that than his twin brother, Joe.

Joe is determined to fly to the Land Of Smiles to find out what really happened to his twin brother. But if he is going to find out the truth he'll need help - the sort of help only SAS Sergeant Matt Standing can provide.

But soon after they arrive they come under attack, leaving Standing to investigate on his own. There are clearly people who want to shut down all enquiries and Standing knows he will have to use all his SAS jungle skills to survive. This will be the toughest of assignments but nothing will come between him and the truth . . .

HODDER &
STOUGHTON

THRILLINGLY GOOD BOOKS FROM CRIMINALLY GOOD WRITERS

CRIME FILES BRINGS YOU THE LATEST RELEASES FROM TOP CRIME AND THRILLER AUTHORS.

SIGN UP ONLINE FOR OUR MONTHLY NEWSLETTER AND BE THE FIRST TO KNOW ABOUT OUR COMPETITIONS, NEW BOOKS AND MORE.